The
Seminole
Seed

Books by Robert Newton Peck

The Seminole Seed

ROBERT NEWTON PECK

Pineapple Press, Inc.
Englewood, Florida

Inquiries should be addressed to Pineapple Press, Inc.,
P.O. Box 314, Englewood, Florida 33533.

Library of Congress Cataloging in Publication Data

Peck, Robert Newton.
   The Seminole Seed.

   1. Seminole Indians—Fiction. I. Title.
PS3566.E254S4   1983   813'.54   83-61758
ISBN 0-910923-03-5

Manufactured in the United States of America

Bucky Copeland

Acknowledgment

It took me several years.

I had to find a tennis professional to help me write *The Seminole Seed*, preferably a young person raised in Florida who could play the game superbly, teach it expertly, and also enlighten the author.

Luckily, I found Bucky Copeland. Though Bucky will never see this book because of his tragic death at the age of twenty-six, it is dedicated to him.

Years ago, I attended Rollins College with Norm Copeland, Bucky's dad, who is now the Rollins tennis coach. Norm introduced me to his son, and Bucky sort of became the model for our hero, Kirby Tree.

Thank you, Bucky, for your countless and patient hours. Without you, I could never have written this novel. It is your story too. And thank you, Norm and Harriett, for giving the game of tennis so admirable and delightful a son.

The Seminole Seed is grateful.

Robert Newton Peck

The Seminole Seed

1

"Are you a mad bull?"

Sitting on the top rail of the fence, Little Man Tree watched big Isaac paw the Florida sand. The beefy Red Angus looked back at him, and snorted. Again the boy spoke.

"I do not fear you, Isaac Stern."

Jumping down from the fence rail, Little Man's ruddy feet slapped the dust. Uncurling his young body, Little Man stood motionless and erect, feeling the evening sun try to toast his naked chest. He wore only trousers which were held up by a frayed rope.

"My father, Wilbur Tree, gave you your name because he closes his eyes at the radio and listens to violin music."

A white egret floated across the bull pasture to melt along the palms and cypress trees of the south swamp. Little Man smiled. To see a bird made his heart sing. Yet only for a breath did he stop watching the red bull.

"You and I are the same age. I'm coming up eight and so are you. But all I weigh is eighty-five pounds."

Isaac, he knew, weighed well over a ton. A ton and a quarter, his father had told him. Full grown.

Little Man took one step closer to the bull. Then he stopped. Father, he thought, would not be happy to find me stomped to death. Nor would my sister be pleased. Flower will scold me and give me a spank. So if Isaac Stern charges at me, like a rabbit I'll run.

Little Man clenched his fists.

Before her trouble came, he thought, Flower would sometimes chase me through the bull field; and we would frog jump over the pasture prickers. But now my sister no longer runs. She walks slowly, because her belly is full of baby.

"Do you hear, Isaac? Flower is soon to drop her baby, like a herd cow does a calf. My father will be a grandfather and I become an uncle."

From a safe distance, Little Man's dirty toes kicked more dirt at Isaac. "She has no husband." He scowled. "Joe Orange comes to see her, but Flower does not smile at him with her heart, so he goes away with a slow walk. But father does not ask my sister if Joe Orange is the one."

Perhaps, Little Man thought, he is.

Flower is silent and beautiful more than ever; yet she will speak no boy's name to our father. So he listens to his soft music on the radio and does not ask. He is lonely for my mother who was killed on the road when I was coming up two. Flower tells me that sorrow presses down on him, because he carries a curl of Mother's hair in his boot.

"Isaac, you are a daddy. Many times. That is why we keep you and the other bulls, to daddy the herd cows that belong to Mr. Ledger."

The red bull bent his head, causing Little Man to retreat a step closer to the fence. I am a rabbit, he thought, and I do not fear bulls.

"I am a Seminole and you will be wise to remember it," he said to Isaac. "The white soldiers came to our swamp, with guns, but never defeated the Seminole. My father says this. And he warned me not to speak of such things to Mr. Ledger who is a white man, because it would not be polite."

Isaac Stern snorted.

"Isaac, do you think that Joe Orange is the sire to my sister?"

Bulls do not tell things, he thought, and neither does Flower. Her belly swells, yet her face does not darken like a thunder sky. Father tells me that this is a happy time for her, for within her body a new life kicks.

A new Seminole.

We will soon have a new Tree. If my sister drops a girl, the baby will look as Flower looks. Always pretty. Her face shines like a wet pebble.

"But," he said to the bull, "if my sister drops a boy baby, he will look like me . . . or maybe Joe Orange."

Little Man stood high on a fallen log, stretching his coppery arms upward. "Come and chase me, Isaac. You can try, but the red Seminole is too rabbity for the Red Angus."

Isaac turned away.

Silently, the white egret returned from the swamp, gliding to a leggy landing only a step or two from the bull.

"Mrs. Egret does not fear you either."

Jumping down from the log, Little Man ran toward the red bull. Reaching him, he yanked his tail, then turned and raced for the fence.

I did it, he thought.

My father would not be pleased to watch me do such a foolish thing, but he is not here to grab me and spank the sand off my trousers. I am Little Man Tree and I will do anything I want. I am the son of Wilbur Tree who fears no white man and no red bull.

"Isaac, I will teach the new baby not to be afraid of you and to be a Seminole."

I hope Flower's baby drops as a boy.

Again he sat on the top rail of the old fence, watching the sun in the west burn into a crimson ball. The sun is cooking, he thought. The sun's face flames like the face of Joe Orange. He does not know that I heard his talk to my sister when he was by himself on the dirt path, down among the pines. Joe Orange was alone, yet he talked to my sister with heat in his voice. He even spoke her name. Over and over, he asked her the question.

"Who?"

Joe Orange used to love Flower, but now I see no love upon his face. Only hurt. There is love and softness in my sister's face, but it is not for Joe. I know that her love sings for the baby. Only the baby. Joe Orange, when I heard him and he did not see me, said he would cut Charlie No Land who also comes to call out my sister's name. As he had spoken, Joe's hand had rested on the handle of his belt knife.

I asked my father if he hated Charlie No Land or Joe Orange. His answer was no. He also told me that I ask too many questions for a boy who is not quite eight years old. Someday, he said, I would understand.

No!

Little Man wants to understand *now*. Because the baby is now, and I am now, and all things in God's Florida happen now. Not someday.

"Isaac, you must be happy that you are a bull instead of a boy who is only coming up eight." Little Man slowly climbed down from the fence, on the safe side. "You are lucky your father does not make you go to the white school, as my father makes me.

Little Man spat.

Remembering the school, Little Man Tree picked up a mud hunk and threw it very hard. I would like, he thought, to break the glass in the school window. But if I do, my father would pay for it; and so would my bottom. Maybe I will not hate the school.

Wilbur Tree hates no one.

He smiles and touches his hat to the ladies when we go to the store. It does not matter to him if the ladies are white or Seminole, or mixed, and he tells me that it should not matter to me. And he reminds me that my mother's skin was white. It is true, because I can close my eyes, he thought, and feel her brush my hair. I wish I could remember more.

Flower brushes my hair, too.

Even this morning, early, when the pain stabbed her stomach, my sister brushed my hair, so it will grow long and black as my father's. Little Man looked at the pink sky. I hope God knows how much I love my sister.

Flower is sick.

I know this, he thought. Because I saw the hairbrush shake in her hand. Her belly may be large, but her fingers are thinner. And weaker. I can tell by the strokes of the brush. It doesn't pull as much. Also, she does not scold me as loudly for being so dirty. And so fat.

Today, Little Man remembered, when the sun was high, Flower returned to her bed. I read illness on my father's face. They tell me little because I am little.

I hate my name.

2

"Little Man!"

Hearing his father call him, Little Man Tree also heard something more; a different note in his father's voice.

As he trotted through the pines, back toward the house, again he heard louder words from Wilbur Tree. The pitch of his voice was higher now, and yelled out in a rush. Little Man wanted to ask questions as he reached his father at the house.

"What's wrong?"

"Go fetch Mrs. Hood."

"Now?"

"Yes," his father said. "Your sister's water is broken. Run all the way and bring her back sudden.

Ask her to please hurry."

"Flower isn't going to . . . "

"Go."

From inside the house he heard his sister cry out. Not loudly. But her one weak scream was enough to whip Little Man Tree into a run.

He wanted to cry.

No, he ordered himself, don't cry. Just get to the wagon road. Thistles were in the way, yet Little Man's bare feet ran through them, feeling nothing. His path was mostly oak bark and pine needles.

"Hurry," he told himself.

The wagon road was not wide enough for a car. It was used only by his father's wagon and their one mule, Londie. The Hoods had a mule. too, so maybe he wouldn't have to walk back, yanking Mrs. Hood at each step. I would not want Mrs. Hood to fall, he thought, because her face loves people . . . even though she sometimes roars like Isaac Stern. My father says that Mrs. Hood's mouth is hard but her heart is soft.

The Hoods lived a mile downroad. At least that was what Little Man had always heard. Flower knew things like that, about miles and inches and grams . . . because she had just graduated from high school last May. And now she was eighteen.

My lungs burn, he thought.

Yet he did not stop, even though his heart was begging him to rest. Tripping on a tree root, Little Man sprawled into the dirt, got up and raced on. His hands stung with sandspurs.

"Mrs. Hood! Mrs. Hood!"

Please be home, he was praying to himself. How far is a mile? I'll just run until I get there. Flower says I'm too chubby and not built for speed. Maybe I eat too much. A girl told me that at school. Perhaps it is true, because our fence rails groan when I bounce on them.

"Mrs. Hood?"

Up ahead, he could see their shack. Clean wash was hanging on the line, blowing dry. Some of it was Mrs. Hood's underwear, but Little Man did not stop to wonder at it.

He almost fell up the two steps of their small porch. Instead, he managed to keep his feet, until he bumped the rocking chair and banged against their screen door.

"Hello. Is anybody here? Mrs. Hood?"

The door opened and Mr. Hood hefted him to his feet. "Goodness sake, what's all the . . . "

Mrs. Hood was there, too. She was holding a pink and white checked dishtowel and a supper plate that dripped suds.

"Come in. Little Man, what in the name of the world is . . . "

"It's my sister."

Mrs. Hood's eyes widened. "She's early? Ain't due until better'n six . . . "

"Father said that her water breaks."

"I'll hitch up." Sooner than he spoke, Mr. Hood was a streak out of his door and around back.

Mrs. Hood was throwing stuff into a small black satchel. "Poor lamb, I bet you run all the way here." She wiped his sweaty face with a clean rag.

"Yes'm. I ran real fast."

Little Man Tree leaned against the door post, trying to return air to his lungs. Behind him, he heard a buckboard rumble and a mule snort. The mule sounded as if she knew the workday was over and wasn't too fixed to travel.

"Come on, Hoody," shouted Mr. Hood to his wife. "You best shake a leg."

Little Man moved. Yet not smartly enough, he suddenly knew, to please Mrs. Hood. She was a big woman and her meaty hands almost threw Little Man up onto the seat beside her lean little husband.

The mule wouldn't budge.

"Hyah!"

No wheel turned until the mule's brown rump stopped the single whack of Mr. Hood's switch. Wild-eyed, she lurched forward; Little Man felt as if his neck would whipcrack.

"Will she be all right, Hoody?" the man asked.

Mrs. Hood snuffed her nostrils. "We'll know a mite more when we get there."

Little Man was thinking that Jason Hood sure could drive a mule. Yet it was nearing up dark and the wagon road was rough enough to make Little Man thankful that he was seated between the Hoods, and the woman kept two firm hands on his shoulders. As she held him close to her, Little Man enjoyed her warmth. She felt like a cold-snap stove.

"I've knowed your sister all her life," Mrs. Hood said, between bumps. "Ain't a prettier gal this side of Angel Heaven."

"Amen," said Mr. Hood.

"When did she spill her water?"

"I don't know. All I can tell you is that I was out with the bulls, when I heard Father yell to me . . . and told me to go bring you back."

"Good thing."

"Your pa's an honest neighbor, boy," Mr. Hood said. "One of the best."

"Seems like he's had trouble aplenty. You know, your ma gettin' killed by that hit-and-run drunk or whoever it was." Mrs. Hood's hands tightened on his shoulders. "We're almost there."

"Yes'm. Just up ahead."

The wagon brake grated the buckboard to a whoa, and Little Man saw Mrs. Hood jump down and head for the door. She spoke out in her loud voice.

"Wilbur? I'm here! Me'n and Jason come back with your boy."

Wilbur Tree greeted her at the door saying, "Thank you, Mrs. Hood. Come right on in. Please hurry."

Little Man followed.

His sister's bed didn't look clean or orderly as it

usually did. The sheets were all sticky red and twisted. Wilbur Tree held a pan of water and tried to wipe the sweat from Flower's face.

Raising the sheet, Mrs. Hood took a quick glance. "She's due. I'm right handy, Flower, so don't you fret."

Little Man started to step forward to be closer to Flower, but Jason Hood held him fast. "It'll serve best if you don't look, young 'un. Or crowd up close."

"No, I want to see."

"God, she's bled herself furious. Wilbur, fetch me some clean linens. Towels, sheets, anything you can lay hand to."

"Right away."

Little Man struggled, but Mr. Hood wouldn't turn him loose. Pulling out a bandana, Jason Hood wiped grit from the boy's hands.

"Wilbur, I been a midwife for thirty years. If'n you recall, I helped born Flower and Little Man. But dang if ever I seen a cork worse'n this here. She ain't dialationed too much. Not near enough to please birthing."

"Will she . . . "

"Looks to my eye like she's hung. Twisted or some such. Got a sponge?"

"No."

"Rag'll do. Anything to plug off her hemorrhage. She's pumpin' like a boarhog."

"Let go," Little Man yelled at Mr. Hood. "I want to

go be with Flower."

"Not yet, boy. Soon."

Mrs. Hood spat out a word. "Push."

"What can I do to help her?" Little Man heard his father ask Mrs. Hood.

"Pray. And if'n that chances to fail, I may have to lance her a mite. You got any alcohol?"

"Some raw moon."

"Fetch it."

Mrs. Hood fumbled into her satchel to bring out a small knife. "Wilbur, sprinkle some on the blade. And do it sudden. She's quit straining, and I best enlarge her while she's still frisky."

The boy saw his father dump whiskey on the knife blade. Most of it splattered onto the dirt floor, leaving tiny round spots to freckle the brown.

"You best hurry," Wilbur Tree told her.

"Hush. Don't tell me how to work my job, Wilbur. I born you two and I'll spring you a grandchild.

Little Man Tree wanted to go find Joe Orange or Charlie No Land and fight both of them. Maybe then whoever was to blame for Flower's baby, he thought, would be sorry.

Leaning over, Mrs. Hood rested her head on Flower's breast, to listen. To Little Man, she seemed to be hearing with her eyes, as they looked about the small room.

"Weak," said Mrs. Hood. "Lord, don't let me lose her to ya. Not this sweetness of a child."

"She bleeds so much."

"I know, Wilbur, I know. Birthing's a bloody business. Or are you so old you forgot about eight years back and how Hanna bled to sprout Little Man? You old stump, you dang well best remember."

Wilbur Tree nodded. "I remember."

Mrs. Hood felt Flower's pulse. Then shook the girl's wrist. "Oh my mercy. She's sinking. I felt her heart stop, then start up weak, but quit again. She's going, Wilbur. Maybe gone. Ain't a thing I can . . ."

"Save her child. Please."

"I'll try."

Little Man watched Mrs. Hood snatch the knife and then cut a deep gash. Blood spurted. He shut his eyes, hearing his own heart and Mrs. Hood's panting. Without looking, he felt the knife himself, with his own eyes clamped shut.

"Help me, Wilbur."

"Yes."

"Now. Pull! Don't yank, hear? Just a steady pull . . . more . . . more."

Little Man Tree waited, holding all breath, praying, and clinging to Mr. Hood. Then he heard his father's voice speak two words.

"A boy!"

He heard a sharp slap, then another, followed by one tiny screech of life. It reached his ear as a small candle of sound in the darkening room and it was a happy noise. Opening his eyes, Little Man Tree stared at the wet and squirming child that Mrs. Hood was

wiping clean. His mouth opened, in shock.
The baby boy was white.

3

Mrs. Hood sighed.

What a dreary day it's been, she thought. I welcome eve. The old unpainted boards of their narrow porch squeaked as she rolled her rocking chair back, then forward again, and stopped. Swatting a fly with her swatter, she turned to her husband.

"It's a shame, Jason."

Mr. Hood lit his pipe. "Sure is."

"At the burial today, I just kept myself remembering of how beautiful Flower Tree was. To watch 'em rest her into ground was more'n a heart could bear."

"Wilbur's a solid man, Hoody," her husband said. "He'll survive, just like he survived the tragic of Hanna's getting struck down."

Reaching into the pocket of her faded dress, Hoody pulled out the small box of Dixie Gold snuff. With her thumb and forefinger, she selected a dainty pinch; then installed it up into her left nostril.

Lord, she thought, what a sorrow.

"Yes," she said, "Wilbur'll make do. It's his boy that worries me some."

"I s'pect that Flower was more mother to Little Man than she be sister."

"True. Flower raised him."

"He weren't much more than a yearling or so when Hanna got killed."

"You're right, Jay. T'was his sister who mothered him up. How old is he now?"

"Seven. Maybe eight. He sure ain't a minute older'n eight years. Little Man's a chunky little tyke."

Hoody felt her chin tremble. "During the prayer at the graveside this afternoon, I was watching that boy's face."

"So was I."

"Ya know, I feel even sorrier for Little Man than I do for Wilbur. Oh, don't mistake me. I feel for Wilbur Tree and his loss of a daughter. But I swear, Jay, I read the death in that colt's eyes. It was like Little Man was filling up his empty with bitterness."

"I don't guess he's much like his daddy. Old Wilbur Tree don't got an overload of temper."

"No, he don't," Hoody agreed. "But his boy sure do. There's a darkness in Little Man's eyes. Black eyes nesting black thoughts."

Jason Hood blew out a gray wisp of smoke. "Hoody, maybe we best talk of something more cheerful. I just can't sit here, like we're doing, and think on that beautiful dead girl."

"Nor can I. Trouble is, my mind can't abide much else. I was at Hanna's bedside when she delivered her. So then Little Man come along, and soon after, Hanna's accident."

"Yup," said Jason Hood, "and now this."

Hoody rubbed the Bible in her lap. "Saints protect the new babe. No ma and no older sister, only Wilbur and Little Man."

"I was surprised at matters." Jason looked at her. "Wasn't you?"

That's for certain, Hoody thought, and surprised isn't the word. "My heart near to quit. But then, as a midwife, I been on the scene to witness more'n my share of newborn surprises."

"The babe had a white pa."

"For sure. I wonder if old Wilbur even asked her who he be."

Jason shook his head. "I'd guess no. Wilbur's a private soul. He'd probable respect her secrets. After all, when he wed Hanna Kirby, more'n one mouth popped open here abouts."

Hoody grunted. "Mouths always do."

Jason smiled at her. "Like we do right now. Here we sit, whispering about cross-breed matters that be none of our concern."

"Not much to talk about, and never was, save gossip."

"You look in on the new babe?"

Hoody nodded. "Right after the funeral. He was sleeping sounder than innocent, his tiny white hands up by his ears. Bless his little heart. I couldn't resist myself, Jay. So I just bent over and kissed his brow and that silky hair. A baby chick. He's got hair like spun gold. Except for his black eyes, he don't look at all like a Seminole."

"Well, from the glimpse I took of him," Jason said, "he sure don't favor either his grandfather or his uncle. Both of them is browner than wet tree trunks."

"No, he don't look no part of Little Man or old Wilbur."

"He's part of somebody."

"Certain sure. When I birthed that baby, I couldn't believe he'd slid out of Flower Tree. Vanilla out of chocolate."

"Blood questions." Jason knocked out his pipe into the palm of a hand, then shook off the black cinders. "Life's a mystery."

"Nobody can predict where seed will sow. It's true, Jay. Or how fruit'll bear, in humans."

"I seen Mr. Ledger look her over, more'n once. Reckon a whole flock of white men done like him. Flower sure was a looker. Pretty as morning."

Hoody nodded. "Maybe that was her tragedy.

Some men more than look. And if you ever do, Jason Hood, I'll boot your butt from here to Sunday.''

She saw him look up at her and grin. "Not me. Got all the female I can handle, right here to home.''

"Best you remember.'' She fanned the evening heat with her flyswatter. "Still and all, I can't believe it was George Ledger that seeded Flower.''

"Well, it had to be *somebody*.''

Hoody hunched her shoulders, "Yes, but who?''

"Months back, when we didn't see Flower seldom, I finally did see her recent. Up near Wilbur's place.''

"And . . .''

Jason scratched himself. "Damn chiggers. And then I knew why. She was full-out pregnant. I realized there hadn't been no wedding, and then I guess I sort of reasoned why she'd abided so close to their shack.''

Hoody let out a long breath. "Those months are lonely times, I s'pose, for a young gal in her teen years who's unwed.''

"At first I suspected that loner, Joe Orange. He's a dark one. If not him, then maybe Charlie No Land.''

"How come?''

"Because more'n once I been to Wilbur's place, watching his bulls, and I'd took notice both them red bucks sort of coondogging after Flower. She was ripe.''

"But now we know that it couldn't of been either one. Flower Tree took herself a lover that nobody knew about.''

"Except her.''

Hoody nodded her head.

"By the way,'' her husband asked her, "how's Wilbur suppering the babe?''

"I asked him. Seems like what works best is a mix of spring water, honey, and goat's milk. Good thing they got a goat and bees.''

"Somehow,'' said Jason, "I can't see Wilbur Tree nursing a bottle to his infant grandchild.''

"He don't.''

"But you just said . . .''

"Little Man tends him, night and day.''

4

Wilbur Tree watched.

He felt his face smile, seeing Little Man pretending to be a pony with naked little Kirby riding his back as a baby scorpion rides its mother.

"Hang tight," Little Man ordered. "Hold on to my hair, Kirby, and you won't fall off."

Wilbur said, "I can spell you a while. You make yourself a horse all day. Do you want to take a breather and rise off your knees?"

"No, because he's my baby nephew and I can be his horse forever."

Wilbur sat down on the doorstep. "Well, my eyes tell me that Kirby is a baby no more. He can walk as fast as you, and a whole lot faster than a grandfather."

"When will Kirby be two?"

"Tomorrow."

"Can I take him over to the pasture to have a look at Pablo?"

Wilbur stood. "Yes, but I hope you will let me tag along with you. Bulls and boys don't mix."

"Okay."

"Thank you," Wilbur Tree said to his son, trying not to show the smile that grew within him.

"Get off, Kirby. Real slow and easy."

But the baby did not get off. Instead he urinated on the spine of his uncle, darkening the back of Little Man's shirt. Wilbur Tree saw the surprised look on his son's face. "Do not let him wet on his pony. We must teach Kirby manners."

"I know. But he does it all the time. I don't mind. Kirby's only a baby. If he has to wet I let him do it. It doesn't really smell. It's just hot."

Together, the three of them walked through the pines toward the pasture. Kirby walked in the middle, holding Wilbur's hand as well as Little Man's. Wilbur felt his little strength struggle to turn loose and walk by himself. Looking down at the tiny white hand in the grip of his own big brown one, he still wondered.

Who?

"Again," he said to Little Man, "you did not go to school today. I want you to learn to read, as I learned."

He saw Little Man's face darken.

"No, I do not like the white school."

"Flower went to school. Every day."

"Yes, and the trouble came to her. Because of a white man, Flower died. So I hate the white school and I will not go."

"Yet you do not hate her white baby."

Little Man stopped. "He is *not* a white baby! Kirby is a Seminole, like Wilbur Tree and Little Man Tree. He is Kirby Tree."

"Yes," said Wilbur, "he is Kirby Tree, because we name him after Hanna Kirby, my woman who is gone."

"Say it."

"What do you wish me to say to you?" As he spoke, Wilbur saw his son's free hand tighten into a fist.

"Say that Kirby is a Seminole. *Say* it."

Wilbur Tree nodded. "My grandson is a Seminole. He is a Tree. And he will grow up strong and tall as do all trees in God's Florida."

"Good." Little Man smiled.

"Yet he will also learn manners, and his tongue will not snap at his grandfather or his uncle, not as your tongue barks at your father."

"I'm sorry."

"I know. This is a time for patience. Because I watch how you love our baby boy, I understand and forgive much."

He is ten, Wilbur thought. So there are things I must teach him. But how? What words do I speak so that Little Man will understand about the seeds of life?

Reaching down, Wilbur Tree picked up a pine cone. Although light, the cone filled his hand. With his thumb he snapped off one of its tan inch-long wings. Keeping it, he tossed the rest of the cone away.

"This," he said, "is a seed. Planted into the ground, it will sprout, and a pine tree will grow."

"I know that."

"Only a pine. Not a cypress and not an oak."

"Why do you tell me this?"

"Because people are not trees. The seed in Flower was not a Seminole seed. I know now that it was *not* the seed of Joe Orange or Charlie No Land."

"Are you sad?"

"I will always be sad because Flower went early to God's sky. As you are sad. But you and I will be always glad that, as Flower died, she gave us Kirby."

"So am I," said Little Man. "And our Kirby will grow up to be a Seminole, like you and me."

"But it is even better to teach Kirby to grow up to be a man, with manners, and with softness in his heart for all of God's Florida . . . and for all of life that shares a home with us."

They walked further.

Little Man pointed. "Look, Kirby. That's one of our bulls. His name is Pablo and he's a Brangus. Your grandfather named him Pablo after a man who plays a violin."

"No," said Wilbur. "Pablo plays a ccllo. It is Isaac

who plays the violin.''

''Over there.'' Little Man lifted Kirby up to see. ''That's Isaac. Isn't he big? Say *bull*.''

Kirby said nothing.

''When will he start to talk?''

''Soon. Perhaps sooner than Little Man will start to listen.''

''Mr. Ledger was here today, Kirby,'' said Little Man. ''And he wants Isaac to breed his white herd cows. Isn't that right?''

Wilbur Tree nodded. ''Yes.''

''What does he call them?''

''His big whites are from a very far place, from France, and he calls them Charolais cows.''

Little Man scratched his head. ''What color will the calves drop?''

''Spotted,'' said Wilbur. ''Isaac is a Red Angus, so the calves will drop part red and part white, like Flower and Little Man.''

''I'm not white.''

''Inside you are, because your mother was Hanna. Even though you look brown like me. Just as, inside, Kirby is a Seminole.''

Seeing them, Isaac started toward the fence at a slow and plodding walk. Closer he came, until his gray nose rested on the top rail.

Wilbur Tree rubbed the bull's ears. ''You have a stern look tonight, Isaac Stern. Has my son teased you or yanked your tail?''

Isaac snorted a soft answer.

"How did you know?" asked Little Man.

"When you and Kirby are asleep, I walk out here alone, to talk to my bulls. And each bull reports to me, to tell me if my son shows good manners."

"Bulls don't talk."

"My bull that talks the most, you can tell Kirby, is over there . . . standing under the big oak."

"That one is a Galloway and his name is Van," said Little Man to Kirby. He turned to look at Wilbur. "Does the famous Van play the violin or the cello?"

"Van Cliburn plays the piano."

"Father, why do you always name our bulls after the music people?"

"To repay them."

"I don't understand that and neither does Kirby. Do you know those men?"

Dropping the pine seed into his pocket, Wilbur Tree stretched out his hands to stroke the hair of his son and his grandchild.

"Yes, when I listen at the radio to hear the music, I know them. Their music sounds strong. I want my bulls to breed strong, so I name them Isaac and Pablo and Van."

Little Man shook his head. "It sure sounds a bit funny to me."

Wilbur smiled. "You see, my bulls are my orchestra. I own a piano, a violin, and a cello."

"How did you get started on all this music stuff?"

Wilbur sighed. "Because of Hanna. Your mother loved music. So my heart began to love all things loved by her, the way I loved Flower, and like the way I now have you and Kirby to love."

"Are you going to die, too?"

"Yes, but not soon. Kirby is new life to me. And to you."

He watched his son hug the child. When I see this, he thought, my heart is as strong as a bull. Stronger even than the music. Stretching out both arms, Wilbur Tree held both of them close to his chest, and closed his eyes.

"My seeds."

5

Little Man Tree walked slowly.

Above him the early afternoon sun was still high in the Florida sky. His body ached from the work in their small orange grove, the spraying, and from repairing the broken fence. The bulls, Little Man thought, must never bust out loose to trample Kirby.

Stopping to sit on a rock, Little Man reached a hand inside his shirt to pull out the wrinkled photograph.

"Again," he said aloud, "I look at your white face, to let you know how much you are hated. And that you will die."

Over his head, a crow barked at him, causing him to look upward. Wanting to tell someone, Little Man talked to the crow.

"Eight years," he said. "It was eight years ago, just after we buried Flower that I found this picture. It belonged to Flower, as it lay under the pad of her bed."

Among her savings he had found strings of colored beads, and her high school diploma, her Bible, and all the travel folders.

"And a picture." Not a day had passed since Flower's death that he had not looked at it.

It was a color photograph, not just black and white, of a young man wearing a white sweater; its V-neck had a red stripe and a blue stripe. But it was the hair that Little Man Tree stared at.

The white man's hair of gold.

"I know," he told the crow, "that this is a picture of Flower's man. Because of his seed, she is dead."

There was no name on the picture. No writing. The man's face smiled as though he knew what he had done to Flower, and did not care. He looked proud of his shame.

"I am now a man. Little Man Tree is sixteen. Kirby is eight and now it is time. Tonight will be the Night of the Snake."

Standing up, and stuffing the rumpled photograph back inside his shirt, Little Man continued his walk toward the school.

The man in the picture, he thought, has long since forgotten Flower Tree. And the man also forgot the party that Flower and her girlfriend went to at the place called Rollins College. A weekend tennis party,

Flower had told Little Man, when the girls would dance with the visiting tennis players from up north. Yes, thought Little Man, that was the night of Flower's trouble. He gave her his picture. And his baby.

But her brother does not forget. No, I remember. Even if I lose the photograph, I will always know the white face. One day, I will see that face again, and the blonde hair so golden that it is almost white.

Little Man trotted.

I am too fat to run, he thought; yet I cannot be late. Unless I reach the school on time, Kirby might start home alone. Among white children. Some of them, Kirby says, are okay, but not all. Perhaps if Kirby is in a hurry, he will follow the shortcut through the bull pasture and be stomped to death.

"Sometimes," he said aloud, "our bulls are kittens. Not always. They can spook at the bees. And, my father says, our bees help to cross-breed our oranges, so that our orange trees stay strong as our bulls."

Looking ahead, he saw his nephew.

"Kirby!"

To say his name, thought Little Man, is lighter than singing a song. Father says that Kirby's smile dances his heart and I understand this. I did not go to school any more, after Flower died. But I am glad that Kirby goes to school because he is so bright and loves to learn. If he learns the new, yet honors the old, I will be content.

Holding out his arms, he waited for the boy to run

to him. High into the air he lifted him, swinging the boy around in circles, until both of them became dizzy and fell onto the pine needles.

"How is school?"

"Good."

"I hope you were a good boy and used your best manners when you recited to Mrs. Hopkin."

Kirby smiled at his uncle. "I always do."

Little Man nodded. The boy leaped lightly to his feet, trying hard to lift Little Man to his. "My uncle is too heavy."

"No, not heavy. I'm just fat. Even when I was eight, your age, your mother always warned me that I ate too much and got chubby."

"Let's run home."

"Please." Getting to his feet, Little Man held up a protesting hand. "I do not enjoy a run. Your uncle is a bull and not a rabbit like you."

Little Man watched Kirby dance a few steps ahead of him. He moves as Flower moved, he thought. Like violin music.

"What did you learn in school today?"

"A lot."

"Tell me, Kirby. I don't go to school."

The boy stopped. "You should. Grandfather should have made you go. Why don't you?"

"Once I did. Up until I was your age. When your mother died, I did not go any more."

"Why not?"

Without answering, Little Man grabbed Kirby's

arm. "Here, I'll lift you up to sit on my shoulders, so you can ride me like a pony. All the way home."

"Okay."

"Up you go."

"Am I heavy, Little Man?

"No, you are lighter than a cello. As light as a white feather that falls from the wing of Mrs. Egret. You are lighter than a poem."

"Go faster."

"No," panted Little Man. "It could trip me and I could fall on you, to squash you like a palmetto bug. So I will be a walking pony and ask you to be a silent and patient rider."

"Why do you always take me to school and then come to meet me?"

"Your grandfather makes me do it."

"That's not true."

Little Man smiled. "No, it is not. Hang onto my hair like a good cowboy."

"Why is your hair so long and black?"

"Because I am a Seminole, like Kirby, and like Wilbur Tree."

"Why isn't my hair black?"

Little Man stopped. Questions, he thought. My nephew always asks what is hard for me to answer. Against his chest, Little Man felt a corner of the photograph prick his skin. Even inside the darkness of my shirt, he thought, the white face digs into me, and cuts like a spur.

"Why did you stop, Little Man?"

"Because," he lied, "there is a pebble in my boot."

"Do you want me to get off?"

"No. I will just walk on the pebble."

The pebble of stone, he thought, is in my heart. Its pain is sharper than a boot pebble and I have walked upon it for eight years. But I will walk eight more, and eight more, until I finally meet the white face in my sister's secret photograph, the picture that not even my father has seen.

Little Man continued toward home. "Now then, tell me what you learned from Mrs. Hopkin today, so that your fat old uncle can also keep up with the new ways."

"She told us about Cape Canaveral."

"The rocket place."

"Have you ever been there, Little Man?"

"No, I do not go places. My home is here in the swamp, under the trees, where egrets fly instead of space rockets."

"Rockets can fly a lot higher than birds. That's what Mrs. Hopkin told us."

Little Man grunted. "If I owned every rocket plane in God's Florida, I would trade all of them for the dignity of one egret."

"Maybe *you* would. I wouldn't."

"Why not?"

"Because I'm going to be an astronaut."

"We Seminoles are not astronauts, Kirby. The astronauts are all white men."

"Am I really a Seminole?"

"Yes, and Kirby Tree must grow up to be proud of who he is as well as what he becomes. As your grandfather is proud."

"I don't look like Grandfather. Or like you."

"Yes you do. Your eyes are as black as mine. Black as all Seminole eyes."

"But my skin and my hair is . . ."

"It is time," said Little Man Tree.

"Time for me to get off and walk?"

"No. Stay up there and ride your uncle. Your fat pony. I meant that tonight will be a magic night in your life."

"What's going to happen?"

"You'll see. Tonight, when Wilbur Tree sinks into his heavy sleep on his old bunk, you and I will sneak out into the darkness."

"Then what are we going to do, Little Man?"

"I will give you my snake promise."

6

"Kirby?"

He was asleep, dreaming of the giant bulls, and imagining that one of the bulls had whispered his name, telling him to awaken. Nudging him gently.

"Wake up, Kirby."

Again he heard the whisper of his name; and this time, Kirby knew, it was not the snort of a bull. It was only his uncle. Little Man's hand covered the boy's mouth as if to order silence.

"Is it the middle of the night?"

"Yes, but be still. We must not roar like bulls or we will wake up your grandfather."

Carefully, and very slowly, Kirby Tree rolled off

his bunk. He saw the shadow of Little Man hand him his shirt and trousers. Silently they crossed the room and left the house behind.

"What's in the sack, Little Man? And where are we going?"

"To the swamp."

"Why are you wearing a long dress?"

Little Man told him why. "It was Opopkee's ceremonial dress. He was Wilbur Tree's grandfather."

"What's in the sack you're bringing? Potatoes?"

"No, you will see."

"I'm cold."

The boy felt the stout arm of his uncle drop around his shoulders. "Do not be cold. And do not rattle yourself with fear. There is nothing this night, for you, to be afraid of. Only to remember."

"The ground is wet."

"We are near to the swamp. Step where the moon does not shine on the water and you will be drier."

The mud feels cold on my feet, Kirby thought, and I wish that I had stayed home at our house, with my dream. With knuckles, he rubbed his eyes.

"Are we there yet?"

He saw Little Man pause and turn to face him. "Almost. The grandchild of Wilbur Tree complains too much. Does my nephew wish to grow up to be a Seminole, or an old white woman?"

"A Seminole."

"Good."

Kirby let out a yawn. When he saw Little Man turn his back to head toward the cypress swamp, he followed his uncle, sloshing through the knee-deep water.

"How much farther?"

"No further. We are here."

Kirby slapped a bug, watching his uncle fumble inside his long dress in order to produce a match. Little Man pulled straw from the top of his dress as well as a handful of pine needles.

Little Man Tree struck the match and Kirby liked the way it yellowed his uncle's face.

"Is my face yellow, too?"

"Yes. Be still. And do not neighbor yourself too close to the fire. I will now heat my knife."

"This is fun."

Little Man pointed a finger at him. "No, it is all but fun. It is secret. Kirby Tree is not here this night to play schoolroom games."

"Why am I here?"

"Tonight is the Night of the Snake."

Kirby felt a chill crawl over his back. A sudden cold. Squinting, he saw the pale streaks of paint on Little Man's face, one below each eye. The fire reflected its orange on the knife's silvery blade.

"Close your eyes, Kirby."

He obeyed, and waited in silence, hearing only the swamp frogs and the fire's crackle; but then he felt his uncle smear something on his face. "What's on me?" The boy opened one eye to a slit.

"It is my blood." Little Man's hand was bleeding.
"The blood of Creek Indians who became the
Seminole. It is your blood, my blood, and the warm red
of revenge that belongs to our people."

Kirby Tree waited. For some reason, he was afraid
and felt his legs shake. The shallow water around his
feet grew colder.

"Open your eyes."

Blinking at the brightening fire, Kirby saw that Little Man's hand held a small square of paper.

"Look at him and remember."

Kirby took the paper, turned it, and squinted at the
face of a man wearing a white sweater.

"Who is he?"

"Your father."

The boy could not breathe. He wanted to drop the
photograph, yet could not seem to force his fingers
to free it. Yellow firelight danced on Little Man's
face. Never had Kirby seen his uncle stare so intently
at him. His eyes seemed to be two black balls of
death. At last, Kirby managed to choke out words.

"I don't believe it."

No sooner had Kirby said it than he saw the hot
knife flash upward. In less than a second, Little Man
sliced off a hunk of the boy's hair. It hurt. Kirby
wanted to cry. Before he could do so, Little Man thrust
the lock of his almost-white hair into his hand. Kirby
held it.

"Now look. See *your* hair and *his*."

Kirby could say nothing. His eyes darted from his

own lock of hair to the blond head of the man in the picture. The man was smiling but Little Man was not smiling. Kirby did not like the look that he now could see on his uncle's round face.

"This man is your father."

Kirby Tree nodded.

"And more," said Little Man, "he is also the evil man who killed your mother. He ended the life of my sister, Flower Tree."

The boy could not believe what he was hearing. It was all too much, too new. He didn't want to learn bad things. Only good things, the ones that Mrs. Hopkin taught at school. I only want, Kirby thought, to hear the happy stories that Grandfather tells me when I sit in his lap, after supper.

Kirby felt sick.

"And now," said Little Man, "it is time for you to hear my promise."

"What promise?"

"Watch."

Using the knife's hot blade, Little Man Tree again cut his own hand. With the other hand, he threw down his knife to snatch the burlap potato sack. Kirby saw dust cling to the blood-wet fingers. Slowly, his uncle undid the knot in the sack's neck.

Then he violently shook the sack.

Kirby heard it and froze. His grandfather had taught him to be afraid of that buzzing noise; and to first look, then run. But now there was no rattlesnake to see. The snake was in the bag.

"Little Man, don't . . . please don't . . . "

"Tonight," he heard his uncle say, "is the Night of the Snake. And there is one more step in my ritual. One more act."

"Please . . . "

"Do not shiver, Kirby. The snake is not for you. It is for my oath."

Feeling the heat of fear behind his eyes, Kirby Tree wanted to run away from the swamp, back home, to where his grandfather was still asleep and where his own bed would be warm and dry.

"Listen to me." Little Man's face came so close that Kirby could smell the beans they had eaten for their evening meal. "Listen up . . . I swear to you, by all holy in God's Florida, that I will kill this man."

"Kill my . . . father?"

"Yes. He must die, to pay for what he did to your mother, and did not marry her."

Kirby's voice was unsteady. "What did he do?"

"He shamed Flower. So I make you a secret promise. I don't know all of the old words, but I feel my Seminole blood, Kirby. On my hands and on your face. I now give you my promise."

"What promise?"

Little Man's eyes narrowed. Two pinpoints of yellow pierced the two black circles. He spoke very slowly and deeply.

"A white man dies."

Kirby saw Little Man quickly thrust his own big hand into the sack, again heard the rattle of the snake; and then, in a breath, saw the eyes of Little Man widen in pain. Slowly, with his teeth grinning into the night, Little Man stood up and pulled his hand from the bag.

The snake's fangs were still buried in Little Man's hand, until he shook it free. With a plop, the rattler landed into shallow swamp water and whipped off into the night. Little Man sank to his knees.

"Kirby, . . . I . . . promise."

7

"Listen up, Jason."

Standing on her small porch, Mrs. Hood cupped her hand around an ear and leaned toward the early morning sun. "Hear 'em?" she again asked her husband.

Jason Hood nodded. "Yes, I hear 'em."

"We feared it. Knew they was coming. And now we'll hear 'em roar all day. And scatter their dust up yonder into the holy."

Jason sighed. "Bulldozers."

"Can't hear our sweet mockingbirds this morning. Even though the bulldozers are most a mile off."

Her husband sneezed. "There's sand in the air, Hoody. I can smell it up."

"So can I." Hoody slumped down into her porch rocker. "Florida ain't alive no more. Even the gators are leaving the swamp to die themselves at a road-side."

"I guess a gator hears them giant machines, too. We all gotta have a spot to live in, Hoody. You, me, and the swamp gators."

Hoody said, "I don't guess I seen a bear or a cub come by in six months or better. God's Florida has lost her quiet."

She saw her husband slowly shake his head. "Ain't a thing folks like us old crackers can do, woman. Just try to hold ground and swallow their dust."

Mrs. Hood heard the mule snort.

"Jessica don't like it much neither. She hears 'em all threat down on us. And we're all to gray to run. We're only a pair of old crop pickers, and now we're even too tired to stoop and gather up."

Her husband tightened his lips. "Soon there won't be no place to run to. God's Florida . . . they'll soon blacktop it all."

"I prayed last night, Jay. Prayed right hard we'd find us a way to hold our home. Lord knows, our shack ain't too gussy. But it's ours. All I want is to live here and die here. We don't beg Heaven for no more."

Jason spat. "Developers."

"How close'll they come, Jay?"

Before her husband could reply, the distant bulldozers growled an answer. Hoody shuddered.

"Day by day," said Jason, "and rod by rod, they'll come at us, all them city ginks in their yeller helmets, holding up blueprints. Plans to spook off every beast and every human being that used to call it the sweet word of home."

Hoody reached into her pocket for her snuff, then changed her mind. "You told me what they were building this time, and I guess I made myself forget."

"A country club."

She slapped her knee. "If that don't beat all. A real twister. To build a country club they got to wreck the country."

"That's how they do it, Hoody." Jason sat on a barrel. "Them fancy developers all name their places after whatever they destroy."

"So it seems."

"To put up that cluster of new houses, north of here, their bulldozers knocked over every tree on twenty acre. Every dang tree. And what did they finally name the place?"

"I don't recall."

"They called it Sherwood Forest."

Hoody cackled out a laugh. "That's a righteous caution."

Her husband smiled, too. "And west of that, the dozers all but leveled off them pretty little hills into a prairie, and you know what they named their new flat?"

"What?"

"Called it Harwood Heights."

Hoody grabbed her ribs. "Oh, that beats all. It really do. That really eats up the final crumb."

"Hey, You wanna hear my guess?"

"About what?"

"Well," said Jason, "about what all them real estate developers'll name their new country club."

Hoody couldn't wait to hear. "Tell me."

"As I see it, I s'pose they'll bully in with their pumps, drain every drop of water out of our swamp until she's bone dry . . . and then call their dust bowl something like Green Lake."

"Stop!" Hoody's arms wrapped across her stomach. It hurts to laugh, she thought, but it hurts a lot worse not to. "Jason Hood, if'n you don't quit up, I'm to chuckle my bowels loose."

"Does a body good to laugh."

Hoody nodded. "True, it certain does. Let's hoot at 'em, Jay. Maybe we ought to hitch up Jessica and journey over to point our fingers at their big yeller bulldozers, and laugh at 'em until they spook off."

"Maybe we ought."

As he spoke, Hoody saw her husband's face lose its grin. "Don't quit smiling, Jay. Please don't."

"Sorry, I don't guess I got many more smiles left inside me, Hoody."

"Don't talk that way. It grieves me to hear ya. Grieves me down."

Both of them were quiet, hearing the distant engines grinding their gears. They were quiet for a few minutes. Then came a dull blast of dynamite.

Hoody saw her husband's face twitch.

"That blowup we just heard. Know what that was, Hoody? Ya know what just happened?"

"I know. Dynamite."

"Yup, and more'n that. Deep in that earth what they just blowed apart was some little animal's burrow. Maybe a skunk or a coon. Probable a warren of rabbit. Along with litters of rabbit fawns and coon kits. Innocent blind babes."

"Don't say no more, Jason. Please don't."

"I got to. I got to look up to Heaven and tell God Almighty about somebody's home, even if'n the somebody ain't more'n a coon."

He stood up on the barrel, lifting his scrawny arms up toward the sky, yelling.

"Hear me, God? All we be down below is your creatures. Just a mess of swamp possum, and us Hoods. Listen up to'em. Harken their bulldozers and their blasting. This old place of ours is all we got, me and Hoody. We got a mule, our watermelon crop, and a scrub-pine shack. It's all we want. Me and my wife don't ask no more."

Hoody couldn't move. She could only sit captive in her rocker and watch the pain and the fear possess her husband's upturned face.

"No," Jason whispered to the sky, "I don't never beg you for frills or fancy. And no supper gets ett until we bow our thanks for it. Even if'n it be one turnip, we blessing it."

He finally lowered his chin. Slowly he got down

off the barrel to look at his wife. "Hoody, I guess I'm no more than a aging fool."

She stood up. "You and me both, Jay. We're two old fools. A pair of old swamp frogs, you and me, croaking in our night of blackness that things aren't the way they was."

Walking up on the porch, he came to her, to put his thin arms around her, holding her close. Trembling, she felt the sweetness of her man. He smelled of mule, sweat, and home.

"Come inside, Jay, and I'll brew tea."

She felt his head nod.

"There's a rip in your shirt. Skin it off and I'll mend a patch to it."

"We won't spook, Hoody." He looked at her with red eyes. "We won't let 'em beat us back into the swamp. Hear?"

"I hear."

"No, we won't run no more. You and me squat this land and, by damn, we'll keep root."

"Here," she said. "Here to home."

8

Westal Jordanson shouted.

"Hold up!"

Pulling off his white cowboy hat, Wes mopped his cheek with the short sleeve of his white tennis shirt. He walked out onto the court.

"Billy, let me have your bat for a minute," he said softly.

The boy handed his racquet to Mr. Jordanson.

"Here's what you're doing wrong. You tend to hit off your back foot, leaning away from the shot, because you're not prepared. Even before the ball crosses the net, I want to see your racquet back. Way back here, like so. Then you lean forward, lean into the ball with a closed stance."

"Okay."

"You don't hit a tennis ball with your arm. Power comes from hitting with your entire body. An attacking tennis shot is body force. The key is preparation. So you attack the ball instead of allowing the ball to charge at *you*."

Billy Gossage nodded.

"Another thing," Wes told him. "When your racquet's back, keep it low. Then bring it forward, and *through* the ball . . . not *at* it. The racquet starts low and finishes high."

"Why?"

Wes squinted the leather of his face. "Because that's how you'll hit a tennis ball with topspin. And with topspin, once your shot crosses the net, it'll dig its own hole. Bite down into the air and land in the court."

He walked slowly back to his big wicker chair, the one he kept on the wooden platform. From there, Wes could look along the net of the pro court and check the arc of a tennis ball. Westal Jordanson could tell how a ball was hit without looking at either player. The ball said it all. If it floated, the player had hit flat.

"Go to it," he told the two teenagers.

The yellow ball passed back and forth, crossing and crisscrossing the net; but the old professional's head never moved from side to side. The ball's trajectory told him the story.

"I'll know it when I see it," he mumbled, "but this ain't it. Maybe someday I'll spot the boy I'm looking for."

The parents of both these lads, he thought, have paid me thousands of dollars. Plus all the checks they wrote for clothes, balls, and bats.

"Darn," he said under his breath, "If I'm not tempted to give every cent of it back."

Buddy Small, the boy hitting with Billy, popped the ball up high. A short and high lob. Without turning his head, Wes saw Billy charging in, coming under the ball; yet not quite close enough. Bill's racquet cocked for the big overhead smash, the sure winner. He hit it.

But the ball died in the net.

"No," said Wes in a quite voice.

Again he got up from his chair, feeling his face wince. Doggone arthritis, he was thinking. Mornings, such as this, were the worst times. Soon the sun would be stronger and bake him loose.

"An overhead," he told Billy, "is no more and no less than self-explanatory. Right then, you hit the ball in front of you. That's good for ground strokes. But to hit an overhead winner, the ball is just that . . . *over your head*. Straight up."

"I know that. I just . . ."

"Listen a minute, please. As you hit the shot, Bill, do you know what you did?"

"No, sir."

"You dropped your head. Keep that chin up. I want you to watch that overhead ball falling at you; then you keep your eye on it, and knock it out of an empty sky. Got it?"

Billy nodded. "I'll do it."

Wes smiled at him. "In time. A lot of tennis, boys, is just plain old common sense."

The old tennis pro slowly returned to his high-backed wicker chair, pulled his cowboy hat down over his eyes, and thought.

Both the boys would become superb club players. How old are they? Bud and Billy were probably fifteen. What gets me is that constant look of surprise on their faces when they miss a shot. All they think about is that the ball went to the wrong place. Trouble is, they both want to *admire* a shot instead of hit it.

Wes snorted.

That isn't the key. The answer is that the body has to be in the right place. It's all in the feet. A tennis shot is like a fort, he thought, built from the ground up. More dancing than athletics. I look at the feet, then the legs. Feather toes and iron thighs. You don't find the combination under every fern.

"No," he said aloud, "you surely don't."

Westal Jordanson forced himself to sit up straight in his chair. One more hour, he thought, and the ache would hopefully start to melt away. Come on, sun.

"How they doing, Wes?"

Looking back over his shoulder, Wes saw Art Gossage, standing just behind him, wearing a bright pink jacket, plaid slacks, and white shoes.

"Hey there, Arthur. They look better and better. Tell me, how's Florida's most prominent car dealer?"

Art grinned.

"We're movin' the tin. That's all there be to it. Show customers how the chrome shines and whisper 'im a honeysuckle deal."

"Is that your secret?"

"Always has been. Get 'em into the showroom so's they can slam a door, kick a tire, and pretend they can judge an engine when they peek under the hood."

Coming up behind him Art rested his hands on Westal's shoulders and kneaded the muscles. "How's your old back behavin'?"

"Fine. Just keep doing that all day and I'll turn your boy Billy into a club champ."

"That's what I like to hear, Wes. Is he hittin' real good?"

"Real good. How was the board meeting?"

Art chuckled. "Usual bull session."

"Are you gentlemen keeping the Sweetgum Country Club in the black?"

"Surprisin' enough, yes. For a new club, we're more than solvent. Herb Caldwell . . . you know, the funeral director . . . Herb got elected to the board this morning, and *he* owns half of Central Florida."

"Yeah, and you own the other half. If I could sell half as many tennis bats as you do Cadillacs, I'd lie in bed until noon."

Art clucked his tongue. "Don't gimme that, Westal. Take away your tennis and you'd die off."

Wes nodded. "Yes, I probably would."

The diamond ring on Art's little finger sparkled in the morning sun. "You're lucky you can still play the game once in a while."

"Only doubles. Too gimpy for singles."

Art Gossage patted his portly stomach. "And I'm too fat to play either one. I'm just a dumb ol' country boy tryin' to scratch out a livin' selling cars."

Westal Jordanson felt himself grin. I'd easily wager, he thought, that Art Gossage had a million dollars. He saw his friend shake his head.

"I gotta take off a few pounds. Maybe I'll quit ridin' around in my golfcart, invest in a racquet, and letcha gimme a few lessons."

"Anytime, Art."

"Lassie June keeps harpin' that she'll divorce me unless I melt off a ton or two."

"Maybe so."

Wes again saw Art's chubby hand pat his belly. "I tell her *that's* nothin' more than prosperity. Florida's growin' and so am I. By the way, we're extending the golf course to eighteen holes."

"How soon?"

Art pointed toward the pines. "Bulldozers ought to be here Monday, to break more ground. Nine holes was okay for a starter, but now we can financially swing eighteen."

"Where'll they go?"

The car dealer continued to point. "Right over yonder. Due west of here. We'll drain, level and sod . . . then slap in the greens. Folks'll tee off in less'n three months."

Wes sighed. "It's kind of a pity to knock down that stand of big cypress and pine."

"Lassie June says likewise. She was born a swamp rat. I met her workin' in K-Mart. Married her in a week. Lassie's always naggin' at me to spare a tree or two."

"Your wife has a point, Art."

"I tell her that I don't knock down the trees. The bulldozers do." Art slapped his beefy leg.

Wes squinted west. "Still and all, I sort of hate to see so many of Florida's big trees fall."

"Yeah, but that's progress."

9

"Kirby?"

Wilbur Tree looked around for his grandson. The boy was nowhere in sight. Run off again, he thought, as did I when I was his age.

"I know where," he said to Isaac.

The big Red Angus worked his thick neck up and down against the rough bark of a pasture pine.

"Do you itch with ticks again?" asked Wilbur. "Stand easy while I look you over."

I wonder, thought Wilbur Tree, how much this old bull understands of what I tell him. Perhaps much. Then again, perhaps nothing at all.

Moving slowly, Wilbur narrowed the distance between himself and his animal. He grows old, he

56

thought, as Wilbur Tree grows old. In a few more years he will die. Maybe he will wander off into the swamp when he knows it is time. He already is aware, I think, that I no longer lead him to visit Mr. Ledger's cows. No more. Isaac's seed no longer sires calves.

How long will he live?

"Live as long as you wish, Isaac Stern, and rest in the shade and whip the deerflies with your tail. Kill every one so that they will not chew the light skin of my grandchild."

Remembering, he called out again.

"Kirby?"

Yes, he nodded his head, I know where he goes. So does Little Man who is maddened by it far more than I madden. I know where Kirby goes, and why.

"Do not be afraid, Isaac. It is only your old Seminole friend, Wilbur Tree, who comes to visit you."

He is blind, thought Wilbur. Or almost blind. So I must warn my bull that I can now almost reach out to touch him, and I will do that. I will scratch the backs of his ears.

Scratching the bull, Wilbur saw his big brown eyes close. They close often now, he thought, for there is only his own darkness to see. Wilbur Tree will not be sad, for this is the way life sometimes ends here in God's Florida.

Alone, in the darkness, and in the long night of age.

Narrowing his eyes, Wilbur searched the thick red

hair for ticks. He searched for several minutes. Finding none and feeling no scabs, he felt relieved.

"Isaac Stern, you are clean."

Very slowly, Wilbur worked his way around to the bull's other flank, being careful to keep one hand on the great back, in constant contact. There were no ticks here either.

"I will leave you now, Isaac, to rest beneath your big tree, and to dream of your times with the beautiful cows, as old men often dream."

Wilbur walked across the sunlit sand and grass of his bull pasture, waving to Van Cliburn and to Pablo Casals, his two younger bulls. How, he thought, I miss my Hanna. Yet we had our days, our nights, and our many years. So it ends in death; for Hanna, and then for Flower.

How old is my grandchild? Yes, I remember. Kirby is now twelve.

Wilbur Tree walked through the swamp that sat east of his house. Looking beneath his feet, he noticed that the black water appeared to be shallow. More land could be seen. The water was going. Little Man tells me, he thought, that it is because of the drainage people, and their pumps that roar all night and all day.

I hear them, Wilbur thought.

At night, when the two boys sleep, I have heard the distant pumps, their motors groaning in labor. And I smell the exhaust, the fumes, smoke that an eye can-

not see but that can cause a nose to wince. Closing his
eyes, Wilbur inhaled the fragrance of his swamp.

Again he looked down.

In places, where the muck should have been black
and shining wet, the dirt was drying to a lighter gray.
The gnarled knees of the cypress seemed to grow
taller overnight. From his left, he heard the hiss of a
gator, then a sudden splash.

"Catch your catfish," he said. "Eat and prosper, so
that your gator jaws will go eastward to snap at the
hoses of the pumps."

Little Man tells me about the pumps, he
remembered, and I see his face darken. My son lives
by the old ways. Not my grandchild. At his school,
Kirby hears of the new ways, the new life, and reads
to me from his books. Strange things. Often I turn off
my radio to listen and to rest the batteries, while
Kirby reads newspapers that he brings home. I listen
when he reads the advertisements about the show
places.

"Mickey Mouse."

Wilbur smiled as he walked. My grandson is happy
because a mouse has come to God's Florida. Mice
abound here. I name my bulls. So I must accept that
Mr. Disney names his mouse. And his duck. Out
there, beyond the swamp, new things happen that
are foreign to Wilbur Tree and to Little Man Tree.

Yet not to Kirby Tree.

My grandchild is new life. And he wishes to learn,

to read about the new ways, and to switch the number on the dial of my radio . . . to hear the white man's music.

"Ha!" Wilbur Tree laughed. A frog jumped and he said to the frog, "The music that my grandchild tells me is modern sounds more savage to my ear than the handsome violin tunes of Isaac Stern."

As he walked, Wilbur heard the distant sound of voices and knew that he was almost to the place where he would find Kirby.

Tonight, he thought, after my grandson is asleep, I will reset my radio to its old number, the one where I hear the man's voice say, "This is your classical music station." Then I will wait for the music that is played by the men and women whose names I honor.

For so many years, Wilbur thought, the dial of my radio did not spin. All I did was turn it on or off. But now Kirby twists the dial, yet his ear is only rewarded by the harsh noise that he tells me is the new music. Much of it has no tune.

Wilbur grunted. The new music, he thought, sounds like Mr. Ledger's turpentine factory.

Ahead, the voices were louder.

Wilbur kept himself in the brush. There was no need to alarm the white people who might wander into the trees to search for a hard little white ball which was not much larger than an egg from a snapper turtle. This was the ball they hit with sticks.

Golf was a strange game, he thought. The white man hits the ball with his stick and when the white ball flies to hide in the trees, the man speaks a dirty word.

I will watch, said Wilbur to himself, because it is more fun for me than for the golf men. He watched a golfer swing a silver wand. The ball did not move. Instead, a clod of earth flew into the air and the man threw his stick.

Wilbur Tree laughed, shooting a hand upward to cover his laughter so that the golf man would not hear and think that Seminoles do not wear good manners.

He throws the stick well, thought Wilbur.

This man must be a good player, but I do not understand why he hits the little hunk of earth instead of the ball. The white man's game should bring him fun, but the white face does not seem to shine with happiness.

Wilbur moved on, through the dense veil of green brush, making no sound. He would find his grandchild at the place where he always sneaked off to hide . . . to watch the other game, the one with the yellow balls. I cannot remember the name of the other game, but Kirby will again tell me.

There he was.

His grandson was standing, just ahead, in a patch of sunlight. The sun poured gold on his hair. Kirby, he thought, grew the hair of an angel. How beautiful he is. Lighter than Flower. He is light in all ways. Hair, skin, and heart. And the heart of Wilbur Tree, he knew, is lightest of all when I sometimes behold him and he does not yet see me.

The boy turned and smiled.

"So," said Wilbur, pretending to frown, "you have again come to your hiding place, to watch the game of yellow balls."

"Yes," whispered Kirby. "Please let me stay for one more minute. It's deuce."

"You are twelve years old and you must come home and help your grandfather work his orange grove."

"I'll come."

He is a good boy, thought Wilbur. Even though he wanted to stay and watch, he turns away to walk home with me and to be my strong little helper. He does not let disappointment cloud his face. Instead, he carries manhood in his spine.

"Tell me, Kirby. I forget. What is the name of the game you run away to watch?"

"Tennis."

Wilbur noticed that Kirby was carrying something. "You have a yellow ball in your hand."

"It's mine. I found it."

"No, it is not yours. And you must be honest and return the ball to its owner."

"But look. The ball's old." Kirby handed it to him. "They knocked it away, on purpose, over the fence toward the swamp."

"Are you sure?"

"Yes."

"Keep it then. It can be yours. And, because you are a fine grandchild, I have a surprise for you."

The boy's black eyes shone brighter. "A surprise?"

Wilbur Tree nodded. "Yes. It is not yet carved. But I will use the knife and make the surprise for you, because you sometimes do work like a man at the oranges."

"Please tell me what you're going to make with the knife. I want to know right now."

Wilbur Tree smiled. "In time."

10

Westal Jordanson jumped the puddle.

Not bad, he thought, for a man my age who's carrying a flyrod and a tackle box. If there are still a few bass in that pond, they had better be on their guard.

Reaching the wagon road, he continued to walk due west, keeping the morning sun at his back. It felt good. I wonder, he thought to himself, if bass ever get arthritis. As he walked by the gray wooden shack, he looked up and saw Mrs. Hood.

Wes stopped. "Good morning, beautiful."

"Same *to* ya, Westal. Going fishing?"

"Thought I would. Thank goodness for Mondays when the club is closed. Aren't you going to your job this morning?"

Hoody nodded. "Just about to leave. As you know, Monday's the day we cleaning ladies go to polish the place."

"Didn't I see you at the club yesterday as well?"

"Sure did. Me and Jason walk over, now and again, to watch 'em play their tennis. We cotton to see 'em miss."

Wes grinned. "Planning to take it up?"

"Not me. I'm too lame. But we sure do cotton to watch. The golf ain't near as exciting. Far as I can see, them golf balls don't do much more'n go plop into water."

"Hoody, you have good taste in sports."

"I got a question to ask ya."

"Shoot."

Mrs. Hood planted her big fists on ample hips. "You folks don't intend to make the Sweetgum Country Club any *larger*, do ya?"

"I wish they never would."

"Well. Me and old Jason been pushed back as far as tolerable. If'n you'd tole me, two years back, that today I'd be workin' there one day a week for wages, I'd 've called y'all a pack of liars."

"Florida's changing, Hoody."

"Sure as righteous is. Well, I best get myself cranking and go do my day's work.

Hope ya hook a bite."

"So long, Hoody." Wes turned. "And please do tell Jason that the two of you are welcome to come watch the tennis any time you wish. You're my guests."

"Will do. Watching them fat rich folks try to play would make a dog laugh."

Leaving the wagon road, at the tree where he usually left it, Wes cut through the swamp to the northwest. I hope, he was thinking, that no one else ever discovers my fishing pond. Westal sighed. In time, someone surely would.

"Maybe today," he said to his flyrod, "you and I will try our luck on the far side. We've never been over that way before."

Arriving at the spot, Wes rested his tackle box on a fallen log, to unfasten its clasp. But he never completed the act. Something made Westal Jordanson pause.

Thump!

Wes listened. Perhaps, he thought, I'm just hearing things. Yet he heard the noise once again.

Thump!

There's no one out here, he told himself. It's still wilderness, thank Heaven. Still virgin. But then he heard the sound a third time.

Leaning his flyrod on a tree, Wes followed the noise. It grew louder each time he heard it. What, he asked himself, in the name of good sense, would create a *thump* like that? If it's an animal, it sure is one strange beast.

He kept walking. Faster now, cutting through the palmetto, as curious as he ever could be about whatever was causing the sound. Then he saw the **barn**.

And the boy!

Wes stopped, held his breath, and tried to convince himself that he was still sane. Yet, in a matter of seconds, Westal Jordanson saw it all. Motionless, he stood under the trees, to watch, trying to control the leapings of his mind and spirit. Just to see what he saw made Wes sweat.

The half-grown boy was tossing a rotten old tennis ball into the air, serving it with a racquet that was obviously, to Wes's eye, homemade. The serve was superb.

Up went the ball, the makeshift racquet cocked, and fired . . . and a colorless ball almost knocked over the side of the old barn. The barn's gray flank had been painted with a white horizontal stripe, the height of a tennis net. The rusty iron wheel rims of two giant wagon wheels had been nailed, left and right, just above the white painted line. The two circles were targets.

Thump!

"Thirty love," Wes heard the boy say.

He served again, and the ball hit the wood exactly in the center of the iron rim to the left. *Thump*! As it bounced off the barn, the boy attacked its return with a backhand volley, cross count, into the hoop on the right.

As he played, Wes watched.

The young legs bent; then they would spring forward to thrust the lithe body into the next shot. The boy's heels never touched the sand. There was no court, no surface, and no ground strokes. Nothing but serve and volley.

Except for a pair of sorry-looking undershorts, the boy was naked. Golden skin; and hair lighter still, almost a white. A real towhead, Wes thought. How old? My guess is no more than thirteen. Hilda, he said silently, this is the son that you and I could never have. God, he prayed, how I wish you were still alive.

I am going to do my damndest, Wes thought, not to cry.

Nevertheless, Wes felt his own body tremble, asking one hundred questions every second, coupled with his wild fantasies of the future. A tennis champion? Minutes passed before he could think rationally.

"I'm in shock," Wes whispered.

I want to grab that boy and hold him in my arms; to look at his face, and to tell him that *he is the one*. The love I feel is far beyond hope. In moments, I have come to cherish this boy. It is, Wes was thinking, as though I've met the son I never had, the contender I never found.

He's the one.

With both arms embracing a small oak to steady himself, Westal Jordanson, the grayhaired tennis professional of the Sweetgum Country Club, stood and witnessed his dream that had at last come to life.

The boy missed a shot.

An old ball hit the barn just below the crooked, crudely-painted white line; and he pounded his right leg with the strange racquet.

"No!" the boy scolded himself. Walking to his left, he picked up another worthless ball, posed himself sideways, and said, "Ad out."

This time the toss climbed up and back, one that Wes knew would require the perfect six-to-twelve o'clock serve. It came. The cocked racquet gracefully slashed like a sword.

Thump!

On a tennis court, the serve would have been superb and the boy somehow knew it.

"Ace," he said.

Unable to control his reaction, Wes Jordanson applauded. He walked forward as the startled boy turned. But then Wes stopped both his approach and his clapping. The boy's face showed shock. Yet what Wes saw was not the tan young face, but the eyes.

Two black eyes stared at him.

Wes swallowed. "Excuse me, son . . . but please permit me to ask you who you are. Don't be afraid. My name's Wes Jordanson."

"I am Kirby Tree."

Standing still, Wes gently nodded. "So your name is Kirby Tree." Wes extended his hand and the boy hesitated, then took it. Good grip, Westal was thinking. Claws like a young lobster. "Do you live around here?"

"Yes, sir, with my grandfather and my uncle."

Wes smiled. "Would you please allow me to look at your racquet?"

The boy handed it over. As far as Wes could see, someone had whittled it with a knife. Its shape was slightly irregular and it had been strung with fishing line. Wes shook his head in disbelief. Fishing line! Some of the strands were green; some colorless, obviously from a leader.

The knots were crude, yet tight.

"Did you make it?"

"No, sir. Grandfather made it for me."

Go slowly, Wes warned himself. Not too many questions from the thousands that I am urged to ask.

"Do you know who I am?"

The youth nodded. "Yes, sir. I have seen you teach people to play tennis. They do not do what you tell them, and you sometimes walk sadly to your big chair. So I come home and do whatever I hear you tell them. And it works."

Wes felt the pain in his back. Yet, he thought, it somehow isn't going to hurt me much. Not on this day.

"Kirby, would you do an old man a favor?"

"Sure. Just name it."

"Please let me meet your grandfather."

11

Little Man stared at the white stranger.

No, he told himself, this is not the face in Flower's photograph. And he is older than my father—much too aged. This man, who talks of the tennis and calls himself Jordanson, is not the one.

The four of them sat on the pine needles beside the house, talking. Little Man Tree did not like the words nor did he want to listen to so many questions that the white face was asking. We leave people alone, thought Little Man. So why cannot they leave the Trees to work our lives in peace?

"And," the white stranger asked again, "you actually made this wonderful racquet by hand, for Kirby here?"

Wilbur Tree nodded. "I am pleased to see when my grandson wishes to learn new things."

The white face smiled.

"Mr. Tree, I don't really know just how to tell you this, but your grandson, whom I just met less than an hour ago, learns more quickly than any boy I have ever seen."

"Thank you. Kirby also learns to hide from work. He does not yet learn that bugs eat our orange crop, and ticks eat our bulls."

Little Man saw his father pretend to frown at Kirby. I shall frown at him, too, he thought, because it is honest work that hardens the arm of Seminoles. The face of the white man, Little Man thought, wears confusion. He looks puzzled, as if he cannot find the words to ask Wilbur Tree more questions. I do not like the way the man glances at Kirby, as though he wants to take him from us. Yet he does not appear to be a loud man; so I will wait and listen.

"You are a teacher," said Wilbur Tree.

"Yes, I teach tennis."

Little Man saw his father nod and speak. "Teachers are good. My grandson learns many new things at school, but not all that he learns is good."

"I would be interested to know, Mr. Tree, what things you think are important to learn."

"Manners."

"I quite agree. Tennis is a game of manners, sir. The day it stops being mannerly is the day I stop playing it."

"Manners are not enough, Mr. Jordanson. My grandchild will also learn to work, so that he will eat in God's Florida after I die."

The white man agreed.

"Work is first," said Wilbur. "Your tennis is only a game for the people who play at the country club place. Only a game."

"You wish to say more, Mr. Tree?"

"Yes. You talk of manners, but I do not always see good manners when the people play the golf."

"You are wise, Mr. Tree. And you are a gentleman, far more so than some people who play golf. Please don't think me rude to ask, but where are Kirby's parents?"

The pine trunk, against which Little Man leaned his back, became harder. He wanted to move but did not. I do not like to hear, he thought, so many questions. How will my father answer? I hope he does not.

Stretching out his legs, Wilbur Tree crossed his ankles and started to speak. But instead, it was Kirby who spoke first.

"My mother is dead, sir. She died as I was born. I never knew her, but her name was Flower and she was very beautiful."

"I married a white woman, Mr. Jordanson. She, too, was beautiful. White as the egret. That is perhaps why my grandson wears the light skin and the silver-gold hair. My wife was Hanna Kirby."

"I see."

No, thought Little Man, the stranger does *not* see. His face still asks . . . who is Kirby's father? Not a Seminole, he thinks.

"Then only the three of you live here in the swamp with your bulls, bees, and oranges."

Wilbur Tree nodded. "Do you have a wife, Mr. Jordanson? I hope you do not wonder if I have bad manners to ask this."

The white face smiled. "Hardly," he said. "I do not think anything but admiration for your manners, sir."

"Thank you."

Mr. Jordanson shook his head. "No, my wife died. I married a long time ago."

"Are you a father?"

"Hilda and I had no children. Years back, when I was a young man, I wanted us to have some kids, so that I could teach them to play tennis."

Wilbur touched the man's shoulder. "I am sorry you have no children. It is an emptiness. My own life is wealthy with Little Man and Kirby."

"Yes, I can see that."

Little Man saw the smile melt from his father's mouth. "Mr. Jordanson, I feel that you want Kirby."

"I do. I want your grandson more intently than I have wanted anything since Hilda died. Fifteen years ago. Kirby is the boy I have waited for. I'm sixty-one years old, Mr. Tree. Sixty-one, so I have little time left to build me what I must build."

"And what is it you build? I do not understand all that you say."

Little Man saw Mr. Jordanson take a very deep breath. "Mr. Tree, with your permission, I want to build a champion."

The face of my nephew, thought Little Man, looks now like a new penny. Golden and happy. How, he wondered, can I fight this tennis thing that brings Kirby so much joy? Yet it also bruises his leg when he strikes himself with the present that Wilbur Tree carved for him. The racquet toy.

To himself, Little Man smiled. Kirby is still my baby boy, and I will be forever his fat old uncle who walks the long miles to the little store, for ice, to pack on Kirby's leg. So that his hurt marks will not be stiff or swollen to a purple color.

I cannot see Kirby hurt.

But I fear that there is pain ahead for him, if he leaves us to learn the white game with the yellow balls. Yes, thought Little Man, I can close my eyes and see Flower dying. My sweet sister who brushed my hair.

"Mr. Tree, I will not be so unmannerly as to ask you today for an answer." The man stood up quickly. So did Wilbur. " My hope is merely that you consider allowing me to coach Kirby."

Wilbur Tree looked at his grandson, and at the racquet he had made which Kirby was twirling in his slender fingers.

"I will think, Mr. Jordanson."

As Little Man watched Kirby, there seemed to be only one word in the boy's heart. Please.

"He has talent, Mr. Tree."

"But your tennis is only a game."

"To me, it is more. It is my work and my life. And I pray you'll let your grandson be part of my life, as I want to be his teacher . . . more than anything else on earth." He smiled. "More than anything else, as you would say, in God's Florida."

Wilbur Tree held out his hand. "You are an honest man, Mr. Jordanson. I know oranges. Also, I know bulls. And I see strength in your eyes."

"Thank you, Mr. Tree. Thank you so very, very much."

Little Man Tree saw the tennis man turn to go, but then Wilbur asked him one more question.

"I would like to ask, Mr. Jordanson, if you like to listen to music?"

The man nodded.

"And do you know," Wilbur continued, "the music on the radio that is made by Isaac Stern?"

Little Man saw the puzzled look on Mr. Jordanson's face. " I believe I do, yes."

"Will you teach my Kirby to play the tennis in the way that Mr. Stern plays his violin?"

The surprised white face was silent. Little Man could see that he was making an effort to answer his father's question. The white chin trembled before the white mouth could finally answer. When he spoke, his voice was half choked. And very soft.

"Mr. Tree . . . I promise to."

12

"Army shoes?"

Kirby stood in Mrs. Hood's open doorway, watching her face as she raised her eyebrows. She came forward to pat his cheek with her big hand, as she often did, and her touch felt good to him. He wanted to hug her.

"Yes 'm," he said instead. "Mr. Hood was in the Army and he showed me his big shoes."

"And you wanna wear 'em, do ya, and pretend you're a grown up soldier?"

"They're for my legs."

Kirby saw Mrs. Hood react with additional dismay. "You aim to put shoes on your legs? To make your outfit complete, maybe you best wear stockings on

78

your arms." As she laughed, she gave him a joking shove.

Her house smells of cooking, Kirby thought, his eyes wandering over to the stove.

"You hungry?" she asked him.

"Oh, no thanks. I'm just sort of curious about what you were baking that smells so good."

"Corn dodgers." Lifting a white napkin from a lumpy plate, Mrs. Hood said, "Open up." As she shoved half of a warm muffin in his mouth, she smiled. "Jay says I bake up the best dodgers in the county."

The corn dodger tasted grainy, but great. Kirby chewed, and then swallowed. "You sure do. Thank you."

"Well, you're more than welcome, Kirby, I'd like to see a pound or two more brawn on your bones. You're thirteen, ya told me?"

"I'm fourteen. But my grandather says that boys grow up and then grow out. He makes me drink a lot of goat's milk."

"You're spurting up faster than swamp gas." Hoody nodded. "Old Wilbur's right on that score. Now then, where did I squirrel away them old Army shoes?"

Kirby watched her paw through a tan cardboard box, pulling out a worn pair of trousers, a battered hat, and several rolls of printed cloth. Most of the cloth, Kirby saw, was as faded as her dress.

"Here they be." Mrs. Hood straightened up to hand the Army shoes to Kirby. Both were dusty and, to Kirby's nose, still smelled as if they were still in the Army. "Best you try 'em on. Jay always had feet bigger than all summer. I bet your feet'll near swim inside those."

Kicking off his mocs, Kirby pulled on one shoe, then its mate. "They sure are big. But that's the way I want them to fit."

Hoody laughed. "Don't tell me you aim to play tennis in them clodhoppers. If'n you do, your feet'll take three steps before *they* do."

"I'm going to use them to run in."

"Ha! That's a gooder."

"Honest. Are you sure that Mr. Hood doesn't ever wear these shoes."

"Positive. Jay says he wore 'em too long and won't ever put a foot to 'em again. He claims they nettle his arches. So I guess they're yours for keepers."

"Thanks. What I'm going to do is run through the swamp, so that these big shoes will fill up with mud and get heavy as lead."

"What the goodness for?"

"Mr. Jordanson says that I have to build up leg muscle. He told me that my thighs have to be a lot stronger than the rest of me or else I'll crumble."

Hoody nodded. "Westal Jordanson is one good man. And worth heeding."

"He sure is."

"If'n I weren't a wed woman, and a few years fresher, Wes could dance me into a dolly."

"I guess all the ladies at the country club like him a whole lot."

"Imagine so. I wager that old gray fox knows he's got a waltz or two left inside him."

Kirby laughed. It was fun, he thought, to listen to Mrs. Hood talk, shouting her opinions on any subject.

"Where's Mr. Hood today?"

"Back yonder in his patch, I s'pose. Before ya head uproad to home, I'll load you down with a watermelon."

"Wow. Thanks a lot. How's your yield this season?"

"Good as usual. Jay and me's lucky to have the melons for a money crop. My man birddogs them vines like a mother hen, so's they'll hatch out prosperous."

"That's good."

"How's your tennis coming along? Now, don't frown at me. You'll nab the hang of it."

"It's my ground strokes. I'm not attacking the ball hard enough to please Mr. Jordanson. And he makes me use the new pro racquet which I'm not yet used to."

"Ya still got the one your grandpa made? I'll never forget that day you come scampering all the way down here toting that thing, to show it off to Jason and me. You was one proud kid with that new toy to wave around."

Kirby smiled at her. "It really is more than a toy. A racquet is a weapon, like a sword."

"Who learned ya that? Wes, I reckon."

"Yes'm."

"Figured so." Mrs. Hood sat herself down at the table that was covered with a chipped oilcloth which had once been blue. Very little of the color, Kirby could see, was left.

"He's doing lots for you, boy. I see the two of you go at it, hours and hours, every Monday when the club's closed to members and the ladies an' me come to clean. Wes used to take his Mondays off. But now he forfeits 'em all to you."

Kirby worked to untangle a lace on one of the big shoes. "I know he does. But he won't let me thank him."

"How come?"

"Well, he always claims that I'm doing as much for him as he does for me."

"You still practice to home?"

Kirby nodded. "Every minute I can spare away from homework and helping Little Man."

"Your family's healthy these days, I hope."

"Little Man is."

Kirby saw Mrs. Hood's mouth pucker. "You mean old Wilbur ain't? Tell me what his ailment is and maybe I can mend him up new."

"Well, he claims it's just his years. Grandfather's not a complaining man. Yet I can see him slowing down a bit. He doesn't listen to his radio as much or pin as many pictures on his wall."

Mrs. Hood smiled. "Guess I haven't been uproad to your place since the day we buried your ma. Day after you was born and I helped deliver ya. But I recall all the photos that Wilbur had stuck on his wall."

"He used to collect pictures of the people that he admired and respected. All kinds of people. A lot I never heard of."

"Like who?"

"Grandfather remembers all their names, even though most of the pictures are yellow. He's got President Nixon, a man named Adlai Stevenson, Bruce Jenner, Robert Frost . . . he wrote poems . . . and some singers, too. He's got Anita Bryant and John Reardon and George Beverly Shea, mostly people that he's heard on the radio."

"Anybody else?"

"Let me think. Oh, and Mario Lanza. Also a man named Tiffany who made colorful windows that were songs of glass."

Mrs. Hood grunted. "Some of 'em I heard of and some I ain't."

"You know, sometimes when I'm all alone in our house, I study his pictures. He likes all kinds of people. Not just one kind. I can see the pictures he saved and know so much about my grandfather."

"I s'pose so. And it's good to hear you feel so tender toward him, Kirby. You know you're a lucky boy in many a way."

"Sure am."

"Years back, me and Jason couldn't get over the way Little Man tended on you. Maybe you didn't have no direct parents to raise ya, but that uncle of yours served to you like the Lord had appointed him to be ma, pa, and watchdog."

"I know. Now he's sort of my big brother. Little Man doesn't understand me all the time, so I try to understand him all I can. And I know what worries him. One thing, more than anything else."

"And what is it?"

"Tennis. He almost spits whenever he says it. Little Man calls tennis a white man's game. I guess my fat old uncle just doesn't want me to become a tennis player."

"What does he want you to be?

"Little Man wants me to be a Seminole."

"Of course you understnd why. A smart young whelp like you has just got to have reasoned it all out."

Kirby stood up. "Yes, I understand Little Man, maybe more than he realizes I do. All he knows is that I love him as much as he has always loved me. And for him, that's enough."

"You're a good lad."

Kirby smiled. "Little Man does strange things sometimes. Yesterday he came home from the new store with just one purchase. He walked all the way over there, to get it, and all the way home."

"Must have been something real important."

"It was a present for me. And when he handed it to me, with that wide grin of his, it really shook me up."

"Well, what was it?"

"A can of new tennis balls."

Mrs. Hood laughed. "Don't that beat all. You're right about your uncle. He does pull a few strange tricks. Tell me, does Little Man save pictures of people, too?"

Kirby Tree felt his body suddenly sweat, remembering the one picture that Little Man carried with him.

13

"I'm home!"

Hearing the voice, Wilbur Tree turned his head toward his grandson. He saw Kirby coming from the direction of the house, running toward the pasture.

Wilbur smiled. "How is school?"

"Okay, I guess."

Resting his brown hands on the top rail of the fence, Wilbur eased his chin down to a wrist. Kirby, he thought, will be pleased to see our new bull.

"Wow. He's *here*!"

"Yes. Little Man and I led him here to his new home this morning, so now we have a new bull in our family."

He saw Kirby's black eyes studying the new member. Yes, he thought, our bulls are part of us, for they belong to God's Florida.

"Have you named him yet?"

"No," said Wilbur.

Earlier, the old man remembered, Little Man had suggested that Kirby could name their new bull. Wilbur had nodded. And now, he hoped that his grandson would select a strong name, to honor a strong young animal.

"I know what breed he is," Kirby said.

"Tell me."

"He's a Santa."

Wilbur Tree felt very pleased. My grandchild learns, he thought, not only about the tennis, but about the work we do at our home.

"Did he cost a lot of money?"

"Some. Mr. Ledger paid more than half, because we keep the bulls away from his herd, except for breeding, and our partnership helps us both."

"I suppose I'd better learn as much as I can, so I can be a helper to you and Little Man and earn my keep."

Wilbur nodded. "That would be wise. I hear much from you about the tennis. Tell me about bulls."

"Well, to be a smart beef raiser, you have to care for young bulls every bit as much as for young heifers."

"Why?" asked Wilbur.

"Because half the traits of your herd hatch out of bull seed."

"That is good. Say more."

Kirby pointed at the new bull. "He's a Santa Gertrudis. The neck hump is slight and his chest flap is just starting to sprout. He's fresh weaned, probably yesterday, and I'd say his weaning weight was between six hundred and six fifty."

Wilbur Tree smiled. "Six forty-four."

"What's more," Kirby went on, "a bull his age needs to get plenty of exercise, so I'll run him through the swamp whenever I use Mr. Hood's big shoes. That way, we'll strengthen six legs instead of only two."

Wilbur laughed.

"Will you chase him through sunlight when the sun is high and very hot?"

"No, I sure won't."

"Why not?" Wilbur waited. I will see, he thought, how much reason my grandson carries beneath his new cowboy hat.

"If you overheat a bull, his sperm will weaken. It'll thin down. He won't manufacture as much seed."

"Say more to me."

"We won't be in a rush to breed him. And when we do, we won't ever truck him around the way some bull owners do, because the nervousness it causes can downgrade his fertility."

Wilbur Tree tried not to smile his mouth. "What will we do?"

"We'll walk him to a cow. Slow and easy, the way Little Man walks. I'd say we ought to rest him careful for about forty days prior to any herd contact."

"Why?"

Kirby grinned at him. "You know. Because it takes forty days to form a sperm cell. Forty days of quiet, not travel."

I am surprised, Wilbur thought, at how much my golden grandchild learns. His black eyes shine with intelligence. And I am proud to know that my seed lives in his seed. But I will ask more of him.

"Tell me, if Mr. Ledger does not direct you, to which of his pastures do you take your young bull to perform his love? To the old cows who will teach him how?"

"No, sir, not at all. Because even though I love her a whole lot, I wouldn't want to marry Mrs. Hood."

Wilbur slapped a fence post. "My grandson is filled with fun. But if he were a young bull . . ."

"Then I'd feel more easy with a heifer or a young cow. And if I were a young bull, new to breeding, I'd know that one of the Trees would watch me with both eyes, to see that I search out only cows that are wet with eagerness. In heat."

How much he learns, Wilbur thought, and how quickly. Perhaps, even now at the age of fifteen, he knows as much, or more, than Little Man. His white back is not as broad or as strong, but his mind is a sharper knife.

Kirby is Hanna and Flower. A new penny among old coins. My grandson is a wet and shiny seed that a thumb can pry loose from a brown and fallen orange.

Who is he?

The question, Wilbur Tree thought, still haunts me. I must not pain my breast about Flower and her white lover. I will only thank the sky that my life is so blessed by a grandchild of gold.

"I am happy," he said to Kirby.

The boy grinned at him. "Good. So am I, Grandfather. Now then, what are you going to name your new bull? After a musician, I bet."

"Would my grandson wish to name him?"

"Yes!" Kirby looked at the young Santa Gertrudis; and his face, Wilbur thought, brightened into a song.

"Well then, what will he be called?" Wilbur waited for the boy to answer the question.

"I will call him . . . Mario Lanza."

Wilbur nodded. "Good, because the singing of Mario Lanza was bright and strong. He is dead, you know. But even last evening I heard Mr. Lanza sing on the Orlando radio."

"What song did he sing?"

"The man's voice, the one who sometimes speaks about the music, talked about a student prince. So perhaps that was the name of Mr. Lanza's song."

Wilbur Tree closed his eyes, and then felt Kirby's hand rest on his shoulder. It was a sweet touch, like a flower. He is truly, Wilbur thought, the son of my daughter.

"Grandfather, I'm really sorry that Mr. Lanza died. Was he old?"

Wilbur opened his eyes. "No, he died as a very young man. Years and years ago. When I heard the man on the radio tell the news, I wept."

"I wonder why he died so young."

The man on the radio had spoken for a long time, Wilbur remembered, about the death of Mario Lanza. " The tragedy," the announcer had said, "of too much, too soon." And now, Wilbur Tree thought, I think of my daughter.

Flower had enjoyed too much, too soon.

He looked at Kirby, thinking about the country club and the tennis and the new ways.

14

"Hammer it, Kirby."

Shaking his head in disapproval, Westal Jordanson stood in the heat, behind the baseline of his pro court. Turning his back to the boy on the other side of the net, Wes clawed three more yellow balls from his high-leg basket.

"What am I doing wrong, sir?"

"For one thing, you let the floater bounce. Come on back to the net. I want you to stand between the net and the service line. Yes, right there. Now, when I roll a lob over your head, pursue it."

"I did."

"Not quick enough. Tennis is a blend of patience and opportunity."

"Hit me another . . . please."

"I intend to. I'm going to knock a thousand of these rascals over your head, until you realize that your opponent's lob is not a problem. It's an opportunity. Starve for it."

"I was playing it safe, Mr. Jordanson."

The pro snorted. "Another thing. It's high time you let up on all this Mr. Jordanson stuff. Everyone else here at Sweetgum Country Club calls me by my first name."

"Okay . . . Wes."

He saw the young face smile. "Good grief. Kirby . . . you're sixteen years old, and taller than I am. But I appreciate your manners. I really do. And you can thank your grandfather that he raised a kid with respect and dignity."

"Thanks."

"Stop thanking me. You've thanked me every five minutes for over three years. So quit."

He saw the boy spin his racquet. Good, he thought. Gestures relax a player. But why in heck can't he just twist it like a flipped coin? No, he twirls it like a damn drum majorette twirls a baton.

"A lob," Wes told him, "is your big chance. So bang it harder than you hit your serve."

"I'll hit wild."

"Not consistently. It's a matter of geography, Kirby. Look at this service square, this tiny little hunk of real estate that you've proved you can slap a serve into, full blast."

"I don't understand."

Wes sighed. "Against a lob, you've got almost *four times the target*. Four times the area of the service square. So run back under the ball, cock your bat, and belt that mother a ton."

Quickly, before Kirby had time to think, Wes unloaded another perfect lob. Up and over. That'll teach him, he thought. Yet it pleased Wes to see how wrong he had been. Kirby turned, raced back under it and whacked a deep winner into Jordanson's backhand corner.

"Like that?" Kirby strolled with a slight swagger back to the net.

"Exquisite."

"Let's do it again."

"Okay," Wes grunted, "if you think you can."

"I can."

Easing back his racquet, Wes didn't lob. Instead he hit a screamer right at Kirby's chest. It fooled him. The boy had anticipated and had already turned to retreat. As he could not recover in time, the ball ticked the toe of his racquet; and Wes noticed the disappointment on Kirby's face.

"Don't glower at me, son."

"But you said . . ."

"I pulled a trick on you. An old pro has a bag of tricks bigger than Santa Claus. A top player will fire every gun in his arsenal. You anticipated."

"Well, you always tell me to prepare."

"Sure I do. Prepration's necessary, as long as you

coil for the right shot and guess right. You guessed wrong."

Wes whacked another line drive. But this time, Kirby danced to his left, and volleyed a forehand perfectly away.

"How was that?"

"Wrong." Wes pulled a cloth from the pocket of his white shorts, took off his cowboy hat, and mopped his head.

"I hit it."

"You did. But when a ball's coming directly at you, smack into your gut, volley it backhand."

"Why?"

"It's more of a controlled shot. Believe me, Kirby, the backhand defends the body, not your forehand. Your backhand is the short control shot. Take it on faith."

"I will."

He hit one more liner at Kirby and saw him backhand it, handling it neatly, moving his entire body into the ball. He hit it with toes, legs, chest, arm, hand . . . and the racquet crushed it with an explosion.

I can't remember, Wes thought.

Somewhere, maybe twenty years ago or only ten, I saw that identical shot before. I've seen its mother or grandmother. But where? Who?

On purpose, Wes smacked similar balls at Kirby; watching the moves, the dance, the ballet quickness and panther lightness of the feet. Is it only, he wondered, some wild Seminole grace? No, it's too pat. Too cultured. It was as if someone else taught Kirby, he thought, before I came along.

I saw it, Wes recalled, the day I discovered him hitting discarded tennis balls against his grandfather's barn. He was standing barefoot in goat manure, gunning balls into two wagon rims on the side of that barn, nailing each ball with a fluidity of force. Fluid Drive? Wes smiled at his own joke. I'd share it with Kirby but he's far too young to appreciate it.

Quickly, he lobbed over the boy's head, feeling pleased as he saw the hunger in Kirby's retreat to get under the ball. The overhead smash was superb. A rifle shot. A blast of animal beauty.

"Better," said Wes. "Much better. Now let's work on the area where I think is your weak spot."

"Okay. What is it?"

"Your short game. Tennis is a game of art. Beauty is variety."

Kirby smiled. "I thought some old philosopher said that beauty was truth."

"Crap." Wes snorted. "Philosophers don't play tennis. They coach it. Beauty is variety, son. What makes a door buzzer ugly? Because it totally lacks the variety of an orchestrated symphony."

"What do you want me to do?"

"Orchestrate your game. Learn *touch*. Variety shakes up your opponent, throws him off, and destroys his rhythm. Every shot isn't a topspin power drive. I want to teach you to carve a shot."

"Carve?"

"Not a chop. Your bat moves into the ball, with underspin. The ball floats over the net and skids into the dirt. Hardly any bounce. If you keep the ball low, your opponent has to hustle. And then he has to hit up to you."

"I get it."

"There's more. When he hits up, he can't hit hard. If he does, he'll net the ball or hit long. That's the time you move in and drive that ball down his throat. Make him eat it."

Kirby nodded. "Variety."

"Right." Wes tossed a ball and caught it on the strings of his racquet. The ball never bounced. "That's touch. It's surgery, not wood chopping."

"I'll try it, Wes."

"You must not only try it, but master it. Beauty is variety. Right now this stage of your game, you're a baseball pitcher who only throws fastballs."

"Okay."

"I want you to perfect a curve, a change-up, a slider. Vary your pace. Blast deep and then carve short."

"Were you ever a pitcher?"

"Years ago, when I was in college, I tried out for the baseball team. As a pitcher. There was an old pitching coach whose name was Brush Renwick. He was a fat old gent with a gray crew cut."

Wes walked toward the net, watching Kirby do likewise, until the two of them were face to face.

"Brush watched me fire fastballs at the catcher. Each one was a burner. But only about half of them caught the plate. And you know what Brush Renwick's only comment was?"

Kirby waited.

Wes cornballed his words into a cracker accent. "Jordanson, you ain't no pitcher. You're a thrower."

15

"Come," said Little Man.

"Where are we going?" Kirby asked him.

I do not want to show him, Little Man thought, as he lifted the bar to open the pasture gate. Yet I must. Kirby must know about what he is to see.

"We are lucky," said Little Man, "because of the swamp."

"Lucky?"

"We only fence a short line. Our bulls stay put because of the swamp where we need no fence."

They walked across the pasture.

"Mario's growing," Kirby said, looking at their new Santa.

"Yes. How much should he weight-gain each day? To be a wise Seminole livestock man, my nephew must know of such things. He must grow as Mario grows."

"I know."

"Then tell me. Your fat uncle wishes to hear wisdom from Kirby Tree. Not about his tennis but about his *work*." Little Man firmly punched Kirby's shoulder with his final word.

"I put him on Mr. Ledger's scale two or three days ago."

"Tell me," said Little Man.

"Mario's averaging a weight-gain, since weaning, of just over three pounds a day."

Little Man Tree pretended to scowl at his newphew. "Good. But do you mark it down in our book?"

"Always."

He smiled. I am pleased, Little Man was thinking, that he is becoming a businessman so that he will prosper. Not in money only. Also in wisdom.

"Why do we keep records, Kirby?"

"You know. Because the livestock men, like George Ledger, want to evaluate the sire seed. So their beef herd has a higher propensity to add weight."

"Good." Little Man grinned. "I am happy that Kirby Tree does not also keep records on the weight-gain of his fat old uncle."

"Maybe you should run, as I do, in Army shoes, and help me chase Mario Lanza through the muck of the swamp."

"No. Exercising our young bull is a job for a young bullcalf like you. It is not a job for a heavy old cow like Little Man."

He felt Kirby suddenly pinch his stomach, and he winced. "Ow! Your hands are strong for a child."

"I'm sixteen. Not a child any longer. I'm now a man, like you, and like grandfather."

As he walked, Little Man let out a long breath. It is sad, he thought, that my sweet Kirby is no longer my tiny baby boy. Now his golden head is taller than mine. My legs are stumps. His are an egret's legs. A *white* egret. Oh, he remembered, how I miss that little boy that once rode upon my back when I was his pony. But I will not think of these things as they weigh down my heart. Some memories are heavier to carry than a growing boy.

"Where are we going?" Kirby asked.

"Follow me."

Little Man led the way, from the open sunlight into the shade of cypress. The swamp water was lower. The rain comes, he thought; yet the deep water does not stay. Every year, the black earth dries to a crusty gray, and I hear the gators hiss their anger as I am hissing mine.

"There is nothing back here, Little Man."

"Now there is. Kirby Tree will see and understand."

Kirby stopped. "I remember this very place and this tree. It was the Night of the Snake."

"Yes. I also remember. You were so afraid, and I tried to be brave enough for the two of us."

"You could have killed yourself, Little Man. Your arm and your hand were swollen for days and you were very sick. But I never told Grandfather about our secret."

Little Man splashed through a pool of dark water. "No, you kept silent."

"All he believed was that you'd gotten bit by a rattler and he almost made me bring Mrs. Hood the next day to nurse you."

"But I did not die. The Night of the Snake strengthened my life."

"Why did you do it?"

"I wanted the poison in me to turn my blood bitter so that someday . . . someday . . ." Yes, he thought, one day I will even the score and the white tennis player will know about Little Man Tree whose blood has been spiked by a rattler.

He turned to face his nephew. "You are a Seminole. And you will always look at life and death through your black Seminole eyes. Do you understand?"

"Yes."

I tell myself lies, thought Little Man. And worse, I lie to my boy. Kirby looks like a Seminole about as much as Little Man Tree flies like a sparrow. But the seed of Wilbur Tree rests inside his loins.

The Seminole seed.

"How much farther?" Kirby asked.

"Patience."

"I wish you'd tell me where we're going. And why. You and your big secrets."

"Just follow me, Kirby. And try not to step on a gator."

"I haven't seen a gator for over a year. There aren't any in here anymore."

"Yes, they are here. And they no doubt see Kirby Tree, even though he now sees little more than tennis balls. A man can be killed only by the gator that he does not see."

Little Man stopped and pointed. "There," he said to Kirby. "Look over there."

"No!"

"Yes. It is Isaac."

He saw the boy rushing to where the great Red Angus lay motionless, half of his big body lying in the dark water. I hope, he was thinking, that my nephew will not be as sad as Little Man. My own heart aches with sorrow.

"I guess he came out here to die."

Little Man nodded. "Yes, for that is the way of old bulls who know that their life in God's Florida is to end."

"He was blind, you know."

Little Man took off his hat. "I know. Blind and old, almost as old as I am. And older than you are. The day you were born, I was eight years old and I crept up behind him to yank his tail."

He watched his nephew kneel to gently stroke the old head and the silky red hair.

Kirby looked up. "He's cold."

"Yes. The candle of his soul has burned out."

The boy stood up straight. "Isaac was always so warm. Whenever I would stand near him I could feel the heat of his big body."

"His time ends. The ants and the buzzards will come to do their duty. And the reason I wanted you to see is because of Wilbur Tree. Someday, my father's candle will burn low and he will lie cold and still."

"Don't say that."

Little Man Tree rested his hand on the boy's lean shoulder. "I must prepare you, Kirby. It is not only Isaac Stern who looks ahead to see the long darkness."

I am glad, he thought, that the boy does not weep. If he does, it would cause me to weep also. He is strong. Yet his heart is tender. I saw his young hand reach out, to touch Isaac. He is a boiled egg with a soft center. That, thought Little Man, is good.

"Death is sad," he told the boy. "But to grow old and older and never to die, would be sadder."

Together, they left the swamp, leaving Isaac Stern in the spot that the old bull had chosen to be his forever place.

16

"Daddy?"

Hank stood in the center of Orlando International Airport, watching Case's face brighten. Then he felt the joy of hugging her, holding her, and the satin touch of her hair.

"Welcome to Florida," he said, not knowing what else to say to a stranger of seventeen, and wondering why she had so easily recognized him in such a crowd.

"I don't care a hoot about Florida. All I want is to be here and live with you . . . forever."

He swallowed. "Are you sure you'll be able to stand me? Not everyone can."

Pulling back, Case looked at him. "No, not everyone. But I know *I* can."

"Come on," he said, taking her arm. "Let's go pick up your luggage and then we'll see some sights." As he spoke, he was thinking that most of the amusement one sees in Florida are the tourists.

She was almost bouncing along at his side. "It's all so exciting. I never dreamed I'd be leaving Connecticut and coming to Orlando to live with you."

"And here you are."

"Here I am."

He smiled at her. Over the years, the pictures that she had sent to him never fully captured her good looks. She had Pamela's face. The same patrician features . . . clear skin, delicate bones, carefully groomed hair. But, he thought as he looked at her parade at his hip, not the arrogance. There was a sweetness in her that was no echo of Pam's coldness.

"I hope it works out," Hank said.

She winked a bright eye. "It will. But let's not begin our new life with doubts. After all, we hashed it all out over the phone and with our letters."

"Mostly yours," he confessed to her.

She pinched his arm. "Right. You're not too faithful as a writer."

"No," he told her, working their path through the airport crowd, "I've not been overly successful as a correspondent, a husband, or a father."

"That's all in the past."

He nodded. "Yet a man remembers his shortcomings. And whenever I'd forget, your mother was never quite reticent to remind me of at least a dozen per outburst.''

"She's the same with me, Dad. I couldn't live with her either. Nor will I in the future.''

"So you tell me.''

They stood watching the baggage tumble along the belt, as hundreds of hands reached out to claim their property.

"What color is yours?''

"Bright green,'' she told him. "We can't miss it. I brought everything I wanted and the rest I carted down to the Good Will. All my heavy tweeds stayed up north. So you see, I just *have* to be in Florida for keeps.''

She hugged him again. Her arms darted around his neck, making him feel no longer like just one more reformed drunk. Or one more has-been tennis player.

"I'm so up,'' she whispered into his ear, "I'm delirious.''

"Me, too. I'm a strawberry ice cream soda.''

"Mother said that you'd be easy to spot. And that all I had to do was find a tall blond man falling off a barstool.''

"Is that how Pamela describes me?''

"Yes, and I hated hearing it.''

"No more than I loathed becoming just that, while your mother hated watching it, knowing I was destroying myself with each jigger of gin.''

"Was it true?'' Leaning close to his face, she pretended to smell his breath, giving him one pert nod of approval.

"It was, kitten. No longer."

"Good."

"I don't drink anymore. Haven't touched a drop of sauce in five years. Longer than that, eight or nine years. I'm alcoholic, pet."

"But you just said . . ."

He held up a tan hand. "I know. So, realizing that I'm an alcoholic, and that I can't take even *one* drink, I quit. Not even a sip."

"Then you're cured."

"Not cured. I'm only sober."

His hand reached out to snare the green suitcase that she had pointed out as hers. Behind them, an argument ensued, in Spanish. A man pushed another man. Quickly he guided her away, recalling his earlier days when he would wade into any fight, or even create one, in any bar.

"What made you drink? Was it Mom?"

He shook his head. No, his former wife had not prompted his excess, he thought. Yet it was her crowd. They all had too much money and too little balance. Spoiled brats of thirty, even forty. But even before that, he remembered, he had been drinking. So it wasn't fair to blame the Connecticut crew of Ivy League empty suits.

It was the heady wine of fame.

"No, it wasn't your mother."

He had had years to mull it over. The drinking had started with his tennis victories, the celebrations, the parties that always followed the big matches. Big silver trophies full of champagne, and everyone thumping his back, wanting to buy him a drink. Liquor was what he began to thirst for, during the final set, a burning belt of scotch . . . while his opponents only wanted water.

She looked at him. "You never seem to blame Mother for anything, do you? Not one thing."

"I try not to."

"We're strangers, I suppose. You remember me as a litte girl and I remember you only as the tennis player my mother married."

"And divorced."

Hank knew about Jan Dornburgher, the Dutch polo player, that Pam had recently married. But it wouldn't be too polite to ask if this latest love was working out. In fact, he thought, I hope it does for Pamela's sake. She could afford any toy she had an itch to buy, and own. So let it be Utopia for both of them.

I really want Pam to be happy.

His brain snapped back into the present when he saw Case tugging on another bright green bag. She rescued it without his help, then looked at him, smiling.

"You seemed to be off somewhere, gathering wool."

"I was, and I apologize, Casey."

"Accepted," she said. "Today's a jolt for both of us."

More than you know, he thought. He wanted to tell her that he hadn't married her mother for the money.

Not at all. I loved Pamela Rilling and I probably always will. Odd, but I have never loved any other woman . . . except, perhaps, the one I met as a kid. The girl whose name I can't remember and whose face I can't forget.

Maybe I was drunk then, too.

How long ago was it? I'm thirty-eight now. At that wild weekend at Rollins College, I could not have been even twenty. I have been, he thought, deeply in love twice in my life. But only one of those two ladies loved me. The one who loved me wasn't Pam.

"Ah, here it comes," he heard Case say.

"Is this the last of the lot?"

"Yes, there's only three. I hope your apartment has enough closet space."

"It does." He smiled at her. "In honor of your coming. I emptied every drawer and stripped every available coat hanger. All I kept to wear was little more than I now have on."

"How's the job?"

"Nifty." Telling her the lie made him wince.

"For a gent your age, Hank Dawson, you appear to be in the absolute pink. You look lean, mean, and macho. That rich Florida tan really sets off your bullion locks, even if I spy a few wisps of silver among the gold."

"So I look okay for an old man."

"Superb. You look toned, the perfect and poetic male. But please don't try to carry all of my bags. At least let me take the smallest one."

"Nonsense. Be a lady. Being a beast of burden is what masculinity is all about, especially if one gets lucky enough to tote gear for so lovely a princess."

"Thank you, Dad. I'm so glad you turned out to be such a gentleman. Your being so courtly makes me feel regal."

"By the way, I told you a fib a minute ago. It was a real whopper."

"About what?"

They moved through the crowd of tourists (many of whom were grown men in Mickey Mouse T-shirts), heading for the door nearest the parking lot where he had left the car.

"Well, you asked me about my job, and I lied. I've quit. I saved up some money, made a few wise investments, one of which was a real estate deal that really jackpotted, so I'm . . ."

Case broke in. "You're back into *tennis.*"

"Yes. Very much so."

Dropping her one suitcase, she hugged him almost knocking him over with an enthusiasm that felt so welcome, so supportive, that he knew he had made a prudent decision. Letting go of both handles, he ignored the luggage, holding her close to him and inhaling her nearness.

"I just wasn't a stockbroker, Case."

"No, you're not. Time and again, I wanted to tell you on the telephone that you were meant to play tennis. I've watched every match you ever played that was televised."

"Did you?"

"Yes. And when you played at Forest Hills, I never told Mother, but I made Aunt Frances take me."

"Then you saw me lose."

Against his face, he felt her gently nod, and the delicious tickle of her hair. "It was the semi-finals for the U.S. Open, and you played in the mist that Saturday. It was eleven years ago when I was only seven. I saw you weaken and go down."

"It can't ever be that way again for me, Casey. By that, I don't mean the defeat. I can't ever play that way again. I'm playing differently now. Six hours a day. My game is totally new. In a way, I'm better than I was. Not stronger, but a lot more steady."

Pulling away, he saw her look at him. Her hands still reached up to hold his face.

"You'll do it."

"Will I? Yes, by damn, I think I will. I'm foolishly going to try singles. Maybe settle for doubles. I'm thirty-eight. Do you have any idea how over-the-hill that is for the world of competitive tennis?"

"I never wanted to bunk in with a stockbroker."

He laughed. "God," he said. "I'm not swearing. I really said God in fervent prayer. God, I'm happy. And I'm so very grateful, to have you, and to be back at my trade."

"It *is* your trade, Daddy. I've cut out every word that every sportswriter wrote about you. And clipped out every picture. They all made the same remark. It was your trademark, treasure, and trophy."

"All that?"

Hank waited for the phrase he knew so well, the one that had become the caption of his tennis career, the one phrase that he wanted her to say . . . even if no one else even remembered it. And then he heard her say it, very softly, in a young voice ringing with pride.

"You played the golden game."

17

Art Gossage slapped the table.

"By golly, we'll do it! And we can pull 'er off, boys. Cook'er up with good ol' southern style."

Lookng at their faces, Art was pleased by the entire idea; as well as with the expressions of enthusiasm he read on the faces of the board members of Sweetgum Country Club.

"If worse comes to worst," said Herb Caldwell, "each one of us boys can sweeten the pot, out of our own pockets. I'm willing, even if I have to double the price of every funeral."

Art nodded. "What about it, Eugene?"

"I'm game. As you boys all know, it was my bank

that helped to bankroll Sweetgum, back when it was nothin' more'n a swamp. Gook and gators. And I say ol' Art whistles the right tune. It'll put us on the map.''

"Eugene's right," said Ollie Morehouse. "I'm just a dumb ol' country boy, but I know what sells real estate. It's just one simple word. Location."

Art agreed with him. "I go 'long with Ollie on that 'un. Folks want to live where things happen, a place where big names visit and get coverage on T.V."

"What'll we call it?"

"Yeah," said Eugene, cuffing back his cowboy hat, and helping himself to another sip of his luncheon coffee. "We gotta come up with a name that'll undo their undies."

Art Gossage smiled. This would be his moment to shine a mite. Fingering the paper in the breast pocket of his orange blazer, he knew he already had the winner. But why just up and announce it? Might as well, he thought, milk'em a bit; to make sure none of the other boys could conjure up a better handle. He looked at Eugene in his baby-blue suit and white boots.

"Any suggestions?"

Glancing around, Art saw nothing more than thinking faces that seemed to be empty of answers. One by one, the boys began to look his way. No, not yet, he warned himself. Reaching into a shirt pocket, Art pulled out a cigar and slowly slid off the cellophane sleeve. Crumpling it, he tossed it into the enormous bronze ashtray that bore the initials SCC. Then he pestered Eugene Pollet for a match. After a leisurely puff, he spoke.

"Speak up, boys. Don't git bashful."

Belvin Boatright looked at Art. "Seems to me this ought to be up your alley, seeing as your face and your car dealership's on television all the time. Art, you're a lot closer to advertising than the rest of us."

Art waited and then spoke.

"Well, I must confess to you boys, I done a little thinkin' before comin' here to the club this noon."

He saw Eugene poke Herb in the ribs. "Wouldn't ya know it? Ol' Art's got the name all picked out and posters all printed."

Art held up his hands. "Nothin' firm." He reached a chubby hand inside his orange jacket. "Just a rough idea or two to bounce off you boys, to decide whether or no we got ourselfs a hummer."

"Hum it to us," said Eugene. "We're all ears."

Art Gossage cleared his throat. "Last evening, the wife and I put our heads together . . ."

"Is that all?"

The general snort of male laughter died down and Art continued, blowing one more cloud of cigar smoke straight up toward his source of inspiration. "We come up with a few names, but only one that really made us salute."

"Well, let's hear it, Art. Boom it out."

Art smiled. "How 'bout the Big Dixie?"

As he announced his gem, Art was hoping for an

immediate acclaim. But the faces of the Sweetgum Country Club board remained pensive. Herb was the first to brighten.

"I like it."

"So do I, Herbie," said Belvin. "By damn, it's got stature. Big Dixie sounds like it's worth the price."

"Thanks," said Art.

"Speakin' of price," said Eugene, "we boys gotta fetch up a purse. One that'll shake people right down to their Fruit of the Looms."

"Yeah," said Herb, "and attract every top tennis player in Florida . . . maybe even all over the South."

Belvin grunted. "Aint always a leadpipe cinch to get big names to come. There's probable a trick to it."

With a wide and confident grin, Art Gossage tossed his billfold on the table. "You bet there is. It's money."

"Art's right."

"Connors and Lendl and them tennis stars'll play in Hades if'n the fee is fat."

"Right. They're all professionals. And the pros all play for dough. It's their business."

"Maybe we ought to ask Westal."

"Already have." Art Gossage grinned returning his wallet to its orange nest.'

"What'd he say?"

"Wes says maybe the biggies'll come and maybe no they won't. Some'll just plain ignore us."

"How come?"

"Seems like, according to Westal, that the top-seed players, like Connors and Tanner and all them, got so much dough in the bank that they're not always foaming for more. Wes says we might hook one or two big fish but not to count our chickens. He claims folks have tried before to bait the hook with money."

"Reckon he knows."

"Well," said Art, "I bet he's wrong. Maybe, when ol' Wes ain't lookin' our way, we'll just write up a few telegrams to all the tennis biggies and learn for sure if they're as eager as they ought."

"Sounds good."

"But where do we send the telegrams, Art? I hear that they often live somewhere over in Europe or in some other crazy place."

"How'll we reach 'em, Art?"

Within a minute, Art Gossage began to sweat. He wanted to drive home and slip into a fresh shirt; as he so often did at noon. "Now hold on, boys. This ain't the time to turn thumbs down on our big ol' tournament even before she gits up off the ground. There's a passel of good players right here in Central Florida."

Eugene Pollet squinted at him. "Come now, Art. I can see through that ol' notion, even before it passed your lips."

"Don't know what ya mean, Eugene."

"You don't, eh? Well, I certain do, seein' as your boy, Billy Gossage, is our club champ."

"Hey!" said Art. "You boys don't think . . ."

Belvin poured some hot black coffee from his cup into his saucer, blew on it, then poured it back to his cup. "Art, we ain't about to point fingers. But if'n that fat purse o' prize money just *happened* to find its way into Billy's hands . . ."

"Well, why not?" asked Art. "If'n my Billy wins it fair and square, then I say he's deserving. We don't actual *need* it."

Herb's face cracked into a smile. Stretching out a hand, he slapped Art Gossage on the shoulder. "Art, I give you credit, boy. You are one devil of a salesman. And you know what? I *still* cotton to the idea of a big tennis hoedown. Right here to Sweetgum. I go for it, Art."

"Me, too," Eugene piped in. "I'd support Big Dixie all the way, even if Art gets out there on the court and wins every cent for himself."

"Come on, Art . . . smile. Cat got your tongue?"

Art Gossage felt suddenly better. "You boys had me rode wet for a second. Sure, if Billy's to play in our big tennis tilt, I'll be yellin' out cheers for'm. What daddy wouldn't?"

One by one, the men smiled at him, making Art feel a part of things again. One of the boys. Maybe I went too fast, he thought. This gang of gents didn't all become wealthy because they were short on brains. Neither did I. Nevertheless, best I slow down my pace a bit and not risk appearing as though I'm trying to bull my idea through the committee. Or take over.

"You been awful quiet," Art said to Ollie

Morehouse. "How's your feel on all this?"

Ollie grinned. "It'll move land."

"Sure will."

"More'n that," Ollie went on to say, "it'll be fun. If'n a man can't have fun at his job, I say he's in the wrong business. To me, real estate's one hell of a kick. Sort of like playing Monopoly with real money. My only reservation about this Big Dixie deal is that I don't want to see the Sweetgum Country Club turned into some sort of a weirdo tourist attraction."

"Ollie's right," said Eugene Pollet.

"I ain't through. My suggestion would be to limit attendance to our tennis tilt, charge a hefty admission price, and siphon off a few grand to charity."

Herb spoke up. "I'll go along with that. If it works, let's make our Big Dixie an annual charity affair. A deal that'll help all the people and not just us chosen few."

"Sounds good to me."

"We won't ask anybody to donate anything. The tennis pros, whoever agrees to come, will play for a reasonable purse. And we'll tell 'em all in advance, the crowd as well as the players, that us boys intend to skim off a big bite for a worthy cause."

"Why not? Maybe a scholarship fund to help a few kids go to college."

Art Gossage grinned. "You boys are okay. It's all workin' out just dandy. We'll have fun doin 'er, watch some super tennis, add some prestige to the Sweetgum Country Club." And, he thought to himself, I'll be honest about it. "What's more, it'll be good for business, good for some deserving youngsters who can't cough up their own college tuition. And good for ol' Florida."

Once more Art rapped the table.

"Meeting adjourned."

18

"They're calling it Big Dixie," said Wes.

He saw Kirby Tree smile. "Boy, that's one event I won't want to miss seeing, if the Big Dixie is going to be as big as you tell me it is."

Wes nodded, removing his cowboy hat and mopping his white hair. Then he took a healthy gulp of icy orange juice from one of the two tall glasses that Hoody had brought out to the pro court. She had watched for a minute and then had waddled back to the clubhouse to her work.

"You'll see it," said Westal Jordanson. "Maybe even from closer than a front row seat."

He noticed Kirby's questioning glance.

"You're ready, son." Wes collapsed stiffly into his

wicker chair, hearing the familiar creaks. His eyes narrowed, studying Kirby Tree, his star . . . the long and lean body, the black eyes that looked at the world as would two charcoal briquets, and the long strands of golden hair that Kirby held in place with a Seminole headband.

Wow, thought Wes . . . what an image. What a package for the sportswriters to feast upon. Kirby Tree will make every other tennis player look like cold oatmeal. He's almost, Wes was thinking, too beautiful to be a boy.

"You *can't* mean I'm *playing* in the Big Dixie."

"In my opinion, *yes*, you could. And may. But there are still one or two hurdles."

He's still so innocent, so young; totally unexposed, Wes thought, to the eccentricities of a wordly society. Yet he's entirely unsuited for swamp life with Wilbur and Little Man. Kirby has such potential, so much promise. In time, this kid could win it all . . . Forest Hills, Wimbledon . . .

"Hurdles?"

"Yes," Westal told him. "One, you're not a member of Sweetgum Country Club. Two, because of your family, and where you live, there are certain social problems."

"I understand, Wes." Kirby jumped into the air. "Holy crow, the Big Dixie."

"Leave it to me. I've arranged an exhibition match for you and it's to be played here at Sweetgum."

"Against who?"

"Against *whom*. Polish your language, Kirby. Nothing determines your social rank any more than the way you speak. You are quality, and you are going to look like cream and *sound* like cream."

Kirby grinned at him. "I'll try."

"Now then, if you're willing, the match I've slotted you into is against Billy Gossage. You've watched him play and I want your opinion."

"He's good. But with luck I'll take him."

"You're sure?"

The boy nodded.

"Well," said Wes, "you're going to *have* to whip our club champ. The board has hinted that only one player will represent Sweetgum Country Club in the Big Dixie. Billy Gossage is the natural choice, yet the decision is up to me."

He saw Kirby's face become sober. "I've never played *anyone* before. Only you."

"Don't think about that. All you have to do is whack a tennis ball. You and I have played enough tennis, as opponents, to teach you the game. And you can six-oh me any time you please. Even with all my dusty tricks."

Westal Jordanson watched Kirby pace back and forth, gently slapping his right leg with his racquet and shaking his head. Then he looked directly at his coach.

"Billy plays a whole different game, Wes."

"Of course. He's played a lot more tennis than you

have. I'm old and he's in his early twenties, a college boy. He's number one on the Rollins ladder and still improving.''

''Will anyone be watching?''

Westal Jordanson spat an ice cube at his pupil. ''What in blazes do *you* care whether or not anyone is watching when you play? All *you* watch is the ball. You never look at the crowd, hear the crowd, or even *think* about the crowd.''

Kirby sat down on the edge of the platform, spinning his racquet as if it were a baton, then flipped it like a juggler's club.

''I don't like crowds,'' he said.

''Come on, lad. You're a high school graduate, and no longer a little boy from a swamp. So get used to the idea that during your tennis career thousands of people are going to watch you play.''

''I guess so.''

''If you ever qualify for a big tournament, one which is televised, *millions* of people will be watching. So welcome it. Remember, they came to see Kirby Tree play tennis.''

''Wes, I just wasn't expecting all of this to happen so soon.''

''Soon? It's been five years. Doesn't seem possible, does it? Tempus sure can fugit.''

He got up out of his wicker chair to stretch, working the stiffness out of the fingers of his right hand by wiggling them in the sunshine. I won't be able to hold a racquet much longer, he thought. It's over for me. You're through, Wes. Thank Heaven I found me my boy.

Looking at Kirby, Wes again wondered where such a fine young golden god had come from.

Where?

Well, it wouldn't make very good sense to ask Kirby, because, he thought, I'm sure he has no idea. Wes began to hum an old song.

Kirby asked, "What's that tune? I've never heard it before."

"*Just One Of Those Things*. It's a real oldie, from back in my day, written by a man whose name was Cole Porter. To be honest, it's the song I always whistle whenever I think of you. I guess I've always been too busy barking at you to tell you how important you are . . . to me. You're the son that Hilda and I never had."

The boy smiled. "You're awful important to me, too. I have a few questions inside me. One in particular. This may sound a bit goofy, but ever since I was a kid, I sort of wondered who I was."

Wes sat down again and crossed his legs. "We all wonder who we are. Humans are the only living creatures in the bio world that have been blessed, or cursed, with the gift of self-awareness."

"I guess that's true, Wes."

"Yet we all meander through life wondering what and who we really are. All I know is that you're Kirby Tree, you're eighteen, and you are one crackerjack of a tennis player."

"Thanks to you, old coach."

Thanks to me? Wes smiled inwardly, knowing that there was more, the one mysterious element that conceived a white boy with black Seminole eyes and white-gold hair. A secret seed. Well, Wes thought, there's a lot of Wilbur Tree in this kid, and Kirby can be proud of every drop. I don't have to ask what's bugging him about his ancestry. Even if I knew who his father was, or is, I wonder if I'd ever muster up the guts to tell him.

It was just one of those things, Wes was remembering, from the lyrics of that Cole Porter song. Just one of those nights. Just one of those fabulous flights. Kirby's conception was just one of those crazy flings. I wonder how old Wilbur Tree accepted his daughter's misfortune, and her blessing.

"How's your grandfather these days?"

"Fine, thank you. I'd like to have you come over to the house and pay him a visit. He'd enjoy that."

"I will. And I'm glad to hear he's fit."

"Grandfather sits alone in the dark. Sometimes I ask him things and he doesn't answer. Not that he's angry. Perhaps he just doesn't hear me. The other day I followed him as he walked toward the swamp. There is a place out there where he sometimes goes to be alone, not too far from where he told me that Grandmother is buried. And also where he buried my mother."

"What does he do there?"

Kirby shook his head. "I'm not sure. But my guess is that Wilbur Tree prays. Not in words but with his heart. The other day, I watched him lift his head up and look at the top of the tallest cypress. Then he stretched up his hands, as though he wanted to reach for something too far away to touch."

"Have you any idea what his thoughts are?"

"No, nor would I ask him."

Wes said, "I can understand why you would not."

"Not too long ago, Isaac, our oldest bull died. He just wandered off into the swamp to lie down and die. So when I see Grandfather go off like that . . ."

"Someday he may do just that, Kirby. He will be called, perhaps by some compelling voice that only he can hear, beckoning him to follow. In many ways Wilbur Tree has lived as a Seminole and wants to die as a Seminole."

"It's so sad, Wes. I can't bear to imagine its happening. But I can't be with him all the time. Neither can Little Man. My uncle works so hard. He's doing Grandfather's work, his own, and too much of mine."

"Tell me about your uncle."

Kirby smiled. "There's only one Little Man Tree, because God never could have created two. There is no . . . no *self* in him. He seems to live only for Grandfather and for me. When I was a tot, Little Man was my pony, my mother, my father, and my fat old uncle."

"And your big brother as well, I suppose."

"Yes indeed. Little Man was everyone except my grandfather. When I close my eyes to sleep at night, I try to remember as far back as I can sometimes. And the first thing I recall seeing was Little Man's brown moon of a face. Smiling at me, humming at my ear, tickling me in the ribs, feeding me. Ha! And scrubbing my body with suds and a sponge."

"Quite a guy."

"He calls himself a fat old nothing."

Wes couldn't speak. He only looked at Kirby. I want, he was thinking, to hear more about his feelings about his family, because so much of what he tells me makes such beautiful listening. It's like hearing a hymn.

"You know, Wes, as I was growing up, I became Little Man's teacher. I taught my uncle to read, to add and subtract, and as much geography and history and science as he would hold still for."

"Then he never went to school?"

"Only to take me there, and to come to meet me when school let out. Little Man would die for me, if I were to ask him to, and I guess I can understand why. It's because, for some strange reason, I have become my uncle's life. I am the life that perhaps Little Man wishes that he had for himself."

"You believe that's the reason."

"He's a strange man, Wes. There are thoughts he carries inside him that worry me. And a few things he does that bother the heck out of me, almost to the point where I want to scream and make him stop.''

"Such as?''

"Little Man still brushes my hair.''

19

"Three sets, gentlemen."

Kirby heard Westal Jordanson's voice. Yet he did not look at his coach, looking only at his muscular opponent, Billy Gossage.

Extending his hand, Kirby felt the strong grip of Billy's fingers, his firm forearm. Billy wore bands around each of his wrists that were red, white, and blue. His tennis suit was ivory with blue trim, stripes down the hips of the shorts, blue epaulets buttoned on both shoulders. Billy looked hard, fast, and expensive. He also had brought three racquets.

"Good luck," he told Kirby. "I've seen you hit with Wes and you really zap that ball."

"Thank you, sir," Kirby said, and Billy laughed.

"Are you for real?"

"Let's find out," Wes grunted. "Both you young punks get out there and warm up. I'm proud of both of you, but I want to see tennis played by gentlemen. Not with words. With bats."

Hiss!

Wes had jerked on the silver ring to open a can of new balls. He tossed Billy a pair and Kirby caught the third. Kirby saw Billy turn his back and walk toward one of the baselines and so he went to the opposite side, facing the sun.

Billy looked strong and hit even stronger. He was the club champ of Sweetgum and appeared, to Kirby, as though he intended to retain his title. Just an exhibition match, Wes had said. No, Kirby thought, it's a lot more.

It just might mean the Big Dixie. I know it, he thought, and so does the man on the other side of that net.

Kirby tried to watch only the ball. But, in spite of himself, he noticed Billy Gossage's style. Wes had described Billy as the perfect club player. And now, in his senior year under Norm Copeland, he was the top player on the Rollins College tennis team.

They warmed up for twenty minutes.

As Billy went to the sidelines to share a few secrets with his coach, Mr. Copeland, Kirby looked around. Everyone seemed to be staring at him and he wanted to escape, run back to the swamp where he belonged. I sure as heck don't belong *here*, he thought, at

Sweetgum Country Club.

They all belong. Billy belongs. The tennis, Kirby Tree noticed, on all the other eight courts had stopped. The pro court was isolated, off by itself; and now there were close to a hundred people standing around. Many had brought folding chairs.

Damn you, Wes!

Why, he wondered, did Westal Jordanson have to announce it? Well, I guess I know why. To harden me. I wonder if Wes realizes how much I want to throw up.

Kirby recognized Mr. Gossage, Billy's father, who he knew was one of the important bigwigs at Sweetgum, and, according to what Wes had told him, was one of the sponsors of the upcoming Big Dixie. Wes had said that Mr. Gossage was a good guy and a gentlemen.

Kirby walked to the sidelines, looking for a place to hide, but there was no place. No way to escape the stares and the curious faces. A pair of young girls looked at him. As one girl whispered into the other's ear, Kirby noticed the listener's eyes widen and her pretty mouth pop open, as if shocked at the suggestion made by her friend.

I wonder, he then thought, if Billy Gossage knows the two girls.

Forcing his head to turn away, Kirby saw Mr. and Mrs. Hood, both standing in the shade of a huge oak. As he glanced their way, Hoody flashed him a thumb's up sign. She was wearing her church dress on a Saturday. Kirby smiled. Well, he then thought, I now have a cheering section of three. But neither the Hoods nor Westal Jordanson, he guessed, would make much noise.

Wes rested an arm on Kirby's shoulder. "Your outfit's perfect. Who sewed the beads on your shirt? Little Man?"

"No, sir. Mrs. Hood knew all about today, thanks to you, I figure, so she insisted on doctoring my appearance."

"Oh?"

"Come on, Wes. I can see right through it. You and Mrs. Hood cooked up the whole plan, so I'd make my *debut* . . . as you say . . . with flash."

Wes winked. "Trust me, lad. Your new white tennis duds weren't quite enough for a vivid impression. I want you to bash a dent into a crowd's memory. No matter who's watching."

"Okay." Kirby nodded. "I'll go along with whatever you want me to do. I always have."

"Play!" Wes commanded in an authoritative voice. "Spin a racquet, Kirby."

Billy won the call on "up" and elected to serve.

His first service was an ace, hooking wide into the alley; a superb cross-spin service that hit just inside the white tape, then kicked viciously by Kirby's tardy forehand. He never touched it. The crowd muttered appreciation for the shot, with added applause.

Fifteen-love.

Kirby moved to his left. Wake up, he told himself.

Billy's next serve was flat but a foot too long, a fault; and Kirby let it pass him without effort. The second serve was a real looper, a topspin arc that bounced high, but Kirby was ready. Moving into the ball, he belted it furiously to Billy's backhand, just inside the baseline. Billy hustled and caught up to it; sending it back with a topspin backhand lob that wasn't too deep.

Feet dancing, Kirby waited for the ball to drop, cocked his racquet, and whacked a canon of an overhead which Billy could only admire.

Mr. and Mrs. Hood clapped, almost silently, from their distant observation point that was behind the main body of onlookers. They were both still standing in the shade of the giant live oak. As the heads of members turned, they abruptly stopped.

Billy Gossage held his serve. After they had exchanged courts, Kirby double-faulted, won a point, double-faulted again, and lost a point. At fifteen-forty, he hit a flat serve, hitting it so hard that Billy Gossage could only block it. Kirby charged in, to crack a backhand volley cross-court for a winner.

Ad out.

Kirby netted his first service, hit the second looper a bit short, and saw Billy jump all over it, sending it down the line. It was a break, which now meant, Kirby knew, that Gossage would be serving with games at two-love.

Billy held serve.

On the exchange of courts, Billy Gossage quickly

sat down next to Mr. Copeland who talked to him quietly as the young player blotted his face with a towel. Kirby sat next to Wes, waiting to hear the old pro's advice. Wes kept quiet.

"What am I doing wrong?"

"Nothing."

"But I'm losing."

"No, not yet you're not. You've only learning his game, son. It appears to me as though your play is a bit tight. You won't overpower Billy so don't try. Settle down, keep the ball in play, wait for the opportunity . . . patiently, may I add . . . then bang it."

"Okay."

"And spin your racquet. You always do in practice, but you haven't done it even once. Relax. Tennis is a game and it is meant to be enjoyed. If you can't have fun playing a gifted player like Billy Gossage, then you're in the wrong business, Kirby. Go back to your swamp and raise bulls."

"I'll try, Wes. Anything else?"

"Yes. Break his serve."

Back on the court, Kirby held serve to make it three-one. Then he backhanded Billy's first serve cross-court into the far forehand corner. Following his return, he charged the net, stabbed the passing shot, then overheaded a smashing winner. He played the next service return as a soft carve, sending the ball into the green grit with extreme underspin. No bounce. Billy scooped it up into Kirby's eager racquet and then watched it rip by him.

Love-thirty.

Billy Gossage's next serve could have been another wide ace, but Kirby was ready, whacking a perfect forehand down the line, catching the baseline tape. It was now love-forty.

I've got him, Kirby thought.

The next serve had reverse twist, bouncing high to Kirby's left, catching him unprepared. His return was weak and was rapped by a hungry volley that he had no chance of pursuing. Five-forty.

Steady. Settle down, you dumb Seminole, he warned himself as he spun his racquet. You can break him. Do it. But he bunted the next serve into the net tape. It hung on top of the net, rolled, and then fell back. Kirby heared the crowd react. They were liking what they saw.

Thirty-forty.

Ad out, Kirby told himself. No, I mustn't think about a score. Ony the ball, the ball, the ball.

Billy's serve was flat, hard, and blistered the service line tape. Kirby knew his return was short, seeing Billy charge, position, cock . . . and roll an easy cross-court with an extreme angle. Kirby raced for it and dived forward, reaching the ball with the toe of his racquet. And hitting high. Billy waited, then overheaded a yellow blur. Kirby was too close to the net. The ball slammed into his chest; a smarting, stinging yellow fist that had been hit much harder than necessary to win the point.

The club members adored it. As he walked backed

to the baseline, Kirby noticed how every hand seemed to be applauding. Every mouth talking.

His chest hurt.

A tennis ball is a small and hard object that can move, Wes had told him, at speeds of one hundred thirty miles per hour. In one critical match of mixed doubles, Westal Jordanson had actually seen a tennis ball hit so hard by a strong male that it hit a woman player's head and knocked her senseless.

Deuce.

Billy won the next point. Kirby waited for the advantaged serve, hit it long, and saw Billy Gossage's well-earned grin. His opponent, down love-forty, had won five straight points to hold serve, and dominated the set at one-four.

Wes grunted. "How's your chest?"

Seated, and with his wet face buried in his towel, Kirby closed his eyes and mumbled his answer. "It still stings."

"Good."

"I had him down love-forty."

"You let him off the hook. You eased up and changed your game. Your shots were too tentative, too cautious. With a triple break-point edge, go for winners. That's the time to hit deeper, harder, wider."

"I'll do it, Wes."

"Hang back a bit when you're receiving his first service; then move into the left or right, so your body motion attacks. Forget the score. Don't swing at a number. Belt a *ball*. Got it?"

Kirby nodded. I want to go home, he thought, and I wish Little Man and Grandfather were here. Yet, if they were, they might both be ashamed of me.

I want to hug Mrs. Hood.

20

Westal Jordanson winced.

Maybe, he thought, my golden Seminole just wasn't ready. No, that's wrong. I couldn't have picked a tougher first opponent than Billy Gossage. Billy's really come along under Norm. Turning to look at the Rollins College coach, Wes winked, and saw Norm Copeland flash back a chin-out grin.

Never, he then thought, did I think that Kirby would drop the first set at six-two. We're halfway into the second set and Kirby's still unsettled. Jumpy as a cat.

"Come on, kid," he whispered aloud.

Kirby held serve, making it three-all. Good, thought Wes, now break that service game and coast

to a hold-give-hold set. You can do it, Kirby. If I
didn't think so, I wouldn't have tossed you into a pit
with a tough bear.

Billy served a bullet.

Kirby hung back, waited, danced into it and smacked
it a ton. He's quicker than he was, Wes thought. The
kid is moving now . . . waltzing, attacking, charging.
It's always a great feeling to take the first point from a
server and Kirby took it. He ripped it barehanded out
of Billy's guts.

The next serve was a Florida twist, with reverse
spin, that Kirby somehow expected. His down-the-
line backhand made Billy chase it and pump up a high
defensive lob.

Kirby crushed it. Love-thirty.

"Atta boy, Kirby!"

Twisting his head, Wes saw Hoody's big body
dancing a jig. Several others turned to look, too, and
then smiled. Perhaps they wondered who she was.
Perhaps even presuming that the Hoods were Kirby's
parents or grandparents. Well, Wes thought, let them
wonder.

The serve was miss-hit, short. Kirby charged and
neatly half-volleyed a picturesque dropshot just over
the net where it died before Billy could reach it.

Wes grinned, giving his white cowboy hat a tug
down over his eyes.

"Get it now, Kirby Tree. Right now at love-forty.
Break him on four straight points. Let it all gusher on
the first gamble. And you have three shots to do it so

don't lose him. Bang it, boy.''

He saw Kirby twirl his racquet, get ready, and then charge to return the serve with a lashing down-the-line backhand. But this time Billy had leaned to his right, gotten set, and belted a perfect cross-court forehand. Wes saw Kirby go in, crouch, and open his racquet face to squirt a volley down Billy's backhand line. Billy was there. As he hit the passing shot, Kirby leaped, spearing it for a winner.

"Break," whispered Wes.

Wes tossed a towel to Kirby who caught it, sat down next to him, and sighed. "Four straight points, Wes."

"Forget it. Relax and think about girls. Or bulls, or oranges, or how fat Little Man is getting. Rest your mind."

"I can't." Kirby's black eyes stared at him like twin nuggets of wet coal. "I broke him, Wes. It's what I want to think about and savor. I want to sip it, chew it a long time, before I gulp it down."

Wes snorted. "What's it taste like?"

"Cold watermelon."

Westal Jordanson's memory backpedaled about forty years, remembering the first time that he had broken a top seed's serve. The boy who now sat beside him was right. It was a taste, a flavor, abrim with sweet and cooling juices.

"Get back out on your court."

He saw Kirby look at him. "But I still have a few more seconds to rest."

"So what? The time is right to let Billy Gossage see that you're fresher than he is. And tougher. That young opponent of yours has lived a lot of hours in air-conditioned comfort, while you ate and slept in a hot little shack."

"It's not a shack, Wes. It's our home."

Wes caught Kirby's stare. "Sorry, son, and you're right. You *bet* it's a home. Now forget what I so awkwardly said and drag your butt out there."

Kirby served.

The ball nicked the inside corner of the square, a flat serve that practically screamed into Billy Gossage's backhand. He blocked it high, adding little returning power, and it gave Kirby time to follow his serve in. Wes observed how the feet and legs of Kirby Tree danced toward the net, as though they hardly touched the court's surface. Kirby's body tucked into a crouch, then uncoiled at the ball, lacing the volley behind Billy. Gossage had guessed wrong, run to his left, and had gotten fooled.

"That's it, kid," Wes muttered.

Where? That unique form, he thought, was never taught him by me. He had it when he was twelve or thirteen, the day I walked toward that uncanny noise and then saw him hitting against the side of his grandfather's barn. He was serving into wagon rims and then dancing forward with that inimitable grace. A golden boy making impossible golden shots.

I've seen it before, Wes thought.

Years ago, somewhere, on one of the countless

courts of my career. Someone I know plays Kirby Tree's game. But who?

Only two, Westal Jordanson was thinking to himself. Just two players move as Kirby moves and the other one isn't Billy Gossage. Maybe I'm loco. Am I imagining all this history and digging up ghosts? I wonder.

Turning his head, Wes looked over at Norm Copeland. Norm's younger than I am by a good fifteen years, perhaps more, but there's a chance.

Out on the court, Billy Gossage had rested his racquet and was busy retying his tennis shoe. Wes took the opportunity to get up from his chair. Moving a few feet to his right, he slumped down next to the Rollins College coach, cuffing Norm on the shoulder with a friendly fist.

"Notice anything?" he asked Norm's grin.

"Plenty. And it's all good. Both of our kids are playing well."

"Thanks," snorted Wes. "Kirby and I are both grateful that you and Billy would give us a crack at you."

"Our pleasure. What exactly did you mean, Wes, when you asked me if I noticed anything?"

"Well, I just wondered if you see what I see when you watch Kirby move. Does it remind you of anyone special?"

He saw Norm Copeland frown. "Funny you'd ask that. Watching your boy play is like I'm flipping through my scrapbook."

"You keep one?"

Norm nodded. "For close to thirty years, and *one* isn't the answer. At home, I must have close to a dozen."

"What's in them?"

"Pictures, scores, programs," Norm said. "Sometimes I scribble a comment or two. I used to keep a file on players which I must have misplaced a few years ago. Haven't seen it lately. But I sure have seen your boy before."

"Recently?"

Norm shook his head. "No, but somewhere I've seen your Kirby Tree. You lied to me, you old fox, telling me this youngster you discovered was a Seminole."

"Well, he lives back in the swamp with an uncle and a grandfather, and they're both more Seminole than Osceola."

Norm Copeland grunted. "Pig's ear."

"Honest."

"Wes, if you want my guess, I'd bet this kid of yours is some Sweetgum millionaire's son that you beaded up for Halloween."

Westal Jordanson smiled. "If that were true, wouldn't Billy know? They might have gone to Trinity together, despite the age difference, and played tennis at least once."

Norm chuckled. "You got me, Wes. Besides, I've never known you to cheat, on or off the court. If you say your boy's a Seminole, I believe you."

"Well," said Wes, "what's he look like to *you*?"

Norm squinted. "A black-eyed Viking."

21

Billy Gossage sat on his chair, eyes closed, feeling the nap of a dry towel absorb the sting of sweat from his eyes.

"Damn," he said.

How, he asked himself, could I dominate the first set and then give that high school boy the second set? All I had to do was break back and we would have been back on serve. He waited for his coach to say something.

"The kid's good," Norm said.

Billy continued to blot his face. "He's superb. No one covers a court the way he does. He moves like a cat. I have never seen a *pounce* like he pounces."

"I have."

"Who?"

Billy saw Norm Copeland scratch his head and stick his chin out, as if deep in thought. "Can't remember."

"He beat me." Rubbing his soaking neck, Billy felt his scalp begin to itch.

"There's no disgrace in dropping a one-break set. The kid got lucky."

The hell he did, Billy thought. "No way," he told Norm. "Those howitzers he hit at me weren't luck, Coach. He drives the ball like a truck."

His coach handed him a drier towel. "Here, cool off. Just think about *your* game and forget about *his*. Every player has a soft belly, a little spot somewhere that's just waiting for your pig-sticker."

"Really? Where's *his*?"

"My guess is that he's limited."

"In what way?"

"Look at it this way, Bill. For years you learned from Wes Jordanson and he's one of the best, that old gray fox. Then you came to Rollins and worked with me for four years. I know a few tricks Wes doesn't know, even though I'd never tell him that, and I've taught you those tricks."

"And I've hit every single one at him."

"Maybe so. *His* advantage is that this match means *everything* to him. To you, it's just a lark."

"That second set was no fling." It surely wasn't,

Billy Gossage was thinking. But perhaps I let up, eased off, and became too overconfident after my first set.

"You lost a bit of patience during your second set, Billy. I watched you."

"By the way, what were you and Wes talking about? I saw him move over and the two of you were gossiping about something. You weren't watching *me*. Both of you had your eyes on that . . . that quasi-Seminole."

"Just talk. Now get out there and play tennis. You're smoother than he is, and you're stronger, older, wiser . . . plus a lot of your friends are here to cheer you on. So prance out there and chew him up."

"Right."

"He's hungry, Bill. That kid tries to hit winners with almost every shot. It'll cut his probability. So don't try to out-cream him. *Wait* for the chance; and when it comes, *gun* it."

"Okay."

"Keep the ball deep. And you *must* keep the ball in play. Every shot you put into his court affords him the chance to hammer a loser. Offer him the chance and Kirby Tree will beat himself."

Kirby served.

Keep the ball in play, Billy reminded himself. Play a control game. Just wait, and then talon the opportunity. Save your strength for when the door is open, instead of trying to batter it down. I probably can, he thought, overpower him . . . but better yet, I can outthink him.

He broke Kirby's serve, held his own, and broke again for a three-zip lead.

"Better," his coach told him. "You're baiting the trap. I counted seven unforced errors that he handed you on a gut platter."

"I've got him. He's looking as if he wants to run home and cry."

"Don't get cocky, Bill. Just remember that Big Dixie's coming up soon and you just might crack it wide open. That is, if you play tennis and you don't play star."

"Good advice, Coach."

Billy saw Norm look sideways at Wes and Kirby Tree. Then he turned back to Billy. "I wonder," Norm told him, "what that old fox is whispering to his boy."

"I wonder, too."

"Well," Norm said, "it's nothing that *you* haven't heard. Whatever it is, you already know it. And use it."

Billy smiled.

"Okay, get moving. Hold your serve and you've got him at four-love."

Billy held serve.

Then he watched his opponent double fault, hit long, hit the net, win a point, and then miss a deep overhead. The smash missed the sideline for a break.

Five-love.

Billy served faultlessly. Not hard. On the other side of the court, he saw Kirby waiting, playing deep, too far behind the baseline. Billy made sure that his first serves were in, working Kirby forward; then sending him back with looping rolls and deep lobs.

Yet the ball kept coming back. Again and again, he watched the flashes of gold and the sparkle of beads dart to recover shots that should have been winners.

"You're good," he said aloud in a whisper, "but you must be about ready to drop."

Billy Gossage took his time, walking slowly to the net to pick up a ball. Two black eyes stared at him and he stared back. I'm giving you a tennis lesson, kid. You may think you're King of the Swamp, but don't mess with Gossage. Because I'm just about to bang the beads off you.

He looked beaten. The white-gold hair no longer flowed, but hung like wet laundry, drenched in sweat and inevitable defeat. The kid knows he's outclassed, Billy thought, but I'll give him credit.

He's no quitter.

Using his racquet to tap up a lying ball, Billy said, "Hang in there, kid." Walking back to the baseline, he didn't fully understand why he'd spoken. I can thank Wes for that, he thought, remembering what Jordanson had once told him. "I admire winners," Wes had said once, "but I respect men. And real men, Billy, are always gentlemen."

Tossing the ball, he served.

He saw Kirby move in with an open-faced racquet and belt it into his waiting backhand. Club player, Billy was thinking, almost always wanting to play to my backhand. Racquet back, Billy hit a conventional topspin which cross-courted. Let's test yours, he thought. The kid's racquet was low and waiting; then he whipped at it, creamed it with topspin.

The yellow blur hit and bounced high.

Perfect, Billy thought. His racquet reacted, cocked, snapped at the ball, hitting it deeply down the line. It was a short, crisp shot that found Kirby moving to his left. The boy had to guess, Billy thought, and he guessed wrong.

He had not expected to see Kirby stop, reverse direction, and then dive for the ball. It was a suicide shot. Billy saw the boy's extended body become an arrow. No tennis player could have reached the shot. It was a winner in any league, on any level . . . even Wimbledon.

Yet the ball was reached, hit, returned as a high lob that forced Billy to retreat to mid-court where he waited for its fall. Racquet cocked, he banged an overhead smash to win the point, the game, the set and the match.

He had beaten the boy six-love in the third set, and it felt great to win. All the members of Sweetgum were applauding. Trotting to the net, he waited for the blond boy to greet him, and they shook hands. The black eyes stared at him.

"Congratulations, sir," the boy said.

"Same to you," Billy said.

With the net separating them, they both turned and walked toward their respective coaches. Again he looked at this strange boy; and once more, he said words that he didn't have to say. They just tumbled from his tongue.

"I hated to hit that overhead. Not after that diving lob you dug out of the dirt."

"Thank you, sir."

Billy couldn't help smiling at him. "You're not a loser, Kirby. In fact you're going to become a better player, quite soon, than I'll ever hope to be. Besides, I'm thinking about going to law school. A new court."

Black eyes looked into his. The look on Kirby Tree's face almost made him want to back up a step. The boy looked really sick. "Are you okay?" Billy asked him quickly.

"I just fell apart. I'm sorry I didn't give you a tougher match, Mr. Gossage."

"Hey! Don't let it meathook you. All you did was lose your virginity. It doesn't bother me that you lost, because down the road, you're going to be a winner for years."

The country club members were still applauding, but the noise slowly subsided into quiet. People moved away to other courts, toward golfcarts, and to the putting green.

"I'm proud of both of you," Billy heard Wes Jordanson say. Chin out, Norm Copeland agreed.

Billy Gossage threw his towel across the back of Wes's chair, and picked up his extra racquets. He felt tired, aching for a shower. But he couldn't leave the boy standing there without saying what he really wanted to tell him.

"Kirby, just between the two of us, I'll let you in on a little ol' secret."

Kirby looked at him with a red face still awash with sweat, frowning slightly; rather, Billy imagined, more with curiosity than hostility.

"A secret?"

Billy nodded. "I like being Billy Gossage. But if I had to be anyone else, I believe I'd choose to be you."

The boy's frown deepened, then melted away. "Why did you say that?"

"Because," said Billy, "you and I are both going to Forest Hills and possibly to Wimbledon. But we won't ever be together. I'll see *you* there, but I doubt that you'll ever see me."

"Why not?" the boy asked.

"I'll be only in the seats."

22

"The mail's here."

Looking up, hearing her voice as Case entered the apartment, he smiled at this sweet and beautiful stranger who now shared his life. She is, he was thinking, the only person in my world who cares whether I live or die.

"I hope it's all for you," Hank said. "And I bet it's all valentines from handsome boys who ache for you with broken hearts."

She laughed, flipping through half a dozen envelopes. "Phone bill, political junk mail . . . and here," she tossed a Mr. Henry Dawson letter into his lap, "this one looks sort of interesting."

He read the envelope. "Sweetgum Country Club."

"Open it," he heard her say.

He did, looking first at the signature at the bottom. "I thought he was dead."

"Who?"

"Westal Jordanson."

"Who's he?"

"Oh, he coached a player who beat me once. Rather badly, during my early years."

Case was quiet as he read the letter, feeling the excitement of the words, plus the anticipation. And the panic.

"Good news?"

"Yes." He looked up. "A real shocker. I can't believe it. Maybe I'll ask one of the butterflies in my stomach to read it to you."

As she quickly sat on the broad arm of his chair, his arm crept around her waist, giving her a quick hug.

"Kitten, I've been asked to dance."

"Black tie? At the Sweetgum Country Club?"

"It's a tennis tournament. An invitational. They're calling it Big Dixie."

"Singles?"

He nodded. "It's like a dream. They want me to play. After all these years and all the disasters where I crashed and burned, they're . . . "

"Steady, old dear. Of *course* they want you to play, because you're still Hank Dawson."

"Am I?" He heard the uneasiness in his own voice. "In the past twenty years, I've been so many different Hank Dawsons, I'm sort of reflecting a bit lately as to which one I am at present."

"You are Hank Dawson, the tennis player."

"I'm still good, Casey. I hit tennis balls for five hours today, and I don't feel thirty-eight. Yet I am, and there's no escaping the hourglass."

He felt Case's strong hug.

"Daddy, you're coming back. People are never washed-up unless they think they are."

Hank Dawson stood up, walked to the window, turned and walked back to Case. "You nailed it. And, despite the odds, I truly believe that there's a waltz or two left in this body of mine."

"Bully for you. Please read me all about Big Dixie. I'm absolutely parboiling with curiosity."

He looked at the letter in his hand. "Only sixteen players. Lose once, and you're out. Standard draw. No seeds. All the horses break from the gate when the bell rings."

"Are you excited?"

"No," he told Case. "I'm terrified."

"Then why are you smiling?"

"Because I just figured it out. If they're inviting *me,* then it means that America's top-ranked won't be there. It's too sudden, too new. Their schedules aren't that flexible."

"Which adds up to mean you have a chance to finish first."

Hank Dawson nodded. "Perhaps. Please don't let me count my chickens. With sixteen players, this means I have to win four straight matches, on four successive days.''

Case punched him. ''You'll do it, Dad.''

Touching her face, he said, ''I'm always so insanely happy whenever you call me Dad.''

''Are you?''

''Quite. When you were a little girl, if you recall, you called me Hanky, and I adored it. Your mother called me Hanky Panky, which, if I remember correctly, was hardly a term of endearment.''

Casey rubbed an index finger along its mate, pointing a no-no gesture at him. ''And did you deserve such a dubious honor?''

Hank shook his head. ''Odd, but I really didn't. Even among all the adoring ladies who hurl themselves at the gritty sneakers of tennis players, I still loved your mother. Exclusively, may I add.'' He wondered how true Pam had been.

''I believe you.''

''Thanks,'' he said. ''Pamela never did. If she could only have seen me, night after night, alone in my hotel room as I watched a TV movie . . . ''

''My, what a waste of a golden god.''

''Tennis kills you, Casey. Five sets in heat could boil the lust out of Paul Bunyan. At sundown, I could barely raise my fork. Afterward, I'd sleep through the television movie and wake up at six o'clock on the following morning and see a test pattern on the tube.''

He watched Case walk into the small kitchen, open the refrigerator, and then pour two glasses of iced

tea. Returning, she handed one to him which he re-
duced in gulps to half-full.

"Tell me more about Big Dixie. It will probably do
you good to talk about it, rather than brood about it
and give yourself the jitters."

Again he stared at the letter. "It just says if I'm
lucky enough to keep winning, I'll play four matches.
Each match is best of five."

Case smiled at him and he saw Pam Rilling; wide-
set eyes, soft hair, finely-sculptured features. Beauty
and breeding. Yet, he thought, this little one really
loves me and always has. Even when I lost. Pam
loved me when I won. Period. She wanted the winner and not the man. The winner, not the drunk.
Thinking about the polo player, Hank hoped that, for
his sake, he would never tumble off his horse.

"Why are you scowling, Dad?"

"Idle thoughts. Now then, to the matter at hand."
He glanced at the letter, even though he already had
memorized all the terms. "Best out of five can spell
trouble for me, Casey."

"How so?"

"It could mean, if Fate smiles my way, that
possibly I will have to go twenty sets in four days."

Wow, he thought. What in the name of sanity am I
letting myself in for? Will my legs buckle? I must be
some sort of weirdo masochist to consider playing
singles. Who'll be playing? A crew of tough kids.
How old? Well, he concluded, they sure as shooting
won't be thirty-eight. Best I don't dare let any match

extend out to five sets. His hands kneaded his thigh muscles.

"I'm scared stiff, Casey."

"Perhaps now. Once you walk out on that court at Sweetgum Country Club, you'll be Hank Dawson. And I'll be there yelling my lungs out."

Hearing her, the glass of iced tea felt sweaty in his hand. How, he wondered, can a man like me float along on *tea*? Nausea mounted in his stomach. He wanted to crumple the letter from Wes Jordanson and file it where it belonged . . . where Hank Dawson would belong . . . in the waste basket.

God, he prayed, I want a whiskey.

23

"Kirby?"

Walking under the tall pines, Wilbur Tree looked for his grandson. Back at the house, Little Man had flopped down on his cot and was sleeping. But the boy had been silent, during supper, and then afterward. It was not like Kirby to be quiet, Wilbur thought. Words so often flew from his young mouth more eagerly than morning bees.

Wilbur found his grandson at the pasture fence.

The boy was still in his white tennis clothes with his chin resting atop a post. His young body, Wilbur noticed, was bent, as if something inside him had been broken.

Moving quietly, he joined Kirby; yet the boy did

not seem to notice that he was no longer alone.

"I lost."

"So you told us. I'm glad."

Kirby's head turned to question him. "You're glad that I lost my match?"

"Yes, because my grandchild must learn that oranges do not harvest themselves. Without our work, the orange does not jump into a bin."

"No, but I don't . . . "

"The orange is wise. She knows that her sweetness pleases only the hand that squeezes her. And so I believe that Kirby Tree must also become as wise as the orange."

He saw his grandson sigh. "What are you telling me? To quit playing tennis and pick oranges?"

Wilbur Tree shook his head. "No."

"What then?"

As he saw Kirby frown, Wilbur said, "There is a sour sound in my grandson's voice that I take little joy in hearing. He speaks of oranges, but his words are lemons and sour roots."

Kirby slapped Wilbur's shoulder. "Sorry. I guess this just hasn't been my best day."

"It is my best day."

"How so?"

Wilbur Tree smiled. "Each extra day that I work becomes my best day. Tomorrow, tennis or no tennis, will be better for us both."

"You still think tennis is only a game."

"To me, yes. Yet I know that to you it has become

far more. I am wise enough to know that the tennis
could be your life, or much of it. Your work."

"After today, I begin to wonder."

"All lives suffer losses. I still live, even though I
lost my woman and our daughter. So I ask now if
Kirby Tree can lose one game, and I answer . . . he
can."

The young black eyes stared at him. "That match
today meant so much to me." Kirby's fist pounded
the fence post.

"Yes, it did. But did the tennis mean more than
Hanna or Flower meant to me?"

The boy's face softened. "You and Little Man are
more to me than tennis. Compared to the two of you,
tennis is zip."

"Zip?"

"Nothing. Zero. So often I find myself wishing that
I had known my mother and Grandmother. But it's
probably foolish to want things that can't happen."

Wilbur shook his head. "No, it is not foolish if your
wishes are honest prayers."

"Maybe I'm wishing for too much."

"Perhaps for too much . . . too soon." As he spoke,
Wilbur remembered what the radio announcer had
said upon the death of the singer, Mr. Lanza. "Your
mother was so young and so fair. She was green
becoming orange. Flower wanted so much."

"What did mother want?"

"To live. Only to live as Flower Tree."

He saw Kirby swallow. "And she died because she

had to give birth to me."

"That is true. Possibly the mission of my daughter's life was to sacrifice herself in order that you might live."

"Why is life so hard to understand?"

"Come. We will walk to a place in the swamp where you may discover your answer."

There is still, Wilbur thought as they walked together, enough light in our evening to see what I hope to show him. Kirby followed him as they cut through the palmettoes and waded through the dense green of a thick garden of ferns.

"Here," Wilbur whispered, "we will sit."

"What for?"

"She will come. Very soon."

Sitting, leaning his back against the trunk of a sturdy sabal, Wilbur jacked up his knees, closed his eyes; hearing the choir of evening . . . bugs and bedtime birds. Somewhere, a long way off, a gator hissed just once and was then still.

He felt thankful that Kirby did not prod him with questions. When she comes, Wilbur thought, they would observe her hunting, and learn.

Hanna had so loved the swamp and all of its life. How it would strike pain to her, Wilbur thought, were she to see the level of black water drop lower and lower. Where does our water go? Perhaps to the sea. Or will the white man's pump also drain the ocean as he drains away life from the soul of Wilbur Tree?

All white men are not the same. George Ledger, he thought, speaks more loudly about the pumps than I do. His face reddens to a deeper and more burning red than even the face I own. To anger is so tiring. Often so worthless, as rage usually does no chores.

I'm tired, Wilbur Tree thought. As tired as my son who sleeps on his cot and snores with heavy dreams. Little Man has earned his rest. No man in God's Florida works harder or longer. His life is sweat and dust and Kirby.

I wonder if Kirby knows . . .

Feeling the gentle nudge from his grandson, Wilbur opened his eyes, without moving. Good, he thought. She comes to the swamp as I promised she would come; to hunt, and to teach my golden grandchild her laws.

The great blue heron swept into the clearing on her silent wings, her lean legs shiny with water. In the fading light she looked more gray than blue. Standing at the shore of the pond, in the shallow water, she became a feathered statue and waited.

Turning, he noticed that Kirby was watching; and the boy's attention pleased him. He will see, thought Wilbur.

They waited.

It happened sooner than the old Seminole had expected. The bubble appeared, less than three steps away from where the heron stood. The bubble became a ring as its swelling captured the heron's eye. Yet she did not move, not even when the head of the cowfrog stretched upward, body afloat.

The blue heron appeared motionless; but now her nearest foot left the water an inch below, and one drop of water fell from her longest talon, making a tiny ring of its own. No movement could Wilbur see. And yet, the raised foot stretched closer; up, over, and then down, a step nearer to where the cowfrog floated. The frog moved no longer. But it had already, for its own safety, moved once too often.

Minutes passed.

Wilbur saw a bug light on Kirby's face and was pleased when the boy did not slap it. Instead, he fed it with his own blood, his payment for the lesson that Wilbur knew he was learning. Nothing of worth, he thought, is given for free.

The heron still seemed motionless, in spite of her approach, nearer and nearer. Even when the cowfrog changed its position, the heron did not lunge. Her restraint, Wilbur Tree thought, was her most-valued weapon.

Only until the distance shrank between huntress and prey did the heron pause. Her neck coiled back slightly, then lanced forward, becoming a straight shaft of blurred swiftness. The rapier point of her beak pierced the black water.

The frog became her food.

With her long bill pointed upward, the thin and feathery neck bulged with swallows until the meal dropped through her gullet to become supper. Her giant wings fanned open. Knees bent, she hopped lightly from the dark water, winging upward, banking through the Spanish moss that decorated the cypress trees, to fly away fed.

Wilbur Tree nodded. "Now," he told Kirby, "my grandson may swat the mosquito that sucks upon his neck."

Kirby killed it.

"Wow! I guess I never watched a heron hunt before. Oh, I've seen it, probably zillions of times . . . but I never really *watched* it."

"Did you learn?"

"Yes. At least I believe I saw what you brought me here to see."

"Good. You are now wise, like Mrs. Heron. There are no words to label her lesson. Only wisdom."

He felt Kirby reach out and gently touch his arm. "I'm glad that you're my grandfather."

"And I am as glad that my grandchild can still be taught by watching God's Florida. I am pleased you waited to slap the bug that was drinking your blood."

Kirby grinned at him in the retreating light. "I guess maybe that was part of the lesson. Was it, Grandfather?"

"Yes. And I believe that the cowfrog died to feed not only Mrs. Heron."

Kirby slapped at another bug. "Let's go home. I'm starting to be a meal myself."

Wilbur laughed. Standing up, he hugged his grandchild, feeling the youthful strength of Kirby Tree's body close to him. Again the old man smiled.

My seed, Wilbur Tree knew, has learned patience.

24

"More coffee, sir?"

Looking up at the pretty airline stewardess, Patrick J. Tipperary said, "No thanks. Two fillups are plenty for an old man's nerves."

She forced a smile. "May I take your cup?"

Tip handed it to her. The used cup crushed into her bulging plastic bag. "How soon do we land in Orlando, Toots?"

The Eastern flight attendant checked her wristwatch. "In about ten minutes. Captain Jenson will be asking us to fasten seat belts any minute now, and we'll be starting our descent."

Tip resisted his urge to pray.

"Is this your first trip to Orlando?"

He nodded. "Matter of fact, yes. Been to Florida a few times. Usually to Miami or the Keys. Never here."

Her teeth were capped, he was thinking. But she sure was a looker. Cute all over. Super tan. Tip was grateful for his aisle seat and its view.

"You'll love it. Are you coming down on business or is it just a vacation?"

Before answering her, Tip reached inside the briefcase that crowded his belly and lay flat on his knees, pulling out a copy of his latest issue. "Here ya go. Keep it."

"What's this?"

"*Tip Top Tennis*. I'm the editor and publisher. The head honcho. So now, if you're really curious, you know why I'm coming to Orlando."

The hostess looked at him blankly, so Tip Tipperary went on to explain. "I'm going to cover Big Dixie, a new tennis tournament that promises to be interesting, if what I hear about it is true. Do you play?"

She shook her head. "I'm a surfer." Adding no more, she moved on down the narrow aisle of the aircraft.

Good legs, Tip was thinking. And the kind of trim body that would enhance a tennis dress. Why, he wondered, are pretty girls all so young? He rubbed his eyes. I'm a bit bored, he thought, with young females in general. I usually wind up explaining who Rita Hayworth is. Or was.

Tip yawned.

Big Dixie, he was thinking, just might pan out a lot less exciting than Westal Jordanson pumped it out to be. Yet, to the contrary, he'd never accused Wes of being a hotshot promoter. Not like some.

Fumbling into several pockets of his jacket, and finding nothing relevant, Tip wondered what he'd done with Wes's letter. On top of that, a telephone call. Old Wes sure was enthused about his discovery. Closing his eyes, Tip remembered the phone ringing in his Manhattan apartment, at midnight no less . . . followed by that rough voice that he hadn't heard in years.

"Wake up, Fatso."

Tip had been asleep, shoes off, on his king-size bed. He recalled fumbling for, and mumbling into the receiver. "Who in hell is it?"

"Westal Jordanson."

"I don't believe it. You old dog, what are you up to?"

"I'm calling about Big Dixie."

"What in the deuce is Big Dixie . . . a steamboat?"

"Tip, you're going to have to load your overweight carcass on a plane and haul yourself down to Florida."

"Why? Are you in the slammer?"

Wes chuckled. "No, not yet. But I discovered gold down here, and I want you to share the strike."

Tip's eyebrows had raised. "Yeah? Well if it's a blonde, keep her. I been in court three times, with blondes, so spare me the misery."

The voice in Florida cackled. "Well, to be perfectly honest about it, he's a blond."

"*He?*" Tip sat up.

"Did you receive the publicity release we sent to you, on Big Dixie?"

Tip had snorted. "Yeah, it came to the office. I gave it a gander. You got a few good names on your roster, along with a couple I never heard of."

"It's only our first year for Big Dixie, and as you well know, building the reputation of a tilt takes a few years."

"Sure does."

"Will you come to Orlando?"

"Maybe. Which kid on your cast of characters is the Great Blond Hope?"

"His name is Kirby Tree."

Tip had grunted. "Weirdo name. Who thought up a Hollywood handle like that? You?"

"No, he comes by it honestly. By a roundabout route, may I add. But more or less honestly."

"What the hell is that supposed to mean?"

"You'll see."

"Wes, I gotta tell ya, blond tennis stars are a dime a dozen. Ask any pro shop. They sell 'em more hair bleach than they do balls."

"I see you're still the New York cynic."

"And you're a Florida cracker. I figure you're promoting Kibby Treetrunk, or whatever the crap his name is, because you're broke. And the last old lady you were giving pitty-patty tennis lessons to probably tripped on her cast-iron garter belt and busted her pacemaker.''

"Tip, you're still the same sweet guy.''

"Bull.''

"I want you to see my boy.''

He had detected an abrupt seriousness in Westal Jordanson's voice. Tip was curious. "What's so special, I mean besides the kid's oddball name?''

"Kirby Tree is a Seminole.''

Tip had let out a sigh, shifting the telephone to his other ear. "I thought you said he's a blond.''

He's that, too. A blond Seminole with black eyes, peachy skin, with hair lighter than Loni Anderson's.''

"Where'd ya find this kid, at Disney?''

There was a pause. "No, I found him in a swamp, Tip. In underwear, wading through goat manure, and banging a rotten old tennis ball against a barn with a handmade racquet.''

Tip burped. "Is this a con?''

As he had asked the question, Patrick J. Tipperary already knew its answer. It was straight. No con, not from Westal Jordanson. He was one pro whose act was always out front.

"Don't take my word for it, Tip. Just see for yourself. Jump on a plane and come on down to Florida. I'll buy you a drink.''

"Knowing you, it'll be orange juice.''

"Ha! If you're really thirsty, I'll procure you a genuine jug of Florida moon.''

"You redneck rebels are all alike. I bet you tool around dirt roads in a pickup truck with a gunrack in the cab, plus a coondog in the bin. And a bumper sticker that tells me to either love Jesus or get lynched."

"Doesn't everyone?"

"Wes, it'll be good to see ya. It's been a while."

"Then you'll come. If you do, we can perform our old comedy routine. It's about time we brought Velveeta out of mothballs to tickle the crowd. Tip, it'll be like old times. Two old hams."

Tip had relit a stale cigar. "I ought to get my head examined. Yeah, I'll come. It'll probably be hotter than the hinges and my Irish skin will get fried to a pink panther."

"Everything is air-conditioned down here."

"Cathouses maybe. Not tennis matches."

"Thanks a lot, Tip. I remember how you always hated airplanes, and I appreciate your agreeing to come to Big Dixie. I'll even have a band at the Orlando airport."

"Make it bourbon. Ya can't drink a trombone. And, instead of a brass band, just send an ambulance. Even if we land okay, I'll be out cold. Cowards die a thousand deaths."

"See ya soon."

"Sure."

Shifting his body, Tip fished around to locate his seat belt. Why in hell, he wondered, didn't they stretch the damn things to a decent length? He yanked at the strap. This stupid belt wouldn't go around a jockey. Well, maybe a jock. But not around a horse like me.

It would be good, Tip was thinking, to see old Westal again. Even before he had received the telephone call, he had almost decided to go to Big Dixie. I got a hunch, he thought, Wes is being straight with me. Yet I'm not being too honest with him, letting him think that I'm flying to Florida to case his new discovery. Not really.

The seat belt warning flashed several times and then stayed on, making Tip check his buckle a third time.

No, he thought, not to see Wes Jordanson's boy. But rather to see someone else, a player I once admired, even rooted for. Yeah, he told himself, that's not why I'm taking this fool excursion. Not to take in Big Dixie or to see somebody win the tin.

I want to see Hank Dawson.

25

"Here, like this," said Kirby.

He stood behind the barn as Little Man held the tennis racquet as though it were a hammer. Handing a ball to his uncle, he kept a second ball for himself, tossing it into the air.

"Okay," said Kirby, "try another serve."

With his tongue protruding from a corner of his mouth, Little Man Tree tossed the ball in the air, swatted at it too soon, and missed. You must not laugh, Kirby warned himself.

"What went wrong?" his uncle asked him.

"Your toss was too high. Don't try to hit the ball as it climbs."

"On the way down."

"No."

Little Man frowned. "Well, it has to be one or the other. The ball will not float up there like a little yellow cloud."

"Yes, it floats. But only for a fraction of a second. At the height, the apex, of your toss it stops. That is when it just hangs there, in space, like a shiny yellow moon . . . aching to be pounded."

"I am aching," said Little Man, "to quit."

"You'll get it." Kirby popped up a ball off the ground with the toe of his racquet. "Here." He tossed the ball to Little Man who fumbled it, bent over with a grunt and retrieved it.

"Okay," said Little Man, "once more." His mouth drew tight with determination as he tossed the ball, lower this time. As he swung at it with the old racquet, he missed; the ball fell into his face. Opening his wide mouth, Little Man caught the ball in his teeth, turned to Kirby and bowed. He spat out the ball, tried to catch it, but failed.

Kirby fell over, laughing.

"The tennis," said Little Man, "is not a good game for fat Seminoles. I hate it."

"Why do you and Grandfather always call it *the* tennis?"

Little Man pointed at him. "Because of you."

"I just say *tennis*."

His uncle grinned. "Ah, but when you were a little colt, you would scoot off to the country club place because, as you said, you wanted to watch *the tennis*."

Kirby couldn't help himself. Again he chuckled. Little Man's logic so often made more sense than anyone else's.

"It is a foolish game,' said Little Man, his bare brown foot kicking at the ball, "and also a foolish name."

Kirby asked, "What name would you call it?"

Little Man's face twisted and his black eyes rolled in thought. Then he brightened. "I would call it . . . Yellow Ball That Gets No Hit By A Fat Old Seminole Uncle."

"You're not old. You are only twenty-six."

Yet he is old, Kirby thought. Little Man has always seemed grown up to me, even when both of us were children. He always looked old and alone. There is a sadness in him that I have never been able to ease, a burden that rides him, crushing him down into a squat body and a squat spirit.

Perhaps, thought Kirby, I shouldn't go away to college, as Wes wants me to. If I do, Little Man will be more lonely still, as Grandfather has become so quiet. When he dies, Little Man Tree will live alone in our little house until he dies alone. He has no pals, no girls, no hobbies. I was his only hobby and I have been his single joy.

"You may never be a great tennis player," said Kirby, "but you are sure a good uncle."

Little Man smiled. "I am?"

"Yes, you're the best uncle in the whole world, and you work harder than two men."

"Work is all I know."

Thinking about working with bulls and oranges made Kirby Tree pause. My future, he thought, is a midnight swamp. I don't know which way to step.

"I'm all mixed up, Little Man."

Kirby sat on the fallen tree and his uncle followed to sit nearby, not much more than a reach away.

"Is my nephew sad?"

Kirby sighed. "Not sad. Sort of confused as to what to do about what sort of life I want to live."

"Well, you graduated. You're all through school."

How, the boy asked himself, do I make him understand that there are colleges for people my age to go to? Careers to pursue. Wes tells me that high school isn't enough anymore, because Florida's becoming so technical. Maybe I'll bounce the idea off Little Man and listen to what he has to say.

"I might go to college."

Little Man spat. "College is a *trouble* place."

"No, it isn't."

The man stood up and his hands became fists. "You are still a child, even though you are now taller than I am. There are things you don't know and never should."

"About what?"

"Shame."

"Please sit down, Little Man. It's your advice I need, not your anger."

"Okay." Little Man sat and sulked.

"First off, I'm not going to college and get pregnant. I'm a *boy*, in case you've somehow forgotten."

"Bad things can happen to boys, too."

"You're right. Unfortunate things happen all the time, everywhere, to all kinds of people. I know you and Grandfather worry when I go over to Sweetgum. But you know Wes Jordanson. Gosh, he loves me as much as *you* do."

Little Man slowly shook his head.

"I didn't mean to say it that way. What I meant was that Wes is a close friend to all of us Trees. He's like Mr. and Mrs. Hood."

"No. The Hoods are swamp people, like us."

"Little Man, nobody's like *anybody*. I'm not like you or Grandfather. And I can't believe I want what Jason Hood wants, or Hoody . . . "

"You must not call her Hoody. It is not polite."

"Everyone else does."

"Kirby Tree is not *everyone else*." Little Man leaned an inch or two closer. "You cannot be just anybody. You are *her* son."

"I know."

"No matter how tall you are, you are still Flower's baby. And *my* baby."

Kirby felt his teeth tighten. He wanted to yell at Little Man, to scream at him that he was now eighteen and was longer *anyone's* infant. Maybe, he thought, I'll give my uncle a jolt. A regular shocker.

"Little Man, you are never again to call me a baby. I'm eighteen years old, and if I wanted to, I could be a *father*!"

"No, do not say evil to me."

"Yes, I will. Because being a daddy isn't evil. My grandfather is *your* father, and Flower's, and *he's* not evil. Wilbur Tree is about as close to a . . . to a *saint* . . . as any man could ever come. If Grandfather has a drop of hatred for anything or anyone in his blood, I've never seen it. Neither have you. He doesn't even like to slap a chigger."

"Why do you raise your voice at me?"

"Because I want Little Man Tree to understand that his nephew, Kirby Tree, is a feathered-out bird who is about to flee his nest."

"You have a good home. Honor it."

"Of course, I truly do honor my home, my heritage, and my family. If you want me to, I'll even honor our *goat*."

"You are shouting."

"Yes!" Kirby hopped from the log and jumped up and down, pounding his bare feet into the sand. "You're darn right I'm shouting. I may even be so bold as to want to go to, God forbid, *college.* And, on top of that, maybe even someday be a *father.*"

"I hope you are through with your noise."

"No, I'm not through. I haven't even started. Never in my entire life have I ever had guts enough to yell at anyone, and I'm sorry it had to be you." Kirby jumped up and down once more. "Do you know what I just might do, Little Man."

"No."

"Maybe I'll run all the way over to the Sweetgum Country Club, stroll up to the fattest and richest club member that I can find and be *impolite*. I've never done that before. I never dared to do it. I've always been polite to everyone, every kid at school, every teacher, until manners are busting out my ears. If a guy punched me, I was polite. And I'm bully well sick of it." Kirby paused for a breath. "I don't want to *hurt* anybody."

"What do you want?"

"I want to be . . . *rude*. Just once. I feel like calling somebody a dirty name, or swear, or throw my Bible and break my window. I'd like to go over to Sweetgum, pee on the tennis court, and then push all the members into the pool. I'll take the mule along to watch and then ride her up on the great big porch and into the dining room where everybody eats, except me."

Picking up his tennis racquet, the new Borg model that Wes had given him prior to the match with Billy Gossage, Kirby smashed it against the log; again and again, until it was no more than strings and splinters.

"I don't even know who I am," he said, out of breath. "But if I did know, I'd hate me."

"You are Kirby Tree. For a man, contentment is when he knows who he is and doing his work with pride. It is not yelling or jumping up and down, and breaking a toy."

Kirby looked at the smashed racquet. "The toy is

not this racquet. *I'm* the toy, Little Man. I am Sweet-gum Country Club's newest toy, to watch and enjoy, and then to discard like a used paper cup."

"You are not a toy, Kirby."

He stared at Little Man. "Wrong. Ever since I was a baby, I was your toy. Your doll. Your teddy bear! Can't you see this, you dumb fat Seminole?"

Little Man stood up, feet apart, his heavy body slumping with hurt. How, Kirby asked himself, can I be so cruel to him? Am I really that rotten?

His uncle stepped close to him, resting big brown hands on his shoulders, looking into his face. "Forgive me, Kirby. I did my best for you."

The strong arms encircled his body and the big head with its black hair and moon face pressed into his chest, beneath his chin. Kirby felt Little Man's trembling.

God, he prayed, what have I done to him?

26

"Kirby?"

As he approached the shack, Westal Jordanson felt out of breath. Yet, he thought, the fast walking did me good. Loosened up my old joints.

"Kirby . . . anyone home?"

Wilbur Tree opened the door, smiled, and stepped outside. Kirby and Little Man also came. Wes noticed a look of surprise on Kirby's face. I'd like to whack him, Wes thought.

"Mr. Jordanson, you have come to visit us," said Wilbur. "I am pleased."

As the old Seminole offered his hand, Wes shook it. "Mr. Tree, it's good to see you, sir. You're looking well."

"Thank you." Wilbur turned to look at Kirby. "Now if my grandson will bring a chair, we will ask you to sit with us and talk."

Kirby reentered the small house reappearing quickly with a handmade chair. Wes sat, looking at all three men in turn, reading the questioning expressions on their faces. Kirby was first to speak.

"What's new, Wes?"

"You didn't come to the club today. So I was worried and thought I'd just take an evening walk, to learn if anything was wrong out here."

"I had work to do."

"Oh, I see." Wes paused. "Well, I waited over an hour at the pro court. I know you people don't have a telephone, so I suspected that maybe there was a reason you didn't show up."

Wilbur Tree looked at his grandson. "Did you have an appointment with Mr. Jordanson?"

The boy shrugged. "Sort of."

"That," said Wilbur, "is not a polite answer. Did you?"

"Yes, I was supposed to practice at the club, but Little Man and I had to prune some of the frost burn, from last winter, off a few of the orange trees."

Wilbur Tree nodded. "That is strange," he said to Wes. "Never before has Kirby allowed his work to keep him from the tennis."

Little Man said nothing. Wes saw the black eyes level at him. There is, Wes was thinking, a distrusting expression on his face that doesn't comfort me a whole lot. He still has misgivings about me. There are urges in him like swamp shadows, creeping inside him that burn not with light but with darkness.

"I'm sorry, Wes. I should have come."

Westal Jordanson forced himself to smile. "Kirby, I honestly can't complain about you. In six years, or so, today was the first practice that you ever skipped."

He saw Kirby Tree sigh. "Maybe I'm through with tennis."

As he heard the boy say it, Wes felt his own eyes clamp; and the ache nag his spine as though his arthritis did not know that it was evening, not morning. No, he thought. Please don't let me hear him tell me he's through. He hasn't even begun. Kirby's a child, just a gifted boy who can't begin to realize his potential.

"I don't believe it," Wes said slowly.

"Well, maybe it's true." As he spoke, the boy looked down at his bare feet.

Wes cleared his throat. "You're only eighteen, son. I'm sixty-seven, and by damn, *I'm* not through."

"I owe you a lot, Wes. So much that I can't ever repay. I let you down against Billy Gossage."

"That's it, then. The defeat?"

"Partly. I guess it's because Big Dixie's coming up, and I'm on the outside, looking in. I'm still the kid who's hiding in the bushes to watch the big boys play."

Saying no more, Kirby went inside as Wes waited. Wilbur sat on the stoop while Little Man backed away to lean his chunky body against a tree. A long moment passed as Wes listened to the evening crickets and the frogs from the swamp. The boy reappeared, carrying a smashed racquet.

"I lost my temper today, Wes, and ruined my new Borg bat. Maybe I was breaking myself along with it. I'll pay you for it."

"Forget it." Wes stretched out a hand, taking the splintered racquet gently from Kirby. Looking at it, he said, "This is how you make me feel, son, when you talk of kissing tennis good-bye. Like a busted old bat."

"I know, and I'm sorry."

"Don't bother to tell me you're *sorry*. I didn't limp all the way over here for an apology. I had a reason for coming lad. And it happens to be a rather important reason, that is, if you're man enough to consider it."

"If it's about tennis, Wes, I don't want to know about it. At least not tonight."

Wes stood up. "Well, I guess I just took myself a long walk for nothing."

Wilbur rose slowly to his feet. "To listen," he said to Kirby, "has no price. Even if my grandchild has no ears, Wilbur Tree can still hear. I would like to know, please, why you come, Mr. Jordanson."

"Mr. Tree, there's a big tennis tournament coming up at the Sweetgum Country Club. It's called the Big Dixie."

"Kirby has spoken of this. If you wish also to tell

me more, I will listen.''

"I do. We had sixteen players lined up to participate. But now, because of a last minute cancellation, we have only fifteen. I got a phone call today from Bernie Gomez, just as I was about to take the program over to the print shop. Gomez sprained his right hand, up north, at some stupid rollerskating party and can't even lift a pencil.''

"Parties are bad,'' Wes heard Little Man say. "They breed bad trouble.''

Turning quickly to where Little Man leaned against the thick pine, Wes agreed quickly. "Yes, they can ruin a player worse than the way Kirby wrecked his racquet.'' Wes threw the bat into the dirt. "Like that! Kirby, listen to your uncle.''

"I always do.''

"Now,'' said Wilbur, "I wish to learn more about the tennis, where Mr. Gomez cannot play.''

Smart old crow, thought Wes. Behind that wrinkled brown face, and beneath that long gray hair, lurks a mind. A swamp fox. Instead of raising bulls and a few oranges back here in the scrub, Wilbur Tree ought to be a judge. To himself, Wes laughed inwardly. If he ever, Wes thought, becomes interested, we'll have to appoint old Wilbur to the Supreme Court. If he ever could be senile enough.

"Mr. Tree,'' said Wes slowly, "we have fifteen players and need one more. I want Kirby Tree to enter the Big Dixie.''

"But,'' said Kirby, "I lost to Billy Gossage.''

"No matter. I've already talked to some of the committee members and they want you, too. You're in. That is, if you are man enough to play and not complain, to lose and not crumble. Or to win . . . if you can bat that ball the way I taught you."

Kirby looked confused. "I thought I was out."

"No, you're in. Up to your golden locks. It won't be easy, son. Nothing worthwhile is. So what's your answer?"

Kirby grinned. "Count on it."

"Good," said Wes.

Wilbur closed his eyes and nodded.

27

"Butterflies," said Kirby.

As he spoke, he glanced at his coach. The two of them walked east, along the wagon road. Inside Kirby's stomach he felt the fluttering. Whoever, he thought, first described the feeling as butterflies really nailed it down.

"I know," said Westal Jordanson. "You'll inherit a whole flock. All colors. Your bowels will loosen and you'll throw up or dry heave. You're going to notice rashes crawling on your skin, pimples, sudden dandruff, plus mysterious cracks between your toes."

"All that?"

"Worse. By the way, it's decent of you to walk

back to the club with me. But I could have found my way alone.''

"Forget it, Wes. I figure I owe you a lot more than just an escort.''

"You do.'' Wes mussed Kirby's hair. "And don't think I intend to let you forget it.''

I feel terrific, Kirby thought. Earlier today, fighting with Little Man, I was so down. And then I was about to let Wes down, too. Somehow, he thought, I'll make it up to Little Man. If he still wants me to be his teddy bear, I'll try to oblige.

"Big Dixie,'' he said to Wes. "I can't believe it.''

"It's true, son. You're invited.''

"Who else is going to be in it, besides Billy?''

"A rugged crew. Seasoned players. They're tricky and they're tough. When you meet them, they may smile your way; but once on the court, they'll try to stomp the breath from your bones.''

Kirby grinned. "Good, because I'm ready.''

"One of them is Skip Osage. He's a Californian, lives in Miami now, and serves like it's World War Three.''

"Who else?''

Wes walked slowly. "Carp Carpenter, also a Miami boy. He's a Negro and an inch shorter than a telegraph pole. He hits a slice serve that kicks into the next county. Hardly ever double-faults.''

"I hear ya. Keep talking.''

"Tommy Tilson, an Australian pro from a club up in Georgia. He's got a picture backhand, and he can drop a ball into your court on a dime. Tommy keeps the ball low and the Har-Tru at Sweetgum is the surface he owns. His opponents will think they're digging clams."

All these names, Kirby thought, I've read about in the magazines Wes is always giving me, like *Tip Top Tennis*. "And now," he said aloud, "I'm actually going to meet these guys. Wow."

Wes punched him. "Meet'em and beat'em. They're all human. No robots, except for Gus Wallingford."

"Isn't he the one they call The Wall?"

"Right. He gets everything back. Gus is a blond boy, like you. When the tennis press or the broadcasters don't call him The Wall, he's the Golden Retriever. Wallingford is the type of player who just wears you down. And wears you out, using your pace against you . . . blocking, bunting . . . hitting flat, the way a wall hits. It's judo tennis, using your strength to defeat you."

"Boy, this is exciting." Kirby jumped up into the air to yank a leaf off an overhanging limb.

Wes snorted. "Save your energy. You'll need it for the next gentleman I'm going to preview for you."

"Who?"

"Hector Alvarez."

"Where's he from?"

"Mexico. I've known Heck for a few years and they got his name wrong. It should have been Hell. He's quicker than a desert rattler, with venom in every shot. Uses his racquet like fangs."

Kirby swallowed. "You want *me* to play guys like *that*? Okay, it's your reputation."

He heard a grunt from his coach. "No way it is. It's *your* reputation from now on. You're the monster while I'm just kindly old Doctor Frankenstein."

Arms out, Kirby walked like a robot, growling, looking straight ahead as he lurched forward on unbending knees.

"Great." Wes was laughing. "You're loose, son. And that's a healthy indication. Tennis is fun. It isn't war, so never make it that. Revel in it, enjoy it, and respect it . . . because a lot of fine men and women love tennis as much as I do."

Kirby crossed his heart. "I promise."

"Good. By the way, you won't be necessarily starting out against the toughest opponent. You may draw a lamb."

Kirby looked at Wes. "A lamb? From all you just told me, they all sound more like wolves. Or jackals."

"Some will be softer than others. I talked with one entry on the phone recently. Yesterday, as a matter of fact. He might be one of the lambs as I see it."

"What's his name?"

"Hank Dawson."

"It doesn't ring much of a gong. I never read about him in any of the tennis mags you gave me."

"No." Wes shook his head. "You wouldn't. Hank's been away from tennis. A few years back, a decade ago, he was a top seed in more than one tilt. A super player; but I guess I'm getting old, and I can't seem to pinpoint his style in my mind. A lefty, as I recall. I knew him, years back. Liked him, too. Everybody did.''

"Is that why you invited Mr. Dawson?"

"Maybe so. I'm a sentimental cuss, Kirby. Perhaps I feel sorry for what happened in his life; and when I heard he was training for a comeback, I felt some pity for him.''

"How's his game?"

"Like I say, it's been a decade or more, so I can't describe it too well. Hank's a boozer. Heavy drinker. A party boy who plays the piano, sings drinking songs, and dries out his tonsils. Then he wets 'em again and again. Hank's a drunk. It's a tragedy, but it's true. I don't weep very often, Kirby, yet the memory of Henry Dawson almost makes me cry. I can't explain why. Maybe it's because I can't bear to watch self-destruction. I'd make a poor president of a suicide club.''

"Who wouldn't.''

"I saw Hank play at Forest Hills.''

"Did he win?"

"Not hardly. Hank really got wiped. Maybe by bad weather and bad whiskey. Who knows? The pro at the Orlando Country Club is a friend of mine, and he told me that Hank's changed his style. He plays a different kind of a game, so I guess you and I will just have to cool our heels and take whatever comes.''

"Okay.''

"My friend also told me that Dawson's making an honest effort to dry himself out. Doesn't drink anymore." Wes snorted. "I'll believe it when I see it."

Kirby looked at him. "You mean once a drunk, always a drunk, like they say?"

Wes nodded. "People never change, boy. So I never try to change people. I only try to understand a man or a woman. Have I ever tried to change you?"

Kirby Tree thought for a long moment. "No, I don't guess you have. You sort of accepted my barnyard style of hitting a tennis ball and enlarged upon it, but you really never tried to change it."

"Right. I didn't want to warp you away from your natural gifts." Wes stopped, staring at Kirby's face, shaking his head.

Kirby felt his eyes ask the question along with his mouth. "Now what did I do?"

"Nothing." Westal Jordanson kept walking. "Just a feeling, Kirby . . . as though you are, at odd moments, somebody else."

That, Kirby was thinking, is the spook in my attic. He sighed. Soon, he thought, I'll stop in and have a long talk with Hoody. She probably knows. People around here claim that her memory has filed away more facts about birth than the county clerk's office. The emptiness wouldn't go away. The pestering question never did. Before he could stop himself, the words popped from Kirby Tree's mouth.

"Who am I, Wes?"

28

Case Dawson heard the whistle.

Involuntarily, she turned her head, along with a brief moment of mild self-disapproval, just prior to recognizing the creator of possibly the most suggestive whistle she had ever received. She smiled.

"Thank you, Mr. Tipperary. I'm flattered."

"You are far less delighted than I that you'd remember my name. Say, this rich-rebel dump is quite the fancy place, eh?"

Case nodded. "Sweetgum Country Club. The club in Orlando where Dad introduced us yesterday doesn't quite measure up to this one. At least, for unrestrained elegance."

The big Irish face squinted in the late-morning sun, as his pink hands gestured at their surroundings. "For posh, Sweetgum's got 'em almost all beat. Your old man's here I s'pose. Or are you alone, helpless, and undefended, so I can make a pass at you and win you over with all my puckish and poetic charm?"

Case laughed. "He's here, over on court ten, hitting with Hector Alvarez."

"Yeah, the Mex. He's sharp. By the way, how's old Hank behaving? I hope he's bypassing the barley."

"Totally."

Case read the doubt on Mr. Tipperary's face. "Sure," he said with a shrug. When I ran into the two of ya, yesterday in Orlando, I wouldn't 've recognized Hank. He's not as gray as I am, but he's gaining on me. All I gain is weight."

Feeling the sun's increasing heat, Case Dawson took the older man's arm. "Come on. I'm going to escort you into the shade. You tourists from New York require some guidance in matters of sudden pigmentary alteration."

Tip beamed. "Well said, Sweet. It'll be my pleasure. To be seen with a great-looking bomber like you will buff my tarnished image."

Together they walked around one of the swimming pools, up some stairs, and sat in a breezy cupola. Case watched him fan himself with his battered notebook.

"So," she said, "you're here to cover the Big Dixie for *Tip Top Tennis*. I wonder who induced your coming all the way down to Florida."

"You met Westal Jordanson yet?"

"Yes, but only this morning. I'll admit I liked him right away. He impressed me as being the complete southern gentleman."

Tip spat over the edge of the railing. "Yeah, that's old Wes. Us two go way back, baby. Lotta years. Like me, he worships the game of games. I s'pose the two of us differ completely as observers."

"In what way?"

"Wes builds the kids up until they get good enough to write about, and then I tear 'em down. I write about men players and women players like I see 'em, toots. Some got big serves and others got big boobs. I gotta tell ya straight out, kid . . . if a player falls down drunk, I report it, whether he hits a ball or hits a bottle."

He sounds so crass, Case was thinking. So hard. I wonder, she asked herself, if he really is that way, or is it merely a patina of big city bravado. How tough will he be on Hank Dawson?

"It's a bit uneasy to believe that you'd want to destroy a player who is no longer young but wants to battle back and once more be a credit to himself and to tennis."

"I don't destroy nobody, honey bun."

"Well, you sound as if that's precisely how you get your kicks."

Tip snorted, took a sip of his drink, and said, "Not

altogether. I know ya got your old man in mind. Me too. Yet not like you suspect. Okay, so you're apprehensive that if Hank stumbles, Patrick J. Tipperary will run out on the court and knee him in the jewels."

"Perhaps not in those words."

Tip touched her hand. "Fear not. I'm an Irishman, kid. In the world of top tennis, I am not the high executioner. What I am is a ward healer, a big fat mama, to whom players confess things they wouldn't tell another living soul. So don't try to be my conscience."

"I assure you I won't, sir."

"Besides, you ever seen an Irishman who don't take care of his friends?"

Case Dawson laughed. Perhaps, she thought, there was more to this cynical New Yorker than appeared evident in his rough-cut personality.

"Miss Dawson, I have known your old man more years than you have. Watched his rise and watched his fall. I always liked Hank. He's got the soul of a sad Irish song."

"Sung, I suppose you're itching to add, in an Irish tenor that's tippled on Irish whiskey."

Tip shook a warning finger at her. "Lucky for you, and Hank, we slobs are sentimental. I've been known to knock back a jigger or two. That, my dear, is one of the twin weaknesses of Irishmen."

"And the other?"

The big man looked at her; thoroughly, Case noticed, with blue eyes that probably had admired the ladies for close to half a century. "Love," he said. "Without love and liquor, I'd buy a one-way ticket to my reward. I'd even hop a plane."

"I'll bet those blue eyes of yours could woo and win many a heart."

Tip winked. "Come off it, kid. With scores of handsome young bucks around, all willing to croon beneath your balcony, and, if you'll pardon a fervent remark of rapt appreciation, climb a vine to your bedroom window, I know why you're being so sweet to this aging scribe."

"Of course you do, sir. We both know, and I won't deny it. If a forthcoming issue of *Tip Top Tennis* is in Hank Dawson's cheering section, it could mean a big boost to a pip of a guy."

Tip Tipperary clucked his tongue. "You sure are one loyal little broad."

"Perhaps loyal. But allow me to correct you on calling me a little broad. The term is beneath you, beneath me, and I'd dislike calling *you* a womanizing old reprobate who constantly deprives society of his inner feelings—which, I might add, after only the most cursory observation, are possibly sensitive and caring, far beyond the sentimentality of old barroom Irish ballads."

"Holy mother. You're the first female who ever told me off without raising her voice." Tip lifted his glass to her. "I dig spirit. How the hell old are you?"

"Eighteen. How old are you?"

"A hundred 'n ten. In the shade. Excuse my asking

your age. For a teenager, you're damned articulate.''

"Thank you. I try.''

"Besides that, you got a face like an angel and legs up to your mastoids. Most of all, you're honest enough to tell me straight out that the reason you're being indulgent with my crude presence is because you want that tennis rag of mine to haul Hank Dawson out of an attic trunk, tie pink ribbons in his hair, and sell the old guy to the public as though he's Heidi.''

Case Dawson looked down at her hands. If I'm so damned articulate, she asked herself, why can't I think of something really great to say to this man about my father? Perhaps, she thought, if I just voice my feelings, he'll respond.

"Have you ever,'' she asked, "wanted one thing more than anything else?''

"Yeah. A redhead in Vegas.''

"I'm serious. Right now, what I want most of all is not for me, Mr. Tipperary. As you said earlier, you *have* known Hank Dawson longer than I have. Yet I know today's Hank Dawson better than anyone.''

"I'll buy that.''

"Ten years ago, possibly more, I guess he was a playboy, an alcoholic, and an eventual loser. Yet he only blames himself for his fall. Dad's not vindictive. Even though the marriage didn't last, I'm glad he married my mother . . . and recently, since coming to Florida to keep house for him, I have become prouder and prouder that my name is Case Dawson.''

"Nifty." Tip snuffed a melodramatic snuff. "All that was missing was a violin. You're slathering it on a bit thick, aren't ya, kid?"

She felt the sting of his words, regretting that she had not asked Hank to brief her on how to handle a tough walnut like Patrick J. Tipperary. But as she looked at him, she saw his face soften.

"Easy, young lady. I don't fully mean half of what comes through my teeth. My purpose in covering Big Dixie, in person, is not to lean on Hank. But I got a nose, kid. This old nose of mine may look to you like I swiped it off W. C. Fields, but it works. It's my living."

"I don't quite follow you."

Tip shrugged. "I'll go slower." His chubby finger lifted to touch the tip of his pinkish nose. "This here beak tells me that there's a story in Hank Dawson. Part of it's Big Dixie, part tennis, and maybe a hunk of it is even you. Wes Jordan asked me down to witness the debut of his darling little discovery."

"Kirby Tree?"

Tip's eyebrows raised. "You know the kid?"

"No, but when I met Mr. Jordanson, his new star seemed to be one of his chief topics."

Tip Tipparary shook his head. "Sometimes old Westal says more than his prayers. Enthusiasm is maybe what's keeping him on a tennis court instead of in a rest home. That's the trouble with us aging bulls of the herd. We don't have sense enough to limp off into the sunset."

Case said, "I hope you old bulls never do." As she spoke, she was thinking about neither Patrick J. Tipperary nor Westal Jordanson.

She thought about Hank Dawson who had been practicing in the noonday heat, for over three hours.

29

The wind whipped the trees.

Out in the bull pasture, Little Man's hand pressed his hat to his head, giving the brim a tug, so he would not lose his hat to the swamp water.

"No," he said, thinking.

Wilbur and Kirby, he knew, were back at the house, helping each other to fix supper. Soon he would join them, as always. But not yet. Little Man Tree wanted to be alone, to feel the hot wind of God's Florida billow his shirt and dry away the day's sweat.

He did not quite sit.

Instead, he hunkered down, knees bent, to lean his back to a tree trunk. Hearing a splash, he looked at the black water and saw the snapper turtle. Its jaws held a large cowfrog and the turtle would feed.

"No," he said again, "I will not again give my time, as I did today, to listen to the words of the rodeo man."

The man's name was Rockwood. His teeth were yellow. He claimed that he was a friend of Mr. Ledger and that he wanted Wilbur Tree and Little Man Tree to raise bulls for his rodeo.

Joe Orange had gone to the Silver Spur Rodeo and then had talked about nothing else. Charlie No Land had gone, too. The music was loud; and the clown looked funny because he could dive into a painted barrel whenever a bull was loose.

I do not care, thought Little Man.

We do not have money to spare on fancy shows, not if Kirby is going to go to college. I do not, he thought, want my nephew to go away. Yet I suppose he will. Kirby has heard the call of white voices, as Flower heard them, long ago. They are devils of darkness who sing as angels of light, to tempt good people to do bad things.

"Turtle," he said, "your jaws snap at a frog, to hold, the way the white jaws snap at my little Kirby. Ha! My *tall* Kirby."

Well, thought Little Man, no matter what Kirby decides to do, I may help him do it. I will cheer and yell and throw my hat into the air, to tell all of God's Florida that even if I am nothing but a fat uncle . . . I am his. And he is my baby boy.

Little Man Tree shook his head. "No, I best not call him a baby anymore, because such words give him pain. I love him now, yes . . . but is it wrong to still love the little white baby who rode my back when I stooped in the dirt as his pony?

I want to love somebody.

If only Kirby were once again small, he thought, so that I could heat water on our stove, fill the wash tub, and give my little Kirby a bath. Little Man closed his eyes, smiling. How, he remembered, Kirby would giggle and splash the water, until the floor of our house was mud.

Often I would sing to him, as I rubbed him dry with the new towel I bought, singing the same funny songs that Flower sang to me. Ah, the sadness of loving a baby so much is when the baby boy grows up to be a young man, and the baby is forever gone. The child cannot return to me as he used to after school, when I would see Kirby run to me, his black eyes glistening with happiness. Then I would lift him high to let the wind and sun dance with him, touching him softly.

Eyes closed, Little Man remembered.

I do wonder, he thought, if people could ever guess that each day I do this. Little Man Tree dreams awake. Being alone with Kirby, he knew, was one of his secrets. But I am not, he was thinking, alone with Kirby anymore. I am just alone.

Kirby is right. I'm only a fat dumb Seminole. That is all I can ever be. Wilbur is old and wise; I am stupid, while Kirby Tree is beautiful. He is another

Flower. Thinking of her, Little Man's eyes squinted tighter, and the hurt hardened his bones.

"Flower," he said aloud, "you listened to the call of white voices, and you were punished. And now will your son also be broken?"

Perhaps, he thought, I should not let my mind show me bad pictures. No, I will remember the sweet days . . . the times when I comb the corn silk of my little Kirby's hair, and tell him stories of brave Seminoles.

Above his head, the fans of the palms rattled, causing Little Man Tree to open his eyes. The wind is so clean, he thought. All of God's Florida gets a bath of breezes. No, that is wrong. The rain washes us; and then the wind returns to towel us dry and clean.

His fingers dug into the soil.

As his fist packed the dirt into a ball, Little Man tossed it from one hand to the other. It is only dirt, he thought, yet it is *our* dirt. Part of our home. I wonder how many of the rich people, at the white country club place, know that the land is holy. Wilbur Tree told me this thing. My father is wise. His heart, Little Man knew, is cleanest of all.

From close by, Little Man Tree heard a sharper noise. A crackle of paper. Turning, he saw the patch of white about to sail by him, and his hand grabbed it. Looking at it, he wondered whether it was a letter.

Slowly, and with much effort, he read some of the words, except for the long ones with too many letters.

The paper had blown into the swamp from the Sweetgum Country Club and its words told about the Big Dixie, the tennis thing that Kirby talked on. There were too many words to read, but there were also pictures of the tennis players.

One photograph was familiar to Little Man, the one of Mr. Westal Jordanson, Kirby's teacher. My father, Little Man thought, speaks that Mr. Jordanson is a good man, and Wilbur Tree always knows about good people. Besides, he is kind to Kirby.

One by one, Little Man looked at the faces. His heart danced.

"Kirby!"

There was a picture of his nephew, right there with all of the important men who play the tennis. And beneath his photograph were printed the letters of his name. They spelled out Kirby Tree.

Little Man kissed the paper.

With a grunt, Little Man got up from his crouch, slowly feeling the prickle in his legs where his squat had rested too long. I can't wait, he thought to show the paper to my father and to Kirby.

Little Man ran. Trotting across the open bull pasture, he yelled to one of his animals, holding the publicity leaflet high into the air.

"Mario Lanza, do you know that your friend Kirby is famous? See?" Little Man showed the paper to the bull. "I want you to tell Pablo and Van Cliburn. Tell them that your owner boy is going to win!"

He spotted the black Brangus nearby.

"Hey! Look at this, Pablo." He ran to the bull and waved the paper. "Now you can see how grown up my Kirby is. Aren't you proud?"

Little Man danced in circles, puffing from one bull to the other, until his breath shortened and he had to stop. He was dizzy. Falling onto the Bahia grass, he waved his hat and the paper at the evening clouds that had colored the sky into curds of peaches and cheese.

Getting up slowly, Little Man hurried toward the house, feeling the excitement in his heart. His hat blew off in the wind but Little Man Tree did not care. Nor did he even bother to run and fetch it. Again he looked down at the paper and stopped.

But now he was not looking at his nephew's picture, but rather at the face beside it. The paper trembled in his hand. Slowly he read the name beneath . . . Hank Dawson.

Little Man spat at the face.

30

"Mrs. Hood?"

After tapping the unpainted wood of the torn screen door, Kirby waited until she appeared, smiling, with both of her big hands white with flour.

"Jason, we got company."

Mr. Hood came up behind her to grin at Kirby. His pipe puffed up one welcoming little cloud of smoke. "So I see," he said.

Hoody dusted her hands on a pale gray apron that had once been, Kirby suspected, a light blue.

"Me and Jason see you run by a few times, on your way to the club to practice your tennis. And every time you fail to stop, we both cuss the dickens to ya."

209

They both came outside. Hoody flopped herself onto her rocker and shook her head. "Any soul who tempts baking on a hot morn like this ought to be locked up and the key throwed off."

Jason Hood shook his head. "She won't ever slow down, Kirby. Hoody's a regular home-headed mule. Can't begin to rein 'er in."

Hoody snorted. "Ya never could. My stars, we ain't seen your handsome face around here in near a week."

"Sorry. I guess I've had a lot of matters on my mind. You know I'm going to play in the Big Dixie."

Mr. Hood sucked on his pipe. "So you told us, the night you walked by with Westal and then stopped in on the way to home."

Hoody lifted a warning finger. "And you best win first prize, or whatever they call it, or I'll put the dingbats to your bottom. Won't we, Jay?"

"Darn right."

"Well," said Kirby, "I just wanted to say thanks and for you to know that I'll be wearing the tennis outfits that you made me."

Hoody snorted. "I should *hope* so."

Mr. Hood pointed the wet stem of his yellow corn pipe at his wife. "All them beads. Hoody cut apart near every string of beads she owns, to sew 'em to your shirt. And you should've heard her cuss up each time a bead would fall and drop between the floor boards."

Kirby smiled and then swallowed. Saying thank you to the Hoods never felt adequate. They had nothing, yet they somehow shared everything with everyone. Real folks, he thought—the kind of people who owned little but gave so much.

"My grandfather always says that we're lucky to have neighbors like you. So does Little Man."

"Shucks," said Hoody. "What good does it do to own beads ya never wear. I don't hanker to gussy up."

Jason Hood took a step closer to rest a gentle hand on his wife's ample shoulder. "She used her church beads, too."

"Now hush off," said Hoody, adjusting her apron as though she didn't know what else to do. "I'm too old to fake up pretty. Besides, the purpose of church-going ain't to dolly up your person. It's to tidy your soul."

"Oh," said Kirby, "I almost forgot."

Reaching into his new tennis bag that Wes had given him, from the club pro shop, Kirby pulled out the small jar and handed it to Mrs. Hood.

"Here," he said.

"Mercy, more honey?"

Kirby nodded.

"We ain't quite used up the jar you brung to us last week. Kirby Tree, you'll spoil us both rotten . . . not to mention fatten me up to a fall hog."

"Thank you, son," said Mr. Hood. "We're obliged. By the way, are ya going to win that big do at the Sweetgum?"

Kirby smiled. "Well, I'm sure going to try. I'm not going to let Wes down the way I did when I played

Billy Gossage last week."

"You done good against him," Mr. Hood said quickly. "We seen it all. Both you boys done real good out there under that heat."

"Thanks. I guess Billy did a bit better. You know, I learned a lot from that match, and it was lucky for me that Wes arranged it."

Hoody nodded. "You'll do fine in the Big Dixie. And even if ya lose, hold your head up proud and walk prosperous."

"Will you be the youngest?" Mr. Hood asked.

"I sure will. In this heat that could work to my advantage, according to Wes. There's an old guy playing too. He's thirty-eight."

Hoody slapped her leg. "Goodness! I'd sure hate to grow that old. When I reach thirty-eight, I reckon it'll make time to just lay down and quit breathing."

Kirby Tree felt his face flush. "Sorry, I didn't mean to be rude. It's just that thirty-eight is sort of heavy for singles."

Hoody winked at her husband. "Well, if'n that be the case, then I sure am thankful I ain't single."

"Not that I'm trying to change the subject," Mr. Hood said, "but how's your family?"

"Fine, thank you. I don't really know how excited Grandfather is about Big Dixie, because he isn't a man who lathers up a whole lot."

Hoody nodded her gray head. "That's for true. Wilbur always was a collected article . . . even on the night you got yourself born."

"We was there," said Jason.

Mrs. Hood held up the jar of honey, looking at the morning sunlight turn it into a tiny lantern. "You was born as gold as this honeypot. Creamy as a peach. I recall. You come into the world as Flower Tree's most pretty and precious."

"And we was all proud to behold ya," Jason Hood added. "Both us Hoods."

Hoody wiped her eyes. "If you can excuse an old woman saying so, Kirby, you and Flower and Little Man all been sort of *ours*. Y'all been a joy to watch ripen, as if me an' Jay had growed you up our own selves."

Mr. Hood silently agreed with a bow of his head and pipe.

"But," said Hoody, "the one you rightful belong to was Little Man."

"I know."

Little Man had not come home last night, Kirby was thinking. Yet he was at work early, out in the orange grove, spreading a wheelbarrow of bull manure under a yellowing tree.

"My uncle sort of keeps to himself these days. He doesn't talk as much as he used to, and Grandfather hardly says boo. I read a book in school last year about the silence of the Seminole. They are still, the author had written, and more quiet than a midday swamp."

Jason Hood pulled off his battered hat to scratch his thin white hair. "Your uncle's a tough one to figure. I always had me a hunch that there was a sad story behind those black eyes."

Hoody patted the honey jar in her lap. "Yes, I know what Jason means. Little Man's face so often looks to me as if he's hearing music that no other heart could listen."

Kirby Tree sighed, then he leaned against a gray porch post. "He's so alone. Lately, I spend less and less time with him, because Big Dixie's coming up. That, plus I'm thinking of maybe trying college this fall, or next. So I guess Little Man feels that I've already left him, in a way."

"College, eh?" Hoody smiled at Kirby. "You'll have book-learn spouting out both your ears."

"What are ya fixin' to take up?" Jason asked.

"I don't know yet."

Hoody chuckled. "Tennis, I bet."

"Billy Gossage is going to law school."

Mr. Hood grunted. "Well, that's what we need more of in Florida. One more dang law-book thumper."

"Well, I guess I better get cracking. If I'm late for practice, Wes'll drop a calf."

"Good luck, laddy," said Hoody.

"Yeah," added her husband, "and be sure to watch the ball instead of all those young sweets that'll probable widen an eye for you."

"So long. I hope you like the honey."

Hoody waved. "We usual do."

31

Little Man Tree counted slowly.

"Five, ten, twenty, twenty-five, thirty-five, forty, and fifty."

The small tin box, that he always kept beneath his cot, pushed into a dusty corner behind a pair of old boots, was open. There is enough money now, he thought, to pay for what I want to buy.

Folding the dollars in half, he stuffed them into the pocket of his faded jeans, then closed the box, pushing it back to its hiding place.

"My father must not know about this," he said aloud, patting the money in his pocket.

Unbuttoning the flap on the breast of his blue shirt

he removed the paper, unfolded it, and looked at carefully. With it was the old photograph that he had saved for so many years . . . the picture that had once belonged to Flower.

The face of the tennis player in her photo was young. Yet, thought Little Man, it is the same face that I found yesterday, on this other paper that blew into my hand, carried by God's wind.

He saw the stains of his spit, still spotting the man's face. Now he had an older face, he thought, but faces do not change.

At last, he was thinking, Little Man is sure.

I am lucky, he thought as he got up off his knees from the dirt floor of the shack, that I know Charlie No Land.

Leaving the house, Little Man Tree opened the gate, closed it behind him by again slipping the old rope noose over and around the two gray posts, and headed west. Pablo, the black Brangus bull, stared at him from a distance of fifty yards, looking at him in the silent manner that only a bull can watch an intruder.

"No," said Little Man. "Not today. No girlfriend for you to visit so that you can plant your seed."

I'm glad, thought Little Man, that Wilbur Tree has gone off with the mule to talk business with Mr. Ledger, as it gives me time to take the money to Charlie No Land. Slowly, he stepped over a wide ditch in the pasture, remembering.

"Flower," he said aloud, "you and your fat little brother used to run here and try to jump across this ditch. I wonder if the ditch remembers and still hears our laughter.''

One time I fell in, Little Man recalled. And my sister had to fish me out of the black muck and polish me clean. Stopping to look back at the ditch, he sighed.

"Flower," he said, pausing to look at the sky. "I wonder if you know what your brother must do. Would you scold me?''

Cutting throught the oaks and pines, he left the grassland, and entered the swamp where the moss hung thickly to trim the trees. The Spanish moss was gray, like the hair of an old Seminole . . . the hair of Wilbur Tree.

Dodging puddles of muddy water, Little Man headed south and west, seeing wetter land and more water everywhere. The swamp lives, he thought. She is alive, so warm and dark, the womb of a Seminole woman that kicks with new life. The land is female. Seed in her will bear green children. But the wind, that blows the strands of moss, is male. The breezes carry pollen, Kirby says, as the bees do.

The wind is a bull.

And now, he was thinking as he reached the old rowboat, Little Man Tree must also be a bull. A red bull. The murky water steams this morning as does the promise of Little Man to his baby boy. Water climbed his legs as he pushed the boat from the mud.

"You are heavy, boat. Old and slow, but you will float me to the place of Charlie No Land.''

Using a long pole, he nosed the boat ahead. Its hull

was green with algae. Frog spit, thought Little Man. Even the cowfrogs in God's Florida spit upon the white face in the picture.

Boughs hung down to block his passage, causing him to stoop into the belly of the boat, in order to squeeze by. The hot swamp does not want me to enter her, he thought. She fights me, perhaps wanting to tell me to turn back. But I will not hear her nagging. The old woman of the swamp, with moss in her hair, is a witch who swallows up the white man. She snaps at him to eat his reason and then cackles at his screams of terror.

Opopkee said this.

He was, thought Little Man, the grandfather of my father and whose blood was blacker than swamp water, whenever he spoke of the white soldiers. The tip of his lance had reddened wet with soldier blood.

"I am a Seminole," he whispered.

I wonder, he was thinking, if the ghost of Opopkee still howls in his cave beneath the root nests of cypress. If so, the ghost eyes now watch Little Man Tree. My body sweats. As I breathe, the swamp seems to deny me her air.

He looked suddenly back over his shoulder.

"No, I do not fear you, ghost of my great-grandfather. Your blood is now my blood and your war is my war."

Ahead, the swamp thickened. It was not evening. It was day. Yet he heard the night orchestra; midnight music, a choir of frogs and bugs and owls. The ghost of Opopkee, he thought, hears the splash of Little Man's pole. Deep in the water, he looks up to see the long shadow pass over his eyes, made by the boat.

Little Man's shirt became wetter.

Swamp grass choked his passage, forcing him to heave the old boat forward, an inch at a time. Not much further, he thought. Only once have I been to this place, but I will know it.

"Charlie No Land?"

I will call out his name so that he will not run. Did I come the right way? The swamp changes her disguise. She is an old witch with many torn rags to wear, to trick the fools who dream that she smiles the same smile. It is an evil smile, and her frogs sound like they laugh at a fool.

A dog barked.

He heard a voice grunt a curt order to the hound. Then a splash! Little Man squinted in an effort to see. Someone, or something, was now coming. Ahead of the boat's rounded prow, he saw the swamp grass move, yet nothing more. Pulling the pole from the water, its dripping tip black with muck, Little Man stood in the center of the leaky boat, feeling the water sloshing at his ankles.

Then he saw the dog.

A dog's head swam toward him, creating a V in the black surface. Yellow teeth bared to snarl as Little Man's fingers tightened on the pole.

"Charlie?" he yelled.

"Did you bring the money?"

"Yes."

"How much?"

"Fifty dollars. Call off your dog."

"Hyah! Hyup!"

Abruptly the hound's face relaxed, turned, and returned to the voice, its long ears dragging in the water, half wet and half dry.

Dipping the pole, Little Man resumed his approach, feeling relief that the dog no longer threatened him. Now he could see the shack. Yet he could see no sign of Charlie No Land.

The pole felt heavier in his hands as he continued to move the boat toward the old shack. A thin wisp of smoke curled from the stump of a stubby pipe in the roof. Ahead, the dog scrambled out of the water, shaking himself in a sudden cloud of silver drops.

"Charlie?"

"Over here."

Turning his head, he saw Charlie No Land. The man was naked, standing in a thicket of ferns, hidden from his knees down. He looks dirty, thought Little Man Tree, as always. Already my nose is aware of his smell, stronger than the swamp, the odor of an animal. His brown body shines in the heat and his smell howls wetter than his hound.

"Show me the money."

"I have it in my pocket," Little Man answered, stumbling out of the boat and onto the slime of the bank. His boot kicked one of the crumpled beer cans and it went clanking into the watery slime, to disappear.

"Show me. Now."

Little Man Tree does not like the tone of Charlie's voice, he thought. He sounds mean. Seminoles are not all alike; and when my father says this, he has wisdom in his words. Little Man pulled the bills from his pocket and took a step to Charlie No Land.

"Fifty dollars."

Snatching the money, Charlie knelt to finger marks in the mud as he counted the money. Then he smiled, without joy.

"Stay here," he said. "I'll get the gun."

32

"Excuse me, please. I'm sorry."

As he apologized to her, Case Dawson felt the Pepsi smarting her left eye. Boys, she was thinking, are always so clumsy. What an ox.

"Here," he said, pulling a small towel from his red tennis bag, "let me at least help you blot the mess I made."

"Thank you." Taking his towel, she began to absorb the amber drops of cola from the front of her white dress. Only then did she apply the cloth to her face and look at him. He was beautiful. Never before had she ever considered such an adjective to describe a boy. Yet he was, hair so light that it shone like silver, a lean body . . . and those eyes! His pupils seemed to penetrate her.

"Is this how you meet girls?"

He smiled. "I'm not mean. Just clumsy. There's a difference, you know."

She could see the white of her dress in his dark eyes. Two tiny stars of white that made her very aware of how he was staring at her. As she returned the towel to his hand, he took it, dropping his racquet. It clattered onto the stones of the Sweetgum Country Club patio.

"I hope," she told him "that you're a bit more graceful on a tennis court than you are at dashing around corners."

He shrugged, his grin widening. "Me, too. By the way, now that I've spoiled your day and stained your dress . . . I'm Kirby Tree."

"Case Dawson."

And, she was thinking, meeting a handsome hunk like you hardly ruins a girl's day. Only her life.

His smile faded. "Are you Mr. Dawson's . . . "

"Daughter," she said, almost too quickly.

He smiled again; it was instant, she noticed, and without premeditation, as though her own animal reaction to him reflected across his face.

"I'd buy you another drink, but I guess I didn't bring any money with me. Is it okay if I owe you one?"

"It would seem," she said, "as if that's my best

shot. When it's the only game in town, you play it."

Bending over to pick up his racquet, his head bumped the arm on one of the patio chairs. She looked away quickly, not wanting him to see the smile that she couldn't resist. He was, Case Dawson thought, a blend of manhood and boyhood that had somehow united into a raw charm. But, she warned herself, he could be Hank's opponent.

"I'm not very smooth," he said, "around girls."

"So I notice. Not to change the subject, but I read your name on the roster for Big Dixie."

He nodded. "I'm a last-minute entry. Sort of a fill-in."

Case sat in the chair his head had bumped. "Then fill me in. Where are you from?" She gestured at an empty chair. "Perhaps if you sit down you'll do less damage."

She saw him grin, and then heard his laughter, a musical sound that seemed to echo his irrepressible happiness. He sat, pointing the handle of his racquet over his shoulder.

"I live nearby. I'm a swamp rat."

It must be one heck of a swamp, she mused, to spawn a rugged-looking rat like you, Kirby Tree. Aloud, she said, "Kirby Tree is really quite a ringer of a name."

He looked surprised. "Is it?"

"To my ear it is."

"I like *your* name," he said. "Case Dawson isn't the sort of name you'd hear every day."

"That's funny," she told him. "I hear it every day. But enough of that. As you're the first swamp rat that I've ever, pardon the expression, crashed into, tell me about your little ol' swamp."

"Well, I live with my grandfather and my uncle. We raise bulls to breed beef. And we have an orange grove, a small one, some bees, a goat, a mule, and a lot of bugs. I know, it doesn't sound like much, but it's a pretty place to live. Very quiet. I'm lucky to have such a good family and a nice home."

As she listened, Case wanted to touch his face with her hand. For years, she was thinking, I've met boys who resented everything. Kirby seems to respect everything. Wow, he's hitting me hard. There's so much color in him. He's three dimensional, not just a stick figure; he seems as though he belongs in a painting, but as sculpture. Unpolished polish. In only a few moments, he has become a lantern in my life . . . a special someone that's always been missing. But if he plays against Hank . . .

"You're staring at me," he told her.

"Oops. Didn't mean to. Right out front, Kirby Tree, I've never met anyone like you before."

"Thanks."

"Honestly, I'm a mite overwhelmed. People can't say what they mean any more. A pity, yet it's true. So I decided that whenever I meet someone that chemically zaps me, I'll just blurt. I like you, Kirby. What really struck me was the way you described your home. And I'd love to see it. Providing, of course, you're willing to tell me all about the bulls and the bees.''

He laughed again. ''That's super. Very, very good. Usually I don't talk to girls a whole lot. Guess I'm sort of unswift.''

''That's hard to believe.''

''Honest. Because my tongue works into a knot and I drop stuff. In school, I dropped my history book on Beth Warren's toe, just as I was working up the courage to ask her if she'd be my date for a dance.''

''And did this poor wounded girl accept?''

''I never asked.''

Case intentionally sighed. ''Another mood-wrecked moment in the exciting and romantic drama of Kirby Tree.''

''Well, I suppose it was all for the best, because I can't dance a step.''

''A narrow escape for Beth Warren.''

Looking at her, he seemed not to know what next to say, so he zipped and unzipped the cover of his tennis racquet. ''For years now, I really haven't had time for ladies. At home, there's a lot of chores to handle, plus the fact that I've spent hours and hours here at Sweetgum, hitting tennis balls.''

''Apparently you hit them rather well.''

''Tennis isn't my religion. But it's up there very close to it.''

''Do you have a religion?''

Before answering, he looked at the sky. Then, with a lean hand, he leaned over to pick up an acorn which he tossed to her. Case caught it.

"My religion is God's Florida."

She was thinking how much she enjoyed the manner in which he expressed himself, in tangibles. Concepts rooted in soil. He was clean dirt, a creamy lily floating in some placid pond of swamp water. Yet beneath the surface? I'm almost hungry to hear more from him. He seems so vulnerable and yet so vivid. Kirby Tree is an orchestrated man. How, she asked herself, could all this happen so suddenly? Inside her, Case Dawson felt a mounting rush that made her warm. Not heat, but a warmth. He seemed to be so floral, and pure Florida.

"God's Florida," she finally said, "is what I would call a beautiful and befitting phrase. Is that a term you created?"

He shook his silver-gold hair. "No, I can't claim it. Perhaps it's Grandfather's."

"You swamp rats are poets."

Kirby smiled softly. "In school, we studied English poetry. American, too. Yet no poem I ever read is any wiser than my grandfather's stories."

"Well, you can't stop there," she said. "What are his stories about? I'd really like to hear one, you know."

"He talks about the seeds."

"Seeds?"

The boy nodded. "That acorn you hold in your hand is a seed, Case. It's all male. Bury it into earth and an oak will be born, because the land is a woman."

Case Dawson took a deep breath. "Your grand-father must be quite a gentleman. And I'd consider it an honor if you'd introduce me to him. Does he come here to the club often? I suppose your grandfather is a member."

As she passed her last remark, Case regretted that she had said it, although somehow wondering why. Swamp rats, to use Kirby's term, were not fre-quenters of expensive country clubs. Why, she asked herself, did I make such a crass remark? She was men-tally phrasing a hurried retraction as Kirby's answer came.

"Wilbur Tree is a Seminole."

33

"Kirby?"

Hearing his name, he turned to smile at the girl he had run into that morning, while waiting his turn for a practice court. Now he was wet from the workout, and to see her twice on the same day, he thought, was really his good fortune.

"Hi there, Case."

She was standing on the deck that overlooked one of the pools. With her was a man in tennis shorts and a white jacket. A towel hung around his neck. They both smiled as Kirby walked their way.

"There's someone I'd like you to meet," she told him. "Hank Dawson, this is Kirby Tree."

As the older man held out his hand, Kirby took it.

For his age, the old guy had quite a grip, he thought.

"Wes Jordanson," the man said, "has been singing your praises, Kirby. He told me all about you, and Casey added a bit of frosting."

Kirby shifted his weight. "There's not that much to tell. I don't even belong on the same court with players like you and the rest of the gentlemen."

Mr. Dawson said, "Wes thinks you do."

"I'm just a kid, an amateur."

"We were all kids once. And we all had to take our turns at the first big one. Oddly enough, you and I have something in common. You're the youngest entry and I'm easily the most senior."

Kirby looked at the girl and then back to her father. "Yes, I guess that's true."

"If both of you hotshot athletes will kindly sit down," said Case, "I'll go fetch us some cold drinks. Even in the shade I'm aware of the heat. That sun is brutal."

She left.

"Yes," said the man, "let's crash ourselves into a chair. And we'll save a seat between us for Case."

He's as nice as she is, Kirby Tree thought. Mr. Dawson's a good guy. I wonder if I'll have to play him. Well, if I do, I do. And maybe Case will sort of root for us both.

"I really like your daughter, sir."

"Thanks. So do I. We haven't seen very much of each other for a number of years. Casey's been up north with her mother, but now she's here with me, in Orlando.''

"She's a super girl.''

Hank nodded. "And one dickens of a mother hen. I'm too old to need mothering, yet I must confess that I adore having her around. She's my cheerleader.''

"I bumped into her this morning.''

"So she said.''

"While I was waiting for court time, the two of us got to talking. I guess I don't chat a lot with strangers, but your daughter was so outright friendly.''

"Good. We all need a friend or two.''

"Wes told me about you, Mr. Dawson. You know, stuff about your coming back into tennis, and I really salute your courage. Please don't think, sir, that I intended to be rude by that remark.''

"Of course not. And no offense taken. I'm a tough old dog with a few new tricks, Kirby. By the way, please don't call me Mr. Dawson, or help me across the street . . . or I promise you I *will* be offended.''

"You know, other than Billy Gossage . . . I hit with him today . . . I haven't talked to any of the other players.''

"No?''

Kirby shooked his head. "Wes introduced me to Mr. Osage, Mr. Carpenter, and to Mr. Tilson. But we never had any conversation.''

"How come? Wait, let me guess. They all frighten the hell out of you, don't they?''

"They sure do. Mr. Carpenter, the big black guy, looked at me as if he'd let his dogs eat me for breakfast.

It made me feel like I was a kernel of bird seed and the vultures were here."

Hank Dawson frowned at him. "Maybe I'll try that, if you guarantee it'll work you over or melt you down."

"No way. After meeting your daughter, I sort of decided that you'd be a good guy."

"Kirby, don't let the gorillas shake your tree. Sorry, no pun intended. Some players use psych. They'll hit you with a stance of superiority, to try to intimidate you."

"It sure works." As he spoke, Kirby knew it was true, also remembering his brief introduction to Hector Alvarez. "I met Mr. Alvarez, too."

"Heck's a tough gent."

"If a handshake could snarl, his sure does."

Hank Dawson tossed back his head, laughing. "Hector's okay. All you'll have to do is let him know you intend to stand up to him. Alvarez respects a hard hitter, and from what Westal Jordanson tells me, you can hit like a howitzer."

Kirby sighed. "When you were my age, did the big boys always try to sort of *lean* on you, up front?"

"Some did. Shake it off, because all of it's just a form of weaponry. Each one of our big cats wants to win Big Dixie and some will do anything short of mayhem to claw at the cheek. But," he continued with a wink, "you can't let moxie spook you. Remember, if you're playing in the Big Dixie, it's for one reason. You belong in our gang."

Kirby let out a long breath. "I hope so. It's probably an error on my part to tell you this, but I'm almost scared out of my jock."

Hank grinned. "Kirby, so am I. Pretty soon now, I'll be blowing at a cake with thirty-nine candles. I'm more than twice your age. Compared to you, I'm a senior citizen. I lie awake nights, sweating, and worrying about appearing like some rusty old relic that ought to get a job rolling a court instead of competing on it."

"Honest?"

"Straight out. Years ago, back in my princely prime, I was a top seed. Even then I was scared. Fear comes with the territory, my lad. Nerves are just one ingredient in the recipe. Jitters, and crowd reaction."

At the mention of the word *crowd*, Kirby Tree felt his stomach cringe. "Will a lot of people come to watch? That's dumb. I already know they're coming. Sometimes I feel all those eyes are already here, watching me play, and seeing me get splattered like a broken egg."

"Hey! Quit torturing yourself. Big Dixie isn't the fork in the road of your young life. All it is is just one more tournament. One of many. Only in your case, it happens to be your first."

"Maybe my last."

"Cut it. If it will help you to feel any happier, let's imagine that you and I draw each other on the schedule. This could be your one hunk of luck, you know. You just might tear me up."

"Hank, is that reverse psych?"

The man smiled easily. "Whether it is or isn't, if you and I play, we'll have fun. Regardless of outcome, it won't be our last match together. If we both stay in tennis, and it's my hope we will, Kirby Tree and old Hank Dawson could be face to face across many a net."

"How come you're not like the others, Hank?"

"I never was."

"Boy, am I glad you're here. This may sound nuts, but I hope you really shred some of those guys." Kirby grinned at him. "I hope you finish second if I'm still in and first if I'm not."

Hank chuckled. "That's fair enough. Now then, no more jitters. Let *me* toss and turn at night and fret for both of us. Or, better yet, we'll commit the unforgivable and hand the job over to my daughter."

"What about your daughter?"

Hearing her voice, Kirby and Hank both turned to see her coming with a small tray that held three tall glasses filled with ice and lemonade.

"Thanks, pet. Kirby, here's to you." Hank raised his glass. "And here's to tennis, and the oven of hell that the next four days will be. A toast to yesterday, me, and to your tomorrow, and to that yellow bitch of a ball that we shall valiantly, if I'm not waxing too corny, struggle to dominate."

"Hear, hear," said Case.

All three of them took a sip. The cold burned Kirby's throat, yet he chewed on an ice cube until his back teeth ached. Looking at Hank's face, he felt that he had somehow met this man before. Maybe in a dream. Perhaps it was a feeling spurred by his being Case Dawson's dad. It sure felt great to make friends, especially ones as pleasant as Hank and Case.

I'm glad, he was thinking, they have each other. Everybody ought to have a family.

34

"Stay up" said Little Man.

Due to the wind, the rusty-edged gasoline can blew off the stump. As he bent his heavy body to lift the can from the black soil of the swamp, Little Man grunted.

"There," he said.

Two bullet holes had already pierced the two-gallon can; its red and yellow shape was slightly crumpled. Little Man Tree poked the tip of his finger into one hole, then into the other. Reversing the can, he saw the exit holes that were circled by jagged teeth of torn metal. It is easier, he thought, to shoot at a hunk of worthless tin than it is to fire at a man.

Yet the man must die.

Standing the metal target once again on the brown table of the stump, Little Man looked at his right hand. How many years have passed since the night I took Kirby to this swamp? The Night of the Snake, the promise, the knife and the fire and his blood on the boy's face . . . all of these Little Man remembered.

I cannot, he was thinking, go back on my oath to my nephew, the vow I made on the night that I wore Opopkee's sacred dress. Again, he thought, I will wear the dress, and soon. One more time; so that the man in the photograph will see me inside it, and he will know before he dies why a Seminole takes his life.

Little Man studied the pistol that felt heavy in his hand, the one he had purchased from Charlie No Land.

"Yes," he said to his weapon, "the bad tennis man must know, as he dies, who his killer is. So I will tell him, slowly, as he stares into the black hole of my gun, that I am Little Man Tree. And that I was coming up eight on the evening that my sister died, in childbirth. Her name was Flower. Do you forget, Mr. Dawson?"

Then, he thought, I will help you to remember. He pointed the gun at the can, seeing the white face and the terror mounting in blue eyes that would never again smile at young girls.

His hand trembled.

"No, you no longer think of Flower Tree, do you, Mr. Dawson? Nor do you recall the party when you planted your seed in her, without love."

With his eyes still on the gasoline can, Little Man backed up to a distance of twenty paces, counting silently. Out here, he was thinking, no ear will hear my gun. Not even the ears of Charlie No Land's coonhound. I do not like that dog, he thought, and I must keep warning Kirby never to go into the swamp alone.

I wonder, thought Little Man, if the ghost of Opopkee now watches me or hears the bark of my pistol.

Was he with us, years ago, on the Night of the Snake? There are spirits in God's Florida that I do not understand, as they sing in their swampy voices, echoing in the night. Even in daylight, the deep swamp is always dark, where the old witch paints her home in black and green. Flower, he remembered, had called the long strands of moss the garlands of a ghost.

Although sweaty, Little Man shuddered.

I must not, he then warned himself, allow my mind to rest upon the swamp spirits. Instead I will learn to use the gun. Raising it slowly, keeping his right arm rigid, Little Man was careful to squeeze the trigger slowly. To jerk it would only serve to pull the bullet off its course. Soon, the target would no longer be a red and yellow gasoline can.

The target would be Dawson, the white face, who would no more play the tennis. Or shame the daughter of a Seminole.

He fired.

The can did not fall. Again, he thought, I have missed. Perhaps the gun that I paid Charlie No Land for is crooked. Is its aim sour, as sour as the face and words of Charlie when he speaks?

Lifting the pistol, squinting along the barrel until the tiny steel bead marked a black dot on the yellow rectangle, Little Man fired twice more. The first shot was wild; but the second must have nicked the can's edge, causing it to spin backward and fall, screaming its metallic scream.

"I am lucky," said Little Man Tree, "that guns are not my business. I do better at bulls than at bullets."

Walking back to the stump, and beyond, he kicked the can with the toe of his boot. The container still wore only two bullet holes. His last shot merely tore the seam of one corner.

Little Man scowled.

I would like, he thought, to throw this gun into the swamp and let it sleep with garfish or turtles. My gun gives me no joy. I feel unclean. Slowly he sat on the stump and closed his eyes. His neck itched. I am ugly, he thought, and the thing I must do is an ugly deed. But I cannot ask Wilbur Tree to do it for me, nor Kirby. The revenge is only mine. Perhaps, he wondered, I just tell myself that I do this for Flower. Or is it because the feeling that my father calls bitterness floods through me, like an illness, which even poisons the taste of my breakfast?

Inwardly, he almost smiled. How strange it is, he thought, when Little Man Tree no longer sits to his supper to fill the yawn of my belly's emptiness.

"No longer," he said softly, "do I think of breakfast, or supper, or my noon meal."

When I ate an orange today, at first light, the meat tasted like acid in my mouth. Father said once that hatred is sour, like the crackle of a storm that fouls the music of his radio. I would like, he thought, to be a man like Wilbur Tree. His heart smiles, and he breathes in all God's Florida and the orange blossoms of March. The thoughts of my father's mind are always a gentle sweetness. Sorrow would press down upon him were he to know that Little Man Tree can no longer fill his lungs with sunlight.

My home, he thought, is now a shadow.

Kirby looks at me and I see the candle of happiness glows inside his soul; and he tells me about meeting a young girl at the country club place. My nephew did not tell me that the girl was white. Yet I know. Her blue eyes have looked at him, and he will be tempted.

He wants to bring her to our house, as this is what he told me last evening. When he speaks of her, his voice is a violin, and it sings like the music of Isaac Stern. Kirby is a violin and I am a bull. I'm thick and stupid; so when Kirby's new friend looks at me with her water eyes, a fat bull is what she will see . . . a dirty Seminole who wears swamp mud on his boots and smells like his bulls.

Looking down, Little Man saw a mouse darting through a nest of ferns. The mouse stopped to nibble a seed.

"No," he told the mouse, "I do not want Kirby to be ashamed of me. Perhaps, if the girl comes with Kirby, to visit our home, I will hide, so that the country club girl will not look at me, or point her white finger and laugh."

Kirby did not tell me her name, he thought. Names don't matter. What is important is that she is a nice girl and that Kirby wears good manners with her. He is growing up. No, he is grown. Now he is a tall and golden man and each morning ripens him with sunshine. I am so glad, he thought, that Kirby is as beautiful as Flower.

He looked at the gun. Raising it to his nose, he smelled the barrel, sniffing the strong odor of burnt powder. My gun, he thought, does not smell like a blossom. Instead, it smells like Little Man Tree, a stink of swamp, sweat, and hot work.

I remember, he then thought.

Yes, I recall the day last week when I took Van Cliburn to breed Mr. Ledger's cows, and the rodeo man with the yellow teeth was there. He does not like me and I do not like him. When the rodeo man thought I could not hear, he told Mr. Ledger the joke.

"Why," the man had asked Mr. Ledger, "do Seminoles smell so bad?" Then he said the answer. "So blind people can hate 'em too."

Mr. Ledger did not laugh, even though the rodeo man was slapping his own leg; and then he told the man to go away. My father is right, as usual. Wilbur Tree always says that George Ledger is good and that is why he prospers in God's Florida. Mr. Ledger's herd grows and many cows dot his pasture.

I feel sorry, he thought, for people like the rodeo man. He might walk through orange trees, in March, and never smell the blossoms. And, thought Little Man, the rodeo man will never know the way that my nose, and Mr. Ledger's can smell him.

With a deep sigh, Little Man Tree reached into his pocket, pulled out six more cartridges, and reloaded the gun.

"Soon," he said.

35

"Well," said Case, "a new bonnet?"

As she waved to Patrick J. Tipperary, she felt genuinely glad to see his slow waddle along the long white veranda of the Sweetgum Country Club. On his head was a beige pith helmet.

"Howdy," he said and bowed. "Meet the great white skirt-hunter with the crimson face."

Case walked three steps to meet him. "I warned you about the sun and your fair Irish complexion."

Removing the hat in a pool of shade, he said, "So ya did, toots. That's why I invested in a new lid. Yesterday broiled me to a beet."

With a cautious fingertip, she reached up to lightly touch his inflamed brow. "A few more rays," she

243

said, "and you'll be a burnt offering."

Tip quickly put his helmet on, giving her a ridiculous leer that no one could honestly resent. He really is fun, she thought.

"Well," he said, "today's the start of it. Sweet Thursday at little ol' Sweetsop Country Club, the Big Hickie, or whatever in hell you unshod rebels call it."

"Oh, *suh*, you Yankees is so clevah. Even when Y'all's . . . pardon my plural southern possessive . . . neck is so redneck from sunburn."

"Hey, that's pretty good. C'mon and sit your faultless fanny in a chair and talk to me. I'll even spring for a coffee."

"No thanks. Hank and I ate a mountainous breakfast only an hour ago. But it's a pleasure to join you. I like you, you know, in spite of my better judgment."

Tipperary beamed at her, then winked. "I like you, too, babe." They both sat. "In fact, were I half my age and half my size, I'd marry ya."

"Thank you, Mr. Tipperary." She faked a dramatic flutter of her eyelids, in fun. "Sweet talk like that just might turn my little ol' itty-bitty brain."

Tip grunted. "Come off it."

"I declare," Case went on, "y'all so sweet. Yore just honey and the bees don't know it."

"Hey! Let up, before I lose my breakfast and flip my flapjacks."

Case crossed her legs. "Seriously, Mr. Tipperary . . ."

"Enough already. No item as cute as you can call me

that. It's Tip, okay? Now then, tell me what's so serious."

"Well, if you think you can stand to hear it, what really bugs me is the way you New York types constantly portray the South."

"Yeah?"

"Orlando, sir, is beautiful and prosperous while your town, New York City, is dirty and broke. We're not crawling to Washington to whimper for federal funds."

"For a relative newcomer, kid, you seem to be pretty hip to Orlando."

"Hank grew up here. But he went to college up north at Yale. My home's here now. His too. And we're a lot more than your T.V. stereotype of pickup trucks, fat lawmen with reflecting sunglasses, and crashing cop cars."

Tip lifted a bushy eyebrow. "You mean I've been wrong?"

"Orlando's more than a truckstop with Mickey Mouse as its maitre d'. Yes, there's cowboy money in Florida. A ton. There's oil, beef, and citrus. Our tycoons don't look like some drab ole Wall Streeter. They parade around in flowered slacks and drive pink Lincolns. The difference is not in dress, Tip. The difference is in attitude. In Florida, people make money and have a ball doing it. That, dear sir, is what makes New York yesterday and Orlando tomorrow."

"Easy, kid. I ain't here to bomb the place."

"Well, your general attitude concerning

southerners sounds so superior, and so slanted. New York, and I know a bundle, chatter about bigotry as if they're immune. And they're the worst geographical bigots in America. I grew up around New York City, and if those hooting Yahoos I met in Shea Stadium are cultured patricians, then I'm glad that I have become Lula Mae Gutbucket.''

Tip grunted. ''You all through?''

Case Dawson took a deep breath. ''Not quite. I want to shift gears. You're a nifty gentleman, Tip. My father reads your magazine.''

''Hope he approves.''

''I'm sure you don't care about anyone's approval, or disapproval. Mine, or Hank's. But he reads your *rag*, as you say, and enjoys it. He claims you get a few things wrong but a lot right.''

''I can dish it out, if provoked. Honest, kid . . . I don't ever write heartless. Headless, maybe, but not with no heart.''

''Don't tell me again that you're a tear-in-the-beer Irish sentimentalist, even if I darn well know you are. Hank Dawson likes you and that's a glowing recommendation in my book.''

''You're pretty high on your old man, aren't ya?''

Case nodded. ''You bet I am. Hank's a southerner, but he's no Bubba Joe Sixpack. He's bright, sensitive . . . and I'm totally biased, but Hank Dawson wouldn't ever do a rotten thing to anybody. He's one of the most *together* . . . I dislike that term, but it fits . . . the most *with it* guy around. He's a good human."

Tim smirked. "If I had a flag, I'd wave it."

"You and your cast iron mask. I bet you enjoy this kind of heated exchange, don't you? That's your style. Drop an epithet and then sit back and bask in all the blood you boil."

"That's me. Ya got me pegged."

"There you sit, in that absurd pith helmet, judging without observing. Perchance you have forgotten, you and I are guests here. Dad and Mr. Jordanson introduced me to some of the brass and they're rather charming. All of them seemed to be so happy that we're here at Sweetgum Country Club."

"Oh, so you met all the opulent wheeler-dealers who are throwing this bash?"

"Daddy and I had dinner here, last evening. The women are gracious and ladylike. They're all marvelous hosts. And the men were explaining about how they wanted Big Dixie to stand for charity and community service, as well as big tennis."

Tip muffled a burp. "Hooray," he said in his boredom-edged tone. "Three cheers for the Rebel Rotarians and their diamond-studded tieclips. I bet some of those colonels got the Stars an' Bars flagged on their undershorts."

I will not, Case Dawson warned herself, lose my patience with him and his cynical poses. He's not going to prodpole me out of my cool.

"Not to change the subject," he said, "as I'm always so entranced to listen whenever the gentility of the Confederates are enumerated . . . usually, may I add, by themselves . . . but let's talk tennis. I know more about a tennis tilt than I do about charm."

Case smiled. "Old sir, you'd have to."

"Agreed. Who'd our pal Hank draw?"

"He's going against Hector Alvarez in the first round. At noon. Just yesterday, I saw Alvarez hitting, over on court eight, and I'm scared to death."

"Yeah, you oughta be. Tough little taco."

Case Dawson knotted her fingers, pressing them together until her tan hands whitened. "Do you think Hank has a prayer? I'd hate to see him knocked off in the first round."

"Don't sweat it. All these guys are good and Hank Dawson used to be better than any that's here."

"Honestly?"

"Straight up, kid. Like I told-ja, I know tennis. That, and broads, are the only things I'm expert on."

"Then he has a chance?"

"Case, I gotta tell ya, on any odd or even day, any one of these whippers can get hot and shellack the be-Jesus outa all the rest. Or, any one of 'em can, just as sudden, be standing in the heat, wet with sweat, and wondering why he's holding an icy racquet. Somedays, ya can't hit a cow in the ass with a snow shovel."

She was aware that he was watching her sigh. Turning her head, she looked at his blue eyes, seeing no meanness in his sunburned face. And that wonderfully ridiculous pith helmet.

"Here," he said, reaching out to her, "lemme hold your hand, kid. I just washed with lye, so you won't catch V.D."

His hand felt cool as his thick fingers covered hers. Of all the mysteries of tennis life, she was thinking, Patrick J. Tipperary surely had to be one of the deepest. I really would pity Tip, she thought, were he actually as shallow as he pretends. As for knowing about the game itself, he was, as his magazine was so aptly entitled, tip top.

"Have I been bitchy to you?"

"Not to me, kid. So you got a case of the regional prides, and you're hooked on Florida and your new home. God bless ya for that. Ya know, I never got married. The rabbits kept living and I probably lucked out, like Irish roulette. But I hope you'll let me say one thing . . . I envy Hank Dawson."

"Why?"

"I sure wish I'd sired a daughter like you, Miss Gutbucket."

He patted her hand.

"Yeah, I sure wish. I'm all alone in the world, Case. Nobody married me because no woman could stand me. I'm loud, I get drunk a lot and when I drink I turn ornery. Or sing, which causes even more pain. I been tangled up into more barroom fistfights than I got replaced teeth. I s'pose I reek with little more, at the moment, than selfish self-pity."

"I know." She squeezed his hand.

"This old tongue spits vitriol. But I'm not here in Florida to gloat, or to lie, or to let my typewriter spew venom on anybody . . . or, if I can add . . . on any kid's dad. Yours included. Maybe I owe you an apology, too. I sounded off a whole lot bitchier than you did, giving ya the needle and all. So, I'll letcha in on a little secret."

The blue eyes were bluer, she thought as she saw how serious he looked, how sincere his gruff voice sounded.

"Kid, I'm silently rooting for Hank Dawson."

36

It was almost eleven o'clock.

Billy Gossage groaned silently as he picked up his racquets and walked off court four. With a sideward glance, he stole one more stunned look at the man who had just wiped him out, in three straight sets, the player who had demolished him so easily this morning. Tommy Tilson, the veteran Austrailian.

Westal Jordanson was there to shake his hand. "You played well, Billy, and I'm proud of you."

Billy forced a heartless smile. "Wes, you're too kind. I played like Little Mary Sunshine."

The old professional patted him on the shoulder of his soaking shirt. "Tilson's tough."

The boy sighed. "Well, you swore he would be.

Big Dixie, however, turned out to be a bit heavier than my usual college competition. The guys I've opposed in the last four years don't play tennis. And I don't play it either. Tommy Tilson plays tennis."

"I understand. I was strolling around this morning, in an effort to watch all four matches."

"Sorry you had to arrive back here in time to watch me stumble. However, I appreciate your coming over."

Wes nodded. "You're right, with regard to what you said earlier. Tillie plays for bucks. Unlike you, he's not thinking about going off to law school."

Wiping his face, Billy said, "I just couldn't find my game against him. Wes, it was like trying to hit mush. He forced me to where I was having to dig every ball up out of the grit. No bounce. And his placement was almost surgical. Had he wanted to, Tilson could have sliced his shots into one of my pockets and out my fly."

The old man grunted. "Soft game."

"You warned me. It's two hours later and now I'm an official spectator. And here comes Dad."

Billy saw his father, Art Gossage, shrug his beefy shoulders. He was wearing his white suit with a pink tie and pink shoes. "You did okay," he said. "You took a few games, Billy."

"I took three. Tilson only took eighteen."

"Are you glad you're going to pursue the law instead of a yellow ball?"

Billy grinned. "And if I flunk out in Gainesville, I'll just come home and help you sell cars."

"You won't flunk," said Wes. "Art, you and Lassie June raised yourselves a good lad. He's a gentleman, both on and off the court, so the two of you can hold him proud. He'll be a good lawyer."

"Thanks," said Art.

Billy looked around. "Now that I'm out of it, who's still in? What's happening in the other three matches?"

Art shaded his eyes with a chubby hand. "Who's the ten-foot black guy? I keep forgetting some of the names."

"Carpenter," said Wes.

"He's winning," said Art Gossage. "Or so I just heard from Ollie Morehouse. Herb, Ollie and Eugene Pollet are trying to watch everybody at once, like kids at a three-ring circus. As for me, my arches are below the sod."

Billy looked at the people. "We drew quite a crowd, Dad."

Art smiled. "Thank goodness. The handsome turnout's a load off *my* mind. Herb said the same. Big Dixie's off to a peachy start, and it's only Thursday. Now, if we can pull a big gate tomorrow, we're financially in the clear. Saturday and Sunday'll pose no problems. It'll be a jam."

Billy felt pleased. His father, he was thinking, had willingly invested a lot of work into Big Dixie, and so had his cronies. Our chunky old car dealer is an okay guy, right down to his pink loafers.

"How's Kirby doing, Wes?" Billy asked.

"They're in the fourth set. I just left to sneak over and check on you and Tillie."

Fourth set? So, Billy knew, our golden Seminole must have taken at least one set to stay alive. How, he wondered, could Kirby have possibly won a set against the Canadian?

"Let's go check," said Wes.

"Not me," Billy heard his father say. "I'm fixin' to search out an air conditioner and a tall gin fizz. Anybody want to join me?"

Billy could see that Westal Jordanson wanted one thing—to audit his young star. "You go ahead, Dad. Please order me a Gator, lots of ice, and I'll be along in a few minutes."

"Will do. By the way, Wes . . . thanks for drifting over to see my boy play. I know you can't be everywhere at once."

Billy felt Wes punch his arm. His father headed for the comforts of the Sweetgum Country Club bar.

"How's the heat?" Wes asked him as the two of them moved through the crowd to another pair of courts.

"Steaming. I pity the eight guys who are slated to crank up at noon. How come all sixteen of us weren't scheduled for nine o'clock?"

"Because," he heard Wes explain, "it's a weekday. Herb Caldwell figured, and perhaps quite properly, that on a Thursday we'd have a decent chance of pulling a good business lunch crowd. Hope he's right.''

"Lots of strangers came," Billy said. "I see the usual faces of club members, but they seem to be in the minority."

Wes didn't answer.

He doesn't see a soul, Billy thought, except Kirby Tree. I can't blame him. Wes Jordanson never really became a seeded player, nor was he ranked as one of the big-money coaches. But he's a great old guy. I hope Kirby respects this gimpy old geezer as much as I do.

Noticing Wes's somewhat hesistant walk, he asked, "How's the arthritis?"

"My back knows it's morning. It'll ease."

A makeshift scoreboard had been neatly erected for each of the tournament courts. This one, Billy read quickly, told him that the fourth set was over. Yet no one was shaking hands. Good, he thought. Kirby's rolling. As he and Wes walked closer, Billy saw the black numerals on the white squares.

Arnold	6	6	5	6
Tree	1	4	7	7

He saw Westal's unrestrained grin.

"The kid's hanging in, Wes."

The pro snorted. "Skin of his teeth and the seat of his pants. Don't ask me how. I didn't rig the draw, and quite honestly, I was a bit apprehensive for both you and Kirby in the first round."

Two days ago, Billy remembered, he had seen Kenny Arnold hitting with a man he did not know. The Canadian was, he judged, about thirty. He looked lean and hard, hitting the ball with plenty of pace. Vicious topspin on the forehand that bent the ball's final trajectory into a magnetic arc, as though it was electronically homing into the court.

Damn, he thought, I should have drawn Kenny Arnold. Idle dreams. It's over, Gossage, and you blew it. Your bubble's popped. Ha! I'm probably the only living soul here at Sweetgum who is amazed that I lost so badly.

Billy sighed. Why do we all think we're so much better than we really are? Not one turkey at the club thinks he deserves his club rating. Even in a tilt of social doubles, all the men and women think they ought to get paired with a stronger player. He smiled. That's the trophy for doubles. You always have someone else to blame.

Kirby served.

As the final set matured, Billy watched the strain pulling on Westal Jordanson's face. His old fists clenched into leathery hammers. How come, Billy asked himself, I never noticed Wes's twisted fingers? That blond bomber out there, the one in the headband and beaded shirt, is old Westal's last prayer. Kirby's his big roll of the dice.

Lord, he thought, I'm twenty-two. If I was uptight against Tilson, it might be easy to imagine how Kirby

Tree, at eighteen, feels when he's looking across a net at somebody like Ken Arnold.

Both players were toweling their faces, necks, and arms. The sun was higher, almost overhead. The crowd was, as usual during the bi-game break, discussing players. And the weather.

"I guess," said a lady in a flowery dress, "that the mad dogs and Englishmen play at noon." She fanned her damp face with linen.

"Sit quiet, Sugar," said the gentleman beside her, "and I'll just hustle up to the clubhouse and fetch us back a libation. What's your pleasure?"

"Ice tea. And make it a double. You're a dear." The lady was a friend of his mother's. "Billy," she said with a smile, "did you beat?"

Billy shook his head. "No, I didn't, Mrs. Beaufort."

"Oh," she scowled, "you poor lamb."

Yes, he wanted to tell her, he was one of the lambs. Just one of the first-round patsies that are added to invitational rosters in order to round out full complement strength. In football, we would be called tackling dummies, I believe.

In tennis, we're just dummies.

"No," he heard Wes grumble.

Kirby Tree had just double faulted at ad out and had given Kenny Arnold a gift; the first break of a fifth set.

Billy saw Wes hide his face in his crippled hands. The fresh numeral slid into its scoreboard slot. The boards were being tended by clubmember youth, and both the scorers and ball-boys had thus far, Billy was thinking, performed quite diligently. The score read 5-4, Arnold's favor; and Arnold's service.

"Wes, don't ask me how I know," said Billy, "but it's not over. I think your Seminole superstar is going to break back. Arnold's serve isn't that strong and this Canada goose is one heck of a long ways from Hudson's Bay. Look at Arnold's face."

Westal Jordanson looked and nodded. "You're right. The Florida heat's starting to bake him raw."

Kenny Arnold's cheeks were tomatoes. As he served into the overhead sun, he hit a poor toss and the ball kicked off the toe of his racquet.

"Stay in," whispered Wes.

The ball did exactly that, and Billy saw Kirby quilt it for a winner. The Canadian whacked the court with his racket as he moved to the opposite end of the baseline. He served and Kirby Tree returned another beauty. It happened twice more. Four straight points. Arnold threw his racquet in total disgust.

"He blew a fifty-four," Wes hissed to Billy. "I don't believe it. How in Hades did you know?"

"I've played Kirby Tree, remember?"

Wes touched his shoulder. "I recall. I'm proud of *all* my boys, Bill. You know that."

Billy nodded. "Let's watch Kirby take him."

Kirby did, in a tie-breaker.

37

"How's it feel?"

Hearing her voice and seeing her face, Hank Dawson grinned. "Great," he said, and it did. Hector Alvarez stood nearby, staring at him, no doubt wondering how he'd been beaten in three straight sets by a thirty-eight-year-old has-been alcoholic.

He saw Alvarez kick over a folding chair.

Case rushed in to hug him, even though his tennis clothes looked and felt as though he had just stepped from a steam bath. Kirby Tree was there, too, and shook his hand.

"Good match, Hank."

"Thanks," he said, looking at Case. "Please don't

259

ask me how I did it. It was pure luck. Just happened to be my day instead of Heck's."

Behind him, Hank could still hear the little Mexican muttering in Spanish. Perhaps it was fortunate, Hank thought, as he recognized a salty word or two, that Sweetgum Country Club was not entertaining too bilingual a crowd.

Case wrapped an arm around his waist, the other around Kirby's. "Wow," she said, "I've heard the expression Sweet Thursday, and this is it, come to life."

Hank kissed her hair. "Thank golly I don't have to play tomorrow. Guess I'll just stay home and watch T.V. soaps and forfeit."

"Like fun you will. You're playing, sport . . . Friday, Saturday, and Sunday. All the way, Hank."

"Hey!" said Kirby. "What about *me?*"
Hank punched him. "You're still a colt. You don't know what pain is yet. Kenny Arnold was easing up in those last three sets because he felt sorry for you and because he so fervently adores Seminoles."

"Oh," he heard Case's voice almost sing, "I could touch the sky. Really and truly. Both of you played superbly. Yet I never doubted that you'd both win, not even this morning, when Kirby was down two sets."

Kirby grinned. "I sure doubted it. During those two sets, Arnold had me spooked out of my skull."

I like this boy, Hank thought. He lets a victory go to his heart and not to his head.

Slowly they walked through the crowd, stopping several times to allow Hank to shake a few congratulatory hands. "Good match, Hank," he heard. "Great playing."

"Thanks. Thank you," he said over and over. It felt great. He wasn't thirty-eight, he thought. I'm still a kid inside. I was out there having fun with Heck Alvarez, tormenting him, hitting shots almost the way I hit them fifteen years ago. I was pre-bottle, pre-booze, and better still . . . pre-Pam Rilling.

"You did it." Case squeeze his arm. "You led in every set, holding serve, conserving your strength. . ."

"I guess I look pretty pathetic on that lob."

Kirby held up a finger. "That," he said, "was just smart tennis. The lob that Alvarez rolled over your head was long gone. Superman couldn't have run it down. So you just ignored it, then turned to Alvarez, and bowed."

Hank said, "That's the difference between my style and yours, my boy. You'd have run it down."

"Wrong. I'd have hit it in the air."

"Confidence," said Casey. "So beware, my dear and darling papa, of brazen youth."

A few minutes later, the three of them sat on the clubhouse veranda, the one that faced the adult pool. Hank was aching for a scotch. Please, he was thinking, just one to celebrate. I won't be this lucky two days in a row. Just one drink?

"Root beer," he told the waiter.

His daughter stared at him as he'd said it. She *knows*, he was thinking. I wonder if the hunger for booze ever stops. Will it eat away at my guts for all eternity? The veranda was crowded. Liquor was everywhere. Scotch and soda foamed up fresh in a glass on the next table. God, he thought in preventive prayer, am I going to grab some guy's tinkling highball and knock it back?

They don't know what it's like.

No, they'll never understand. It's been called a disease, alcoholism. But it isn't. Disease is hardly the word; and such a term, Hank thought, was probably minted by some tea-drinker . . . some low-key Puritan who never tasted the first drop. He never felt that beautiful burning rush as the initial swallow pours down his throat. Disease was far too limp a handle. *Death* would have been more apt.

Somewhere, from a million miles away, yet at his table, Hank Dawson heard Casey bubbling on and on about how great it all was. He heard Kirby, even higher. The two of them were in Heaven. And here sit I, he thought, waiting for a root beer. How putridly benign.

Maybe, he thought, I could sneak just *one*.

What would it be? His eyes closed; he felt the furnace of his body still pumping in the afternoon heat. Who in hell, he wondered, scheduled such midday masochism? His mind returned to its fantasy . . . what would he order, were he to have *just one drink*?

Gin. Not over ice. Just one colorless hooker of Boodles in a shot glass. One, maybe two. That's it, Hank, order a double. A belt of gin in each fist and he'd feel like King Kong. Eyes still closed, he felt his mouth ease open, then the rim of the imaginary glass lightly touch his lower lip. Just two, and no more.

Who was he kidding?

Maybe a bourbon. For some reason, he couldn't halt his fantasies. Old Grand Dad, just one quick slug, right out of that beautiful bottle. First you snap the seal, then crack the cap, then. . .

"Good one, Henry."

Opening his eyes, feeling a hand tap his shoulder, Hank twisted around to see Tommy Tilson, the Aussie.

"Hey! Good one yourself, Tillie. As I'm still in a daze, I can't recall whom you went against this morning. Refresh my memory."

"Nobody," said Tilson. "I can't remember the bloke either. Billy Nobody. Every tilt's menu has its rack of lamb."

Hank grinned. "Baa," he bleated at the Austrailian and then saw the chortle of Tilson's appreciation.

"Hank, I have me a hunch, old cobber, that there's a surly little Mex around here somewhere who is not calling you a lamb. About now, he's referring to you as the illegitimate son of a *puta*."

Hank laughed. "Tillie, I guess perhaps that you've met my daughter, Case Dawson. And you know Kirby, I presume."

Tilson nodded. "Yes, we've all met. I saw the tail of your match this morning," he said to Kirby. "Arnold let you off the hook like a lover's telephone. Congratulations."

"Thanks, Mr. Tilson. And, by the way, the name of your opponent this morning was Billy Gossage. He's a good guy."

"You're right. Sorry if I offend, *Mr*. Tree. Won't muddle about like that again, old chap. Call me Tillie. Everyone does, even me mum."

Bowing to Case, Tommy Tilson moved away, heading for the bar. The lucky devil, Hank Dawson was enviously thinking.

"Well?"

Hearing the one gruff word, Hank turned to see the smile that beamed from beneath a beige pith helmet. It was Tip. He offered his beefy hand and Hank took it.

"Contratulations, Hank. I saw ya take him."

"Thanks."

"Mind if I join you people?"

"Please do." Hank pulled a chair into the group and watched Patrick J. Tipperary fill it with his generous bulk. The chair squeaked its legitimate gripe.

"How in hell do you old soldiers fight in heat like this?" Tip asked. He mopped his face as he looked around for a waiter, waving a futile hand.

"It was tough, Tip. And I was lucky. By the way, thanks for watching us."

Tip grunted. "I always watch Alvarez."

No sooner than he'd said it, Hank saw Case fake a slap at Tip's shoulder, but with a sly smile. "Now," she said to Tip, "there you go again, trying to stir up trouble with every idle dig."

Tipperary winked at Hank. "Casey's become my self-appointed moral chaperon. I made one big mistake when, in my cups, I must have confessed to her that I was sentimental."

Kirby was being unusually quiet, Hank thought. Tired perhaps. What right did a cub have to feel fatigue? Especially after he'd played the early round. Yet he'd gone five sets against Kenny Arnold. Add to that the pressure of his first tournament and his tender years. So there he sits, taking it all in, and looking at Casey as though she were some forbidden dessert. Hmm, I wonder how much forbidding I can exert.

The waiter finally came with a round tray, to set three glasses of ice and refreshment on their little table. Hank signed the tab. As he scribbled his name, he saw Tip Tipperary stretch out a pudgy hand. Raising the glass, he helped himself to an uninvited sip of Hank's drink.

Tip looked at Hank and grinned. "Root beer," he said with a slight burp. "Haven't had any of that junk in a generation." To the waiter, he said, "Make it the same for me, son. One more root beer, please. When ya get a chance."

Hank looked at him. "On the wagon, Tip?"

"Not really." The Irish eyes looked bluer. "But

every once in a while, a guy's gotta do decent for a friend. Besides, if you can do it, Dawson, so can I.''

Hank Dawson looked at his root beer, raised it, took an ice cube into his mouth and crushed it with his teeth. The cold flooded his mouth, but the mild pain felt oddly welcome. He swallowed.

"Tip, you're a good gent.''

"No I'm not. But there aren't many guys on this planet that I'd order root beer with. And, just in case you're wondering why I helped myself to a gulp of your drink, I was just checking. Okay with you?''

Hank grinned. "Okay with me.''

38

A gun shot?

Wilbur Tree listened, looking westward toward the swamp, seeing nothing but his bulls and an evening sun. He leaned against the top rail of the pasture fence, resting a moc on the lower rail, waiting to hear again what he thought he had heard.

Mario Lanza walked slowly toward him, skirting an alligator hummock nesting in the saw grass.

"My grandchild," he said to the bull, "washes his new tennis clothes and hums music. Never have I seen him so happy."

The bull strolled closer, to within twenty feet of the fence, then stopped for a munch of his meadow.

"Today, he played the tennis and won. He beat a man whose name was Arnold, a Canada man from a far away place. Up north. It is the land of the great white bear and this is all I know."

Mario snorted.

I wonder, Wilbur Tree thought, where my son is. Little Man said nothing during our supper. Today he ate little, as though a worry is eating at him. He seems gnawed by his thinking and cannot fill his belly with cooking because it is already abrim with matters of the mind. My son and my grandson are now men, Wilbur thought; so it would not be righteous of me to pry into their daydreams.

"Do you dream, Mario?"

I do, Wilbur Tree silently answered his own question. Yes, I still dream of Hanna, my woman. Yet there are no stirrings within me, no woman pain; the urgings that I once had burned hotter than charcoal. A man discovers peace only in age. I am now the brown leaf, a thistle that hardens upon its stem to stiffness. He looked up at the pines. No longer, he thought, am I a sprig of green-needles that brush an evening wind.

I remember, thought Wilbur Tree.

Closing his eyes, he was momentarily young again, youthful enough to run beneath the moon, even after a long workday under the sun. Many times, he remembered, he had run ten miles to see Hanna Kirby. Not even to speak to her. He'd waited alone outside the house of her family, hoping to catch sight of her through the window. That was all. His heart had called to her without sound.

"Hanna Kirby! Come outside," he had whispered, "to where Wilbur Tree stands in the shadows and feels the tongues of bugs feeding upon his flesh. Walk outdoors, Hanna, and Wilbur Tree will bind you with his arms and climb your face with his lips."

No one imagined, Wilbur recalled, that I would marry such a prize of a woman. Charlie Deepwater told me that I was a fool Seminole to long for her, and that my longing would knot my bowels and flood my mind with poison. Yet I would not listen to his sour words, for there was too much music singing in my heart; and I did not run the ten miles. Instead, I flew. Back then, my legs were egrets and my feet feathered as hawks. For her, I would have run from one shore of God's Florida to the other, without pause, with no rest. Each fill of my lungs pumped fragrance into me, nourishing my body to be strong and hard and hungry for her.

My eyes saw no other woman . . . only Hanna.

When the time ripened for her to look my way, she saw no one other man than Wilbur Tree, as I knew she would. And she said that my body shone browner than the buckeye nut from the Ohio place. As she touched my chest with her hand, my heart fired, burning her fingertips. She hurt to have me as I hurt in wanting her.

Wilbur Tree smiled; his eyes were still closed, in order to read all of the beauty on Hanna Kirby's face.

Then, he recalled, I was alive, deer swift and bear strong, my Seminole blood a hot spring that steamed among morning cypress. Again and again, Wilbur remembered, he had grabbed handfuls of sand and scrubbed his wet body with its grit, to feel pure.

He had waited, without women.

The daughter of Jack Whiskey had raised her skirts for him but Wilbur had refused her treasure. The running helped to water the fire in his blood. Twenty miles. Almost every evening. When he had finally told Hanna of all the acts that he had seen her perform, as he hid outside their shack, she knew of his devotion. And she figured that, all in all, he had run over a thousand miles merely to see her through a window.

Then she knew that she would become the woman and the wife and the love of Wilbur Tree. No other man would do.

When he had first told her his name, she did not laugh. Hanna had looked at him with softening eyes and had repeated his name in almost a whisper, like praying.

"Wilbur Tree," she said, almost in silence.

He had nodded.

Over and over she had repeated, "A thousand miles to worship a woman through a window."

"It poured iron into my legs," he had confessed to her. "And made my lungs hurricanes. My seed for you, Hanna, is a grainery. I will fill you with the whole of my life and all of my children."

The two of them had wept with love.

"Hanna," he said aloud, remembering.

Walking closer, Mario stretched his big face toward the gentle hand of the Seminole he knew so well. Wilbur scratched his head, watching the big bull close his brown eyes, as though he also had sweet memories.

Little Man has no woman, Wilbur thought, as he stroked the warm fur of his animal. He is alone. Little Man Tree is one love-bug instead of two. Lee said this to me. Lee Roy Wilkerson was a black man who did business with Mr. Ledger; and, Wilbur was recalling, Lee had once told them an African proverb.

"One bracelet," Lee had said, "cannot jingle."

Ah, thought Wilbur Tree, that is quite true, because my son, Little Man Tree, is only a single bracelet with no woman to ring his life into chimes. I say nothing to my son on this matter, for a man must rein his own wagon; and to lead him would only make me a blind mule who becomes lost on a strange road.

The Florida sky grew darker.

This is the sad time of the day, Wilbur thought, when an old man and his bull stand, with a fence between them, to watch an evening die.

"A day passes us, Mario, and she returns to us never again. She flies west beyond treetops."

Where, he wondered, do days go? Is there some secret home in a western sky where flocks of evenings gather on the limbs of a giant tree, to fold their wings and welcome darkness?

Where is Hanna?

I know, thought Wilbur Tree, that her body rests in earth . . . but where is Hanna Kirby Tree? Where is her smile, her laughter; and does she still hear the classical music that closed her eyes with its brilliance?

Mario snorted.

"Do you hear music, Mario Lanza?"

The bull licked his face, causing Wilbur to pull back his head, away from being again the target of so rough a tongue. Taking a red bandana from his pocket, he wiped his neck and cheek, inhaling the strong fragrance that could only be born of bull. Once more he blotted his face, returning the bandana into its torn pocket. As he did so, his fingernails felt the pocket's gritty bottom. I must, Wilbur Tree thought, dunk my trousers soon into soap and water, before I smell like Charlie No Land.

I am glad, Wilbur thought, that Charlie No Land comes to our home no longer. Not for years has he come. Yet, early this morning, I heard the whine of his voice. Looking, I saw his slump-shoulder stance at the edge of the swamp, in shadows, talking to Little Man.

They seemed to be arguing, about money. Yet, Wilbur recalled, I could not hear all of the words. Charlie uses more words than he needs to fill his bucket. His mouth runs over, like a pail that is too small to hold its water. Then, as Charlie No Land talked, I watched the ears of our mule, Londie. She is old and wise, and I think that the sound and smell of

Charlie No Land scrapes her ear, because back it flops and then she kicks at a bee.

Does my son have business with Charlie No Land? I hope not. If true, then it may prove that Little Man trades his money for sadness.

"Mario, you do not know your children. If you met your son, he would be strange to you, as my son is becoming strange to me. The sunlight of my reason no longer lights him. I praise God that this is not also true with my grandchild."

Kirby is sunshine.

He is day, thought Wilbur; while Little Man is a night's inky shadow. My son is my moon child. Opopkee told me of this, when I was a boy, foretelling that I would sire two children but live with two others. Half of this ripens true. Perhaps even all. Opopkee whispered as he read the smoke of the fire about one child in sunlight, the other beneath the stars whose mind is darkened by his destiny.

The bull spooked just before Wilbur Tree heard the gunshot. Mario bolted away, trotting about forty paces, then stopped. Wilbur listened to the ensuing stillness and the bugs of the swamp.

Yes, he knew, it was a gun. Yet he did not know why the gun was fired.

39

Wes Jordanson yawned.

He sat alone out in the gazebo that stood fifty yards away from the main buildings of the Sweetgum Country Club. Behind him he heard the noise of the members and players celebrating the finish of the second day. Another evening party he was attempting to avoid.

Today is Friday, thought Wes. Two more days to go, and so far, Big Dixie certainly had produced its share of shockers.

"Kirby's still alive," Wes said aloud to himself. He whacked his thigh with his hand. "By damn, my youngster's still in it."

Gosh, he thought, but I'm tired. I feel as though

I've hit every ball that was hit today. And what a day it was. Had anyone told me that Kirby would last two rounds, I might have accused that person of wishful thinking. Yet he did. My young Seminole's still alive. And now, it comes down to the final four, tomorrow. The semi-finals.

Kirby plays Carpenter.

Carp just might finish him off in straight sets. Kirby's only chance is to resist any attempt to cream that big serve. He's got to block it, using Carpenter's pace and turning it against him. So, if Kirby can just get that serve back, he can play out the point. That's what he must do. He can't get too eager, or become jumpy. If he does, Carp's serve will put holes in his chest.

"Bullet holes," Westal Jordanson laughed.

I saw Tip watching Kirby today, taking notes, opening his battered old notebook after almost every point. Well, whatever Tip Tipperary writes will be honest. Perhaps not always so kind, yet truthful. To read *Tip Top Tennis* is sort of like being back on the court. His typewriter has a way of rubbing your face into the grit. You feel the heat right up through your sneakers. And into your jock.

Tillie sure played well today. Better than I've seen him play in years.

Tilson demolished Kelly as easily as he did Billy Gossage yesterday. Perhaps even easier. That's sort of how it goes, Westal thought. For some tournaments, your racquet just has the magic touch. You can't miss. Every first serve nicks the tape and kicks every way but where your opponent expects it. Every lob hits a baseline.

Yes, Wes thought, Tommy Tilson was a pleasure to watch. So was Hank.

Wes shook his head. "I still don't believe *that* either." And now Hank Dawson is the only lefthanded player that's still in it. Davidson's gone and so is Ally Blackmoor. Will wonders ever cease?

What a nifty line-up for Saturday. We've got Carpenter, Tilson, Dawson, and Tree. I wonder how Hank'll handle Tilson. My guess is . . . not well. Tillie's just too superb a tennis player, too smooth for Hank Dawson. But, Wes then recalled, Tillie's never had a ton of luck against lefties. Connors eats his lunch and McEnroe cleans his clock on every serve.

Hank Dawson's a lefty.

Wes snorted. "I forgot about that. Yessir, I surely did . . . Hank's lefthanded bat against Tommy's surgical chops." Wes nodded. That, he thought, warrants a moment or two of reassessment. Hank Dawson just might pull it out. Stranger things have happened in our maze of yellow balls.

Getting up, Wes stomped a foot that had gone to sleep, feeling the prickle of awakening nerves climb the shank of his right leg. "Wake up, you lazy old codger," he told his own foot.

It was a warm evening. Usually was this time of year in Florida, Wes was thinking, great place to live. At my age, *any* place you're still on your feet is a thankful residence. Guess I'm just one more senior citizen. That's what's so relaxing about our state. People in their eighties are so plentiful that it makes me feel youthful, he thought. Smiling, he danced a single step, walking along the shadowy walk of lights that circled the putting green.

A brown palmetto bug crossed his path, scurrying from one edge of the flagstone walkway to the other, finally scooting into the groomed carpet of Bermuda grass.

But then something else, another movement, alerted Wes's eye.

Beyond the eighteenth green, a sudden motion captured his attention and held it. Something, or someone, was standing in the heavy brush of palmettoes and then quickly darted away . . . as though not expecting, or wanting, to be spotted. A furtive gesture.

Wes saw the form for less than a second, but it was a familiar shape, one he'd seen more than once. The more he thought about it, the clearer the picture crystallized in his mind and memory.

Little Man Tree.

Never before, Wes was thinking, have I seen Little Man here at the Sweetgum Country Club. Not even once. I asked Kirby if his grandfather and his uncle wanted to come to Big Dixie, but, as I recall, he didn't give me a very enthusiastic response. Kids! Maybe he's too occupied with the pressures of professional tennis. Or, he added to himself, the burdens of romance. Earlier, he remembered, he'd seen Kirby and the Dawson girl walking back to the edge of the pond, near the tenth tee, and they were holding hands.

Wes sighed. "Young love," he said aloud. "Hilda, sometimes I miss you so much," he told the moon, "that I can't bear living."

Wes squinted across the open and treeless area of the eighteenth green.

Walking slowly, he passed between a pair of kidney-shaped sandtraps, climbed the very low hill of the apron and crossed the green to stand near the pin. Its flag, with eighteen on it in Sweetgum colors, orange and green, hung limp, lifeless, as though it, too, was exhausted. He touched its roughness with his hand. "Little Man?" he asked in a conversational voice.

There was no answer. No fat Seminole came out of the brush to reply to his questioning call. Somewhere, deeper in the blackness, an owl screamed and then was still.

Wes waited.

Well, he just wasn't sure. Perhaps it was Little Man Tree or perhaps he had been mistaken. If so, maybe the uncle had merely come to look for his nephew. That was logical. Uncles behave in a like manner. Don't they? Why, he asked himself, does my stomach hurt, as if something is about to *happen* to someone? Nonsense. I'm letting the mystery of a tropical evening master my mind. Perhaps it's just a vignette of Florida Voodoo.

But the pain was there.

With one hand still on the golf pin, Westal Jordanson covered his gut with the other. It hurts . . . as
though I've been stabbed by some uncanny attack.
Shucks, it's probably gas. Ate too much. Gas and mid-
tournament jitters, even though I'm not playing. It
was a good dinner, he thought, leaving the pin in its
cup, walking across the closely-cropped grass and
down the apron knoll.

"Gas," he muttered.

But, he told himself, walking, he had seen Little
Man Tree . . . a man, if one can tell by his sudden surprise to my presence, who did not at all wish to be
discovered.

The shy Seminole.

A curious people, Wes thought, from what little I
know of them. Shy as crabs. They keep to their holes
in the sand.

Westal Jordanson looked back, over his shoulder,
into the shadows where he had seen the man.
Nothing. The bugs were there, courting in their
nightly chorus, but no one else. He saw no Little Man
Tree, no shadow in flight, and no Seminole.

I wonder, Wes was thinking, how many white
people in Florida have been silently and secretly
observed by the black eyes of a Seminole. Countless,
no doubt. Well, were I a Seminole, it's safe to say that
I'd be a tad distressed over the way Florida's changing. Wes looked at the luxurious Sweetgum
clubhouse, the main pavilion. And to think, he said to

himself, I used to hunt deer where I'm now teaching tennis.

Westal Jordanson shook his head.

Again, he looked up at the moon. Maybe, he thought, I'll crash myself early into the feathers. Used to be, I could play tennis all day and party all night. No more. Good thing, too, because nothing destroys a player more quickly than a two-flame candle. From what I hear, it surely did burn out Hank Dawson.

I like that man, Wes thought. Even more, I admire the way he's playing, yesterday, and again today. An entire new style. Years ago, he danced a ballet on a tennis court. More of a dancer than an athlete. Superb grace.

The pain came again.

Not a physical pain, but rather a strange little barb of unexpected memory, which widened Wes's eyes, and opened his mouth in awe. Good God, his brain almost screamed . . . now I know! Not quite in shock, Westal Jordanson leaned against the trunk of a pine, feeling short of breath from the surge of mental exertion.

Closing his eyes, the images began to focus in his mind, as he saw two players, both with golden hair, both dancers, the same face and build. He saw Kirby Tree and remembered the young Hank Dawson. *Yes!* Wes knew now what he had tried so many years to figure out . . . the big question . . . where had he seen Kirby before?

Wes couldn't breathe. He could only sit down on

the grass and ponder which was worse . . . for Kirby to know, or never to know.

40

Case checked her wristwatch.

"Please don't tell me what time it is," Kirby told her. "I don't want to know."

As he spoke, she felt him squeeze her hand and it was a welcomed touch. Without thinking, her fingers answered his.

"For you," she said, "it's just about bedtime."

Kirby shook his head. "No way. I don't feel tired at all. Not a bit. I could stay up all night and play all day tomorrow."

Case shook her head at him. "Athletes," she said. "You all think you're chiseled out of bronze."

His fingertip touched her face, very lightly. "We are," he told her. "But am I glad you aren't."

"Oh, but I am. I'm Henry Dawson's daughter, which means there's a bundle of bronze in me."

She saw him smile at her. "You know, I really like your dad. Sometimes, when I'm talking to him, it's all I can do to stop myself from, you know, coming right out and telling him what a great guy he is."

"You're a good guy, too."

"Thanks." He said the one word with a self-conscious shrug of his shoulders, as though he didn't know what else to say or do.

He's so innocent, Case Dawson was thinking, and so beautifully pure, almost like a flower one would discover in some very secret and personal spot.

They walked slowly along the flagstone path, one of the many that twisted, seemingly without destination, through the giant oaks and the expansive lawns of the Sweetgum Country Club. Yes, she thought, I could stay up all night, too. Just walking and talking, and being alone with Kirby Tree. Her eyes copped a quick glance at him. Amazing, she told herself, but he really doesn't seem to be aware of himself, or know how beautiful he is. Or how charming.

"I'm glad," she told him, "That you like Hank."

"I sure do."

"He's rather protective of me, you know. In his subtle way, he acts out the role of Father Hen, if there is such a character. Well, at least he does with some people."

"That makes sense. If you were *my* daughter, I'd post guards, or keep you surrounded by snarling dogs.

Maybe even a moat, with gators and gars.''

"No, you wouldn't. The way you bring up a child is, quite simply, to instill standards that the child will employ in making his or her own selections. Daddy knows how fussy I am and how macho males turn me off. My guess is that he's slowly beginning to trust my judgment, and he's starting to relax. Quite a bit, actually.''

As they sat on a bench, Case noticed that he didn't sit too close to her. Some boys were always making moves, but not Kirby. If he does, she wondered, how will I ever fight off *myself?*''

"Were you a macho male," she said, "I doubt if you and I would be seeing much of each other. The marauding macho types bore me as much as the feminists do. I don't care to live in a macho-feminist world.''

"Where do you want to live, Case?''

"Well, given my druthers, I'd say in a civil society of ladies and gentlemen.''

Kirby grinned. "Grandfather would like you. Ever since I can remember, he was lecturing me about good manners.''

"Bully for ol' Gramps.''

"Wilbur Tree is a true gentleman, Casey. He's a lot like Wes Jordanson and your dad. I've never heard him raise his voice, not once, not in eighteen years. He doesn't swear or smoke. Every so often, I guess when he's feeling lonely, he'll help himself to a pull on the jug. But I've never seen him smashed.''

Casey sighed. "Good," she said. I wonder, she was thinking, why I left Dad in the bar. And I know why . . . to go for a walk with Kirby. So, like an idiot, I left him there. Again, she looked at her watch.

"You're doing it again," Kirby said.

"I'm sorry. Checking the time, with *anyone*, I suppose can be interpreted as the inexcusably rude gesture. Yet my reason for keeping tabs on the time has nothing to do with you."

"Honest? I know I'm not too smooth around girls."

"So you keep telling me."

"It's true. I wouldn't ever want to tell you a story. Never."

Once more, she felt his fingers close upon hers. Well, she thought to herself, here goes! "What *would* you like to tell me?"

Kirby swallowed. "A whole lot. First off, I want you to know that, since Wednesday, I've had the best three days of my whole life."

"Same here."

"Really?"

She nodded. "For several reasons. My father's making his comeback, Kirby. He just about cultivated a mental ulcer, prior to Big Dixie. Hank's got another problem, too, one which perhaps is too personal to discuss outside the family."

"Booze?" He said the word softly.

"Then you know."

"Everyone does, at least that's my guess. Wes Jordanson told me about it, way before I met you or your father, back when Hank Dawson was just one more name I didn't know.''

"Reputations," she said, "have a way of hanging around. Hank earned it. In his golden days, I guess he knocked back his share of sauce and paid for it, because it destroyed a marriage and a career.''

"He's okay now, Case. Hank's into root beer.''

"Is he?'' I wonder, she was thinking, what's in front of him back at the bar. Darn, I've got to go. Keeping tabs on Daddy's bar tab isn't the job I can delegate to Patrick J. Tipperary. That old gent, I'll wager, has a reputation, too. Not dunked in root beer.

"You're doing it again, Case.''

"I know, I looked at my watch. Come on, you.'' She stood up. "It's beddy-bye for tennis players, of all ages. I can't permit you to sit here all night, working up the courage to kiss me.''

Kirby looked surprised.

"We women know more than you men think we do. And we want more. If we have any brains, we shall even *demand* more, Mr. Tree. So, stand up, and give me one zinger of a goodnight kiss that'll knock my socks off.''

As he stood up quickly he stepped on her foot. I love it, she thought. He's so preciously un-Ivy. With her arms around his neck, she looked at his sweet face and said, "I absolutely adore you, you know.''

"You . . . you *do*?''

"Totally."

With her hands on his ears, she moved his head from side to side, watching him smile at her with his dark eyes. "Okay, big sport . . . knock off my socks."

His lips came to hers and she felt his gentleness, ever so lightly upon her mouth, her cheeks, on both her eyes. He didn't seem to know what to do with his arms and hands, so he did nothing. Yet his lips did it all to her. There was no crushing embrace, no bullying of her body against his, no muscle.

Lighter than a wren, his mouth fluttered against her face, as though he were too timid to do more. More than anything, Case wanted to be close to him, far closer than a mere discovery of one face to another. But only their faces loved. He did not charge at her, or grab; it was a loving lightness that she had never known.

"Wow," he said at last.

"Double wow. You do professional work, Tree, for an amateur."

"Was it really okay?"

"For starters." She answered him in an uneven voice, trying not to let her body tremble. Her knees had become liquid.

"Case, I want to say a lot of stuff to you, but I don't know how to say it."

"How about . . . thanks for a delightful stroll?"

Kirby laughed. "I think *my* socks got knocked off. Wow! I kissed you, Case Dawson. I really *did* it."

"Go home," she told him. "I've got to round up

Hank, rescue him from his bar buddies and let my dear old pa make a Z."

"Goodnight," he said. "See ya tomorrow."

He kissed her fingertip.

41

Patrick J. Tipperary burped.

"Saints preserve me," he said, rolling out of bed; his bare feet padded across the rug of the hotel room to where a worn brown suitcase yawned open on its stand.

Fumbling into the pouch, his fingers finally found what he was after . . . Alka-Seltzer. At the bathroom sink, Tip ripped apart the envelope, dropped the wafer, and watched the bubbles fizz.

He looked at himself in the steamy mirror as he drank, making a face. Draining the glass, he rinsed it and rested it with a clank on the edge of the sink.

"I don't believe it," he told the tired reflection of his face. "It's midnight, and I already got a hangover

. . . on *root beer*.''

How in hell, he wondered, could a guy like me sit in a country club bar as posh as Sweetpea, or whatever its name is, and sop up a gallon of root beer? You're cracking up, Tipperary.

Flicking off the bathroom light with a brush of his big hand, he stumbled back toward his bed.

Punching the pillows, he made an effort to create comfort for his pounding head. What a day, he thought. Worse, what an evening! If there's anything I can't stomach it's a roomful of nice people saying nice things. Maybe I'll telephone Rickles in California, tell him to get here and rescue me. I'm drowning in southern sweetness. Don't these dames know I'm a diabetic?''

I miss New York.

"City," he mumbled to the pillow corner, "I miss your goddam guts. You're my town, even though you are just a howling hooker, in a million doorways, waiting in garbage for a John.''

Yeah, he thought, I wanna go home.

Why in the deuce, he wondered, did I pack along my portable. I haven't typed a word. Not a blessed comma. I roll in a fresh page and stare at it, and there it lies, like a little white virgin, untainted and untouched by the hairy paws of Tipperary.

How come?

Good tennis today. I can't hang my hat on a peg of no action. We all saw plenty. Dawson surprised me.

Tip nodded. Indeed, he thought, Hank Dawson surprised me a lot.

I'll write it all up once I'm back where I belong,
Central Park West . . . back with the broads and the
booze and my big-bake city. Babe, I miss ya, toots.
You're a bawdy brassy band that never quits blowing
your horns. You sweet old trombone, ya.

Maybe I'll sleep. Good thing, he was thinking, that
I tossed off a couple of bourbons after Hank left with
his daughter. Boy, that kid's a looker. If I was
younger . . . hell, who am I kidding? *Whom*? I oughta
be ashamed of myself. Well, it won't hurt to look, or
dream. A long dream, all night, about Case Dawson is
just what I don't need. Even dreaming about legs like
that would wear me out.

There should be, Tip thought, a law against girls
with legs like hers who wear tennis dresses.

Maybe, he thought, I'll offer her a job. Get her to
come back with me, to New York, and put her to
work at the magazine. For a night with her, I'd make
her the editor-in-chief. Only I'll be the editor and
she'll be the chief, he thought, smiling into his
pillowcase.

She and young Seminole make a cute couple. Cuter
than two baby ducklings. I wonder what Henry's
thinking. Well, maybe he's too busy worrying about
Tilson tomorrow. Tillie'll finish Hank off, and easy.
Three sets? Huh, maybe four.

"Hank *won* today."

Shut up, Tip, he ordered himself, and get yourself some shut-eye. Saturday'll be a big day. Sunday even bigger.

My face hurts, he thought. Burns like hell. Darn that crazy broad who borrowed my pith helmet. Took it right off my stupid head; and like a dumb Irishman, I let her do it, merely because she was packing so much gorgeous gear . . . biggest boobs this side of the Rockies. Tomorrow, he thought, I gotta get that pith helmet back. All I did today was squint and hold my hand over my head until I thought my arm would drop off. Shoulder's killing me. Well, maybe the Alka-Seltzer will work on that, too.

Yeah, good tennis today.

And, he recalled, that Tree kid won. How, I'll never know. Yes, I know. He played super, that's how. Eighteen years old. Nobody's eighteen any longer. It's a cussed outrage for anybody to be eighteen and be as handsome as that kid is. When he hits the circuit, he's gonna have chicks waiting in line, just for the honor of rinsing the sweat from his shirt. And that won't be all they'll do. Lucky little bastard. Ha! I guess that's also true, what Wes tells me. The kid's illegitimate.

Nice boy, that Kirby Tree.

Tip rolled over. Gee, I gotta get some sleep, he thought, or I'll be falling on my face, come the morrow. But my mind keeps watching tennis, every stroke, point after point.

"I'm glad," he mumbled, "the kid won."

Nice boy. I didn't think people raised kids like Kirby Tree anymore. Tip remembered their conversation, after the match which Kirby had won. Yeah, he recalled, the lad's got manners like Sir Lancelot. He makes me feel like a bag of turnips. Polite kid. It's a joy to see Westal Jordanson looking so proud, hugging the boy, almost jumping the net himself to carry him off the court.

I can't blame Wes, he thought. It's his dream come true. At last old West has found himself a potential champ, a real seed, and he's going to milk it. Good for you, Wes. Do it, for yourself, and for Kirby Tree. Wes told me a dozen times already where he found this youngster, something like five or six years ago.

Tree can play, even if he's half white or half alligator, or whatever the hell he is.

A lot of bucks were lost today. Big odds, Tip was recalling, against both the Seminole and Hank Dawson. Yet they both survived. Yipes, I sure don't dare to tell Wes that it ain't Kirby I came down to this hot hellhole to catch. I came to see Hank.

"Ha!" Tip laughed aloud. "Wouldn't that be a panic, if Sunday's finals turned out *not* to be Carpenter against Tilson." Well, it probably will be. At least, if what I heard in the bar tonight holds any water, the smart money is guessing right. But today they guessed wrong, twice. Right on Tilson and Carp, wrong on Tree and Hank Dawson. Yeah, wouldn't that be a regular riot . . . if the big match-up on Sunday turned out to be Dawson going against Carpenter?

Even more absurd, Dawson facing the lanky lad in the beaded shirt, young Kirby.

Eyes closed, Tip imagined seeing just that, Kirby Tree on one side of the net and Hank on the other side. Interesting, he mused. Intriguing. Two distinct styles. It would be the aging pro versus the inexperienced cub, a cub's quickness against seasoned wisdom. Hank can't punch as hard, but he's the street fighter, which he has already proven against Heck Alvarez.

"Pity," said Tip.

Yes, it was a shame that the merciless clock of time ticks away the years, because, he thought, wouldn't it be a ball if you could freeze time, or reverse it, so we could see a young Hank Dawson go against Tree. I remember, he told himself, how Hank played when he was nineteen.

Tip smiled, as his mind envisioned a youthful Hank Dawson . . . sleek, gifted beyond measure, and golden . . . belting shots at Wes Jordandon's young star.

"Holy crowbar!"

Throwing back the sheet, even ripping one leg of his lavender pajamas, Tip trotted to find his notebook. He flipped to the back cover, stirred in one of the pockets, until he found the old bundle of photographs. One by one, he tossed them on the floor, until he held only one. It was yellow, bent, fading . . . a full shot of Hank, at age nineteen, serving a white tennis ball.

The photo shook in Tip's hand. Locating his glasses, he looked at it again, studied it, not quite able to believe what he saw in the harsh light of a hotel-room lamp.

He saw Kirby Tree.

Rolling a fresh page into his portable, Tip lit a cigar and stared. How, he asked, do I scoop a story like this and not go to jail? Worse, and not kick a few nice people in the guts. Shaking his head, he pulled the blank paper out of the typewriter, crumpled it, and missed the wastebasket. Then he said a dirty word.

"Damn root beer," he burped.

42

"Hoody?"

Hearing her nickname, Mrs. Hood turned to see Wes Jordanson. He was waving to her, beckoning, so she slowly waddled to meet him. It was always good, she thought, to see Wes. She smoothed her gray hair with a hurried sweep of her hand.

"Nice to see ya, Westal."

"Where's Jason? Didn't he come to see the day's action?"

"No, he's to home. Feeling a mite poorly. I offered to abide him, but no, Jay insisted that I march down and root for Kirby. My, but he played good, didn't he?"

Wes grinned. "Hoody, my love, he sure did."

"You done lots for that boy, Wes. Both me and Jason admire ya for it. We certain do."

"Here, sit down. I'll fetch us both a cool drink. What may I get for you?"

"Oh, no thanks, Westal. I best get back uproad and check up on my man."

"I'm glad you saw Kirby win."

"My stars!" Hoody shook her head. "Never in the world did I foresee it. The young lady who sat beside me knew lots about tennis and kept me up to date after every homer, or whatever they are. It was the Dawson girl."

"Case."

Hoody nodded. "Yes, that's her name. And if she isn't the sweetest thing. Treated me like I was a real somebody."

Wes touched her hand. "You *are* somebody, Hoody. You and your husband ought to hear Kirby brag about the two of you. In his eyes, you and Jason just about created the world."

She smiled, feeling her cheeks flush. Things like that were certain good to hear, she thought, near welcome as watching Kirby grow up to be such a credit to Wilbur and Little Man. And to be such a good tennis winner.

"Where'd Kirby go?" she asked Wes. "I just want to run up and hug that child."

Wes looked around. "I imagine he hit the shower.

What you just saw, dear lady, was one thunder of a match."

"Mercy me, *yes*. That big black fellow sure does hit the ball hard, don't he?"

Westal Jordanson nodded his white cowboy hat. "Indeed he does, sweetheart. Carp's a superb player. He just had an off day. Carpenter was off and Kirby was on."

Hoody stepped a foot closer to Wes. "Ya know, I was watching the way our young Miss Dawson was looking at Kirby. I got me a hunch she just might be a trickle sweet on him. Think so?"

As she finished saying it, she saw Wes's smile disappear. Goodness, she thought, I hope I didn't up and say wrong about anybody. Looking at Wes's sober face, she wondered what so suddenly seemed to upset him. He looked like he'd come up with a gut ache. His hand touched his stomach.

"What's wrong, Wes?"

"Nothing, Hoody. Nothing at all."

"You don't look too fettle to me. Maybe you come down with a touch of the same malady that's ailing Jay."

Wes seemed to force himself to smile. "Oh, it's all this fancy country club food. Upsets my digestion."

Hoody touched his arm. "Maybe you best bring Kirby along to our place, so's I can whip us all up some supper on simple. Just turnips and possum." Hoody smiled at him, whispering. "If it's your bowels, Westal, a belly of possum'll set ya free."

"Hoody, you'll have to excuse me. And do give me a raincheck on supper. Good of you to come, and I hope you can drag Jason here tomorrow, because Kirby's in the finals."

"Yes, so Miss Dawson said. Who's he to play?"

"Her father. Hank beat Tilson this morning. So tomorrow, Kirby will be playing Mr. Dawson."

"I seen *him*, too. My, but he's a good-looker of a gentleman. Ain't met him yet, on account of if I do, he'd just up and steal away my heart. See ya later, Wes. And thanks again kindly for the good seat."

"You're welcome, Hoody. Regards to Jason."

"Sure enough."

Something's bothersome in Westal, Hoody was thinking as she walked slowly through the milling Saturday afternoon crowd. My, she thought, I can't wait to get to home and share news with Jason. He'll be so happy that Kirby won, three times now, that I don't guess he could knuckle to no misery.

"Mrs. Hood?"

Miss Dawson was smiling and coming her way, so Hoody waited. What a beauty of a gal, she thought, and such refinement. Real breeding, and on top of it all, Hoody was thinking, she ain't even a minute worth of stuck up.

"Come on," Miss Dawson said, taking her by the hand, "because there's someone I want you to meet."

"Well," said Hoody, "okay, but only for a breath, because I best get myself uproad and home. Miss

Dawson, who ya got for me to shake hands with?''

"My father.''

"Mercy.''

They walked along one of the long flowerbeds and toward the clubhouse. I like this young lady, Hoody was thinking, and I sure am honored to meet her pa.

Seeing them, Mr. Dawson came to meet them both. This was the first time, Hoody thought, that she had seen Mr. Dawson close by, and he grew handsomer with every approaching inch. Besides, he had a good face. Kindly, like Jason's, and like Westal's and Wilbur's.

"Mrs. Hood,'' the girl said, "Please allow me to present my father, Henry Dawson.''

"Pleased,'' said Hoody, wondering if her dress looked smoothed out to near Sunday morning condition. It was the second time in years that she'd worn her church dress on a Saturday. The first time had been to watch Kirby play the Gossage boy.

Mr. Dawson bowed slightly and took both her hands. "Mrs. Hood, I feel as if you and my daughter and I are already old friends, because Kirby Tree speaks so often about you and Mr. Hood.''

"Well, Jason and me . . . I guess you might say we're near to being Kirby's second home. I born him, ya know.''

"Really?''

As though she were taking an oath, Hoody raised her hand. "Hope to tell ya. I born all three of them young, right back yonder in the swamp.''

Mr. Dawson seemed a bit confused, from what Hoody could see on his face.

"You mean," he asked her, "that Kirby has brothers or sisters, or one of each?"

"Nope," she told him. "Kirby's an only. What I meant was, I helped born his uncle, Little Man. And before that, thirty-six years ago it was, if'n my old memory serves righteous, I helped born his ma."

Miss Dawson said, "Then you knew Kirby's mother."

"Hope to swear I did."

The girl smiled. Yes, Hoody was thinking, this young lady cottons to Kirby, and I couldn't ask for a nicer thing, from all I see of her. Oh, she thought to herself, I just can't wait to scamper home and tell it all to Jay.

"Indeed so," Hoody went on to say. "Wilbur . . . that's Kirby's grandpa . . . lost his wife when his two was real young. Ya know, me'n Jason, my husband, we couldn't never ask for no better neighbors than the Trees."

The man smiled. My, Hoody thought, he sure is a charmer. Reminds me of somebody, but I can't recall just who. It'll come to me, I suppose. Funny, but Mr. Dawson don't favor his daughter much. But they're both good lookers.

"Kirby certainly respects you, Mrs. Hood," Miss Dawson said. "He told Daddy and me how you sewed the beads on his shirt. Your *church* beads."

"Well, he sports finery a mite more fitting than I

do." Hoody looked down at her dress. "He's a precious boy, Miss Dawson. Jason and me didn't have no kids of our own, so I guess we just sort of adopted all the Tree children."

"And I bet," Miss Dawson said to her, "they all adopted you and Mr. Hood, too."

Hoody nodded her church hat. "They sure did. Hardly a day would go by that one of them Trees didn't stop and look in on us. Play jokes on us and all."

The girl touched her hand. "I guess there's so much about Kirby that I'm eager to know about."

Hoody smiled. "Dear, I can see that. An old swamp woman like me knows more that she tells. But I just wanted you and Mr. Dawson to learn what a nice boy Kirby is, that's all. He's from good folks. I want y'all to know that."

"We do," Mr. Dawson said. "He has good manners and a lot more . . . as everyone here today would agree."

"Mrs. Hood, would you please excuse me? I'm meeting Kirby for a Coke in about a minute or so. Will we see you tomorrow?"

Hoody nodded. "Right as rain you will. Leastwise, I'm fixin' to come and . . . bring Jason, too . . . if'n I have to drag him bed and all."

She watched Miss Dawson dash away, as Mr. Dawson turned back to her. "My daughter and Kirby have become good friends in only a few days. And I confess to liking Kirby as much as Case does."

"He's from good stock, my Kirby. I didn't know his pa, God forgive him, but his mother was one of the sweetest girls to ever walk this earth."

"You knew her well, I suppose," Mr. Dawson said.

"Of course I knew her. And loved her. You couldn't find more of a blessing of a girl, rest her soul, than Flower Tree."

Hoody saw Mr. Dawson's eyes widen. There was a sudden flash of alarm that clouded his face, a look that Hoody couldn't understand. He bit his lip.

"No," she heard him say.

43

"One more."

As he emptied his glass, tapping its bottom on the bar for a refill, he saw the bartender at the Sweetgum Country Club take a cautious breath.

"Mr. Dawson, sir, don't you think you've had enough? After all, tomorrow's your big day, sir."

If there's one thing, Hank thought, that ticks me off, it's when some watchdog bartender tells me that I've had enough. They're paid to pour liquor, not advice.

"If I get drunk, it's *my* business, ol' buddy."

"With all due apologies, Mr. Dawson, the club has a policy. It's sort of my responsibility to . . ."

"Kiddo, it's your responsibility to dump sauce into an empty glass . . . get what I mean . . . and see to it that everybody has a wild Saturday night. Okay?"

The young bartender said nothing. Taking the empty glass, he turned it upside down on the scrubber, pumped it, then rinsed it to a sparkle.

"Whatever you say, sir."

Hank grunted. "Hey, that's more like it, sport. Live a little. That's what I did when I was younger than you are. I *lived*, kid. I got loaded and . . . and . . ."

He couldn't finish the sentence. Yeah, Hank was thinking, I got myself tanked and grabbed girls. Isn't that what's expected of young blond tennis stars? The public eats it up. Knock down a drink and then knock up a girl.

I never knew, he thought.

Yes, that was the name of the beautiful girl. It all came back to him now . . . Flower Tree. No, it hadn't been just sex. If two people can meet and fall instantly in love at a college party, we did it. No brains involved. Just bodies and souls. What a poem of a girl, all beauty, outside and inside. She wanted me as much as I wanted her. And I promised to write, but I was on tour, a tennis vacation from Yale. But, I swear, had I known about the baby, I would have married her . . . instead of Pam Rilling.

"Here you are, Mr. Dawson."

As the barman set a fresh scotch in front of him, he raised it to his lips and gulped in that blistering taste.

306   The Seminole Seed

Heat flooded his stomach, burning all the way down from tongue to gut. God, he thought, I love it. I'd rather drink than make love, or eat, or play tennis. Or live.

Tennis?

"Ha!" he said aloud. I'm through with that rotten game. It's over for you, Hank. You're washed up, so wash it down, boy, because it's quitting time. My big victorious day is now nothing more than bitterness and shame. I didn't deserve to beat Tilson and I don't deserve one damn thing.

Spinning slowly on the barstool, being careful not to tumble to the floor, Hank raised his glass to the lounge full of club members, players, and guests.

"Hey, you people. Let's have a toast, okay?"

He saw several faces smiling at him, so he made himself return a smile. As some of the scotch spilled from his glass, a lady at a table blotted her blouse with a napkin. "Some people," she said, "ought to call it a night."

"Everybody listen," Hank yelled to an unhearing and indifferent crowd. "Here's to tennis, you bums. Here's to that little yellow bitch of a ball that none of you country clubbers have ever hit correctly in your entire filthy-rich lives."

"Take it easy, Hank," he heard a voice telling him.

"Sure, I'll take it easy. Sorry, folks, if I offended anybody. I heartily do apologize. Madam, I didn't mean to slop scotch on your best Bergdorf-Sears."

He saw Tommy Tilson, the Aussie that he had
beaten today, come toward him. Tillie wasn't smiling. Hank grunted at him. "Poor loser." Reaching
out, he tried to yank Tilson's necktie.

"Henry, old cobber, how's about it if I take you
home?"

"No way."

Hank felt Tillie gently taking the glass from his
fingers. "You've had plenty, old bean. A snoot full.
You haven't forgotten about tomorrow, have you?"

"Tillie, I want to forget about everything, you
bloody Aussie. You hear? I want to forget who in hell
I am and all the rotten stinking things I've ever done.
Plus all the lives that I've managed to foul, including
my own."

"Come on, Hank. What say we take a walk and get
some fresh air, eh?"

Hank stumbled against a stool. "I better drive, Til.
I'm too drunk to walk."

"Damn you, Hank. We all thought you'd licked it.
And there's not a soul in this room that wants the
barley to lick you, you bloody fool."

"Yeah?"

He saw Tommy Tilson nod. "You whipped me today, you blessed bugger. Gave me a trim, Hank, you
did. And I don't feel an ounce of shame when I get a
trouncing from Hank Dawson."

"I beatcha, buddy." Throwing his arms around
Tillie's neck, he hugged him, trying not to fall over.

He kept his balance, but only with Tilson's arms around his shoulders.

"Let's go, Hank. It's time we got you a cold shower and a good hot cup of tea."

Hank shook his head as the two of them, guided by Tilson, weaved their way through the boisterous crowd. He looked at the face of the tennis player, his old friend, who was half-carrying him toward the door. Tilson was apologizing for him in a choked voice.

"Hey! Whatza matter ol' buddy. Defeat too bitter for you to swallow?"

Tilson stopped and looked at him. "You're right, Henry. Some defeats are more than a man can watch happen."

"Yeah?"

"You're forgetting, old bean, that this isn't the first time. I saw you do this to yourself years ago and a lot of us wept for you, you bloody ass."

"Forget it, Tillie. Let's you and me forget it all. Forget . . . forget . . ."

"You could have been the best of us, Hank. The king. And we all leaned on you. I wish to hell I'd punched your handsome head, every time I saw a glass of booze near it. I wish to hell I had. May the Almighty forgive me for not choking you with both fists."

Hank giggled. "You're okay, Tillie. Hey! Here's a piano. Let's have a song to celebrate. Here we go, folks."

He eased himself down on the padded bench, looked at the blurring black and white keys. "Where did they put middle C? Yeah, here it is." As the song came back to him, he started to play. It didn't sound good, but he didn't care, as long as the music could drown out her name.

"Its . . . a . . . long way . . . to Tipperary. It's a long way . . . to go . . ."

He was singing now, hearing other voices join in, and somehow his fingers, more or less, were locating the right keys. People crowded in around the piano, holding their drinks and raising their voices to the lyrics.

As he studied their faces, he found the one he was looking for . . . Tip's. He saw the big Irish face and the pearly blue eyes on a face that was red with sunburn. But no joy.

"Come on, Tip, you old dog. Sing your damn song. I'm playing it for *you*, aren't we, Tillie? So sing it, Tip. Sell it, baby!"

For some strange reason, everyone else seemed to be singing the song . . . except for Patrick J. Tipperary. The big man just stood, not leaning on the grand piano, but standing, staring at him. And then he looked down at the glass in his hand.

Tillie was singing in Hank's ear, yet it didn't sound like his heart was totally in it. "Just like the old days, Hank. If that's the way you want it, the old days are back. You're a kid again, Henry. A drunken kid, blessed with more damn talent than you deserve. And cursed, with the inability to give thanks for it."

Hank took a sip of somebody's drink and turned. "I want to die, Tillie. So maybe I'll just kill myself in booze."

Tommy Tilson shook his head. "Swell."

Looking at Tip, Hank said. "Hey! Another chorus, folks. One more time . . . for that august editor of *Tip Top Tennis* . . . who can write all about the rise and fall of one more irresponsible tennis bum . . . who doesn't know or care what he does to the people he loves."

"No," Tip said, "you really don't."

Again, he was playing the song, and the gang was singing, so he didn't care about a damn thing . . . except getting drunk . . . just fall-down, shirttail drunk, so that he'd pass out and not remember.

"And to think," Tip said, "that for you, Hank Dawson, I switched to root beer."

The song went on, finally stopping, with voices ringing out the very last of the lyric. *And my heart's . . . right there.*

Tip leaned forward. "By the way," he said, "I was just wondering. Are you giving any thought to how much you're going to hurt Casey?"

Hank stopped playing. People were urging him to play another song. "We wanna sing," a man was yelling. "Do you know *Who's Sorry Now?*"

He tried to play, but the keys seemed to be in the wrong places, as though they, too, were trying to escape. Nothing made sense, he thought. Except booze. Tillie was trying to keep him from falling off the piano bench, as Hank looked up at Tip's sober blue eyes. God, he thought, Tip Tipperary is one heck of a guy. What a face.

No one can cry like an Irishman.

44

Sunday morning, thought Little Man.

He lay on the peaty earth, on his belly, feeling the warm dampness rising up through his work shirt. Looking eastward, through the spines and oval tips of a swamp cactus, he saw the dawn. No sun, only a long yellow streak that serpentined along the jagged horizon.

Even though he had not slept all night, Little Man Tree did not feel tired, or even dull. He was wide awake, knowing that today would be his day. He had waited for Sunday and, at last, it was here.

Sunday, he said silently.

His hand felt the gun that was stuck into his belt,

unloaded. In his pocket were his last three cartridges. Charlie No Land had warned him about the dangers of purchasing ammunition for a handgun.

"When a Seminole walks into a store and asks for bullets," Charlie No Land had said, "he asks to kill himself. The store owner will excuse himself and call the troopers."

Little Man had been prudent. Yet he had, he knew, wasted too many cartridges, firing at the gasoline can, back beyond the swamp where no ear could hear his firing or the clank of the lead ripping into the can.

Rolling over on his back, he looked at the lightening sky. And a bird. It was a black water turkey, a snakebird, one that his father called an anhinga. As it circled over his head, flying to the edge of the swamp, he saw it light up the lifeless trunk of a dwarf cypress. The water turkey hen was wet, and so she waited to dry her wings in morning sun.

"Today is Sunday," Little Man said to her, "and it will be the Sunday that my life has waited for."

Little Man Tree remembered the Sunday morning, nineteen or twenty years ago, when Flower did not wash him up for church. Or brush his hair. There had been a quiet sadness in her eyes, a black sorrow, and she had told him that she would not go places anymore, but must stay close to the house.

"Why?" he had asked Flower.

"Because," she had tried to explain to him "I have been shamed, and I do not deserve our church."

Flower had hugged him tightly and then had explained to him about a baby that she knew was growing inside her body. He wanted to ask how the baby got there and how she knew. Yet he had remained silent, knowing how often he had been chastised for asking too many questions.

She had told him that she would soon be a mother and that both of them would love the baby, and bathe it, so its skin would shine. And brush the baby's hair.

"Will the baby be a Seminole?" he had asked his sister.

Flower did not answer his question, because her eyes were closed, and then she held him very close to her, almost rocking him in her arms.

That, thought Little Man Tree, was a long time ago. I wonder if people have forgotten that once there lived a girl who laughed and sang, whose name was Flower Tree. Sometimes, he was thinking, I suspect that even Wilbur Tree forgets. When my father spaded holes in the sand with a shovel, and then buried Mother and Flower, I wonder if he also buried his remembering.

Little Man sighed.

On this day, on this very Sunday, I will get even for my sister's sorrow and then I will run away, deep into the cypress swamp, where I will live alone and never again see my father, or Kirby.

Reaching into the pocket of his jeans, Little Man pulled out the wrinkled Country Club paper, unfolded it, and squinted to see the man's face. The name beneath the picture said Hank Dawson.

"Today," he told the face, "you will die."

I am a stupid man, he thought, and people point at me and laugh because I look as plain as I am. But I will show them that a Seminole knows at least one thing. Little Man Tree knows how to pull a trigger and keep a snake promise.

Opopkee would understand.

Even before my father and his father were born, the grandfather of Wilbur Tree fought the white man. And won. The white soldiers were driven from the swamp. Yet not all of them. Some of the soldiers, the father of Joe Orange told me, still lie rotting in the swamp, to make the golden plumes of sawgrass grow tall.

The barrels of their cannon became rust, and they, too, died as the soldiers had died, in black water. The water turkeys came to peck at the white faces with beaks as sharp as a Seminole lance.

I will be proud, thought Little Man.

It is important, my father always told us, to carry our backs straighter than a Seminole arrow. But then he said that the swamp wars were over, so we must quiet our lives with peace and forget the fighting. No! Little Man Tree does not forget. He remembers. It was the white tennis man who forgot the Seminole girl.

Today, before he dies, Hank Dawson will remember. Before he dies, I shall tell him that I am Little Man Tree, the brother of Flower Tree, the woman that he shamed. His blue eyes will see my gun and his white ears will hear my first shot, into his white belly. Then, a second bullet will stab his heart, and my last I will fire into the white mouth that spoke of love to my sister . . . on the night that he felt no love.

"I still love you, Flower."

And, he thought, I cared for Kirby because he was *yours*. Your child, the baby boy who grew to become my child. My baby boy.

Little Man smiled. Oh, he thought, how I wish Flower could now see Kirby, how fair he is. How fresh, with a face as pure as a wet white lily that floats among green pads. Flower, your son is quicker than a swamp frog, and brighter, too. He is as wise as his fat old uncle is dumb.

Yanking the gun from his belt, Little Man weighed it in his hand. With his fingertips, he carefully wiped grains of black sand from its barrel and trigger ring.

"You must kill today," he said to the gun. "And then I will throw you into the black water of God's Florida, where you will lie silently with the old cannons of white soldiers and keep your Seminole secret."

Little Man Tree looked at his right hand. The fang marks were gone. Ten years ago, he remembered, was the Night of the Snake. I took Kirby, he recalled, into our swamp and lit a fire to heat my knife. Then I bloodied my face, and his, to make him my promise. My oath. No one saw us that night. No eyes, except the dead eyes of Opopkee's ghost. Perhaps his gray mouth smiled a cold smile, because he saw me in his sacred ceremonial dress. It is the dress, Little Man thought, that I will again wear, this day, when I go to the Country Club place, to keep my snake promise.

"I will be silent," Little Man said to the pistol, "for I have learned that I must not be seen, as I was seen by the white eyes of Mr. Jordanson, the other evening. I had not gone there to kill, only to learn, because it was my first trip to the Country Club place. Today will be my last. But I now know, he thought, where the buildings are, and where their paths go, in order to escape quickly as soon as the promise has been paid."

Now, he thought, I will pray.

Pulling off his clothes until he was naked, Little Man waded into the water, washing himself. I must be clean, he thought. Pure, to show the spirit of Opopkee that Little Man Tree prepares both his soul and his body for war. He scrubbed his brown skin with his fingernails until his flesh was burning. Yet he did not stop. I want to feel the pain on my body, as Flower knew the hurting when she bore the white man's child.

On the way to the Country Club place, he thought, I will hide a straw basket of oranges near the shack of Mr. and Mrs. Hood, so they will discover them to eat. I love them, too. Never have I told them so, yet they both know, even though they are white people. Mr. and Mrs. Hood loved Flower, as they also love Kirby, so I will hold them in my heart. And bring oranges.

After allowing the morning breeze to dry his body, Little Man put on the old dress. The early sun danced the colors, all colors, red, blue, green, yellow, white, and purple. Some orange, too. Opopkee had worn the dress, to pray in, and so Little Man Tree lifted his arms to the tallest cypress.

"Help me," he whispered with closed eyes. "Help me to avenge my sister. And to run away forever. Watch over my father and my nephew. Keep them warm. And let Kirby find the paper that I wrote on, the one that I hid in the cover of his tennis toy."

Little Man remembered unzipping the cover, carefully, placing the note inside, near the strings, and then zipping it closed:

GOODBI KIRBI
TODAY IS SUNDAY SO
I WIL KIL THE MAN
DAWZON
YOO WIL NOT SEE ME
AGEN FOR A LONG
TIM SO PLEES DONT
FORGET YOOR FAT OLD UNKEL
                LM

45

"Please go away."

"No," said Case, "I won't go away."

Hank felt her hands on his ankle, not too gently, yanking, twisting his body until he hit the floor beside his bed. Pain hammered his head, and he wanted to throw up, or die.

"It's ten o'clock. You're playing at three, and you are going to parade onto that court, if I have to drag you and rope the racquet into your hand."

He tried to lift his exploding head off the carpet. "I'm sorry, Casey."

"You certainly are," she said, lifting him up onto his hands and knees. "You're one sorry mess of a man. However, one evening of relapse does not necessarily convince me that your life is over, at age thirty-eight. Stand up, sir.''

''I can't.''

''Rot. You can and you will. Even if I have to kick your behind into the shower and out of it.''

Her voice, he was thinking, was merely resolute, not strident, the way Pam's always sounded on mornings after. Pam was a screamer. Her molten words had stabbed into his ears like icepicks.

Hank opened his eyes. ''No pajamas?'' He was aware that he still wore last evening's clothes.

She lifted him up until they both sat on the edge of his rumpled bed. ''We didn't really think of your sartorial appearance at two o'clock in the morning, at which time Tip and Tillie and I finally got you this far.''

''Thanks.''

''Don't give me words. Talk is too tawdry to mean anything at the moment. Okay, so you managed to make yourself into a disgusting mess. But there's no law that says you have to *stay* one.''

With her help, he stood up very slowly; wondering how he had forgotten, for years, how hard a hangover hits a head.

''I feel dirty, Case. It's why I got tanked. Something . . . a long time ago . . . things happened that I didn't learn about, until yesterday.'' It hurt to talk, but Hank knew he'd have to tell her. *Now*, before her feelings for Kirby Tree deepened into a disaster.

''I know.''

"You really *know*?" he asked. He had to sit down again. His world and his head spun too much to stand.

"No, I don't understand any of it. After we tumbled you down, Tillie left, threatening to get drunker than he'd ever gotten. Yet I think he just went back to the club and sacked out. He looked dreadful, probably because of you."

"Then what?"

"Tip and I sat in the kitchen and drank the coffee that you wouldn't drink. He said that perhaps you'd want to explain a few matters to me, if you ever got sober, things that it would take plenty of gumption to say."

"Is that what Tip said? How in the deuce does *he* know?"

"Whatever it is, he *knows*, Dad. And, from what he told me, between sips of coffee, he's guessing that Westal Jordanson knows, too. I concluded that Tip talked to Wes about it, yet I can't say for sure. I'm thoroughly confused."

"So am I, Kitten."

"Apparently, I'm the only living soul in Florida who doesn't have an inkling as to what's going on, or what your destructive secret is, and why you so stupidly got smashed into oblivion."

Hank Dawson's hands gripped the edge of the bed. "I don't know how to tell you, Case. It's a horrid truth for a man to suddenly learn about himself . . . and admit to."

He felt her arms around him, holding him close to her, as her hands gently touched his face and hair. God, he thought, I've got the two most wonderful children in the world, and I'm absolutely unworthy of either one.

"Case . . . Tip was wrong. I don't have the guts to tell you. But it's why I got so drunk."

"Tell me. I'm a lot tougher than you think, Hank. Inside, your little girl is cast iron, and by damn, you're going to toughen up, old Tiger, and share the family load with me."

He forced himself to look at her. "It's about Kirby and me. Honest. That's what it truthfully is."

Hank saw her face become ashen and her head slowly move from side to side, denying what she was hearing him tell her. Her eyes closed, just prior to her hands rising to cover her face.

"God," she whispered, "you had a sexual relationship? No. Please don't say it, Hank. Please don't."

"*No!*" He almost hollered the word. "No, Casey, not at all. Good grief, I didn't mean *anything* like that. I guess I can't seem to say what I'm trying to tell you."

Taking her in his arms, he held her, softly, feeling her body tremble . . . knowing now just how unimportant he was and how priceless Case and Kirby both were. But, he thought, I have to tell her. So here goes. They both have to know, I suppose; even if it means that I lose the two of them forever.

"It happened a long time ago, Case. I was just a kid your age at the time. And I never knew the consequences. Never even imagined."

"Tell me, please. Right now. Whatever it is, I'll understand, because you're my father and nothing will ever erase that. Or destroy it."

"This may."

Her fist pounded his shoulder, but he was numb from any physical pain, too hurt inside to be aware of his own body or his own feelings. Other feelings were to be damaged and torn, the feelings of two kids that mattered. I don't matter anymore.

"Say it, Hank. Tell me, or I'll hate your guts. What is it about you and Kirby?"

His voice was little more than a whisper. "There was a party, at Rollins College, and I met a girl, and got drunk and played the piano, and we fell in love. At least I did. We both did, Case. And she died because of me."

"Who was she?"

"Her name was . . . Flower Tree."

"God."

"Kirby is my son."

Her eyes closed. "I don't believe you."

"It's true. Look at me, Case. Can't you see it all?"

"No, it's not true."

"Yes, my darling, it's all true. Every blessed word of it is the God's honest truth. Flower Tree and I made love, and we were *in* love, both of us. And I left, to go back up north to Yale. He was born about eight months later."

"No, it's all impossible."

"Wrong. All I can see is Kirby's face. His hair, his young body, even the way he plays that panther style of tennis which I admire. To watch him, Casey, is like my being allowed to view my own boyhood."

She sighed, shaking. "Kirby is my . . . brother?"

"Half brother."

"Does he know?"

Hank shook his head slowly. "No, I don't imagine he has any idea that he's my child. My son. Case, I really couldn't understand why I liked him so suddenly. It was somehow instantaneous. I actually felt an urge to hug that kid, thinking that the reason was because he was so sweet, so endearing . . . and because the two of you became so instantly . . ."

"Compatible."

Her single word sounded so brittle. "That's the rest of the tragedy, Case. Please try to treat Kirby as a brother. Anything more would be . . ."

"I know. We'd breed idiots."

"Yes." Looking at her, all Hank Dawson could see was the agony that he had thrown into her face. A clumsy clown's pie.

"When I said that, I sounded so insensitive. Daddy, right now, you and I can't think of ourselves and our own emotions. This isn't too easy to accept, you know. But I'm going to have to stand up to it. Kirby and I almost . . ."

"Made love?" he asked her.

"Yes. You have no right to know such personal things, nor do I have the right to confess them. It's just fortunate that the two of us are rather sensible, that's all.''

To him, her voice sounded twisted and empty. Hank hugged her. ''I guess I wasn't fatherly enough to ask about you and Kirby, as I was counting on your judgment, and his. But when I was drinking last night, I knew you were out somewhere with my son, and that neither of you knew . . .''

''Well,'' she said, touching his face, ''I guess I know now. Even though I'm shattered by it, I'll recover. The world hasn't ended, Hank.'' She paused. ''But I almost pray it will.''

Casey, he was thinking, you are one devil of a strong young woman. And you were correct about your cast iron. But it's entwined with petals. Staring at her, he saw her early happiness with Kirby turning from green to brown. Her face was wilting under the weight of all he had confessed to her. Case was biting her lip, looking at him; actually looking through him as if he were nothing at all. But then she spoke to her hands.

''You'll have to tell Kirby.''

46

Tip opened his eyes.

Squinting, he saw that his bedside alarm told him that it was almost eleven o'clock. Even though both drapes were pulled, Florida's persistent sunlight filtered through, painting a determined yellow slash on the wall and floor.

Reaching for the stub of a cigar, Tip jammed it into his mouth, tasted it, and then returned it to its overflowing ashtray. "Why," he muttered, "do hotels always have big windows and small ashtrays?"

Slowly, he sat up. He spat a shred of the remaining taste of the cigar from his tongue.

Moving a heavy body inside his polka-dotted Kelly

green pajamas, Tip staggered toward the bathroom, reached it, and kicked up the toilet seat with a bare foot. As he stood there, performing the day's first chore, he relieved himself of close to half a gallon of last evening's root beer and coffee.

Tip flushed the silver handle and positioned himself at the tiny sink. One numbing glance into the bathroom mirror produced an only word.

"Yuk," he said.

Sunday morning, he was thinking. And what a Sunday this would be for a whole crew of people. Trouble is, they're all nice folks, every dang one of them. It sure is a rotten feeling to be *trusted*, and that's how Wes laid it all out in front of me. Off the record. Odd, he thought, how Wes Jordanson and I tripped over the same root.

Tip snorted. "And it wasn't root beer."

He almost smiled, reaching for his razor, thinking about a book he'd read called *Roots*. The word means a lot more to me now, he mused. Even more ironic, the roots of Kirby Tree. "Ha!" he blurted out a mirthless laugh. "I oughta write an article called *Tree Roots* for the magazine."

It's not funny, Tipperary, he warned the stubbled face in the mirror. Not at all. In fact, it's so damn sad it hurts. Sad, yet beautiful, like an Irish ballad. On many a Sunday morning, he thought, smearing Rise on his face, I hated waking up and knowing I had to tote Patrick J. Tipperary's hangover.

"Today," he told his razor, "sure as the devil, I would hate to be Hank Dawson. Not with his head and his conscience."

As the blade halfway harvested the wart under his chin, Tip saw the sudden stream of blood create a thin riverlet down his neck. He grabbed a towel, reddened it, and said a dirty word to the cut.

Blood, he thought. Guess I'm lucky I won't be bleeding the way Henry Dawson will bleed today. My heart bleeds for ya, Hank. And I bet your stupid eyes are bloodshot this morning, ya stupid oaf, ya.

Tip shook his head. "Here I am," he said to his bleeding neck, "leaning on some poor guy . . . one drunk reviewing another. It's irony. Or unpoetic justice."

I wish, Tip was thinking, that I hadn't found out. Ah, the bliss of ignorance. For a journalist, Tipperary, you sure can coin a crumby phrase. Yeah, you certainly can. And to think I was bitching that there was nothing to write about at sweet ol' Sweet Tooth, or whatever they call their poshy palace. Wow, there's a lot to write about. But the catch is, I can't write it up. None of it.

He rinsed a gob of lather and whiskers under the chromium hot water tap. Down the drain, he thought. Sort of akin to the greatest scoop of my life for *Tip Top Tennis* and it's even too personal for my crappy column. If I pulled out the portable to write about Hank Dawson's bastard kid, I'd feel like a Peeping Tom.

"It sure would sell magazines."

For that, Tip was thinking, I'd double the damn press run. Flash a photo on the front page of Kirby and Hank, color; spread shots in the body copy of Case and her leggy limbs. Jesus, am I really that incestuous?

"Those two kids are courting it up," he said to his undershorts, "so Hank had best get his ass in gear and tell 'em both that he's Kirby's sire."

That, thought Tip, as he snapped the elastic on his size 48 baby-blue undershorts, would hardly be a leadpipe cinch. Not for any gent with feelings. How in hell do you tell a nice youngster a thing like that?

"By the way, kid," Hank would have to casually blurt out, "I'm your old man. I sort of made it with your ma and knocked her up, so I thought you'd get a few jollies to learn about it. Prior, that is, to our facing each other in today's final."

Tip grunted.

That would be a ringer of a speech. Then, to top it all of, he's got to tell Kirby, on the biggest day of his young life, that the young lady with whom he is so smitten, is really his half sister. Neat. Real cute act, Hank. So lot's of luck, baby. Now I think I can understand why you swilled down so much sauce and fell off the wagon. Trouble is, Henry, the root beer wagon was rumbling over a bridge, and you fell off into Grand Canyon.

Back in the bathroom, Tip stirred through his enormous toilet kit until he found the can, then sprayed each armpit with Right Guard. With a click, he replaced the plastic cap, tossing the can back into its toothpaste-stained nest.

Tip spat into the sink.

Yeah, he thought, there's a rotten taste in my mouth, and it has the foul flavor of somebody's pain. Today'll be heat, hurting, and a whack of heartache . . . for Hank, his daughter, and his son.

Funny, he thought, how Westal and I felt each other out, testing one another to learn which one of us knew exactly what. He doesn't know what to do and neither do I. So the two of us look each other in the eye, pretending we don't know, and the whole sorry little saga is naught but pure conjecture. What beats me is . . . how did Hank find out? Or *did* he? Maybe he just got soused because that's usually what drunks do.

Tip shook his head.

"No," he said. "Hank Dawson *knows*." Nothing, except for a jolt like that, would have spurred him to throw away a comeback final, and break his daughter's heart . . . complicated by the fact that he's observed her feelings for the boy. Hank must have noticed how Kirby and Case are holding hands. Maybe more than that. Kids today! Well, maybe they're not so bad. Hank's two are terrific.

Another irony, Tip was thinking as he buckled his belt, is that Henry Dawson didn't raise either one of his kids. Yet there's a lot of Hank in both children. You're lucky, Hank. I'd settle for either your son or your daughter, and *you*, ya lousy lunatic, ya got yourself *two*.

From the dresser, Patrick J. Tipperary stuffed his wallet, some loose change, and his hotel key into his pockets, then ran a brush over each ear. The mirror again reminded him how little hair there was to groom. His face was still red. He must, he was thinking, relocate his pith helmet. A face as pink as his couldn't take three more hours under a Florida sun. But, so what's a sunburn?

Tip felt empty, without hunger.

Nothing, about himself, seemed to matter. A bit of sunburn's minor pain was insignificant compared to the crunch that somebody was going to get today . . . a real kick in the crotch, from cowboy boots.

Today, Tip thought, could be a horror.

47

"Wow," said Kirby, "what a day."

Wes Jordanson looked at the grin on the face of his young star, as the two of them shared a small table at the west end of the Sweetgum Country Club's luncheon veranda. The boy was already in his white beaded tennis clothes.

"Eat up," he told Kirby.

"I can't, Wes. I'm just too excited."

Wes nodded his white hair. "I know." A fork was in his hand, but he didn't feel at all like eating the sliced steak that he and Kirby had both ordered. "Nerves. I've got the same butterflies that you have. But I want you to eat *now*, because it's noon, so your stomach will be nearly vacant by three o'clock. I want you to feel hungry out there.''

Again he saw Kirby grin. Only three more hours, Wes was thinking, providing Hank Dawson doesn't become a no-show. What a disappointment that would be, he thought, as it would dump a pail of cold water on Big Dixie. The crowd would grumble. Kirby would, ergo, win by default; yet it would't be much of a victory. Soon the spectators would be coming, but surely *not* to witness a pathetic default. So, all I can hope for, is that Hank Dawson proves to be every bit as much of the man that I have always judged him to be.

''I wonder where Case and Hank are,'' Kirby said, twisting around in his green and white chair. Inside, knowing what he knew, Wes winced.

''They'll be along. I don't want your mind on that girlfriend of yours. All you're to concentrate on is the match.''

''Okay, Wes. Anything you say.'' Kirby forked a chunk of rare beef into his mouth, chewing mechanically, as though not able to taste its succulence. Finally, he swallowed. ''Gee, it sure was nice of you to invite me for lunch, Wes. This is my first meal at Sweetgum. Thanks a whole lot.''

''Don't mention it. Enjoying a quiet lunch with the first champion of the first Big Dixie is my pleasure.''

''Wow,'' said Kirby, ''who would ever have guessed that Big Dixie was going to boil down to Hank Dawson and me?''

''Life is full of surprises, son.'' And so, Wes was

thinking, I pray you'll be able to weather the ones that are bound to be coming your way. Maybe, he pondered, I ought to tell Kirby now. Get it over with. Rejecting the idea, he figured it wasn't his job. It was Hank's.

"I still can't believe it, Wes. I'm so happy I could bust. I feel like a pink balloon, so full of gas that I could float a mile up."

"Settle down." Westal Jordanson pointed at Kirby with his knife. "I just want you to relax, that's all. You've got to stay loose, lad. Key up now and you'll be burned out by three o'clock. Incidentally, Billy Gossage is going to warm you up, while Tip and I rehearse our routine. Just to polish it up. So, try and enjoy this wonderful day."

"Okay, I'll try."

When I look at his face, Wes was thinking as he chewed, all I see now is Hank Dawson. Damn all drunks. Eventually the drunkard always manages to wound somebody, and so often the victim is someone who loves him. A mother, a wife or girlfriend, maybe a daughter. Why in hell does life have to be such a snarl?

Wes took a sip of tea. "By the way, did you notice the parcel I so carefully placed under my chair?"

Kirby looked down at it. "Sure. What's in it?"

"Well, it's a present for you. Fetch it up here and we'll open it up and see if it fits."

Kirby tore open the brown paper and removed his

gift, along with it's bright red and white beaded oval case.

"A brand new racquet! Gee thanks, Wes. I really appreciate it." Kirby unzipped the cover and slowly pulled out the expensive racquet, as he held its handle.

"It's a USA Pro-Am. They're calling it the most perfectly balanced bat that U.S. Pro ever designed. And it's the first tennis bat I've *bought* in years, but I want you to have it, and use it today."

It seemed to Westal Jordanson as if Kirby was holding his breath. Finally he let out the held air. "Wes, I don't even know what to say. It's so beautiful."

"How about thanks? You usually thank me twenty times an hour, even though I ordered you to quit the habit. However, for a bat like that, I'll accept gratitude."

Kirby grinned. "Coach, you got it." The boy's fingers dug into his shoulder to shake him. The kid had a grip, Wes mused. Well, he'll need every ounce.

"I suppose you brought your other racquets."

Kirby nodded. "Two others. The one I've been using, plus the first one I ever had, the racquet Grandfather carved."

Closing his eyes for a second, Wes remembered the boy of twelve and the old balls that thudded into two wagon rims on the side of a mule barn.

"What are you doing, Wes? Sleeping?"

Startled, he opened his eyes. "No, just recollecting.

Remembering all the years you and I worked, son, for a day just like today. And it's finally come."

The boy pinged the new bat against the heel of his hand. It rang with a musical sound, a strong echo that sustained its tone and then melted.

"Use it," Wes told him. "I think it's the right bat for you, against Dawson. If he shows."

Kirby stared at him. "Why did you say that? Of course Hank'll be here."

"He got drunk last night, son. Tip Tipperary and Tillie had to help his daughter cart him home."

"No, I don't believe it. Hank wouldn't . . ."

"I'm afraid he did. But forget it. Hank Dawson's been into booze before, and he plays better hung over than a lot do healthy. I know. I've been around tennis courts for a passel of years."

Kirby was silent, then spoke. "You know, Wes, I really love those two people . . . Hank and Case. I want today to be so perfect, for all of us. For you, too. For you and everybody here. I just want to play my best, against a great guy who's playing *his* best. A picture day, all around."

Wes was choking, inside. I'm just a soft old man, he thought, with too much sentiment in me. Kirby has no idea how *right* I wanted this day of days to turn out. Well, it was too good to be true. The only thing missing was that Hilda isn't here to see it, so I could share our banner day with her. And now, will it all fade into so much less than the dream? How I wanted this for Kirby, his big victory, his debut . . . yet certainly not at the expense of a Hank Dawson tragedy. No way, Wes was thinking. The price of a trophy comes high, and low. Only the gods of fate will determine what happens between now and sundown.

Just One of Those Things, he was thinking, singing the lyric silently as he looked at a half-eaten lunch. "You're right, son. Hank will shape up."

"Case worries about her father a whole lot, Wes. All the time. You know, because he drank so much when he played as a top seed, years ago."

"Son, we can't always watch over the people we love. Sooner or later, if we truly care for someone, I guess we just have to allow him his liberties, and his follies, so he can steer by his own star."

Kirby nodded slowly. "I guess so. Maybe I'll have to explain that to Little Man sometime, because of the way he's always taken such good care of me."

Wes smiled. "I hope your grandfather and Little Man come down here to watch today. Any chance?"

"Grandfather won't. He's old, Wes, and becoming sort of stubborn. He insists that a man ought to know his place, and that Wilbur Tree's place is not the Sweetgum Country Club. Little Man won't come either. They're too shy, Wes. And I can understand how both of them would feel out of place. If anything, Little Man is even more mule-headed than Grandfather."

Wes smiled at his pupil. "You know, the other evening I could have sworn I saw Little Man here."

"Here?"

Wes Jordanson nodded and poured himself another cup of tea from the pot, then squeezed in five drops from a bent wedge of lemon. "Maybe I just thought it was your uncle. Could be wrong."

"That's funny. He doesn't leave our place very often. Hardly at all, except to go to Mr. Ledger's with one of the bulls. But, come to think of it, he's been straying off by himself lately, as if there's something bugging him."

Westal set a cup down on a saucer. "I've tried to understand Wilbur and Little Man. More for your sake, son, than for my own. But, to be straight out about it, I have probably failed." Wes smiled. "At least I succeeded with you, my boy. You're playing just the way I knew you'd play."

"Maybe it's all luck."

"Some of it, surely. Not all. Now, I'm asking for one more win. I want you to take Hank Dawson. But don't be in a hurry to do it. In fact, I wouldn't care if the match endured for five sets."

"How come?"

"Because the longer he stays out under that afternoon sun, sweating in that heat and bleeding booze out of every pore, the weaker he'll get. His legs will wilt, Kirby. Believe me, I know the feeling. I was thirty-eight once myself, about thirty years ago, or darn close to it."

"Okay, so he's thirty-eight. It doesn't mean Hank's a relic."

"Listen to me. Don't try to win it all too early or

you'll fall in three quick sets. Rubber it out and make it last. Force that old boy to run. Just remember, Hank Dawson's thirty-eight. God, kid, he's old enough to be your . . ."

Kirby was staring at him. His black eyes didn't truly react. Then he reached over to punch Wes's arm, and smiled very slightly, just enough perhaps to make his coach feel at ease.

"Kirby . . . I'm sorry. It's just an expression, son, that slipped out before I fully realized how clumsy my tongue is."

The boy smiled. "Forget it, Wes."

48

"What time is it?"

Case Dawson checked her watch. "Well, it's exactly five minutes later than when you asked me five minutes ago. It's one-thirty."

She pulled the car smoothly into the parking lot of the Sweetgum Country Club, cut the engine, popped the keys into her purse, and looked at her father.

Hank sighed. "Ninety more minutes."

"Right on." She started to open the door on her side of the Buick, but then, seeing that Hank hadn't offered to budge, stopped. "How's the head?"

"Better, thanks to V-8, raw eggs, and your devotion. Physically, I'm fit. Oh, I'm aching for a drink, to be honest with you, but that's not too unusual."

"If you say so." Her own voice sounded cold and she meant it to be. "This isn't going to be the easiest day of your life, old timer, as you well know."

Looking at her, he smiled; but then his face hardened, perhaps with the grim thought of what lay ahead. "No," she heard him say softly, "it won't be a picnic. But I'm stronger today than I was last evening. It hit me awfully hard, Case. Worse yet, how hard I hurt you. And will hurt Kirby Tree."

She touched his hand. "I know. You're a sensitive man, and you care about people. Perhaps so much so that you tried to run away from yourself and hide in a bottle."

Hank nodded. "There's no escape. The answer is to face up to who I am, what I've done, and what I have to do."

"You *have* to tell him. Kirby's lived eighteen years, wondering who his father is, or was. Sorry. *Was* sounded like you're a has-been, and the past three days have proven that you're not. You're a finalist, a winner."

"I won't ask you to root for me."

"Dad, I have rooted for you ever since I was old enough to watch tennis. Until you die, I'll root for Hank Dawson. Even when you play your own son. I'll be cheering for *both* of you, don't you know that?"

"Yes, I know."

"However, you have to tell him. Were I you, I'd wait until after the match, for Kirby's sake. As well as for yours."

"You're right. I just can't walk out there on the stadium court, shake hands with him, and say . . . oh, by the way, Kirby, I'm your father. Let's play."

"Hank, I believe you'll find a way to tell him. But it has to be today. You can't run from it. Yesterday, you ran. And you saw how much it helped."

He opened his door. "Okay, let's be off to the war. The bugles are calling."

"Wait, old soldier." Her arms went around his neck, and for several seconds, Case hugged her father as hard as she could. "It's a good day, Hank. On the positive side, I just have a hunch that Kirby Tree wants to know what only you can tell him, and he's wanted to know all his life."

She felt his head nod. "I ought to be comforting you, my sweet princess."

"Really," she said, "if you stop to think about it, something beautiful is going to happen today. Kirby already likes you, as much as he likes me, in a way."

"Are you sure about that?"

"Yes," said Case, "I'm quite sure." She looked at him squarely. "There's so much you can do for Kirby Tree. Today, because of you and your honesty with him, for the first moment in his life he'll feel like he's somebody's son."

"I hope so."

"Until now, Hank, he's only been a grandson and a nephew. No parents. It's tough to grow up as a bastard."

"It is, Case. I've been one."

"No, you haven't. You're just a human being. But now you're so much more. You're a boy's dad. And believe me, old dear, Kirby is one whale of a kid."

They both got out, looking at one another, smiling without mirth. He came around the car to rest an arm on her shoulders. "I also," he said very quietly, "have one whale of a daughter."

"Cast iron." Inside, she was telling herself, I feel like a gob of melted butter.

"Well, here we go, Case. Into battle. And thanks forever for becoming so wonderful a woman. You really warm up an old man."

"Who's warming you up on the court?"

"Tillie. When you were in the shower, he called and said to get my guts together. I didn't explain about my being Kirby's father. I just let him think that I had an alcoholic relapse, because of the pressure."

Good, she thought. Enough about parental bloodlines until after the match.

"Dad, just in case, it might be helpful for me to know who else is aware that you're Kirby's father. Who knows?"

As they walked toward the club, he said, "Oddly enough, to answer your question, I learned it from Mrs. Hood. Yet I'm sure that the dear old lady has no idea. Only four of us know . . . Tip, Wes, you and I.''

"Today's the day you have to tell him.''

"You have my promise on that.''

"You know, Dad, I've lived a lot of my seventeen years without having a father to love. Please, I'm not soliciting sympathy. Yet at least, even though you weren't around, I knew that I had one, and that I was Hank Dawson's daughter.''

He winked at her, without smiling. "Thank Heaven you are.''

"It's been Kirby who really shouldered the load, Hank. He never knew about any of it, and I'll wager he's been more than curious. Curiosity is hardly the word to denote an emptiness as deep or as painful as that.''

She saw Hank drop one of his racquets. Stooping, she picked it up and handed it to him. "You'd better not fumble on the court.''

"No, I've fumbled enough for one lifetime. Thanks,'' he said, taking the racquet. "There's an old maxim that says how responsibility sobers us all.''

Pinching his arm, Case said, "Sober's a nifty idea for you, King Henry. Besides that, do you have any idea how much both Kirby and I want you to play your best?''

"How do you know that?''

"I was with him last evening. He adores you, Hank. He even said that he wants to be like you when he's thirty-eight. And then, in later years, he wants to mature into somebody like a Westal Jordanson.''

''Wanting to be like Wes I can savvy. Not like me. I'm not sure that I'd wish that kind of misfortune on a dead rat.''

''Buck up. We're just beginning, Hank. You're going to be Kirby's dad, and I'm going to be his *sister*, God willing.'' It hurt to say it, and Case Dawson felt her fists clench, involuntarily. The edges of her nails bit into her palms. Come on, you cast iron gal, be as tough as the family menfolk. No, that's inadequate, she was thinking. Be tougher.

Closing her eyes, and taking her father's arm, she let herself go for a moment. No, I don't want to be his *sister*. What I want . . . Stop it, Case! She tore open her eyes to look at the Florida day as it really was. Face, it baby, she commanded herself. It's up to you to pour concrete into Hank's weak spot. Perhaps, she thought, before this uncanny Sunday ends, I'll have two men leaning on me. A pair of big brutes to hold up.

They met Tommy Tilson.

''Henry, old cobber, it's bloody good to see you alive and erect.''

''Thanks, Tillie, for last night and today, and for all the rest . . .''

''Can it. Let's go hit.''

Turning to face her, her father looked at her and softly begged, ''Tell me I can do it, Case.'' His eyes weren't too clear, and the blue seemed to be centered

in suggestions of Saturday night excess. Reaching upward with both hands, she lightly touched both sides
of his face.

"Play your proudest," she said. "Play the golden
game."

"I promise. You're so strong, Casey. How in the
devil did I ever sire so well? You're cast iron, kid.
Compared to you, I'm not tough at all."

"Maybe," she told him, "you're as tough as you
look, old Tiger."

"We'll see. I owe you so much, Casey. Words can't
express it. But I'm just one lucky guy. See ya later."

As they were leaving, she looked through the
gathering crowd and saw Kirby. He was talking to
Billy Gossage, or rather listening to him, as his head
was twisting about, searching. Without allowing Kirby
to see her, Case darted up the veranda stairs, around a
corner and into the powder room.

Seeing her face in the mirror, she touched a
wayward lock of her hair, without really caring about
the cosmetics of her life. How, she asked herself,
bracing on the edge of the lavatory with both hands,
do you groom your *guts*, lady?

"Stand up, Case," she told herself aloud. "You're a
Dawson. Ha! Isn't *everybody*?"

And, she thought, the males whine about the
agonies of masculine desire. I want Kirby Tree more
than sanity. I swear, she was thinking, that a bitch in
heat could lick the world. No, our proud males will

never know, and we women would be fools to squander our time in telling them.

Besides, she thought, the jolt would be too detonating to their male fragility. So get your guts together, girl. Hank couldn't ever dream how I feel about Kirby, and neither could he. Five days of thunderbolt emotion. This was *it*, for me. Perhaps for us both, but I pray that Kirby's not burning with the same level of fire. God, she thought, I'm too hurt to cry.

Men, she was thinking as she went through the motions of running the water to wash her hands and her face, will never know. At least, not *my* men! Again, she looked at herself squarely in the long restroom mirror.

"Miss Cast Iron," she said, "it's time for you to march out there and watch your father and brother play games."

49

"Easy, old man. You'll tire."

Hank saw Tommy Tilson hold up a hand, almost in self defense. The Australian flashed a warning grin. He's a good guy, Hank thought.

"Well, how am I doing?" Hank asked him.

"Save some of your gunpowder for the Seminole, cobber. Feel like taking a breather?"

"Not really. I just want to hit. I'm coming around, Tillie. Coming back, and I don't want to cool off, if it's all right with you."

It was true, Hank thought. I suddenly feel stronger than ever. Maybe, oddly enough, today's my day. He saw Tillie cock his racquet to bang another ball at him, which Hank waited for, and returned, a down-the-line screamer that nicked the tape.

"You're tough, Henry."

"Keep hitting. Give me more, all you can crack. I've seen Kirby play, as we all have, and he'll be tougher."

Tillie continued to hit more balls at him, changing his style. And then Hank understood why. Tommy Tilson was whacking the ball like Kirby Tree, emulating the boy's technique. Same savage strokes.

"Okay, old Henry," he said, "here's how he'll look to you. So best you be prepared."

The next serve came harder, yet Hank chopped it short with underspin. The ball drifted over the net, fell, and died in the dust. Tilson never even tried for it. Yet he held up a warning finger, even though a ball was in his hand.

"The Seminole would have gotten that, Hank. So don't get cocky. He's got touch. Move him around, so he doesn't get set, or he'll overpower you. You can't outhit him, old man. Not for five sets in this heat."

"Any suggestions, coach?"

Tommy laughed. "Yesterday, you gave me a lesson in the third round and finished me off proper. But you can't play the kid the way you played me. I'm not a belter. He *is*! Cracks it a ton, he does. Yet he's patient, and he waits for his shot. Then turns it into yellow powder. So beware, and keep the ball low on him."

For another twenty minutes, Tillie was Kirby Tree, with smashing backhands and forehands, peppering vicious volley shots into Hank's feet. He was a great old Aussie, Hank was thinking. Last night he carried me to bed, and today he grooms my game. Tillie's really a friend. Odd, but until Big Dixie, I never knew how much our friendship meant, to either of us.

"Okay," he told Tilson, "I'm hot."

"You are, man. Sharper than yesterday. How in hell you do it with a hangover is more than the saints can solve."

"Conditioning," said Hank. "That, and also knowing that I have youth and speed."

Tillie grinned and towelled off. "I'm for a quick shower, so's I can watch it all in comfort. I'll be pulling for you, Henry. We senior citizens have to stick together."

"Thanks again, Tillie . . . for everything."

"By the way," he told Hank as they left the court, "Wes and Tip are performing their act at three o'clock. Haven't seen it in years. Knowing those two, it'll be its usual riot. This crowd will eat it up."

Tillie left.

Hank Dawson walked toward the club, feeling the heat in his legs and arms. It felt good. I mustn't tighten up, he thought. Keep moving, leisurely, just to stay loose. This is my day. I feel it. It's a flavor you can taste that's way back in your throat, sweet and sour, like honey and vinegar.

"Hank?"

He heard her voice even before he saw her face. Not wanting to turn, he stopped, feeling the muscles in his legs harden. It was the way only she could say his name. Then he heard her voice once more.

"Lost your balance, dear?"

Turning, he saw Pam.

It took him a moment to steady himself. Funny, he thought, but she doesn't look much older. A bit more mature, yet still with the same sleek body, long legs, and, as always, exquisitely dressed. Her suit was a subtle shade of pink and peach, with flowers here and there. On her head was a perfect white hat, wide brim, tailed with a flowing pink bow. Her blouse was low cut, open and invitational.

She looks so much like Casey. And I'm so glad, he thought, they're not a bit alike in character or personality. Somehow, he had known she would come to Florida to see Casey. But why *today*?

"Hello, Pam."

He was surprised when she walked to him slowly and then kissed his cheek; not quite, he was noticing, the way one might greet a dear old uncle. He smelled her. Pam still wore that intoxicating fragrance. And she furthermore knew it, hovering just close enough for a second or two, to allow him to know her scent. In a way, she was confident of being a woman, the way Case was confident.

"It's been awhile," she said.

"Years."

"I must say Florida agrees with you, darling. You

look like a tropical deity in those white tennis togs. But then, you always did."

"Thanks for the flattery."

Her look pleased him. No, he thought, please not today. It's just one more chemical element I can't take added to the formula. The lab is going to blow up.

"Where's your polo player?"

Her mouth fell softly open. "Gone."

"I'm sorry to hear that."

Pam's voice softened. "Are you?"

He shifted his racquets to the crook of his other arm, as, he thought, an awkward schoolboy might do. "Yes, I really am. You may not believe it, but I hoped you and Polo Jan would be happy."

"Polo's so dull. And polo players eventually always reek a bit like their horses."

"I see."

"Besides," she said, her finger caressing the handle, "tennis racquets are so much cheaper to buy than ponies."

There was that same note in her voice, that bragging tone, proclaiming that Pam Rilling could buy any toy she fancied. And wind him up, Hank thought, just as she's turning my key right now. Click, click, click.

Looking down, he saw how her slender fingers were teasing the racquet's handle with an overt sensuality, knowing that he would observe it, or worse, feel her touch himself. Pam Rilling was still one of the most desirable women that he had ever encountered. On their first date, following a tennis match, they had dined together, and he had, he recalled, fallen completely in love with her.

"Well," he said, hardening, "what brings you to the Sweetgum Country Club?" Trolling for a male, he silently mused; and in that outfit, with that body that looked like female tinder, she would easily attract attention, and company.

"Big Dixie, darling. What else?"

"No," he said, "there's more. Please don't chide me about your becoming a tennis fan. I don't buy it."

Her voice strengthened. "Are you forgetting the fact that you blatantly stole my daughter, Hank?"

"I didn't steal her. Case is almost eighteen, and she is free to live where she chooses, and with whom."

"My, you sound so noble. But then, drunkards have a knack for holding up a mask of feigned nobility."

He wanted to bite his lip or run. No, he thought, what I really want is a drink. Just one. She's right about that.

"Pam, it's nice to see you," he lied. "But neither you nor I have the right to start yanking Case around like two dogs pulling on a rag doll. Please don't cause trouble for her. Today's a tough day for *her*, too."

"In what way?" she asked.

"Well, it really isn't any of your business, if you'll pardon my being so candid."

Pam Rilling raised her eyebrow. It was a practiced

gesture, he recalled, always a harbinger of some forthcoming vitriolic epithet that she was cranking up to hurl his way. "Oh, it *isn't*? I suppose you're now about to announce how *you* raised her."

"No," he almost sighed the word, "I didn't raise Casey. You did. And you raised her rather well, so please accept my gratitude on that score. We have a wonderful little lady, Pam."

"Spare me the chatter, darling," she said, using her fake smile, "because I'm considering taking her back to Connecticut."

He felt ill. "You can't."

"Oh, *can't* I? I can do whatever I please, and if you try fighting either Father or me in a courtroom, let me warn you that Rilling money shops for judges as easily as we drop pennies in a gumball machine."

"Pam . . . ," He closed his eyes, hurting, then reopened them to look at her, "it's unfair of me to say this, but Case is *my* daughter, too. I know, I didn't raise her. I wasn't around. But a small part of Casey is mine, and I really have gotten used to having her with me."

"How touching."

"Yes, it's corny," he said. "But everything in this world that means anything to me is corny. *You're* corny, Pam. You are a prototype of patrician poison that I'll never understand. Or get over."

"And what are *you*, besides a lush?"

"I'm a father. Don't laugh. For the first time in my

stupid life, I *am* a father today. Yes, *today*. And I intend to be the best father I can."

"You're in for a smashing surprise, Henry, so perhaps you'd better brace herself." Her face was leaden, cold, and her voice was stiffer than it had earlier sounded to him. Far more resolute.

"What surprise?"

"You, my darling, are *not* Case's father."

"I don't believe you."

"Don't doubt me for a second, darling. In matters like these, Rillings don't play softball. We play hardball."

Hank shook his head. "I don't . . . "

"Our attorneys have it all on paper. Complete records, of your blood tests, mine, and also my daughter's. Lawyers and medical testimony are all in the file, dear."

"Then *who* . . . ?"

"I'll let you guess, Hank. Besides, that's a question that a gentleman never asks a lady."

He felt stunned. But he believed her; especially when she had talked about the blood tests and the proof. His head hurt, and he knew that he was glowering at his former wife, wanting her, and hating her.

She smiled. "Enjoy your game."

50

Art Gossage cleared his throat.

In his pale lemon suit, he knew he looked about as elegant as any Florida business man could look. The diamond ring sparkled on his little finger as he held the hand mike close to his mouth. Taking a deep breath, Art spoke to the crowd.

"Ladies, gentleman, Confederate sons and Confederate daughters . . . (he was interrupted by exuberant applause and more than one rebel yell) . . . members of the press and of Sweetgum Country Club, visitors, friends, and athletes . . . welcome y'all . . . to the finals of our very first . . . Big Dixie!"

Hearing the applause, Art grinned. It was one grandmother of a crowd, he thought. Fifty bucks a couple. At last, he sighed inwardly, he knew that Big Dixie would balance in the black.

"As y'all know," Art said, winking at his wife, "today you're to see the final match, best of five sets, between, I am proud to say . . . two good ol' Florida boys."

Damn, he thought, I sure wish Billy was still in it. But he's not, so best I show the same sportsmanship that my son exhibited. My boy makes me stand real tall.

"Today, in about five minutes, y'all are gonna see Mr. Hank Dawson and Mr. Kirby Tree have at it."

Art paused for the applause.

"But first, it is my pleasure to introduce our very own tennis pro, Mr. Westal Jordanson, *and* his most charming lady pupil, Miss Velveeta Sweetspot."

Even Art Gossage was not quite prepared for what he saw trotting onto the stadium court. Wes looked as he usually looked, in tennis whites, prepared to give a lesson, and carrying his familiar wire bucket of balls. But across the net, at the other end of the court, was Tip Tipperary, wearing hightop sneakers, long black stockings, and a pastel blue-and-white-dotted tennis dress that could have housed a sideshow. On Tip's head was a hooker-red wig that framed a heavily-rouged Irish face, complete with false eyelashes that were at least two inches long.

The people loved it. So did Art.

Wes pretended to instruct Tip who was holding a giant racquet, the head of which was shaped like an enormous heart. Tip swung at a ball and missed, spinning around and around, yet catching the ball between his generous thighs. As Tip pretended to search for it, the audience almost fell out of their seats.

Art wiped his eyes. Tip, he thought, sure is a caution. A good guy, too, even if he does come from New York.

Wes hurried over to Miss Sweetspot and pretended to help Tip look for the lost ball. Tip was pointing, Wes was groping, and everyone else was on the verge of hysteria. Looking confused, Wes bent down to look up Tip's skirt, and Tip banged his butt with the giant racquet. Wes bounced like a ball on a yo-yo.

When the ball fell out of Tip's skirt, Wes scurried to retrieve it, picked it up, and then dropped it quickly, as though the ball was too hot to hold.

The audience hooted. Those two, Art was thinking, would make a coondog laugh.

Wes then positioned himself behind Miss Sweetspot and proceeded to instruct her on how to hold the racquet, the handle of which constantly seemed to get caught between either Wes's legs or Tip's. The facial expressions, Art was thinking, on that Tipperary gent were not to be believed. Tip was some actor.

Wes seemed to want to continue the lesson, but Tip started to pull tennis balls, one by one, from his ample bosom. If'n I was fixing to guess, Art was thinking, I'd say he pulled out at least a couple of dozen. Maybe even more.

Art looked over at Lassie June, his wife, to gesture his head in approval. "Aren't they precious, honey?"

"Sure are, sugar."

"If'n you ask me, we ought to get them boys to act up for us at every Big Dixie we ever throw."

"Sugar bunch, I just bet they'd do it."

"Doggone it," Art said to his wife, "I sure wish ol' Billy was playin' today. Don't seem right."

"I know what you mean," she said. "But he played his best, like a young gentleman. And you and I had druther raise a gentleman than a brat who's a tennis bum."

Art gave her a quick hug. What she had said was true, and Art felt good, knowing that they'd have a lawyer in the family. He looked at Kirby Tree in his beaded outfit and at the headband that held his golden hair. Well, Art thought, maybe it was time that Florida gave a break to a Seminole. High time. Billy was saying lately that Kirby was a nifty kid, and his son was on target. Nobody had ever uttered a sorry word about Kirby Tree.

The laughter of the crowd brought Art Gossage's attention back to the antics on the court.

Tip, in his oversized dress, had attempted to leap over the tennis net and was caught midway, a leg down on each side. Wes was pretending not to know what to do about it, and all of Sweetgum was appreciating it. Art studied the many faces. This, he thought, is just what a tennis tournament ought to be, good old-fashioned fun. A Sunday picnic.

Earlier, a few days ago, Art had chatted with
Westal Jordanson, talking a bit about Billy's future.
Wes had said that he was just as pleased that Bill was
headed for law school. Tennis today, Wes had com-
mented, sadly, wasn't what it used to be. Money had
replaced manners. Crowds had somehow lost their
gentility and had become more like the boo-birds in a
baseball stadium. It had, Wes had admitted, only
served to cheapen the game of tennis.

But, Wes had continued, Billy Gossage and Kirby
Tree had both turned out to be courtly, which was
one of Westal's favorite puns. Wes had sounded
pleased, Art recalled. Both his boys, the old pro had
told him, would play tennis for the love of the game;
and would be a credit to the sport, and to Florida.

Remembering the conversation, Art smiled.

"Today's a right proud day," he said to Lassie June.
"For a whole raft of reasons." Yes, he thought, this
would be a Sunday that people would never forget.

Everyone was laughing or pointing.

Out on the court, Wes was attempting to teach tennis to his ridiculous pupil, but Miss Velveeta
Sweetspot suddenly seemed to be more interested in
cultivating a romantic relationship with her coach.
Tip's big arms kept creeping up and around Westal's
neck. Tip seemed intent on trying to blow into Wes's
ear.

Tip couldn't cuddle up too close, so he remedied
the situation by extracting a pair of footballs from his

brassiere. The footballs tumbled madly onto the court and Wes tried to kick one. When he did, Tip screamed, grabbing his own chest in horror.

The laughter of the crowd, Art Gossage noticed, was continuous and genuine. They were all amused. As he looked about, Art observed that every mouth sported a wide Sunday grin.

All except one.

Hank Dawson didn't seem to be looking too happy, Art was thinking. Kirby Tree was laughing, but not Dawson. Well, Art mused, maybe it's the tension of tennis, because I sometimes get a few jitters on the golf course. Especially on the first tee. Once I start hitting, I'm okay, even if'n there's a couple of hundred bucks riding on the final putt.

Sure, Art told himself, that's it.

Dawson's making a comeback, and maybe he needs the dough. At thirty-eight, he's probable near to milked out. Yet he's playing real professional, so Billy says. Bill knows.

Art Gossage noticed that his son was sitting next to Kirby Tree. I'm glad they've become friends, Art was thinking. So many kids today aren't interested in sports, or in clean living. Lassie June and I are lucky that Billy turned out so well. A lot of what went into Bill I owe to Westal. He's an okay gent. And our son's a credit to us, to Lassie June and me, and to Florida.

Again he looked at Hank Dawson.

I bet Dawson's proud of his daughter. Who

wouldn't be? Billy talked to her and told us she was real nice, and a lady, too. Sure is a looker. And, Art was noticing, so's that other lady in the flowery suit. Never seen that one before. She's not a member, that's certain. I wonder how come *she's* not laughing either. Just sitting there, staring at Dawson's daughter. Case Dawson, he saw, sat between Hoody and her husband.

I suppose, Art was worrying, that I dasn't root for either player today, seeing as Big Dixie is sort of my baby. Best I keep my engine in neutral. There I go again, Art smiled to himself, always being a car dealer. At least it's an honest profession, the way we do it at our dealership. In the long run, if'n you give folks a good deal and hospitality treatment, you wind up with more than just customers.

You make friends.

Money's okay, but it's folks that matter, Art was thinking. Folks and family. I got myself Lassie June and Billy, and there's not a happier man today in all of Florida. Not in the whole world.

I don't know why Hank Dawson's appearing to be so glum, Art was thinking. Well, maybe it was too fat a Saturday night. Herb and Eugene were in the bar yesterday evening and told me at lunch that Hank Dawson really tied on a beauty. Well, they said he had a reputation for booze. So I reckon, Art thought, that maybe old Hank's a bit broke and poking through his socks. He's probable thinking about winning the purse and working himself back to Easy Street. That's why he looks so sober.

Yeah, Art thought, it's the money.

51

"Up or down?"

Hank Dawson spun his racquet, covering its butt plate which bore an HD, with his right hand. Kirby was less than five feet away and Hank studied the boy's face, seeing himself, and the beautiful girl whom he had not forgotten, Flower Tree.

Kirby grinned at him. "Up."

As he glanced at the racquet end, Hank felt happy that Kirby had won the spin for first service. "You got me, you rascal. It's up."

"I'll serve. Good luck, Hank."

"Same to you, old top. You're a worthy opponent."

Wes Jordanson motioned to the officials to take

their positions, as Kirby and Hank shook hands. In Hank's hand, Kirby's fingers felt young and strong. Casey's right, he was thinking. I have to tell Kirby today, but not before his first big final.

They were both allowed five minutes to hit balls back and forth and to take a few practice serves.

"Gentlemen," the head official in a high chair at the net commanded, "please begin play. And good luck to both of you."

As Hank walked to his corner to receive Kirby's opening service, he was telling himself not to dwell on the past, not about Casey, or Kirby, and not at all about Pam's unexpected and ill-timed surprise. The ball, he told himself. Only the ball. His left hand tightened on the handle.

Kirby's first serve hit the tape, so Hank moved in a step, crouched, and waited. The second serve was a high looper, a yellow oval of topspin that bounced into his backhand. Hank sliced it down the line. Kirby had moved to his left, prepared, to whip a steaming backhand cross-court. Again, Hank went down the line, chasing the boy to his right. The return was not the driving groundstroke that he had expected his son to hit. Instead, it has a short chopping dropshot that barely cleared the net, skidded, and made Hank come up with it. Kirby slammed an overhead winner.

"Fifteen love," intoned the judge's impartial monotone.

Kirby held serve. They rested for one minute, then

exchanged courts.

Hank's first service game went to deuce, yet he hung on to win it, and then Kirby Tree did likewise. He's good, Hank said silently to his towel. The kid is too strong for me, if I let it go to five sets. I've got to gamble early, while I still have wheels, the legs, to cover the court.

The first set remained on service until they exchanged sides with a score of five serving six. Hank knew he had to hold serve. He tossed short, then caught the ball and retossed. This time the ball climbed up and back, perfect for a Florida twist, hit with reverse spin. The serve fooled Kirby who was breaking to his left.

Gambling, he did it again, pleased that the serve had worked twice in a row. Tennis, he mused, was a lot like offensive football. Find a play that clicks and run it until the defense adjusts.

Each point was applauded by the audience, but not loudly, Hank Dawson noticed, as the match was yet too young to prompt crowd hysteria. So far, they clapped more from politeness than from enthusiasm. Leading at thirty-love, he missed his first service, and gambled on the second, blasting deep, to catch Kirby who had crept in a bit too close.

He held on, holding serve, then winning the tiebreaker more easily than he had anticipated.

"First set to Mr. Dawson," came the electronic voice through the P.A. system, "at seven games to six."

Kirby nodded to him. "Good set, Hank."

"Thanks. I got lucky."

The boy's face was open, without any show of defeat or disappointment. I'm so proud of him, Hank was thinking; yet I mustn't think of him as my son. Soon, but not quite yet. After the match, regardless of its outcome, I'll have to tell him. How very odd, Hank thought, but I *want* to tell him. I can't wait to say, "Kirby, you're my son. And I'm your father."

Sitting on his chair, Hank wiped his hands on the towel. Here, he was brooding, there was no ball to command his concentration. Turning, he saw Case who sat between Mrs. Hood and a man who, Hank presumed, was Mr. Hood. Case flashed him a thumbs-up sign, as Hank winked back.

Not being able to help himself, Hank looked at Pam. Well, he thought, I guess I'm only shocked at her news, but not amazed. I was away a lot, he remembered, on tour, while she stayed home a few times to party with her friends . . . to play around!

My head hurts, Hank thought.

"Time, gentlemen."

Kirby held his serve to lead by a game. I want to win, Hank told himself, preparing to serve. Damn, I want to win at something, just to show the world I can still do it, and that Henry Dawson is more than a drunken loser. No, he said, I won't think about Pam.

His serve was working. Almost all of Hank's first serves were good, with a balance of spin and pace, cutting into Kirby's backhand. Again and again, he followed his first serve in to volley for a winner. The report of the ball's leaving his strings sounded sharp, crisp. His drop volley, whenever he had cause to employ it, he hit with underspin, cross-court, keeping his young opponent off-balance.

Kirby held serve, yet so did Hank. The set progressed on service; few games went to deuce, and when they did so, the server continued to prevail.

His forehand felt better than ever, stronger, exploding the ball cross-court and deep into the boy's backhand. Hank's own backhand was almost entirely underspin, to keep the ball on the racquet's face longer, which enabled him to place the ball with a canny accuracy. He forced Kirby to hustle, chase, and made him scamper from line to line. Hank used all of the court for a target, going for sidelines, dropping shots with underspin that cleared the net by less than inches.

I have to take the second set, he thought, and I can. Keep the kid trucking, ignore him, work only on the ball. Never allow my young opponent to get set and hit his howitzers at me. He hits harder than I do, and deeper, with topspin that's almost inhuman. The way, Hank mused, I used to play at eighteen. All power. Kirby's racquet whips at the ball, lashes it, almost with hatred. Or with love.

He worships tennis, Wes said.

Somehow, Hank broke the boy's serve in the seventh game, then held his own, to lead by two.

Kirby served at three-five.

Now, thought Hank, I'll break him again. It's gamble time, folks, so prepare yourselves to witness a few thrills. The only way to crack his serve is to break his rhythm, as I did before, by constantly altering the profile of the point.

The serve blistered the dust, rising upward, but Hank chopped it, using its own spin and its own pace to force the ball to skid back into Kirby's feet. He failed to come up with it.

"Love-fifteen."

Three more, Hank was telling himself. Three more points and I've got the second set. The serve came, exactly where Hank hoped it would come. As the boy followed it in, to volley, Hank uncorked a driving shot into the body, waist high. Kirby's volley was short, weak, one which Hank rolled up and over. It was the unnecessary lob, the unexpected maneuver that Kirby wasn't looking for. Nor could he chase it down. The audience applauded with an augmenting appreciation.

"Love-thirty."

Only twice more. Hank was ready for the serve, carving it low and down the line, watching the lad lunge for it, reach it, and return a shot that would have not been returned by many a professional player. But the ball bounced into center court, at the T, where Hank could jam it for a winner.

The loudspeaker announced, "Love-forty."

The serve came like a cannon, clacking the service line tape, skidding low, forcing a flabby return. It was a fat ball and Kirby nailed it with a flat volley that sounded as though it had originated from a rifle instead of a racquet. Fifteen-forty.

Be careful, Hank warned himself. You can't hit slop at him. You just did, and he forged it into an ingot. His next serve, Hank told himself in preparation, may hit the tape again. All his serves are deep, so be ready, old tiger. Don't let him catch you again with your knees locked. Bend, crouch, and pounce.

Kirby's first serve caught the net, kicked upward, then faulted uselessly into the alley.

"Fault."

The second serve was a superb spinner, but Hank Dawson did not wait for the ball to reach its bouncing apex. Instead, he punched it on the rise, before Kirby's charge could cross the service line, and whacked it, backhand, down the line. The volley came, hard, wide, low. Somehow, Hank caught it with the upper strings and toe of his racquet, hitting it more into the middle of Kirby's court than he had planned. Hank was caught. The boy was there, racquet back, with the option of angling either way. Hank guessed correctly, instantly gambling to his right, and the ball tore at his strings. Half, even more than that, of the court behind him had been totally undefended, naked.

Hank felt his racquet bunt the ball into the corner,

reading the surprise on Kirby Tree's face. His son's licorice eyes stared at him, with a respectful disbelief.

"Mr. Dawson wins the second set, six games to three."

52

Kirby Tree sat and sighed.

"He's cleaning my clock, Wes," he said to the old gentleman who was sitting beside him. He broke me two times in a row."

Wes grunted. "Indeed."

"What am I doing wrong?"

Kirby saw the professional shrug his shoulders. "Nothing, to be honest about it. You're playing well, son. You are doing your level best and that's all that a player can ask of himself."

"But I'm losing."

"So far, yes, but you haven't *lost*. In the third set, time and heat will start to get our friend Henry."

"Well, they haven't yet."

"You're wrong, son. From here on the sidelines, while you're watching the ball, I'm watching Hank Dawson. Even though he broke you twice in the second set, he's a step slower than he was in the opener."

"You mean it?"

Kirby saw Wes firm his mouth and nod. "I mean it. Hank's not waiting to play out the point. He's gambling. Rolling the dice on almost every shot. The old fellow can't go five sets against you under that afternoon sun. His legs will buckle."

"I hope you're right, in a way. Even though I want to win, I sort of hate to make Hank lose."

Wes grinned. "In the third set, you'll realize why I had you run through swamp mud in Jason Hood's old Army boots. You know what those soggy shoes are, Kirby? They're the two final sets. You'll see."

Closing his eyes, Kirby listened to Westal Jordanson droning on about leg muscles and mud. He felt a bit easier just listening to Wes's voice.

"Now then," Wes went on to advise him, "in the upcoming set, I don't want you to hit winners."

"You want me to hit *losers*?"

"No, not that. Yet I want you to exercise a modicum of moderation. Extend the points. Stretch'em out like taffy. Make every point last, last, last . . . so you'll run Hank Dawson around in the heat."

"And don't go for winners."

"Right."

Kirby felt Wes's twisted fingers touching his

shoulder. Looking down, he saw the swollen joints, hands that wouldn't be able to hold onto a racquet much longer. Westal Jordanson, he knew, was getting close to seventy. I'm his last chance, he thought. I'm his one final stab at coaching a tennis champion, and I can't fail him or disgrace him in any way. Not today and not ever.

Wes said, "In the third set, I want you to hit down the middle but keep the ball deep so Hank can't kill you with angles. He'll hit short on you because that's his style so be ready to pounce and hit *control* shots at his corners. Hear?"

"I hear."

One of the line judges, a lady who was a member of Sweetgum Country Club, had asked to be excused for a minute. Therefore, the rest continued in her absence.

"This break could work in our favor," Wes told Kirby. "It'll let old Henry possibly stiffen up. Now, as I was telling you . . . what was I talking about?"

"You were telling me to keep the ball in play."

Wes nodded. "In the first two sets, you went for winners, lad. Don't do it. Let's soften your game a mite. Time and again, you hit long or netted the ball. From now on, don't give Hank Dawson a point. Make *him* hit the winner."

"Okay."

"Force him to play the ball, rather than watch you err. You've got to demand his exertion. Tire him out. Every time he runs, swings his bat, and serves, will wear him down an ounce."

"I'll do it, Wes."

"Do it. Especially on *his* service games. Bear down only if he has the advantage and is threatening to hold serve. Edge him back to deuce. Dropshot him. When he charges, don't try to overpower him. Go over the top."

"Lobs?"

Wes snorted. "Yes, but be careful not to lob long. A ball that doesn't land in the court is a tennis ball hit by a fool."

Even though he was paying attention, Kirby Tree felt confusion. Wes taught me one game, he was thinking, and now he's jerking me into playing Hank's. As he listened, he looked at the racquet that leaned against his chair, the new USA Pro-Am that Wes Jordanson had given him at noon, during their lunch.

"Wes, it's just a thought, but if I'm going to change my game, it might work better if I play with the other bat."

The old man shook his head. "Well, I wouldn't if I were you. That new Pro-Am looks good on you, son. Don't switch now."

No, Kirby was thinking. The new racquet was a boomer and the strings felt tighter and harder. The racquet that he had used to reach the finals wouldn't be quite as taut.

"I want to switch bats."

He heard Wes mumble. "It's your match. Maybe

you're right. You're the one who has to whack the ball off the grit.''

''Then it's okay if I swap?''

''Suits me. I sure as Hades don't want my boy standing on a court and swinging a sword that's making him uncomfortable. I'm against changing bats, but it's your decision.''

Kirby slid the USA Pro-Am into its red case and reached around his chair for his old racquet. Wes had given him this one, too, along with others. Unzipping the zipper, he slid the racquet from its cover. Something rattled. There was paper inside. A note from Casey? As his fingers unfolded the scrap of paper, he knew that Case Dawson had not written such a mess.

Wes, perhaps thinking that the message was a private matter, turned away. Kirby read it.

> Goodbi Kirby
> Today is Sunday so
> I wil kil the man
> *Dawson*   Yoo
> wil not se me
> agen for a long
> tim so pleez dont
> forget yoor fat old
> unkel
>   L M

The paper shook in Kirby's hand. Holding his breath he read it a second time, and a third. He thought, *why*? Is it because Little Man wants me to

win? Is that why he's threatening to kill Hank? Little
Man, he was thinking, doesn't even know Hank
Dawson's name.

"Time gentlemen. Continue play, please."

"She's back," Wes told him. "So march out there
and do what I told you. And forget your love letters
from your girl."

Kirby couldn't move. Slowly, his hand crumpled
the crude note and shoved it into the racquet cover.
He tried to think. What am I going to do? Little Man
loved to play jokes, but this, he was reasoning,
wasn't just some idle prank.

"Mr. Tree," he heard the voice from the highchair,
"please take your position. Mr. Dawson's waiting for
you. We all are."

Dazed, he stood up, looking out on the court at
Hank who was smiling and waving with an inviting
sweep of his arm.

"Let's go, Kirby," said Hank. "You're nowhere
near as hot or as hurting as the old folks."

The crowd laughed and clapped.

Kirby tried to move his legs, but suddenly they had
become concrete. He stared at Hank Dawson. In his
mind, thoughts that made no sense tumbled over one
another, in confusion. Little Man wouldn't kill
anybody. Little Man Tree, he remembered, was a man
who bent over to lift drowning bugs out of puddles.
He couldn't hurt anyone. Why the note? Why is he
warning me that he wants to kill . . . ?

The Night of the Snake!

The picture, the one that Little Man had carried inside his shirt, the face, the tennis player . . . and his mother, the mother that he had never known.

Mother, he thought, *who am I?*

"Resume play, Mr. Tree, if you please."

Hank was smiling at him. He's got *my* face, Kirby thought. My hair, my body . . . my God. I'm *his*! Closing his eyes, Kirby's memory could see the old wrinkled photograph. Then, eyes open, he saw Hank Dawson.

Little Man would not lie.

"Mr. Tree, are you ill, sir?"

How, he thought, can I reach Little Man, to stop him? He's so stubborn and when he decides to do something . . .

Kirby could only stand, hearing the impatient drumbeat clapping of the anxious crowd, a noise that came from a million miles away. Hank, he thought, must never know. He would be too ashamed, even though I'd want him to understand that I could never be ashamed to be his son.

Hank walked toward him, with a puzzled look on his face. He came closer, resting a hand on the side of his neck and ear. Kirby almost bolted at the touch.

"What's wrong? Are you okay, Kirby?"

"Something's up, Hank," said Wes. "We were sitting here, and then I looked away for a second or two . . ."

"I'm okay," Kirby heard himself speak. "I can play."

He looked at Hank Dawson. *You're my father*, his brain was screaming inside his head. But I can't ever tell him or tell anyone, because I love this man. And I'm proud to be his, but I mustn't tell Casey. It would hurt her too much.

God, he thought, Case and I are . . . we're . . .

53

Wilbur Tree looked at the sky.

It is time, he thought. The dead sisters of the swamp sing their song to me and their singing is too sweet not to listen. So they bid me, to come, and Wilbur Tree will answer.

"I come," he said softly.

It is strange, Wilbur thought, but I am not afraid, now that my silent darkness awaits me. My days in God's Florida have been many, and full, and my young bulls have sired calf upon calf. The orange has run her rivers of juice into my throat, as her flowers feed our honey and our bees.

My son, Wilbur Tree thought, is almost as thick as our bulls. Little Man Tree is a tree himself, one that hurricanes will not topple. He is a short cypress stump, hard and tough. Inside, he is tall, and the boughs of his feelings shelter my grandchild beneath their shade.

"I am lucky," he told the sky. But in his mind the swarm of memories made his brain a hive of confusion.

Wilbur tried to remember it all. Kirby rides Little Man's back, and wets water on his shirt, while my son smiles with devotion. Soon my grandchild will learn to walk, and run, so that I can watch him jump the pasture cactus to chase Flower. Yet they will not catch her because breezes carry her feet. And also because Little Man is too heavy and Kirby is too small.

I must, he thought as he opened the gate to the bull pasture, see to my animals. He closed it behind him.

Seeing the bull that he had named Van, after a piano person, Wilbur walked slowly through the Bahia grass toward the animal. "Van, you stand in low shade and you are wise. But I want you to listen to the radio music that comes from our house, so that you will breed mighty calves."

I will miss George Ledger, he thought. For years, the two of us worked without even one word of haste or anger passing from a lip to an ear. I never asked George to be more than a white man, nor did he require that Wilbur Tree change into a man that was no longer a Seminole.

He stroked his bull. "My heart will always miss you, too, Van Cliburn."

Softly, with quiet steps, the bare feet of Wilbur Tree walked through his pasture, heading toward the darkness of the swamp. Yes, he thought, fortune created me as a Seminole, and gave me my Hanna. She is cooking possum now, my nose tells my belly, and the white meat steams in its black pot.

Mrs. Hood is coming, too.

Very soon, the sisters of our swamp will sing her song, and Jason will weep his sorrow at her bedside. Then he will hitch up his mule and take her to church for the last time. Ruby Hood is a good woman, and when she dies, the frogs of the swamp should still their croaking and feel colder because she is gone.

Turning, he looked back at the small gray shack of unpainted pine. "Home," he said. "It is a music word to say and any ear dances to hear it."

I must help the Hoods to eat, because trouble comes, and their money crop of watermelon rots with blight. Jason Hood is a good neighbor and would hunger himself to feed my children his last turnip. He does perhaps not yet know that his Hoody is to die, very soon, but Wilbur Tree hears the sorry song that sings among leaves of live oak. Sad breezes hiss the high needles of our pines.

Bending, he picked up a large cone, breaking off a tan wing, a seed, remembering how he had told the story of life to Little Man and to Kirby, years ago. He slipped the one seed, the size of a postage stamp, into his pocket, to save.

He reached the swamp, invading the quieter and

darker places that were prepared to greet his arrival. His hand touched the lace of a fern. Hearing the husky old voice of his grandfather, Wilbur Tree nodded his head, continuing his final journey.

"I come, Opopkee."

Wilbur Tree frowned. Early this day, he recalled, I searched in my house to find the ceremonial robe, the dress of my grandfather, which I could not touch with my fingers. It was gone. I wonder, he thought, if Flower took it. Then he smiled. Yes, because she wore it to go to the party, at the college place. No, he remembered, it was not the dress of Opopkee, but rather the gown that her own needle fashioned, with thread, and with beads and many strips of colorful cloth that Mrs. Hood saved up for her.

Flower will be home soon, with her school books, singing as she cooks for Little Man and me. Then she will pile his plate high with possum, even though she scolds her brother because he grows so fat. Like a bull. He is strong and stubborn, even though Little Man is yet a boy. I see pictures in my mind, he thought, of all the food . . . the orange potatoes, carrots, and the biscuits that Flower bakes, spilling their honey.

My fingers feel sticky, he thought. It is from the honey of the biscuit bread that Flower pulled from our oven this morning. I should have brought a hunk to Opopkee to fill his old belly, so that he will smile a toothless grin at me, and let me sit on his legs to listen to his white-hair stories.

As Wilbur leaned against a cypress, the loose bits of bark dusted the shoulder of his shirt. Water sloshed around his legs and half of his trousers darkened with wetness.

"Tell me, Opopkee," he whispered, closing his eyes. "Once again I want to hear your old voice crack, telling me about the guns of the white soldiers that could no longer spit flames. And how the stench of burnt gunpowder was finally wafted away, so that white lilies once more floated without fear of white hands. Each lily bloomed for a dead white soldier.

"Kirby is white."

I do not understand, Wilbur thought, frowning, why my grandchild has such golden hair and light skin. Well, I will ask Flower why. This I must know before I die, because it is a question that all eyes who see Kirby ask. Deeper still, it is the question he also asks himself.

Who?

"No," he said. "It would not be good manners for me to question my daughter. Not now, not when Flower's body swells and ripens on the stem that is within her and joins mother to child."

The sisters sang to him, causing Wilbur to slosh through the water, away from the shack where he knew Flower was cooking, and where Little Man was milking the goat. The milk will feed my grandchild, he thought, and should mix with honey to sweeten his heart into a tiny biscuit. Looking at his hands, as once again they felt sticky, Wilbur bent over to wash his palms in the black water.

I must be clean today, he thought.

What I will miss very much, Wilbur was thinking, is listening to the radio . . . and to the early mockingbird who calls to God's Florida and welcomes each sun. The mockingbird sings all bird songs but her own, for she does not know who she is, and that is sad.

Kirby does not know. "Perhaps," he said to the water on his hands, "Kirby may sing another song, too, like Mrs. Mockingbird." That, he remembered, was what Flower called her. And always she said Mrs. Egret, in the manner that she would say Mrs. Hood.

Names are strange, he thought. Jason Hood calls his wife Hoody, instead of Ruby, because he so loves thinking of her as his very own.

The water is warm upon my knees, he thought, and the swamp's black earth sucks at me, wanting to claim all of Wilbur Tree. My eyes tire, so I will lie here, in the warmth and let the waters cover me. The swamp is my night blanket.

I wish now, Wilbur thought as he lay back, half in and half out of the water, to thank God for my life . . . for Hanna, for Flower and Little Man, and for my golden grandchild, little Kirby.

Did I think to empty my pockets?

Reaching a hand into his soaking trousers, Wilbur felt a small object. Wondering what is was, he withdrew it between two of his fingertips. Without opening his eyes, he felt it, with recognition.

A seed.

It was from a cone of pine that he had handled, earlier today. Now he remembered. With a slight smile, he allowed the pine seed to rest in his hand, to sleep, and, he thought, perhaps when all was gone, the seed would be found by the fox squirrels.

"I am glad," he whispered, "to be Wilbur Tree."

"My seeds live," he said, breathing now very easily, though hardly at all. The choir of swamp bugs and frogs seemed to be rocking him in his watery cradle. Only once did his body shudder from fear of the long sleep among the ghosts. Perhaps the gators will come. If so, I will feed God's Florida as she has always nourished me.

So it ends, he thought. Not nearly as frightening as folks dread. My work is over. Wilbur Tree will sweat no longer, nor will he regret too many careless deeds. I ask Joe Orange and Charlie No Land to forgive my thinking ill of them, suspecting them of Flower's shame.

In his hand, he felt the raw edges of the seed press into his palm. This is wrong, Wilbur thought. Releasing his fingers, he allowed the seed to float away, perhaps, he hoped, to be a sire in black soil and parent a pine. It would not be polite to hold the seed a captive inside his hand. No, he thought, it would not be . . . good manners.

Now, he was thinking, there is no chore left to do. Except for the waiting. Death, like birth, is not a mule that can be switched into a trot. Perhaps, beyond God's sky, there is a Mrs. Hood angel who serves as the midwife of Heaven. Lying very quietly, Wilbur Tree began his long journey.

The smile melted from his face, as he lay in dreams that only a dying Seminole can dream.

54

He's changing his game, Hank thought.

The third set was underway. Kirby was still banging his burning serves, yet hitting them, Hank Dawson noticed, with absolute precision. The boy didn't seem to be smiling anymore. Something had happened, Hank reasoned, during the rest that followed our second set.

Bouncing the ball prior to his serve, Hank stared at it, ordering himself to think about the ball, and nothing else.

"One yellow ball," he whispered. "Concentrate."

Hank served. Kirby's return was not the usual blistering shot that the lad had been hitting in the earlier sets. His returns landed well inside the baseline, forcing Hank to hit shot upon shot. The points lengthened. No problem yet, Hank thought. My legs are somehow holding up. But something happened on the sidelines to boil the starch out of Kirby. His face had looked drained, blank horror had burned in those two black eyes.

Worrying about it, Hank carved a routine backhand into the net, swearing under his breath. Dumb and careless, he thought.

"Advantage, Mr. Tree."

Then, to worsen the situation, Hank double-faulted, to lose the game. Kirby held. The set continued, grinding on in its slower, yet more grueling demands, ending in a set-win for Kirby Tree.

On the sideline seat, breathing heavily, Hank felt the roughness of the towel against his face. He knew why. The sun was getting to him. No lotion would stop it. Neither suntan cream nor any brand of sunscreen would adhere to facial skin in this heat. Sweat rinses most of it off, in seconds. Nonetheless, he tenderly applied cream to his nose, brow, and cheeks, being careful to use his right hand and not his racquet hand, his left. An oily palm, he thought, wouldn't do. Hank winced, as the tip of his finger smarted his face.

Glancing to his left, he saw Westal Jordanson talking softly to Kirby. I'd give anything to hear, Hank thought, just what that old fox is telling him. Plenty, I bet. Whatever he told him after set number two certainly paid off. Kirby's switched racquets, too. He's resting his new Pro-Am.

Kirby's lucky to have Wes.

He's my *son.* Hank couldn't stop his brain from clicking out one remark after another. And Case *isn't* mine? Damn that Pam! Why, he wondered, do so many bitches have to be so beautiful? Well, she didn't hurt me any more than I hurt her. Looking up, he saw Pam in the crowd. Casey had her face.

"Are you hanging in, Henry? Or hanging over?"

As he felt a big paw on his shoulder, he turned, and there was Patrick J. Tipperary in his pith helmet, carrying his floppy notebook.

"Hiya, Tip."

The big Irishman sat in the empty seat at Hank's side and groaned. "This cussed heat is roasting me alive. I wonder how the heck you Spartan gods can take it, out on that oven of a court."

"Comes with the territory."

"The Seminole's starting to look tougher."

Hank sighed. "So I noticed. In case you didn't, I just dropped the third. And he's not a Seminole."

The big hand squeezed Hank's shoulder. "I know. It took me a while, Babe, but the dawn finally came burping up through my root beer. And I know you're proud of your boy."

"I suppose you're outlining the spiciest genetic story ever to run in your rag."

Tip snorted. "Wrong, kid. Maybe, when the time

comes, but only when you and your son are united, the way I hope it happens, I'll dust off the Underwood and bang it out. Yet only with your permission, Henry. Yours, and Kirby's.''

"S'matter, Tip? Are you getting soft?''

Tip let out a chuckle. "Maybe I'm just getting senile. Ten years ago, I would've scooped that story, with a cover photo of Hank Dawson with his pants down.''

"Yes, you would have.''

"*Tip Top Tennis* is becoming respectable. We're maturing, creeping out of the jungle and into the sunshine of civility. That's how come I'm wearing my pith helmet.''

"By the way, Tip, you're still the funniest damn Miss Velveeta Sweetspot that the tennis world will ever see. You and Westal knocked 'em dead out there.''

"Thanks. It's a good feeling to know that when I die, I've left at least something of a legacy that this crowd of rednecks can remember.''

"We'll remember more than that about you, Irish. A lot of us will. Casey finds you adorable. She calls you her lovable leprechaun.''

"You got yourself a dilly of a daughter.''

Inside, Hank Dawson cringed. "Indeed so. She's a super little lady. Not until this morning did I know how much cast iron . . . her term . . . is behind her belt buckle.''

"Time, gentlemen.''

"Okay, kid," Tip told him, "don't let me down. So drag your lucky freight out there and play your best. Your son deserves it."

Hank stood up. "I'll try."

"Henry, you're the sole reason that I'm down here in this hellpot. I came to Dirty Dixie, or whatever they call this tilt, to cheer your comeback. Go do it."

"Thanks, Tip . . . for a lot."

As he took his place back out on the baseline, Hank was thinking that he *had* to win this set, the fourth. His legs felt tighter, warning him that he might not be able to last for five. Well, he thought, if I can't outrun him, at least I can outthink him.

The idea came to him.

If Kirby can change his game, so can I, he thought. He belted Kirby Tree's first service into the net.

"Fifteen-love," said the speakers.

It's okay, Hank was thinking. That's just the first point, and it doesn't prove I can't bang that yellow banshee and force the points with winners. The first serve came wide, into the alley; but Hank laced the second with a lashing forehand, feeling the jolting impact of his racquet's face all the way up and into his brain.

Sweat stung his eyes.

The sun lotion was dripping to cloud his vision, and Kirby's next return was a masterfully carved dropshot that Hank dived for. The ball popped over the net, too high. His son was there, charging on his young legs faster than a frisky stallion. A yellow blur smashed into Hank's belly, just as he was regaining his position.

"I'm sorry," the boy said. "Honest."

Hank forced a grin. "Part of the game, Kirby. And I'll do the same to you if given the chance."

"Thirty-love," said an electronic voice.

Kirby won two straight points, taking the game with an easy four. Too easy, Hank scolded himself. He then served hard, feeling the heat climbing up through his sneakers and penetrating his baking body.

No pity, he was thinking. Don't feel sorry for yourself, Henry, because that's all that a drunk can ever do. You, he thought, are more than that. You're a tennis player, remember? This is your game. So get cracking and whip the headband off that young beaded bull. I'll have to hand it to Westal Jordanson, he thought, because he sure knows how to package a pro for publicity's sake. On or off the court, Hank had noticed, people always seemed to be watching Kirby Tree.

Hank hit harder.

But the boy was keeping the ball low, slicing his shorts with underspin, making Hank hustle. In order to hit deep driving shots, Hank had to crack a full-out topspin which started to tire his left arm and shoulder. He was hurting, yet he wouldn't quit. This, the fourth, had to end as his.

He started to gun serves that he had not hit in ten years . . . flat bullets, that Kirby could only block, bunting each one back into Hank's charge. He forced his legs and body to follow his serves in, racing toward the net, crouching, coiling to uncork a flat volley, aiming for corners.

After each point, Hank felt his heart working, trying to pump cooler blood into the boiling tissue of his flesh and skin. His shots were not scoring, because Kirby was always there, oatmealing, punching the ball back, making Hank scramble. The boy's touch was superb.

Kirby broke his serve. They rested, and the time flew by. The rest seemed only a second long to Hank.

Now his son was serving at five games to three. I need a break, Hank thought. I *need* it? Crap! The world is bored with needs. What counts is what a man wants, grabs for, wins. *Need* is a beggar's wail.

The services coming from Kirby's racquet were softer, Hank noticed, and carried more spin. No longer could Hank use Kirby's pace to blast back a return that was hard and deeper. He had to use his own ebbing strength. The boy was playing brainy tennis, Hank was thinking, and he smelled Westal Jordanson's advice. Punching a down-the-line forehand, he saw Kirby moving to his right, to hit a high topspin lob which Hank had to chase. The yellow ball melted into a yellower sun. Hank squinted, losing the ball, then dodging to let it bounce high and toward the zonie crowd, the people who sat at his back.

Backing up, he heard the warning of the audience as his foot stumbled into one of the countless geranium pots that decorated the one court. Yet he hit the ball. Kirby waited calmly, dropping it short, tapping the ball just over the net tape for an easy winner.

The fourth set went to Kirby Tree, at six-three.

55

Case Dawson wiped her palms.

There was no action down on the court. Both players, she noticed, were seated on the sidelines, neither looking at the other. Her father and Kirby were grinners, but not today. Now they were battlers.

"Miss Dawson," said Mrs. Hood, "I think there's a lady sitting back a few rows, in that other bunch of seats, who's trying to get your attention."

As she turned around to look, Case Dawson saw only strangers, most of them in hats, holding fans, or sipping tall icy drinks. Then she saw the last face that she ever expected to see.

"Mother?" Case said the word so softly that it apparently was unheard by either Mr. or Mrs. Hood.

She saw her mother nod and then the hand that beckoned to her. Why? The question seared Casey's mind. Why had her mother come here, today of all days, except to cause trouble? Again, her mother motioned to her to leave the Hoods and come to her.

"Excuse me, please," she told the Hoods. "But do save my seat. I'll be right back. Okay?"

"Hurry," Mrs. Hood warned her, "because I don't guess you'll want to miss the next have-at-it, or whatever it is."

Stepping carefully, making sure her white sandals did not step on all the other pairs of white sandals, Case worked her way upward for several rows, to join her mother. She was greeted by a slight and not-too-motherly smile.

"Hello, dear." Her mother's voice sounded coldly sweet and forced.

Quickly she sat down beside her mother, wondering what she'd say and whether there were still any words remaining to be said.

"Have you seen Hank?" Case asked.

"All too often, darling."

Then stay away from him, Case wanted to yell at her. No one begged you to come. I didn't, she was thinking, and I'd bet a bundle that Dad surely didn't.

"Yes, I saw Henry the Hapless just prior to the opening ceremonies. I can see by his eyeballs that he's still swallowing swill."

Pam lit a cigarette, with a series of graceful motions. How few women, Case had often observed, could improve their appearance by smoking. Most of them inhaled like sink plungers and then belched out fumes like a starch works. Pam, she had to admit, still smoked as though each gesture had been choreographed by a French ballet master. Smoking strangely enchanced her mother's patrician personality.

I don't have to defend my father, Case was thinking. But if I'm put in that position, I'll attack first. So here goes.

"Where's your polo player?"

"You mean Jan? Oh, I guess we'd both become victims of ye olde *ennui*. So he took his mallet and balls somewhere else. Not that it's any of your affair."

"You're quite right. It isn't." Inside, she was pitying her mother, an act she thought impossible.

"After all, I am still your mother. And we Rillings rather do what we please, without being grilled by our progeny."

Case pressed her palms together. "Today, of all days, is hardly the perfect timing for your little surprise visit."

"Well, you certainly aren't rolling out too many yards of red carpet, I must say."

"No, I guess I'm not really unrolling any. Not that I mean to be rude to my own mother. And if I sounded rude, I apologize. It's only that there are circumstances you have no way of knowing about, and . . ."

"Dear, your mother knows nearly everything that requires knowing. And, if I may add, perhaps a jarring fact or two about which my daughter doesn't even have an inkling.''

She recognized the tone in Pam's voice, an edge, the one that warned the world that Pam Rilling held a trump card, one which she was about to flip onto the table . . . a card to rake in all the chips. But she would pick up only the blues. A Rilling, her mother had said, never creates a scene.

"Mother, do us all a favor. Just because you're currently bored with the pastimes and pleasures of polo, please don't tell me that you've come all the way down from Connecticut to stir up trouble.''

Her mother arched a brow. "Heaven forbid.''

"And if you're here to order me to come home, even though I'm seventeen, please let me inform you that I *am* home. I live in Florida now, with my father,''

"Perhaps in Florida, baby girl.''

"I don't understand.''

"There's no need for you to understand anything, except that I know what's best for you. I've been to the lawyers, and I'm changing my own name from Dornburgher back to Rilling.''

"Very well. I don't see how your reverting to Rilling affects me.''

"It does, because I'm on the verge of changing yours, too, dear. Legally speaking, you're not Case Dawson. But I don't want to bore you with all the tedious legalities. Just accept the *facts*. Your legal name will soon officially be Case Rilling.''

She stared at her mother's cool face, the only face in the audience that was not perspiring. It would have been beneath Pam Rilling to sweat, like other people.

"I don't believe you'd consider doing such a thing," Case told her, "without at least checking me out first."

"It's already being handled."

"Did it ever occur to you," Case tried to hold her voice down, "that I possibly don't *want* to be Case Rilling?"

Her mother nodded. "It did. But remember, mothers know best, dear. And your being a Rilling certainly won't hurt you socially. Not in Connecticut."

"I've left Conneticut."

"You'll come back. Florida will bore you very soon, dear, just as Florida continues to bore anyone with either brains or breeding. Unless, of course, your plan is to throw yourself away and marry some braying southern jackass."

Thoughts of Kirby Tree flooded Casey's mind. Why, she wondered, couldn't she and her mother talk without a constant scrap? "No," she said, keeping an even voice, "I don't plan to get married. Maybe I've seen too much marriage, and, may I add, possibly so have you."

"Ouch. You're twisting the blade, dear. And that's considered to be shabby form."

Out on the court, Hank and Kirby had resumed play, yet Case couldn't seem to watch the game. She felt her dress begin to cling to her body. Closing her eyes, Case tried to think of what to say, or do. To just get up and leave her mother would be little more than bratty, and she didn't feel like crawling in front of rows of spectators during the play of a point.

"So you, Grandfather, and your crew of lawyers have just stepped into my life, without even bothering to learn how I feel about the situation. Is that it?"

"Quite."

Her mother's solitary word seemed to hang coldly in the heat as an ironic icicle.

"By the way, dear," Case heard her mother ask, "who's that handsome young heathen Hank's playing?"

"His name's Kirby Tree. He's part Seminole."

Her mother's eyes widened. "Really? From up here, one would never know. It's odd, but that boy reminds me a bit of our dear Henry of years ago."

Case felt herself stiffen. "All tennis players look alike to me. You know, the proverbial blond-haired stereotype. Just the way all polo players look alike."

"Touché."

"I'm sorry I said that, Mom."

Pam touched her hand. "I know. I've said a few things today that even I actually regret. Odd though it may sound, in my own unfathomable way, I want you to always remain loyal to your father, because I so adored my own."

Out on the court, her father was closest to her, with Kirby Tree playing on the far court. Hank

Dawson's body seemed to glow redder with each whip of his racquet.

Around her, she heard several people complain about the heat, as well as the lack of shade. Yet, she thought, all we're doing is sitting and watching. Hank had to play. Case recalled how her father had worried about five sets and whether or not his aging legs could stand up in the fifth.

Case watched him darting from one white line to another, his racquet hitting shots that seemed almost inspired by some mystical tennis god, belting balls that no average player could ever have even toed with the tip of a desperation dink. Kirby Tree was returning every one.

I so love the two of you, Case said silently. And I'm so proud to be who I am, and of what I have. Her mind toyed with her heart, causing her to imagine that Pam and Hank were still married, and that she and Kirby were brother and sister, in a home where everyone cared for everyone else.

"How," she quietly asked, turning to look at her mother, "could any woman not love a Henry Dawson?" Or, she added to herself, a Kirby Tree.

"This may sound odd to you, Case, but in my own strange way, I still do. Perhaps what rubbed me raw was the way you loved him more than I ever could, so I guess I resented both of you, knowing what neither of you knew, yet lacking the character to be honest enough to . . ."

"Mother, I'm not following all this.

"Nothing, dear. Just ancient history, another yellowing and self-pitying chapter in the life and times of Pamela Rilling, socialite and fool."

Both players were seated, resting, allowing the spectators to converse, reviewing points with one another. Others had gotten to their feet to stretch their legs. Case saw her mother stand up quickly. "I'm leaving," she told her daughter.

"The match isn't over," Case said. "But I suppose that's not why you came today."

Leaning forward, her mother kissed her face. "Go back to your friends, the elderly couple you were sitting with, and see it through. And let's just write it off with one of my flippant remarks that tennis still bores me. As to your name . . . I erred. Don't fret about it. I'll change it back to Dawson."

Her mother's face looked as it always did; calm, in control, cool and unfeeling . . . yet Case saw a distant look in her eyes that didn't belong. Pam hurriedly flanked her perfect nose with a pair of sunglasses. "Take care of your father for me. I butchered the job. So see that you don't."

To Case, her mother's voice sounded a bit throaty, lacking its usual ring of New England solidarity.

Case touched her mother's hand. A child only gets one mom, she was thinking. Only one, and this lady is mine. It's so unfair to demand that a mother has to be a madonna.

"Mom, something's wrong, I just feel it. You're not ill, are you?" As she asked the question, she thought she heard her mother sniff; for her, an unusual act.

"No, dear, I'm physically in fettle. I guess when I heard you wonder how anyone could not love a Hank Dawson, it hit me. Your father and I hurt each other, rather deeply, with lasting pain for which there is no balm. Yes, I came to wound him one last time, but it backfired. Our handsome Henry possibly deserves more than my loyalty, yet surely no less than yours. So perhaps, as I gallop off into the sunset, it's best that you just continue to tend your father. I no longer can, Case, yet I confess I want somebody to. One of us ought to have someone to love."

"Mother, are you crying?"

"Darling, a Rilling never cries."

56

Little Man waited.

Never, he thought, have I seen so many people and heard so many voices. I do not like crowds. And I did not know that rich white persons make so much noise. I can see all of them but no eye sees Little Man, or sees the Seminole paint on my face.

It is good that I am hidden in shade, he thought, even though my legs begin to ache, and the old dress itches my skin. Little Man Tree scratched his belly. With his other hand, he held the pistol that he had purchased from Charlie No Land. For some reason, the gun seemed to feel heavier.

"Like a young bull," Little Man said in a soft voice, "my gun gains weight every day, every hour."

At the edge of the swamp, the earth he stood on was dry. Thorn bushes, scrub oak, and the stand of thick palmettoes hid him well, he thought, and there was no sunlight here. By only a slight movement of his head, Little Man could peep through the vines, between the saw-toothed stalks of a palmetto to watch Kirby playing the tennis. He looks tired, Little Man was thinking. Earlier, hours ago, Kirby hit the yellow ball much harder, but no longer does he do this.

Little Man was still puzzled about why his nephew was playing the tennis game with the man whose name was Dawson. The boy does not know, he concluded, that the man is the evil one who did the shame to Flower; because the Night of the Snake was too long ago for him to remember the face in the picture. He saw it only once.

Little Man remembers.

"Yes," he breathed, "and I will keep the promise that I made to my baby boy that night, when the two of us stole away to the swamp, and I let the rattler stab my hand with its fangs."

I will get revenge for my sister and show the people that a Seminole treasures a vow.

Why, he wondered, do they play so long? And how will I get close enough with my gun? Little Man did not guess that so many people would be here at the country club place. Looking at Kirby, he smiled. He is a fawn, thought Little Man, and dances like a young deer who chases his mother, the way I used to run after Flower across our bull pasture.

Closing his eyes, Little Man Tree was once more a child, playing tag with his beautiful sister, or vainly trying to catch the goat. His sister had always been there whenever he fell.

"Flower," he said softly, "I still miss you so."

His body stiffened. I must act brave this day, this Sunday, he told himself. Little Man Tree must do battle and fight like a Seminole, because all the people here at the country club place do not know that where I stand used to be a swamp. Beauty grew here. But now only ugliness sprouts up with its noise. And the white people who watch my nephew play the tennis are the white soldiers who came to kill the Seminole and steal our women. The Dawson man stole Flower. Yes, thought Little Man, and he will pay for the theft of her life with his own.

"Little Man Tree."

No, he thought, his eyes quickly popping open. I do not hear my father's voice. It cannot be Wilbur Tree, only the wind calling to the leaves, because my father sleeps each afternoon on the cot in our house, and in his sleep he says "Hanna."

Wilbur Tree naps, he thought, but Little Man Tree feels his foot almost asleep because I stand too long here. The yellow ball still hits back and forth, across the fishnet fence, even though I can see how tired Kirby is . . . as tired and as hot as the bad man that he faces.

When, he asked himself, will the tennis end so that

I can end the white man? The rich people seem to be clapping their hands together more, each time the yellow ball stops bouncing. He saw Kirby hitting his own leg with the racquet toy, as though he wished to punish himself. Only white men do this, he thought; and now Kirby Tree begins to act as white as his looks.

"No," he said, "he is a Seminole."

Little Man sighed. Perhaps, he thought, I lie to my own ear once again, for the last time. I tried to make a mule into a goat, a folly that only a fool would make in God's Florida. Wilbur Tree knew. So did I, yet I closed a fool's eyes to the golden hair and the light skin and tried to dance Kirby to a Seminole drum.

Inside, he thought, my blood drums and flows through my body hotter than the water from the steam spring that bubbles in the swamp, near where the Hoods live. Before I came here today, I stopped only to see the Hood people, just once more. Not to say hello, he thought, but hoping only to see their good faces from where I was hidden behind the sawgrass. No one was there, except their mule.

I like Mr. Hood and Mrs. Hood very much.

Even if they are white, he thought, they are both good people. Kirby showed me the beads on his tennis shirt, the pretty ones that I touched with my fingers that had been Mrs. Hood's church beads. Mrs. Hood would be a good Seminole. Even so, she is still a good neighbor, because she tried so hard to save Flower.

His thoughts were disturbed by a sudden burst of noise that came from the tennis place. Looking, Little Man saw all the people suddenly stand, and then rush from their seats. Something had happened. Out on the flat place, the game had stopped, and he saw Kirby and Dawson hugging each other, almost as though each was trying to hold up the other.

"Now," said Little Man. "I must do it now, even if some of the people see me, or hear my gun."

Stumbling out from the darkness of the tall trees and lower palmettoes, Little Man ran toward the crowd, pistol in hand, trying not to trip on the hem of the long dress. With his strength, it was no problem for him to push his way through the crowd. A few people stared at him, yet everyone seemed to be yelling or talking; their hands were in the air. Several people threw their hats, dotting the late afternoon sky, and the hats scattered into the wind, a flock of cloth birds.

Little Man hurled his big body forward, pushing people out of his way, trying to see the man whose name was Dawson.

"Hey!" he heard a woman crying out. "He's got a gun!"

People stood in Little Man's path, but he threw them to one side or the other, as if they weighed no more than toys. He felt stronger than a bull. He had become, he felt, a Pablo or a Van or Mario, a red bull after a white cow. I am Isaac Stern, he thought. The ghost of our dead bull lives within me, charging inside with the heat of my body, and my arms are stronger than horns.

"Watch out!" someone was screaming.

Little Man Tree did not stop. Now he saw the hair, the face, the man that he had to reach. A man threw a punch at him, but to Little Man, it felt no heftier than the beat of a wren's wing. All he saw was Dawson. The man was still hugging Kirby. I must, Little Man thought, tell him who I am and why I come here.

"Dawson," he tried to yell.

Yet he knew that all the white faces were also yelling too much for anyone to hear. They were all trying to reach the two tennis players, extending open hands, pounding both Kirby and Dawson on their backs and shoulders. It was then that Little Man Tree could not believe what he saw. Many white men were lifting both the players up on their shoulders, shouting their names. Women and young girls crowded in closer, trying to kiss their sweaty faces; and no one, it appeared to Little Man, would stop hollering.

"Look at that clown in the dress," he heard someone say.

Another voice said, "It's gotta be a size forty."

Bodies moved in against him, from all sides, with such mass that even Little Man's strength momentarily failed to move him forward. As he was almost brutally jostled, he somehow dropped the gun, feeling it fall to his feet. Bending, he fought his way downward, touched it, and then felt his fingers close on it. He used both hands to lift it upward, his body choking among the scores of other bodies that crushed against him, on all sides.

"It's a *gun!*" several voices were crying out.

Looking up, he saw Dawson, high on several shoulders, smiling. Kirby was there, too, up above the crowd. No one could move much more than an inch or two in any direction. He saw Kirby's face, also smiling, still holding Dawson as well as being held by him.

With his thumb, Little Man pulled back the pistol's hammer, hearing it click into a cocked position, as the gun was close to his own face.

"Kirby," he tried to yell over the crowd noise, "your uncle is here to keep his promise."

The boy saw him. Little Man saw Kirby's eyes widen, his mouth open, and then he was hollering "No! No! Little Man, *no!*"

Yes, he was thinking, I must kill Dawson for you. A promise will be kept. Bodies surged against him, but Little Man's finger tightened on the trigger, as he almost felt the snake fangs again biting into his right hand.

"I am Little Man Tree," he hollered at the white face of Dawson. "Flower Tree was my sister, the girl you . . . you . . ."

Little Man jerked the trigger, and the gun exploded in his hands, blinding him with smoke, tears, and memories.

"For you, Kirby," he said, "and Flower."

57

The funeral ended.

Tip Tipperary wiped his eyes. An unfeeling emptiness tugged at his insides, along with the question . . .
could he ever write the sweet story that somehow
deserved to be told? How, he wondered, does a
veteran sinner compose a hymn?

As he noticed Case Dawson's lovely face, expres-
sionless now, Tip knew how much he wanted to
shoulder some of her sorrow. Hers, and everyone's
here. Standing in the sunlit meadow at the edge of a
Florida swamp, Tip looked upward to spare his eyes
from the sight of the freshly-dug grave. A hawk, little
more than a tiny dot of brown, drew lonely circles in
the empty sky. One small puff of a cloud looked, to

Tip, to be very young and so very innocent.

Lord, he thought, you created not a blessed one of us sturdy enough to endure the shards of this day. And I am the least of us all.

A man whose name was Ledger, and another man, slowly began to shovel dirt into the grave. Tip heard the sandy gravel hitting that plain and unpainted coffin. As the box was gradually covered, the noise of the dirt grew softer. Nearby were two older unmarked mounds of sand that, according to what Tip had been told, belonged to Kirby's mother and grandmother, two women whom the boy had never known.

"Thank you for coming, Tip."

"Henry," he said to Hank Dawson, "I couldn't have stayed away. You and Case are more to me than just friends, and you always will be. You and Westal."

Tip saw Case Dawson put her arms around the quiet elderly couple who stood nearby, whose names were Hood. "Thank you both," she said, "for loving him so much."

The old woman could only nod. Her small husband seemed to be trying to hold her up. Mr. Hood wore a shabby black suit, a work shirt buttoned at his slender neck, and no tie. They looked very poor, Tip thought, yet they possessed a silent dignity.

Westal Jordanson stood without moving, his face covered by his twisted fingers. Tip took a step or two closer and rested a hand lightly on the lean shoulder. "You discovered gold, Wes. Few men do that in a lifetime. But you did."

Wes shook his head. "A barn," he said softly, pointing to the gray structure. "Right over there. He was only twelve, hitting old . . ." Westal's voice stopped.

"I know," Tip told him. "And he was your child as much as anyone's."

Mr. Ledger and the black man whose name, Tip recalled, was Lee Roy, had finished their work with the shovels, said their goodbyes, and left, promising that they would tend to the animals. Slowly, those who remained walked toward the shack.

"Nobody lives here no more," the old woman said to her husband. "They're all gone, Jason. Hanna, Wilbur, Flower, Little Man, and Kirby. They all are clean gone, our neighbors."

The old man patted her arm. "I know, Hoody. I know. George Ledger figured that it was just Wilbur's time, so he wondered off to die. And they took Little Man away, the police did. He looked serious sick. My guess is he'll die of a busted heart, on account of what he done. They fired him all them questions but it was like Little Man was struck dumb. Couldn't move or talk."

Tip saw Wes Jordanson walk to the doorway of the shack, go inside and then reappear, carrying a tennis racquet. Squinting, Tip noticed that it seemed out of the ordinary, as though it had been handcarved, and slightly warped. Wes stood still, holding the crude racquet and staring at it. The racquet trembled in his hand.

"His grandfather carved it for him," Wes said, looking up at everyone, "and strung it with fishing line . . . . I remember that day so well."

Hank said, "Keep it, Wes. Kirby would have wanted you to have it, sir."

Wes said, "Please don't call me sir. I can't bear to hear it. That's what Kirby called me. Sir."

"Remember it, Wes," said Hank. "I want everyone to remember my son . . . Kirby Tree Dawson."

Tip saw the Hoods look at Hank, in surprise.

"Yes," he walked closer to them, "it's true. I was the father he never knew. And you were the one, Mrs. Hood, who told me." Hank touched her hand. "Even though, as you were telling me, you didn't know yourself, last Saturday, when you told me about Flower."

Mrs. Hood nodded. "I can see it now, Mr. Dawson. Your face favors his. And I'm glad you owned up."

"So am I," Hank said. "For one day, I knew that I was Kirby's father, and I'm honored to say it, even thought I was just about shattered to learn the truth."

Case came to him and Hank held her close, his hands resting on her shoulders. "Kirby knew," she said. "Wes found the note from Little Man. He knew you were his dad."

Wes stepped toward Hank, holding out the hand-crafted tennis racquet. "I think Kirby would have wanted you to keep this, Hank. It's all you'll ever have of him. I had him for six years. Your keeping his first racquet seems fitting somehow."

Hank took it. "Thanks, Wes."

"He belonged to all of us," Tip heard Mrs. Hood say. "Kirby belonged to each of us here."

Tip noticed Hank again approaching the elderly couple. "Mr. and Mrs. Hood, I never knew about Flower Tree's baby . . . our baby. I never guessed. But I want both of you to know that I loved her. We were both very young, perhaps foolhardy, yet we were in love."

"We understand, Jason an' me. Love belongs to the youthful. In your way, Mr. Dawson, you and Flower give us all Kirby."

"Thank you for understanding, Mrs. Hood."

The old woman smiled up at Hank. "We do. Without you for a pa, none of us would've had the same Kirby Tree. Some things get planned, away up in the yonder, and they're things that are intended to be in this life. And maybe in the hereafter,"

She kissed Hank Dawson's face.

"Now then," Mrs. Hood continued, "I'm going to beg y'all a favor. I want us to all join hands," she said to Hank. "You, and Miss Dawson, Westal, and Mr. Tipperary, along with Jason and me."

Hank rested the old racquet on the ground and they formed a circle. Tip held Case's hand and also Mrs. Hood's. He saw the old woman close her eyes and then she lifted her plain and lovely face upward.

"Today," she said, "we buried a boy who belonged to nobody, our sweet Kirby. But I want to ask God to forgive Little Man Tree, who cared for him more than

any one of us ever could. Me an' Jason, we know.
Please pardon him, Lord. We all do, because what he
done was out of love, and not hatred. Amen.''

"Amen," voices echoed.

Case Dawson hugged the old woman. The big arms
encircled the girl, and Tip heard the woman say,
"There, there . . . indeed I know. He was ours, too.
All the Tree children was ours. You're ours now. Promise?" The girl nodded.

Hank bent over and picked up the old racquet. "I
wish," he said, "that bullet could have . . ."

"No," said Tip. "Mrs. Hood said that some things
are planned, up yonder, and maybe they are, Hank.
We have buried your boy, so let it go, my friend. Let
matters rest the way they are. Rest, as they say, in
peace.''

Tip looked at the tiny shack. For some reason, he
thought, it just looks like a home.

Behind their mule, Mr. and Mrs. Hood rode in their
wagon. The rest walked. Tip walked with Wes Jordanson, looking at Hank and Case ahead. They left
the Hoods at their little house. I guess I just have
forgotten, Tip was thinking, that people can be this
poor. And this rich. The four of them continued
down the road.

Well, Tip thought, I came to Florida.

I came for a story, the one I was figuring to write
about the comeback of Hank Dawson. It is surely, he
thought, too tragic a tale for anyone like Patrick J.
Tipperary to tell. I'd like to presume that all Irishmen

are poets. All, except me. Could I sit down at a typewriter to share with a world how Hank Dawson won a tournament and lost his Seminole son?

For some reason, Tip reached over and held Westal Jordanson's hand. The two old men walked slowly together, and neither spoke, because there were no words. I'll come to Florida again, Tip was promising to himself, and maybe Wes and I can go fishing. He'd like that and so would I. We'll take Hank and Casey, too. And we'll also come visit the Hoods.

The old woman, Tip guessed, had been correct when she had said, in her plain voice, how Kirby Tree belonged to no one.

And finally, to us all.

ROBERT NEWTON PECK, winner of the 1982 Mark Twain Award and creator of four television shows, is the author of thirty-four books, including the widely acclaimed *A Day No Pigs Would Die*, *Fawn*, and many books for young people. He now lives in Longwood, Florida, and *The Seminole Seed* is his first novel that finds its setting in his new home. Peck is also a well-known speaker and ragtime piano player.